A BOND
Never BROKEN

A BOND

JUDITH MILLER

Never BROKEN

DAUGHTERS OF AMANA

BethanyHouse
MINNEAPOLIS, MINNESOTA

Cover design by Lookout Design, Inc.
Cover photography by Aimee Christenson
With special recognition to The Amana Historical Society

Published by Bethany House Publishers
11400 Hampshire Avenue South
Bloomington, Minnesota 55438

Bethany House Publishers is a division of
Baker Publishing Group, Grand Rapids, Michigan.

Printed in the United States of America

Library of Congress Cataloging-in-Publication Data

Miller, Judith, 1944–
    A bond never broken / Judith Miller.
        p.   cm. — (Daughters of Amana)
    ISBN 978-0-7642-0644-3 (pbk.)
    1. Amana Society—Fiction. 2. German Americans—Iowa—Fiction. 3. World War, 1914–1918—Iowa—Fiction. 4. Amana (Iowa)—History—Fiction. I. Title.
    PS3613.C3858B66   2011
    813'.6—dc22

                                                                    2010041188

To
My brother, Tom McCoy, and my
sister, Mary Kay Woodford.
I am forever grateful for your
love and support.

Books by
Judith Miller
FROM BETHANY HOUSE PUBLISHERS

The Carousel Painter

DAUGHTERS OF AMANA
Somewhere to Belong • *More Than Words*
A Bond Never Broken

BELLS OF LOWELL*
Daughter of the Loom • *A Fragile Design*
These Tangled Threads

LIGHTS OF LOWELL*
A Tapestry of Hope • *A Love Woven True*
The Pattern of Her Heart

THE BROADMOOR LEGACY*
A Daughter's Inheritance
An Unexpected Love • *A Surrendered Heart*

POSTCARDS FROM PULLMAN
In the Company of Secrets
Whispers Along the Rails • *An Uncertain Dream*

www.judithmccoymiller.com

*with Tracie Peterson

JUDITH MILLER is an award-winning author whose avid research and love for history are reflected in her novels, many of which have appeared on the CBA bestseller lists. Judy makes her home in Topeka, Kansas.

Those who cannot remember the past
are condemned to repeat it.

—George Santayana

CHAPTER 1

October 1917
Amana Colonies, Iowa
Ilsa Redlich

I had failed.

There was no other way to justify our presence at the train station.

My brother, Albert, tipped his head and leaned down to look into my eyes. "Please smile, Ilsa. I don't want this to be a sad occasion. I want to remember your engaging smile and the twinkle in those big blue eyes."

I tried, but even his reference to my eyes didn't help. Gaining control over my trembling lips would be an impossible feat. "Please don't ask me to smile. To see you depart does not please my heart." The headpiece of my woolen cloak had fallen to my shoulders, and I touched my index finger to the black cap that covered my hair. "My head will not accept your choice, either."

Once Albert stepped onto the train, nothing would ever be the same. The war had changed everything, and who could say when I would ever see him again.

As if reading my thoughts, he rested his arm across my shoulders. "They've told me I'll serve all of my time at Camp Pike, and I'll probably get to come home for Christmas."

I nodded. "They told Dr. Miller the same thing. Did that stop them from sending him to Europe?" I didn't wait for my brother's answer. "The same is true for you, Albert. Those people can tell you anything they want, but it doesn't mean they will keep their word."

He tightened his hold and squeezed my right shoulder. "You worry too much, Ilsa. All will be well. You must put your trust in God."

Passengers skirted around us, eager to purchase tickets or locate a seat near the station's wood-burning stove. "Like Sister Miller? When I saw her at the Red Cross meeting last week, she didn't think all was well. She was in tears when she spoke of her husband." I lowered my voice. Speaking against the war was not a good thing, especially for those of German heritage. "And she was angry, too. She said her husband was told he wouldn't be sent overseas because of his conscientious objector status, but still they sent him."

"*Ach!* Who can know what happened with Dr. Miller? Not me or you. I am only certain of what I've been told: I will serve at Camp Pike and then return home."

He wasn't going to listen, so I bit back any further arguments. Not knowing when I would see Albert again, I didn't want to spoil our parting with cross words. Mother had kissed Albert's cheek, said her good-bye, and hurried to the kitchen to prepare the noonday meal for the hotel guests, but I hadn't failed to notice the tears she'd squeezed back. And Father had murmured a hasty farewell and pulled Albert into an awkward hug before heading to the wheelwright shop after breakfast.

Around us, the clamor of conversation rose and fell. A train whistled in the distance. "You promise you'll write? *Mutter* and *Vater* will worry if they don't hear from you each week."

He wagged his finger back and forth beneath my nose. "It is not Mutter and Vater who will worry. They have peace because they trust God. But you, dear Ilsa, are not so quick to find that peace."

"*Nein.* Probably because I prayed you would be spared from the draft, yet you received your notice. Then I prayed you would file a request to be released from military duty because of your religious beliefs, but you didn't. Instead, you only checked the box saying you are a conscientious objector. So then I prayed you would fail the physical exam, but you passed with flying colors. My prayers failed on all accounts, and I find it hard to trust that God will answer my prayers to keep you safe."

"God heard your prayers, Ilsa, but He has other plans for my life, and those plans include serving in the U.S. Army. It's as simple as that."

I glared at a group of boisterous passengers congregated nearby, angry that their lives remained unchanged while mine was being turned upside down.

"I promise I'll write," Albert said, "but you shouldn't expect a letter every week. I don't know what my duties will be, and I don't want you to be disappointed." He grinned. "Maybe you could bake me some cookies and send them."

I forced a tight smile. "*Ja.* You know I will."

He pecked a kiss on my cheek. "I will be happy to have some, even if you burn them."

I gave him a playful shove. He never failed to tease me about the first cookies I had baked without Mother's help. Tearful when they had burned, I fretted there would be no dessert for the hotel guests. Albert had come home and joined me in scraping off the black crust. He'd declared them perfect, though I don't think the guests had agreed.

Tears threatened and I swallowed hard to keep them at bay. I could cry later. But not now, not during these precious final minutes with Albert.

With only an eighteen-month difference in our ages, we'd been close all of our lives, unlike many of our friends who didn't get along with their siblings. Perhaps that was why I'd taken it so personally when he refused to take my advice to remain at home. Then again, maybe it was because I feared his decision would influence Garon and change my life even more. And it had. Not only had Albert's decision wreaked havoc in my relationship with him, it had also caused problems between me and the man I was pledged to marry.

"Unless the elders tell us the government wants us to use even less flour and sugar than we already do, I will do my best to send you something *gut* to eat at least once or twice a month." I did my best to keep my tone light.

The station doors burst open, and a group of travelers flooded inside. Teeth chattering, they hurried to cluster around the stove. A cold gust of wind swept across the wooden floor, and I drew my wool cloak close. It was early for snow and ice, but not so unusual that we hadn't faced the same circumstances in the past. If we were fortunate, this cold weather would pass and warmer fall weather would return for a few more weeks. Garon followed the group inside. He'd been to the depot at Upper South and driven the passengers to Lower South in the special carriage used to transport travelers back and forth between the two train stations in South Amana.

Give or take a few, our population in South had remained at two hundred residents for more than thirty years, but the constant flow of train passengers and visitors made it seem bigger. And though we were smaller than Main Amana with its more than five hundred residents, we were the only village with two train stations. A point of pride, though pride wasn't considered a good trait among our people. Nowadays we didn't worry so much about boasting, for the elders didn't enforce the less significant rules with the same strictness that had prevailed in the early days of the settlement.

Garon stomped the light dusting of snow from his boots and yanked the woolen cap from atop his thatch of coffee brown hair. He grinned at me. "Got a few passengers planning to stay overnight at the hotel. Hope you've got rooms for them."

"Ja, we can take care of them."

"I told them I had to stop at the depot before I could take them on to the hotel, but they didn't seem to mind." Garon clapped my brother on the shoulder. "Didn't want you to board the train without saying a proper good-bye, Albert." He leaned closer. "I may be joining you soon, so be sure to write."

I snapped to attention. "What do you mean, Garon?" Panic gripped my stomach in a tight knot, and I was thankful I hadn't eaten much breakfast. "Have you received your notice to report for a physical?" My fingernails dug into the soft flesh of my palms.

He shook his head. "Nein. For sure I would have told you if it had come." Doubt must have shone in my eyes, for he stepped closer and leaned down until we were nose to nose. "I give you my word, Ilsa. I have not received my notice. If I hear anything from the local draft board, you will be the first to know."

His words didn't soothe me. What I truly wanted was a promise he wouldn't join the army no matter what. But I knew I wouldn't hear that—at least not right now. I had quit arguing with my brother, and look what had happened. I would not make the same mistake twice.

Albert and Garon continued their talk of service and patriotism until the train rumbled into the station. I clung to Albert's arm while Garon strode alongside us, carrying my brother's bag.

"Well, this is it until I get leave to come home. I hope it will be for Christmas." Albert pulled me forward and smothered me in a bear hug. "Don't forget those cookies you promised, Ilsy-Dilsy."

Ilsy-Dilsy—how long had it been since he'd called me by that name? When I was a little girl, I would stomp my feet in anger when he called me that. Now it caused a lump in my throat. I lifted a gloved hand and swiped the tears from my cheeks.

"You'll find a tin of cookies in your case. I wasn't going to tell you, but you might get hungry on the train."

"Thank you. For sure they won't go to waste. If I don't eat them on the train, they will fill my stomach once I get to Camp Pike." He released me from the warmth of his embrace and waved to Garon. "Come and take her home. I don't want her standing on this platform catching a cold. Then she won't be able to bake me any more cookies."

Albert was doing his best to sound cheerful, but his laughter rang hollow, and I detected a hint of sadness in his eyes.

After a slight nod, Garon touched his forehead in a mock salute. "You should not worry about anything except your army duties, Private Redlich. I will take gut care of Ilsa, and I promise to taste any cookies before she sends them—to make sure they are gut enough for you."

My brother laughed and took his bag from Garon. "Better get those folks over to the hotel, Garon. I'm sure they are warmed up by now."

After a final peck on my cheek, Albert turned and loped toward the train. With one last wave, he stepped aboard. I gestured in return, longing to remain until the train was out of sight. But Garon propelled me toward the station before I could put voice to my desire.

"Will only make you sad to remain until the train departs." Garon opened the depot door and gently pulled me along.

Mouth agape, I stared at him. How did he know what I'd been thinking? "But I'd feel better if . . ."

He shook his head. "Nein. You would feel worse. Come with me, Ilsa. We must not keep the hotel guests waiting any longer."

I wanted to argue, but I knew he was right. I wouldn't feel any better if I waited, and the hotel guests deserved to be settled into their rooms. I waited inside while Garon assembled the group and assisted them into the oversized buggy before I stepped outside and joined him.

We hadn't gone far when the train blasted two long whistles. I twisted around on the seat and strained for a final glimpse of Albert. Garon flicked the reins and urged the horses to a faster pace so I could catch sight of the train when it passed. I removed my neck scarf and waved it overhead. The dark wool strip whipped in the wind like the flag that hung outside the general store— the American flag we raised and lowered each day to show our loyalty to this country. At least that was the hope of the elders.

But if waving a flag had helped ease feelings of hatred toward German-Americans, I hadn't noticed.

I wanted to believe my brother's service and the service of other Amana men in the armed forces would ease out-siders' doubts and suspicions about our people, but I remained unconvinced.

CHAPTER 2

Marengo, Iowa
Jutta Schmitt

At the familiar jangling of the bell, my parents and I raised our heads and looked toward the front door of the bakery. "I'll go," I said, signaling for the two of them to continue with their work. I glanced at the clock near the long wooden worktable. "It's time for Mrs. Woods to come in and argue with me."

My father laughed and nodded. He disliked being interrupted in the midst of preparing dough for the oven. Should he stop for even a minute, he worried his loaves wouldn't rise to the proper height or his crusts wouldn't glisten with the perfect sheen. I didn't see how a few minutes could make a difference, but that is why I waited on the customers and my parents took care of the baking. Father said each job in the bakery was important, and I was best suited to help the customers. He said they liked my smile and pleasing personality, but I knew it was mostly because I understood English better than he or Mother.

We were a good fit, the three of us, each enjoying our particular duties in the shop—at least most of the time. I wanted to run and hide when cranky Mrs. Woods came into the bakery to buy bread. Each morning she'd arrive and each morning she'd find fault with every loaf, hoping I'd give her a discount. It had become a game of sorts, a game that had begun shortly after we moved from the Amana Colonies to Marengo when I was sixteen. It was a game I had tired of after ten years.

Swiping my hands down the front of my white apron, I stopped short as I crossed the threshold into the front of the bakery. Lester Becroft stood at the counter with a shiny brass badge pinned to the lapel of his ill-fitting woolen jacket. Strands of red hair poked from beneath his hat. Another man I'd never before seen stood by the door. He was wearing one of the badges, as well. I tried to read the black lettering on Lester's badge, but I couldn't see it from my current vantage point. I considered taking a step closer but hesitated. For instead of his usual despondent gaze, Lester's eyes shone with either defiance or anger—I couldn't be sure which.

"Did Martha send eggs?" I asked. The Becrofts had been trading eggs for bread. And even though my father had made an agreement with a local farmer to supply eggs for the bakery, he'd been unable to refuse Mrs. Becroft's request. "They need our help," he'd told my mother. "So many little mouths to feed." And Mother had agreed, giving the Becrofts any leftovers when they appeared late in the afternoon.

Lester's lips curled in a snarl. "Ain't here to talk about no eggs."

I took a backward step, stunned by his frightening behavior.

He motioned to the stranger, who turned the wooden sign that hung inside the front door to read that the bakery was closed.

I shook my head and waved to the man. "Please, turn the sign so that people will know the bakery is open for business." I forced a smile. "We cannot afford to turn away any customers."

When the man at the door didn't heed my request, I gained courage and stepped forward. The moment I circled around the counter, Lester grabbed my upper arm in a tight grip. "Stop right there, Joota." We'd lived in this town for ten years and still most people couldn't pronounce my name. Instead of dropping the *J* to properly call me *Utta*, they transformed my name into a number of strange-sounding words. I tried to free my arm, but Lester tightened his hold. "*We* will say when the sign can be turned around, not you."

His large frame towered over me. My eyes were now level with the shiny badge pinned to his chest and the black letters circling the outer rim, which read *Iowa Council of National Defense*. On the inside in smaller letters, I read the words *American Protective League*. I swallowed the lump in my throat and did my best to appear calm. I'd heard a number of frightening stories about the men who wore those shiny badges, but never would I have guessed Lester Becroft was one of them. For the past two weeks I'd noticed strangers positioned across the street from the bakery. I'd mentioned them to my father, but he'd said it was only my imagination at work. Now I knew I'd been correct. This stranger was one of those men I'd seen loitering nearby.

The stranger stepped away from the door. "We got questions for you and the other Huns back there." He pointed a thick finger toward the bakery kitchen.

"We are Americans," I replied. "You can ask Mr. Becroft. He has done business with us for years." I turned to Lester, hoping my reference to the kindness we had shown him and his family would halt this alarming confrontation.

"You're Huns—no different than the Huns who are killing our American soldiers."

I sucked in a deep breath. How dare he say such a thing! I wanted to retaliate and defend my family, but anger would likely escalate the situation.

"I hope that your children are all well, Mr. Becroft." I kept my voice low, hoping I could appeal to his sense of decency. For a fleeting moment, regret flashed in his eyes, but the hard look returned as quickly as it had departed, and I knew I had failed to reach him.

In recent months we had been shocked to hear customers talk about the government's encouraging the Iowa Council of National Defense and the American Protective League to help the war effort by reporting on their friends and neighbors. We'd listened with concern to the report of threats and accusations being made by these men—men who called themselves patriots. Never had we imagined that the people who regularly visited our store had joined their number.

Though I'd never before seen the other man, I couldn't believe Mr. Becroft would come into our store and make ugly accusations against my parents and me. For ten years we'd operated our bakery in Marengo. "The people of this town know us." I turned toward Mr. Becroft. "You know that we're as much a part of this community as any other family living here."

The burly stranger tipped back his head and snorted. "Well, one of those people who hold you so dear to their heart has reported that someone in your bakery placed ground glass in loaves of bread you donated for departing soldiers. Ain't that right, Lester?" Mr. Becroft gave a slight nod. Not satisfied with the lackluster response, the stranger slapped Mr. Becroft on the shoulder. "I said, ain't that right, Lester?"

Mr. Becroft straightened his shoulders. "Yeah. Bunch of unpatriotic Huns. Shouldn't be living in this country. It's Huns like you that killed my brother."

My jaw went slack. I'd never heard anything so farfetched in my life. "Killed your brother? Put glass in bread? I don't understand."

"My brother's dead. We got word last week he was killed by Huns." Mr. Becroft pointed a dirty finger at the badge on his lapel. "But now I got this, I'm gonna make sure my brother didn't die for nothing. I'm gonna work with the patriots and make sure you Germans get what's coming to you."

"We aren't the ones who killed your brother, Mr. Becroft. We are Americans, just like you. And we didn't put glass in any bread. We have never donated bread to departing soldiers. We didn't even know there were soldiers departing. When is this supposed to have happened?" I gave a slight stomp of my foot. "I want to know who told you these lies. We have a right to know who has accused us of this terrible act."

I glanced at the front window and was startled to see Mrs. Woods and several other customers peering inside. Why didn't one of them go and get the police? "We have customers waiting outside. Perhaps you could come back later in the day."

I had raised my voice several decibels, and my father stepped from the kitchen into the front of the shop. He glanced at the two men, his gaze resting on Mr. Becroft for a moment before he nodded and smiled at him. "Why are the customers outside, Jutta? There is some problem?"

"There is a big problem. Maybe we should all go into the kitchen, where we won't be distracted." The stranger stepped forward and pushed Mr. Becroft toward the door. "Tell those people to go away, Lester. Tell them the bakery is closed until further notice."

"What? Wait. You can't do that!" My father tried to skirt his way around the stranger, but he grabbed my father's arm and shoved him backward.

"You are Bert Schmitt?"

"Ja, that is my name. Why do you ask? Lester knows who I am. He and his wife, Martha, trade their eggs with us."

The man ignored the remark and continued. "Your wife is Eva, and your daughter is Jutta."

My father bobbed his head. "Ja. That is us. We own this bakery for the last ten years. Just ask Lester—he can tell you."

The stranger poked my father's chest, pushing him toward the rear of the shop. "If I wanted to hear from Lester, I would have asked him the questions. I'm asking you."

As the man repeated the allegations that had been leveled against us, shock and disbelief shone in my father's eyes.

"I said we will talk back here, where I can watch what all three of you are doing."

"We are baking bread and cakes. You want to learn to become a baker?"

The man clenched his fist and sent a bruising blow to my father's chest, causing him to double over in pain.

"This is not a matter to joke about, Mr. Schmitt. You and your family are in serious trouble." He glanced over his shoulder at Lester. "These Huns are too stupid to know what's going to happen to them."

Lester stepped alongside the other man. "You better listen, 'cause we got plans to destroy this bakery and send you off to jail if you don't cooperate." He pointed at me. "And we can turn that pretty face into something no man will ever want to look at."

My father straightened back up and said, "Lester, I cannot believe you would treat my family in this way. We have always been *gut* to you and helped your wife and children."

Lester spit on the floor. "And killed my brother. That was very *gut* of you." He hurled the mimicked words at my father.

The stranger sneered, obviously enjoying the exchange. "What you think we oughta do with 'em, Lester? We got a free hand to do what we want, and I got me some ideas."

A sense of foreboding crawled up my spine and settled like a noose around my neck.

Lester appeared somewhat taken aback. "Not sure. Never done this afore. Maybe we should do the same thing the defense group has been doing with the other German traitors who don't cooperate." Lester made a fist and punched the air. "Put the fist of persuasion into action and let 'em see what it feels like." His lopsided grin revealed the gap between his front teeth. "Or we could do some damage to the bakery. That would serve 'em right." His eyes gleamed. "Maybe a fire. What d'you think?" He turned toward the stranger, now reveling in the idea of their rebellious behavior.

My father faced Lester. "What is this talk of hurting us and damaging our bakery? We have done nothing wrong." He pointed toward the wooden tables where the pans of bread rested. "We bake bread. Bread that feeds your family, Lester. Since when is baking bread a reason to hurt someone?"

The stranger repeated the accusation. "I have signed affidavits from two men, swearing the bread came from this bakery."

"But that is a lie. What proof do these men have to back up these affidavits? We didn't supply bread to any soldiers. How can you accuse us of something we did not do? We are loyal to this country. I kissed the American flag to prove my loyalty when we entered the war."

The stranger folded his thick arms across his chest. "So even then your loyalty was in question." He glanced at Lester. "I'm not surprised." He tapped his jacket pocket. "These affidavits are all we need to prove our case. The word of any upstanding American is proof enough against a Hun."

Anger welled in my chest. Speaking to this man was like talking to a brick wall. "My father's loyalty has never been questioned. You know that, Lester." Again, I hoped to appeal to Mr. Becroft's sense of integrity. "We are highly regarded in this town." My assertion was a little exaggerated. Since the United States entered the war, the residents of Marengo hadn't been as friendly to us. Though my parents and I had been born in this country, we were of German heritage, and that alone cast a cloud of suspicion over us—but I wouldn't admit such a thing to this bully. Besides, Mr. Becroft and the host of spies who'd been watching our store over the past weeks had already convinced whoever was in charge of this so-called group of patriots.

My father pointed to the stranger's pocket. "There must be something we can do to prove our innocence. I would like to confront the men who have signed the papers against us."

The man leaned back, bent his right knee, and rested the sole of his boot against our clean white wall. "That won't happen. The proof has been accepted by the authorities as valid and truthful. But there is one way you can protect your family and this bakery. A way you can prove your loyalty."

"Ja, of course. Tell me what I must do." My father bobbed his head, and strands of dark hair fell across his narrow forehead. "I will do whatever you ask."

"And what about you?" the man asked me. "Will you do whatever is asked?" The evil gleam in his eyes caused me to take a backward step.

My father flattened his palm across the handle of a bread knife. "I hope you are not asking what I think, because I would not want to hurt you." My father spit the words from between clenched teeth and wrapped his fingers around the knife handle.

"Relax and take your hand off that knife, old man. You couldn't hurt me if you tried." He tipped his head in my direction. "Your daughter is pretty enough, but I have no interest in a Hun."

I was silently thankful when he raked his gaze over me with a look that said I was unworthy of his consideration.

My father slid his hand away from the knife. "What is it that you want from me?"

The man grinned and dropped his arms to his sides. "I'll get to that in good time." He removed a small notebook from his pocket and turned the pages. "You know, I'd wager there isn't much of anything the Iowa Council of National Defense don't know about the three of you."

Had I looked in a mirror, I'm sure I would have been met by the same startled reflection I saw on both of my parents' faces. While Lester stood by and listened, the stranger pulled out a sheet of paper and rattled off facts that made my knees go weak. He knew that we had been members of the Amana Colonies and had lived in Homestead until ten years ago. He didn't blink as he read the dates we were born, the names of our customers, and even how we'd managed to purchase our bakery. "You had you a piece of good luck when old Mr. Lotz sold you this place for next to nothing."

My father stiffened at the remark. He believed the circumstances surrounding the purchase had been an act of God's grace, not good luck. "I was most thankful when Mr. Lotz agreed to sell me the business. He knew we had no money, so he agreed I could make monthly payments, but I gave a fair price for the bakery and have paid off my debt. God blessed my family when we moved here, and every day I thank Him for that."

"Well, as of today, I think you've run out of blessings." Using his foot, the man pushed away from the wall. "If you want to stay out of jail, this here daughter of yours is going to move back to them Amana Colonies, and she's gonna be reportin' to us on all the anti-American activity going on in that place."

Air escaped my lungs in a giant whoosh. "Is this some kind of joke? I can't move back to Homestead without my parents."

He shrugged his shoulders and curled his lip. "Then I guess maybe we ought to get to work, 'cause this ain't no joke." The stranger pointed at the worktables and shelves of pans and utensils. "Guess you can begin the damage in here, Lester."

"Wait! We have done nothing wrong. Will no one listen to me?" My father took a step forward, and Lester shoved him against the table.

Father winced in pain, and I stepped between him and Lester. "You don't understand how decisions are handled in the colonies. There are rules. I can't pack a suitcase and move back as though I'd never left—that's not how it works. The elders must give permission. I would have to meet with them and answer questions about why I want to come back. Afterward *they* would decide if I can return—not you." It gave me a bit of pleasure to tell them they couldn't control the elders.

"Then you best convince them elders you had some kind of a vision that proves you should return to the fold. Otherwise, the three of you won't have a place to live or a bakery." He arched forward, and I could smell his foul breath. "And that pretty little face of yours won't ever look the same if I find out you've told anyone about what's been said here today. You tell them Huns in Amana about our deal, and your mama and papa won't be around the next time you step foot in Marengo. You understand?" He chucked me beneath the chin with a thick finger.

Only moments earlier I thought I had deterred him with my explanation of the rules, but my moment of relief faded as quickly as it had arrived. I felt as though I'd taken a blow to the midsection. The burden of gaining the elders' permission had fallen squarely upon my shoulders.

CHAPTER 3

South Amana
Ilsa Redlich

I stomped the dusting of snow from my black leather shoes and entered the front door of the hotel. After hanging my cloak behind the desk, I beckoned the first of the guests forward. "Please write your name and home address in the register." I pointed to the empty space in the thick book and handed a pen to the man standing first in line. He dipped the nib into the ink and scrawled across the line. I turned the book. "You are traveling alone, Mr. Y-young?"

"Jonathan Young. And no, I am not traveling alone." He nodded toward a woman warming her hands near the stove. "My wife, Lillian. I wrote requesting a large room with a sitting area. We plan to be here through the winter. I trust you've made those arrangements for us."

I'd become accustomed to the abrupt manner of some of our

guests. They continued to stay at our hotels because the rooms were well maintained and the food was good, but many of them were unable to hide their anti-German feelings. However, Mr. Young's clipped words bore a disdainful tone that surprised me. I didn't recall seeing a letter from this man, but it wasn't unusual for Father to pick up the mail and make reservations without notifying me in advance.

"Let me check the keys." Long ago my father had developed a system. If a room was reserved for a specific date, the key would be removed from the hook and placed in the top drawer of the desk on the morning of the reservation. Each morning my father checked the reservation letters against the keys. If Mr. Young had requested the largest room, the key to room five should be missing from its hook.

An audible sigh escaped my lips when I stepped to the rack of keys and saw that number five had been removed. I returned to the desk, opened the drawer, and noted the same scrawl of handwriting on an envelope. My father had tucked the key inside Mr. Young's letter.

"You and your wife will be staying in room five—it is our largest, and I think you will find it most comfortable." By now Mrs. Young had stepped to her husband's side and was listening to my every word.

"I do hope the room provides a good deal of sunlight. Winter is such a dreary time of year." She looked up at her husband. "You requested a bright room, didn't you, Jonathan?"

"No need for concern, Mrs. Young. Number five is a corner room. You have windows on two sides." I removed the key from the envelope.

Mrs. Young rubbed her gloved hands together. "I do hope

that doesn't mean the room will be cold. Sometimes too many windows allow for unwanted drafts along with the sunlight."

Could I possibly please this woman? I bit back my urge to tell her she could place a shawl around her shoulders if she felt a chill and forced a smile instead. "If you decide the room isn't to your liking, we can offer you another, once one is empty."

Several guests were pacing back and forth while waiting their turn. Mr. and Mrs. Young seemed not to notice. I extended the key to Mr. Young.

He glanced at a large trunk and several cases. "Am I expected to carry my own baggage?"

"My Vater will be pleased to take your belongings to your room when he returns for the noonday meal. Number five is at the top of the stairs and to the right. We serve our meals on a regular schedule. Breakfast at seven o'clock, twelve o'clock for the noonday meal, and six o'clock for supper."

Mrs. Young touched her fingers to her neckline. "Dear me. I'm not accustomed to eating my meals at those hours. I much prefer to take my meals later in the day."

"It is the same for everyone, Mrs. Young. Here in the village, we have schedules to maintain so that we may worship together each day." I glanced toward the impatient guests standing behind her. "If you will excuse me, there are others who would like to settle into their rooms, as well."

Several men murmured in agreement, and the Youngs took the cue. One by one the remaining guests stepped forward. All of them men, all staying only one night. They signed their names, took their keys, and carried their own bags without complaint. None grumbled about the meal schedule. Of course, most were regulars who had stayed at the hotel on previous occasions and already knew the routine. They were businessmen who traveled for a living and stopped for a meal or stayed overnight depending upon when their connecting train would arrive.

While I was registering guests and assigning rooms, there was no time for thoughts of Albert, but once the final guest headed off to his room, sorrow descended like a crushing weight. I longed to rest my head on the desk and let my tears flow, but there would be no time for self-indulgent behavior. The guests would soon return downstairs and expect their noonday meal.

I passed through the dining room and peeked around the doorjamb into the kitchen. My mother glanced over her shoulder. "All went well at the station?"

"Ja. The train was on time." I cleared my throat. "I registered eleven guests."

"So many?"

I nodded. Usually we had two or three come in on the early train. Today had been unusual.

"Any others joining us to eat?"

"Nein. Garon said there were a few who decided to eat at the hotel in Upper before coming down to make their train connection at Lower." Because the Chicago, Milwaukee, St. Paul, and Pacific Railroad line passed through Upper South, and the Chicago, Rock Island, and Pacific passed through Lower South, hotels had been constructed near both depots. A wise decision, for the needs of many travelers could easily be met.

"Gut. I don't want to stretch the soup until it loses all flavor."

We were never certain how many guests we'd need to seat at the long wooden tables in the dining room. In the winter Mother would sometimes need to stretch a pot of soup and loaf of bread to feed a few more mouths. Although my father enjoyed thick chunks of bread to dip into his soup, when unexpected guests arrived, he had to settle for thin slices. Years ago he told me Mother could slice bread so thin he could read the Lord's Prayer through it. As a little girl I'd been sorely disappointed when I'd placed a piece of the bread atop the Bible and discovered he was wrong.

Moments later came the sound of stomping feet as my father entered the back door. I heard him ask my mother about Albert's departure before he strode into the dining room and greeted me. He looked at the number of settings arranged on the two long tables and arched his brows.

I shrugged. "We had a lot of arrivals."

"So it will be skinny bread with my soup." His blue eyes, so similar in color to my own, twinkled with delight. "This would be a gut day to go and eat with Sister Barbara, where I can get my stomach full."

I grinned and shook my head. "I don't think that would make Mutter happy."

"Ja. Sister Barbara would be telling everyone that I like her cooking better than your Mutter's. And if she didn't, I can be sure that Garon would take great pleasure in passing the word. That boy likes to play jokes even more than I do." He laughed and strode toward the kitchen, where I heard him tease my mother with the idea of going to the neighborhood kitchen house for his noonday meal.

While the guests congregated in the parlor, my father returned to the dining room. "Your Mutter didn't think I was so funny. She said she was too busy to listen to my nonsense." He chuckled and picked up the spoons and handed them to me. "I have some gut news that was delivered to me at work today."

"Ja? And what is that?" I lifted the water pitcher from the sideboard and poured water into one of the glasses.

"The elders tell me they are searching for someone to help you and your Mutter here at the hotel."

Except for the assistance Albert and my father provided after work or when they returned for the noonday meal, my mother and I had been without any additional help for the last three months. And now with Albert gone, an extra set of hands would be most welcome.

"Finally! Who is it, and when will she arrive?"

"You were not listening. I said they are searching. They want to be sure they find someone who can speak and read English and is also well suited to the work. We were fortunate to have Sister Hulda's help for so many years. Finding a replacement is not easy."

My father was correct. Sister Hulda had been a good fit for the hotel. She possessed a cheery personality, and her ability to speak English had improved through the years. But with the passing of time, her aching joints made it impossible for her to continue climbing the stairs or standing at the washtubs. She had been pleased when the elders placed her in charge of the Red Cross projects and even more delighted when she was assigned an apartment next to her sister's. Though I was happy for her, I didn't enjoy the additional work. Especially when the hotel was full.

"I hope they find someone with a gut disposition like Sister Hulda's. They should consider letting you or Mutter help them decide."

"Ach! Such a thing you are suggesting." He waved his hand as if to brush away my comment.

"I think it only right that we should have a say."

My words carried a sharp edge, and my father looked up, his brows knit in a deep frown. "I think you have forgotten how to show proper respect for your Vater, ja?"

"Ja. I am sorry." Ashamed, I fixed my gaze on the floor and continued around the table.

He stepped toward me and lifted my chin. "You are forgiven. I know you are not yourself today. We are all sad that Albert has gone off to serve in the army." His lips tipped in a sad smile. "I should have waited to say anything until the elders have selected someone, but I thought the news would cheer you. You understand it is not my place to question the church leaders. They will tell me what I need to know when the time is right."

"Ja. I know this, Vater. And I am pleased to know the elders have not forgotten we need help."

The moment the village bell rang, my father motioned for the guests to enter the dining room. Mrs. Young wasn't among them.

My mother filled the soup bowls before we passed the heaping platter of sliced boiling beef she had used for making the soup stock, along with bowls of fried potatoes, cabbage salad, and applesauce. I carried the bowls to each of the guests. When I placed Mr. Young's bowl before him, I stopped for a moment. "Your wife is not going to join us?"

He turned his head and looked at me. "She asked that you bring a tray to the room at two o'clock."

I didn't want to discuss his request in front of the other customers. "Could you please remain a few minutes after we've finished the meal?"

Though Mr. Young didn't acknowledge that I'd spoken to

him, I knew he'd heard me, for he stiffened his shoulders and turned away. During the meal he answered when another guest addressed him, but otherwise he remained silent and appeared somewhat uncomfortable.

When the meal was completed, my father carried the soup tureen into the kitchen while my mother cleared the sideboard of serving bowls. The guests strolled toward the parlor or returned up the stairs—all except Mr. Young, who approached. "In the future I would prefer to dine at a table by myself. My wife will take all of her meals upstairs."

"I'm sorry, Mr. Young, but that is impossible. We don't have separate tables. All of our meals are served in the same fashion as we use in our kitchen houses. Although we would like to accommodate you and your wife, we don't have the space or enough help to serve individual tables." He didn't appear convinced, so I forged on. "We've found that our guests usually enjoy sharing our customs. They say it gives them a better understanding of our ways."

"There is a problem, Ilsa?" My father returned to the dining room and came alongside me in four long strides. Though he'd asked me, his gaze was fixed upon Mr. Young.

Mr. Young didn't wait for me to explain his wishes. Instead, he repeated the requests to my father as though he hadn't heard a word I had spoken. "And I would prefer at least two choices for my meals. Is there no menu to choose from?"

My father shook his head. "We offer few choices in our dining room—or in any other dining room in the colonies, especially during the wintertime. In the summer sometimes guests enjoy taking their meals outdoors under the trees in the side yard, but there is little choice during cold weather. Let me assure you that our meals are hearty, and our visitors have never complained about any of the food my wife has served to them."

My father motioned toward one of the benches. "Sit down." The two men dropped to the bench with their backs to me. "In your letter you made none of the requests I am now hearing. Why is that?"

"Because most hotel dining rooms offer a menu and do their best to accommodate their guests. I mentioned in the letter that my wife suffers from bouts of melancholy."

My father nodded. "Ja, I remember, but what is this *melancholy*? I have never heard of this ailment."

I wasn't sure either of the men realized I was still within earshot, but since the initial conversation had been between Mr. Young and me, I decided my presence couldn't be considered eavesdropping. Besides, if I was going to carry meals to Mrs. Young, I wanted to know more about her illness.

"My wife wants to have children. We both want children." He bowed his head. "So far, that hasn't been possible. She lost another only a month ago." He squirmed on the bench, his discomfort obvious. "She's become very despondent, and her doctor thought a change of scenery might be the answer. He said the peace and quiet of the colonies might be good for her."

My father rubbed his jaw. "We are a quiet kind of place, for sure, but most people don't come here for long stays in the winter. Ja, we have some who spend the spring and summers, and even a few who come when the leaves are changing color in the fall, but not during the winter. The doctor didn't think someplace with *warm* weather would be gut?"

I knew my father was thinking of the Andersons, who came

to spend each spring here. Mrs. Anderson went south for the winter months, and her husband joined her when business permitted, which I gathered from what she'd told me wasn't very often.

"I understand Iowa winters, Mr. Redlich, but a warm climate would be quite impossible. I'd be unable to visit my wife if she went to a distant state, and I can't afford to be away from my law office in Des Moines for long periods of time. I want to spend as much time as possible with her. You understand."

"Ja. Of course. Is not gut for a man and wife to be separated. We will do our best to help her while you are gone, but you should explain to her that we do not have anyone who can always run upstairs with her meals. Is better she's around other people, don't you think?"

Mr. Young exhaled a deep sigh. I wasn't sure if he was annoyed at my father's suggestion or with the fact that he hadn't succeeded with his demands.

"I'll explain, but when I'm away, I trust someone will check on her well-being if she doesn't come downstairs to take her meals."

As the bell situated in the woodshed behind the tailor's shop tolled, my father pushed to his feet. "Ja, for sure we will look in on her." My father glanced over his shoulder and spotted me. "Is time for me to return to my work, but first I will carry your belongings to your room."

Mr. Young jumped to his feet. "You go on to work. I'm sure I can manage to get them upstairs."

Strange that Mr. Young was suddenly able to manage his own baggage. His changeable attitude baffled me. For sure, they were a strange couple who would require special treatment.

But without Albert around to provide daily amusement and distraction during the long cold months, perhaps the Youngs would furnish a much-needed diversion during the cold winter months.

CHAPTER 4

Most evenings I looked forward to attending prayer meeting, but tonight was different. Tonight I was at odds with God over my brother's departure and would have preferred to remain at home. But barring illness or other grave misfortune, absence at meeting was unacceptable. The fact that we attended eleven church meetings each week prompted strange looks and more than a question or two from outsiders, but for us it was a normal way of life. Unless something out of the ordinary arose, evening prayer meeting lasted only a half hour or so. Afterward, it was good to relax and visit for a short time with friends and neighbors.

The wet snow squished beneath my shoes as I trudged behind my parents, annoyed that each step took me closer to the Leiserings' residence. Like the kitchen houses where most residents ate their meals, the place we met for prayer meeting was determined by where we lived. Some met in the meetinghouse, while others met in private homes. I'd always been pleased that we met in a home, for I enjoyed the closeness this arrangement permitted. Tonight, however, I would have preferred the formality of the meetinghouse.

Garon smiled and motioned for me to wait as he approached with his parents and sisters. "We are going to make popcorn after meeting, and my Mutter said you are welcome to join us."

I shook my head. "I don't feel like being with other people."

"And that is why you should join us. It isn't gut to sit around and think about Albert. It's better to keep busy."

"Maybe, but I'm not in the best of humor. You'd probably have more fun without me."

He stepped closer. "That is not possible. I won't have any fun at all without you." His dark brown eyes twinkled in the moonlight. "Besides, Albert would be the first to tell you to have fun and quit moping." I knew Garon was correct. Albert had told me as much before he'd departed. Yet it seemed wrong to continue my life as if nothing had changed. Before we entered the Leiserings' house, Garon urged me to rethink my decision.

"I'll come for a little while." The moment I agreed, a sense of betrayal struck like a winter storm and continued throughout the meeting. Except for special prayers asking God for Albert's safekeeping, the service continued as if nothing had changed. And for everyone except my family, nothing *had* changed. I tried to remain mindful of why I was there. I needed to focus on God, but tonight my thoughts of God transformed into feelings of betrayal and anger. So while the others bowed in prayer, I thought about Albert and wondered what he was doing on this cold late-October night. Was he still on the train, or perhaps waiting in a strange railroad depot, or maybe he had already arrived at Camp Pike. If so, I wondered what it must be like to be away from home, surrounded by strangers from all over the country—men who had no understanding of our beliefs. Would they treat my brother with disdain, or would they be at least respectful, if not kind? I shivered at the possibilities.

"Come along, Ilsa." My mother grasped my arm and jarred me from my private thoughts. I stood, embarrassed that I'd needed to be alerted that the meeting had ended. She leaned close. "You were still praying?"

I avoided her question with one of my own. "Garon has invited me to join his family and several other young people at his house to make popcorn. What do you think?"

Her lips curved in a broad smile. "I think that would be very nice. You need to enjoy some time with your friends. It will be gut for you."

Before we departed, some of our neighbors gathered around my parents—all of them eager for news of Albert's departure. Several of the men patted my father on the back and lauded the merit of having our men go off to serve, while others shook their heads and thought they should all remain at home. Of course, I sided with those who thought the men should remain at home. The women who circled my mother didn't voice an opinion either way. Instead, they pledged to keep Albert in their daily prayers. I hoped their prayers would be answered, for I was certain God had turned a deaf ear toward mine.

I bid my parents good-bye and walked down the front steps of the Leiserings' house. My breath puffed vaporous clouds, and I lamented the early arrival of winter as I shivered and took hold of Garon's arm.

"This is Iowa. In two or three days, fall will return and we will forget this bit of snow ever arrived."

I knew Garon was correct, but it didn't erase my dour mood.

As we approached his house, I pointed to the trees, the moonlight emphasizing their drooping leaves. "Each fall I look forward to the changing colors. That is what I truly enjoy. But now the leaves are spoiled from the early frost."

"Then we must make the most of this snow and find something that will cause you to enjoy it, as well." He tugged on my hand.

"Where are you going?" Garon's sister, Christina, tromped after us as he pulled me along toward the rear of the house. "Can I come with you?"

"To the backyard. And yes, you can come."

The layer of snow glistened in the light of the moon as Garon scanned the area. He held his sister's arm when she attempted to run into the fresh blanket of snow. "Over there. We are going to make snow angels."

Christina jumped up and down in delight. Carefully, she dropped onto the snow and flapped her arms up and down. When she finished, Garon pulled her to a stand. "A beautiful job, Christina." After he handed her a stick, she printed her name in the snow beneath her angel. "Your turn, Ilsa."

Christina ran toward the house, worried the others would begin popping corn without her.

"Maybe we should go inside, too," I told him. "It's cold and I don't want to get my cape wet with snow."

He frowned. "Where's the girl who always enjoys having fun?"

I shrugged. "Maybe her joy departed on the train with her brother."

"Such talk! I'm not going to listen to any more of it." Garon removed his coat and grabbed my arm. Shoving my hand into the sleeve, he wrapped his jacket around my shoulder. "Now there are no more excuses. I want a snow angel with your name beneath it."

My heavy shawl rumpled beneath Garon's coat, but I knew there would be no denying his request. I stooped down and fell backward in the snow, flailing my arms up and down like a rooster flapping its wings. After helping me to my feet, Garon lifted the jacket from my shoulders and shook off the excess snow. Just like Christina, I used a stick to print my name in the snow. Garon shrugged into his jacket and fell backward beside the imprint of my angel. While he moved his arms, I leaned down and gathered a handful of snow, formed it into a firm snowball, and backed away from him. The minute he jumped to his feet, I laughed and tossed the snowball in his direction. It hit his arm with a splat.

"So you want to have a snowball fight, ja?" He bent down and quickly scooped a clump of snow from the ground.

I turned and scurried toward the house but not before he hit my shoulder with a perfect throw. "You forget I have a gut aim, Garon. You better keep your distance," I shouted. My foot slipped beneath me as I leaned down to collect another handful of snow, and I landed on my backside with a thud.

Garon raced to my side, his laughter ringing in the air. He scooped another handful of snow and attacked. I rolled away from him. Snow flew through the air as we tossed handfuls back and forth until finally he captured my hands and held them tight inside his gloved ones. We panted for breath while he rubbed my hands for a moment before helping me to my feet.

He gathered me in his arms and held me close. "I think I have a duty to help warm you, since it is my fault you are so cold. I don't want you to turn into an icicle."

I enjoyed the strength and warmth of his arms, but if Christina should happen outside, word would spread all over the village that we had been embracing in the backyard. "I think it might be warmer inside by the fire."

"Maybe safer but not warmer than in my arms, Ilsa." Garon's soft, deep chuckle resonated within me, and I smiled up at him. He leaned down and lightly kissed my lips.

"Now I *know* we must go inside."

The following morning, when Garon stopped at the hotel to pick up guests needing a ride to the train station, I thanked him for insisting I go with him the previous evening.

"You see? I sometimes know what is best. A gut quality for a husband, ja?" He grinned and helped himself to a biscuit while waiting for the travelers to gather.

My mother patted Garon's shoulder and laughed. "A man with gut qualities does not need to brag on himself. He lets his wife do it for him. But since you are not yet a husband, I suppose you must be like the rooster in the henhouse and strut so you are noticed, ja?"

"Ja! I want to make sure Ilsa knows I am a good catch, or she may look another direction before the year is over." My mother and I laughed as Garon lifted his knees high and flapped his arms while circling toward the dining room.

Our laughter gained my father's attention, and he glanced around the corner into the dining room. One look and he stared at the young man to whom I was betrothed. "What is this, Garon? Do we need to call the doctor? You have some new illness?"

Garon raked his fingers through his thick brown hair. "I am imitating a rooster."

"This I can see, but for what reason?" A grin played at the corners of my father's mouth. He loved a good joke even more than my mother. "Ach! If you want to impress my daughter, you will need to do better than that!" With that, my father headed toward the kitchen, performing an even better imitation of a rooster.

My mother shushed him when he started to crow. "Stop, Odell! You will have all the guests thinking we have lost our senses."

My father laughed and kissed my mother's cheek. She blushed and turned away. "Out of the kitchen—both of you." As if on cue, the bell tolled in the distance. "You see? You're going to be late if you don't hurry."

The men didn't appear overly concerned, but my father headed off to the wheelwright shop while Garon collected bags and helped the guests into the carriage. Before leaving, Garon poked his head around the corner. "I'll see you when the next train comes through."

"Ja, and maybe you shouldn't be strutting too much while you're carrying those bags." I giggled and waved. When the house was finally quiet, I was hit by the realization that I'd truly enjoyed myself—both last evening and this morning. Perhaps Garon was right—being sad wouldn't change anything. It would only make time pass more slowly.

A short time later, as I cleared the dining tables, I heard a distinct thumping overhead. I glanced toward the kitchen, where my mother was washing dishes. "Did you hear that?"

She nodded. "Sounds like it's coming from number five. Mr. Young left with Garon, and his wife didn't come down for breakfast. Maybe you should go up and see if she needs help."

I finished wiping the tables, carried the remaining items to the kitchen, and placed them on the counter along with my damp cloth. "Do you think she is expecting breakfast?"

My mother shook her head. Wisps of dark hair fanned from

beneath her small black cap. "I think your Vater made it clear that we do not serve meals in the rooms, but if she is not feeling well, then you should let me know. Some toast and a cup of tea might help her."

"I will ask if she is ill, but . . ." Another thump. I glanced toward the ceiling and then at my mother. "If she is well and says she desires breakfast in her room, what do I tell her?"

"Tell her there are a few strips of bacon, some fried potatoes, and some biscuits, and we would enjoy having her come downstairs to eat. She can sit in the kitchen or dining room, whichever she prefers."

I ran up the stairs, pleased my mother hadn't expected me to carry a tray to the woman. Without Sister Hulda to help, I hoped Mr. and Mrs. Young wouldn't ask for service we couldn't provide. Besides, to treat some guests with favoritism wasn't our way. Since all of us were created in the image of God, we believe all should be treated with equal dignity and respect, without deference to another. Outsiders found our desire to live with equality as strange as we found their desire for excess and favoritism. Still, I didn't want Mrs. Young to be ill and no one to come to her aid.

I turned down the hallway and tapped on her door. "Mrs. Young?"

"Come in. The door is unlocked."

I pushed down the heavy metal latch and opened the door a few inches. "Is there something you need? I heard banging overhead when I was in the dining room."

"Come in, come in. Don't stand in the hallway." Still in her dressing gown, she motioned me inside. "Where is my breakfast? Before my husband left, he said you would bring a tray to me. I'm still waiting." She glanced out the window. "I'm accustomed to having my coffee first and my breakfast a half hour later."

Though she was slight of build, the woman appeared perfectly healthy to me. I didn't understand why Mr. Young would tell her such a thing. For that matter, why would she want to eat alone in her room? It didn't make good sense. Those facts aside, being alone wouldn't help her overcome her feelings of sadness.

"Your husband misspoke, Mrs. Young. If we have an ill guest, we do try to help in any way we can. But through the years we have learned that our guests enjoy joining in our customs when they visit the colonies." I had already explained this to her husband. He'd obviously failed to convey the message. "Why don't you finish dressing and come downstairs? My Mutter and I would enjoy visiting with you while we clean the kitchen. All the others have eaten breakfast and departed."

Mrs. Young twisted the ribbons that trimmed her fancy dressing gown. "I shouldn't go too much longer without eating. Perhaps it would be nice to leave my room."

I smiled and agreed. "There's bacon and fried potatoes, and I know there are a few biscuits remaining—and my Mutter keeps coffee on the stove most of the time." I stepped toward the door. "I'll tell Mutter you'll be down shortly."

She cast a soulful look in my direction. "I don't know what I'm to do with myself in this place."

"The weather has warmed a little, and the sun is shining. Perhaps you could take a walk. We have some lovely trails through the woods you might enjoy." Mrs. Young didn't look like a woman who enjoyed the outdoors, but we weren't a community that offered recreational activities for visitors.

She wrinkled her nose. "I don't enjoy walking by myself—especially when I'm unfamiliar with the area." Her lips formed a childish pout. "What do you do when you're not working in the hotel?"

I recalled playing in the snow last night with Garon, but I didn't think I'd mention that bit of pleasure to her. "I attend Red Cross meetings. And the ladies gather to quilt or knit when time permits. We have prayer meeting each night, where we see our neighbors, and sometimes I go to visit friends afterward."

Mrs. Young sighed and folded her hands in her lap. "I'd like to attend the Red Cross meetings with you—and maybe I could help with the quilting. Otherwise, time is going to pass far too slowly. I must remember to have Jonathan bring me some additional books."

I pushed down the door latch and turned to leave.

"Wait! You didn't tell me what time I should be ready for the Red Cross meeting. I'll need time to change dresses and fix my hair."

I glanced over my shoulder. "You have plenty of time. It isn't until next Thursday at one o'clock. And there's no need to wear a fancy dress. We'll all be in our simple clothing."

"What about the quilting? When is that? I'm not much good with a needle, but I can give it a try." She ignored my remark about attire.

"I think we're supposed to meet the day after tomorrow. I'll check with my Mutter and let you know."

For some reason I took pity upon the woman. Perhaps because her husband had left her alone in unfamiliar surroundings or because I'd heard him speak of his wife's melancholy. She appeared as forlorn as I would likely feel if someone deserted me in the middle of Iowa City.

"After I finish cleaning the kitchen, I must attend to a few errands at the general store. If time permits, I could take you for a short tour of the village, if you'd like."

She immediately brightened. "Oh, that would be great fun. I'll be downstairs quick as a wink."

I nodded and backed out the door. I'd never before heard such a term, but I guessed that she meant she would soon join us in the kitchen. Indeed, these people were going to prove most interesting. Mrs. Young seemed as changeable as her husband.

CHAPTER 5

A short time later Mrs. Young appeared with a coat draped over her arm and a smile on her lips. My mother greeted her and motioned to one of the chairs. "When Ilsa said you would be coming downstairs, I put your food in the oven to keep it warm."

"That was most kind of you, but I believe coffee and one of the biscuits will suffice. I'm excited to begin my tour of the village as soon as possible."

My mother smiled. "Ilsa must first complete her chores. You will have enough time to eat more than a biscuit."

Mrs. Young sighed and set her handbag on the chair. "In that case I suppose I will have some of the bacon and potatoes, though I doubt either will be good for my waistline."

My mother glanced at me, and I shrugged. Mrs. Young didn't miss the gesture. "I mean that if I eat such hearty fare, I soon won't fit into my clothes."

"Ach! We do not worry about such things here in the colonies. Hard work takes care of too much padding around the middle." My mother pinched her waist and smiled.

While Mrs. Young ate, I completed my duties in the kitchen. Between bites, she asked several questions, and I was surprised by her curiosity. Of course, most visitors came to the villages because of a desire to learn about our ways, but I hadn't expected such interest from Mrs. Young. Perhaps because both she and her husband had seemed so unfriendly when they'd arrived.

Mrs. Young wiped her mouth and placed the napkin on the table. "I would like to see the men making bricks."

I carried her plate to the sink and dropped it into the dishwater. I had just explained that because of the clay in South Amana, we had a large brickyard in our village. "They do not make bricks during the winter, and they don't make as many now as they did years ago, but if you return in the late spring or summer, you can watch. And if you visit in the summer, it is very pretty here. All the fruit trees are in bloom, the grapevines are covered with thick, full leaves, our gardens are filled with beautiful flowers, and you can taste the best vegetables in all of Iowa."

"I'll mention that to Mr. Young. We may want to return this summer."

Although Mrs. Young appeared disappointed she couldn't see bricks being made, I assured her we could walk past the brickyard before her departure. "Today there won't be time to go that far—not if you want to see the basket maker or tinsmith, but I'm sure you'll see plenty of bricks during our walk. All but four of the houses in South are made from our brick—even the big chicken house and the outer walls of the granary." I tried to keep pride from my voice, but it proved difficult. I believed we lived in the finest of all the villages. No doubt colonists in other villages would disagree with me.

While Mrs. Young slipped into her coat, I removed my cloak from the peg and bid my mother good-bye. As we walked down the front walkway, she called after us. "Don't be gone too long, Ilsa. I will need help cleaning the rooms."

I waved and nodded. "We will take a short tour, and then we can see more on another day."

Mrs. Young didn't seem to mind, especially when I told her we would end our tour at the general store. "You are a lovely girl, Ilsa. What you lack in beauty is overcome by your pleasant disposition."

Her words stung, for I didn't believe my appearance unappealing. Garon told me I was the most beautiful girl in the village. And though I knew he stretched the truth, I never thought of myself as someone in need of any special trait to offset a physical flaw. Albert had sometimes teased me about the slight crook in my nose, but he'd always told me I possessed the prettiest eyes and brightest smile he had ever seen.

I decided to ignore her comment. Instead, I pointed out the tailor shop as we passed by and was surprised when Mrs. Young asked if he might be willing to hem one of her dresses. "The tailor makes the more difficult pieces, such as suits and coats. Women here do their own mending and hemming." A gust of wind tossed dead leaves across our path, and I lowered my head. "You do not sew?"

"Dear me, no. I detest needlework. I don't know what I would do if I had to perform such tedious work."

I was puzzled, for she'd said she wanted to join our quilting group. Wasn't quilting a form of sewing? The woman was an enigma. We stopped to visit for a few moments with the tinsmith and the basket maker, where she attempted to purchase a gathering basket. She was taken aback when her request was denied.

As we departed the shop, she traced her fingers over the basket. I didn't miss the longing in her eyes. "I truly wanted this basket."

"Our craftsmen work hard to supply the needs of the villagers. To make enough for sale to outsiders would be difficult, but you can buy some of our woolens and calicos at the general store." I hoped the idea of choosing fabric would appease her desire to purchase something made in the colonies.

"Yes, that would be nice. I suppose I could take it home and have some dresses made." We continued onward, and I pointed out a kitchen house and our meetinghouse. She stopped in front of the meetinghouse, her brow knit in a frown. "It doesn't look like any church I've ever seen, and I've seen many churches during my travels abroad and in this country, as well." She meandered up the walkway toward the long brick building. "Most churches have doors in the center, and steeples, and they're much more ornate. If you hadn't told me this was your church, I would have thought it another large residence or one of those kitchen houses. Why does it have doors at either end?"

"The men and women enter through separate doors and sit on opposite sides of the church. It is our custom."

"Just like at meals. You people have strange customs."

Her judgment of our ways troubled me. "I am sure we would say the same thing if we visited one of your cities."

She chuckled. "I suppose you're correct. I'm sorry if I offended you. It wasn't my intent."

Her words of regret surprised me. She didn't seem the type to offer quick apologies. Then again, I hadn't expected her to show such interest in the village and our people. "In what countries have you seen all of these beautiful churches?"

She tapped her gloved finger against her cheek. "Let me see if I can remember all of them. Jonathan and I have traveled extensively, but I also traveled with my parents before I married Jonathan. We met in England. I have visited France, Italy, Germany, Poland, Switzerland, and Norway." She shivered when she mentioned the final two. "My parents decided to live in Norway for a year. I thought I would never get warm while we were there."

I couldn't imagine visiting even one of those places, for I'd never traveled beyond the borders of our villages. "Did you learn to speak all of those languages?"

Her eyes clouded, and the openness she'd first exhibited disappeared like a curtain drawn across a window. "No, of course not. I speak a little French and Italian, and I was forced to learn some Norwegian while we lived there, but I've forgotten most of what I learned. I was a young girl at that time."

"Do you speak German?"

"Only the rudimentary terms such as *good morning* or *good evening*. We were never in Germany for very long. Why do you ask?"

I shrugged. "I was curious if you would be able to speak to some of the villagers in our own tongue. Of course, we do not speak pure German." I giggled. "When relatives come from Germany to visit, some of them have trouble understanding our Amana German."

She tipped her head to one side. I could see the curiosity in her eyes. "And what is Amana German?"

I moved my shopping basket to the other arm as we continued down the street. "Our villages were settled mostly by people from

Germany, but there were some who came from Alsace-Lorraine and Switzerland. The German language has been altered a little by the people who live here."

I waved to Brother Wilbur as he passed by with a wagonload of freshly hewn logs. "Some of our men are busy cutting down trees." We stopped in front of the general store, and I pointed to the west. "We have a large sawmill where they cut up the trees and then deliver the logs to our homes. We chop them for use in our stoves throughout the winter."

Mrs. Young hurried inside the general store without asking any questions. Though she'd expressed great interest in brick-making, she appeared to have little interest in the sawmill or logging.

Brother Peter ambled toward us when we entered, and I made a brief introduction of our guest. After a quick nod Mrs. Young continued down the aisle without giving him an opportunity to ask any questions. The storekeeper's disappointment was obvious to me, though I doubted the woman had noticed. I handed him my mother's list, and while he set to work weighing out sugar and coffee, I joined Mrs. Young, who stood staring at the bolts of fabric.

She looked up as I approached. "I'm not certain how much I should buy. I believe I'll write to my seamstress and ask her opinion before I purchase anything." She surveyed the store with obvious interest and curiosity. "I'm surprised by the variety and abundance of items."

"People from the surrounding communities come to shop here, so you will find most anything you want or need. And if it isn't available, the storekeeper can order it—everything from farm machinery to delicate lace. Many of the salesmen who supply the store stay at the hotel."

Mrs. Young continued through the aisles while I returned to go over the remainder of my mother's order with Brother Peter. As he was listing our items in the ledger, she placed a packet of needles and a spool of thread on the counter. "I'd like to purchase these."

I didn't question her acquisition, though I didn't understand why someone who couldn't sew would want needles and thread. The woman was indeed a mystery.

CHAPTER 6

Homestead
Jutta Schmitt

After Lester Becroft and the threatening stranger had departed, my father penned a letter to arrange a meeting with the *Bruderrat*, the elders who presided over the village of Homestead. Although my parents had chosen to leave communal life in Amana many years ago, they had left on good terms. And in most circumstances, former members wishing to return were welcomed back. My father had been clear that he and my mother agreed with my decision to return. Neither of my parents wanted me to move away, but it was true enough that we'd reached an agreement. I must return to the colonies and a way of life I'd left ten years ago. And for me, there had been little contact since my departure. Occasionally one or two of my parents' old friends would stop at the bakery for a brief visit when passing through Marengo, but otherwise we now lived in a different world.

We had returned to Homestead only once that I could remember, and that had been to attend a funeral a few months after we'd moved away. Now as I sat beside my father in our rented buggy, my thoughts drifted to Lester Becroft and the threats leveled against us. I had hoped that Mrs. Becroft would visit the bakery and I could question her about her husband and his brutish behavior, for in the past, she'd been at the bakery door nearly every day. But we'd seen nothing of her since her husband had made his unwelcome appearance. I wondered if she agreed that we were anti-Americans who supported the Germans in the war.

"Here we are." My father's words drew me from my thoughts.

Not much had changed since my last visit. An automobile parked outside the hotel seemed strangely out of place in the town, and the women weren't wearing as much calico. Otherwise, the village appeared much the same. There were a few familiar faces, but after ten years, I'd forgotten names. I had been thrust into another world, where life moved at a different pace, a place where I'd been required to learn new ways. What once had been common and familiar now seemed strangely foreign and unfamiliar. I was glad my father was at my side. If I was going to gain acceptance back into the colonies, I'd be required to make some misleading statements—possibly tell some outright lies. His presence would make this charade a little more bearable.

My father pulled back on the reins and brought the horse and buggy to a halt in front of the meetinghouse. My heart skipped a beat, and I clasped a hand to my chest. I'd heard of people dropping dead from such episodes with their heart, and for a moment I wondered if I would live until tomorrow. "We are to speak to them in the *meetinghouse*?" The thought of telling lies to the elders was offensive enough, but to do so in church made me shiver in fear. Perhaps I should worry more about God striking me dead and less about my heart skipping beats!

"Ja. You do not remember that the Bruderrat usually meets at the church?" My father patted my hand. "I know this is frightening for you, Jutta. If I could take your place, you know I would."

I forced a smile and nodded. The men from the Iowa Council of National Defense had given us no choice: I was the one who must return. The elders would never believe either of my parents would return without the other—or without me, for that matter. But for me to return without them would not be so difficult to accept. Besides, I had developed a story that wasn't far from the truth—one I thought would make them readily agree to my return.

A blast of cold wind whipped at my cloak, and I clutched it tight against my throat. With my head bent against the wind, I took my father's arm. We were nearing the church when I heard one of the elders welcome my father, and I looked up. The two men exchanged greetings, and then my father tipped his head in my direction. "Do you remember my daughter, Jutta?"

The older man nodded. "Ja, I remember her. You are a grown woman now, and I am told you wish to come back to live in the colonies."

I tried to respond, but my tongue stuck to the roof of my mouth. Finally, I nodded.

He pulled the brim of his hat low to block the sun from his eyes. "You should know that this matter must be addressed by the *Grossebruderrat*. Since you have no family here, a decision must be made about where you will live and work should they agree to your request."

"But she wishes to return as soon as possible, Brother Herman, and she is familiar with Homestead." I could feel the muscle tense in my father's forearm. "Surely the Bruderrat here in Homestead can agree to bring Jutta back without the need of involving the Grossebruderrat."

"Nein." He shook his head. "But there is no need for worry, Brother Bert. We sent out word, and all the members of the Grossebruderrat have gathered in the church to speak with Jutta. I'm certain they will make a decision today."

I don't know what startled me more—to hear my father once again addressed as Brother Bert or to discover the Grossebruderrat was waiting to interrogate me behind the closed church doors. I clenched my fingers into the sleeve of my father's wool jacket.

My father squeezed my hand and took a forward step. "Then I suppose we should go inside."

Brother Herman shook his head. "Only Jutta. She is the one who has requested the right to return and live among us. She is twenty-six and of an age to make this decision for herself, Brother Bert. After speaking with her, I will advise you if the members of the Grossebruderrat wish to make any inquiries of you."

I could see the hesitation in my father's eyes. "But I told Jutta I would come with her."

Brother Herman smiled. "And you have. But this is as far as you can go. Jutta must come forward alone and make her wishes known. The elders have read your letter and know there is no objection from you or Sister Eva."

Brother Herman pointed toward the women's door of the meetinghouse. "You know your way inside, Jutta." Brother Herman extended his hand to my father. While they shook hands, I walked toward the church entrance and wondered if the Kiefer family still lived in the separate apartment inside the church and if they were still assigned to clean the building. Their daughter, Elizabeth, and I had been friends when we were much younger.

As I walked down the center aisle of the church, my gaze fell upon the familiar finger-size hole—the hole that permitted us to remove a square of wood from the floor and slosh the dirty scrub water down to the cellar beneath the church. How I'd loved helping Elizabeth scrub the floor, all so I could do something that seemed so wrong and yet was exactly what we'd been told to do.

Now I was doing something that seemed terribly wrong, as well. Yet returning to the community was what I had to do. When the door on the other side of the room slammed, I looked up to see Brother Herman enter and hurry to the front with the other men.

He stepped toward his chair and waved me forward. Afterward, he extended his arm toward the other men. "We have all read your father's letter, but we need to hear from you."

I folded my hands in front of me and, without any elaboration, stated that I wished to return to live in the colonies.

"Well, this much we already know," said one of the elders. "It is why you want to return that interests us, Sister Jutta. You have been living in Marengo for how long? Nine or ten years now, and suddenly you want to come back and live here? Maybe you want to grow closer to God or maybe you are having problems with a man? Tell us why you want to return and live among us."

I knew I should look at them—it was the courteous thing to do, but I simply couldn't. "I'm sure you know there are many threats against those of us who are of German heritage." The elders murmured in agreement and nodded. "I no longer feel safe in Marengo."

"These threats, they are only against you and not your Mutter or Vater? What kinds of threats have been made?" The questions came from the far end of the table, from an elder I'd never before seen.

My heart plummeted like a rock in water. I had hoped to avoid telling any direct lies. I couldn't mention the Iowa Council of National Defense. That would give rise to even more questions, and I might slip and tell them that I had been sent as a spy to live among them. The men shifted in their chairs, and Brother Herman leaned forward. "Well, Jutta? What have you to tell us in answer to these questions?"

"I am somewhat embarrassed to speak of such things to you—especially in church. But the threats come from men in the town. Remarks about what they will do to me if I don't cooperate and do what they ask."

One of the brothers slapped his hand on the wooden table. "Ach! Such vile behavior. It is no wonder you want to escape from such a place. I can understand why your Mutter and Vater want you to return, but why do they want to stay in a place where their daughter is treated in this manner?"

Perspiration dotted my forehead as I attempted to arrive at a response. "His contract!" The men looked at me as though I'd shot a gun into the air. I hadn't meant to shout, but I'd been so delighted to think of an answer that I'd been overwhelmed with excitement.

"His contract?" Brother Herman arched his brows.

"Yes. My father signed a contract when he purchased the bakery."

Brother Herman nodded and leaned forward to speak to the other elders. "Brother Bert must stay there because of his contract to purchase the bakery. He has a lawful obligation he must meet."

"Ah," they murmured while bobbing their heads.

I uttered a sigh of relief. I hadn't really lied. Even though my father had already met the obligations of his contract, it was

Brother Herman who had delivered the incorrect information to the Grossebruderrat, not me. I shifted my weight from one foot to the other and hoped they wouldn't think of any further questions for me. In truth, I wanted to flee from the room, flee from the village, flee from this country that was supposed to grant everyone freedom from persecution. Instead, I waited for these men to decide my fate. I would either move here and do harm to the people of Amana or return to Marengo and go to jail. If they knew the depth of my deceit, they would never again let me set foot in the villages.

I was lost in thought when Brother Herman cleared his throat. "This does not take long for us to decide, Sister Jutta. We are in agreement that your request should be granted. You may move back to Amana."

"Thank you so much. I am grateful for your decision, and I know my parents—"

Brother Herman signaled me to silence. "You will not move back to Homestead. There is great need for someone with your English skills at the hotel in South Amana. You are young, healthy, and well qualified to help clean the rooms and prepare meals for guests at the hotel."

The elder who had questioned me earlier leaned his forearms across the table. "Ja, and they have a daughter close to your age, so it should be a nice place for you to live and work."

"The Redlich family—did you ever meet them when you were living in Homestead?" Brother Herman had once again taken control of the conversation.

"No. I don't know anyone living in South. I was only to High with my parents one time and over to East when we would go to see the lambs in the springtime."

"You will like it with the Redlich family. And they will be

thankful to have you. They have been waiting many months for extra help, and God has sent the perfect fit." Brother Herman beamed at me.

A fresh wave of fear washed over me, for I knew it wasn't God who had sent me, but the devil himself.

CHAPTER 7

South Amana
Ilsa Redlich

Although Mrs. Young had purchased needles and thread on our visit to the general store, she didn't attend the quilting bee last Friday. A short time before we were scheduled to depart, she declared she wasn't feeling well. I'd been somewhat surprised, for only the day before, she'd appeared eager to attend. The woman continued to prove herself a mystery. One minute she wanted to smother me with friendliness, and the next minute she was withdrawn and aloof. Mother and I agreed that from one moment to the next we never knew which Mrs. Young we would encounter. And though we did our best to make her comfortable, her expectations sometimes exceeded what we could provide, given our lack of help in the hotel.

That morning at breakfast she'd been excited over the prospect of attending the Red Cross meeting, but I wondered if she would change her mind by the time one o'clock arrived. When Mother had mentioned the possibility of her presence to several of the ladies after prayer meeting last night, the news hadn't been met with much enthusiasm. Mrs. Young was, after all, an outsider. But when Mother suggested compassion, kindness, and sympathy, the women softened.

Mother leaned in close to the circle of women. "Is difficult to want a child and never meet with success. I don't think Mrs. Young has the faith to sustain her through this terrible time. One minute she's cheerful, the next she's gloomy. The problem over losing several babies seems to be affecting her mind. That's what her husband told us." My mother tapped her index finger to the side of her dark cap.

"Ja, ja." One of the women bobbed her head. "That happened to my aunt in the old country. All her life she wanted children, but she never had one that lived. After the seventh one died, she was never right in the head again."

The morose talk had sent me scurrying toward home. I didn't want to listen to the ladies speak of such things, but the little I'd heard gave me greater compassion for Mrs. Young and her curious ways.

Still, as the hour to depart approached and she hadn't come downstairs, I felt a sense of relief. We gathered items to take to the meeting, and Mother placed a sign on the door directing guests to the wheelwright shop, where my father would assist them. Though there were no trains due to arrive during our meeting and no expected guests, Mother always put a sign on the door. "Just in case," she would say, hooking it on the door.

I removed my lightweight cloak from the hook, thankful the weather had warmed a bit. "Do you think I should go upstairs to make sure she isn't coming with us?"

My mother glanced toward the stairs. "Nein. If she is resting, we don't want to waken her. She knew what time we planned to leave, and I don't want to be late. Sister Margret will wear a scowl for the entire meeting if we're not on time."

I laughed when my mother scrunched her features into a deep frown. "Ja. I remember how she chided Sister Barbara for being late last month. And now that Sister Hulda has taken charge of the Red Cross projects, there will be double scolding."

My mother nodded. "Oh, for sure. Sister Hulda dislikes tardiness even more than Sister Margret."

I lifted the basket of yarn and needles onto my arm. We'd made it across the threshold when I heard Mrs. Young call from the upper hallway. "Do wait for me, ladies. I'll be down as soon as I gather my hat and gloves."

My mother stepped back inside and cupped her hands to her mouth. "Don't be too long, Mrs. Young. We're expected to arrive on time, and it's close to one o'clock."

Moments later Mrs. Young scurried down the steps, her hat in one hand and gloves in the other. She stopped in front of the large mirror across from the desk. Lifting the hat to her head, she caught my gaze in the mirror. "This won't take long. I promise." She wiggled the felt-and-feather headpiece atop her dark curls and shoved a long jeweled hatpin into place with the precision of a surgeon. "There. You see?" She held her gloves tight in one hand and motioned toward the door. "Well, come along. The hour is late."

It wasn't difficult to determine that the sight of Mrs. Young flapping her gloves in the air and reminding us of the time set my mother on edge. She clamped her lips into a tight seam—no doubt afraid if she said anything to our visitor, the words would be harsh and inappropriate. Though such a reaction wasn't my mother's usual manner, she sometimes failed to hold her temper in check when pushed to the extreme. And Mrs. Young's comment had come close to crossing that line.

As we exited the hotel, I gave Mother a wink. Perhaps it would help to lighten the mood. I inhaled the scent of the fallen leaves, thankful the earlier snow hadn't completely ruined the season. "A lovely autumn day, don't you think?" I tucked my free hand into the crook of my mother's arm and gave it a gentle squeeze.

"It won't be so lovely if we are late."

I glanced over my shoulder. Mrs. Young had fallen behind. I wasn't certain if she'd been taking time to enjoy the weather or simply wasn't accustomed to walking. "Are you able to walk at a faster pace, Mrs. Young? We still have a short distance to go."

"My shoes are pinching my feet. I didn't realize we'd be walking. I thought there would be a carriage, but I suppose not?"

Mrs. Young's question hung in the crisp November air. I turned my head. "We don't use carriages very much in Amana, Mrs. Young. I should have told you to wear your most comfortable shoes." I tugged on Mother's arm and leaned closer. "Why don't you go on ahead. I'll follow with Mrs. Young. You can explain the reason for our delay, and perhaps we will be forgiven." I grinned, hoping to lighten the mood. My mother didn't enjoy being made a spectacle, and if she was late, Sister Margret would surely embarrass her.

"You told her there was no need to wear fancy clothes to the meeting, but she had to change into her finery." My mother sighed. "I suppose you are right. I'll go on and explain to the ladies. Be sure to enter quietly in case the meeting has begun."

"We will be quiet as church mice."

"It is not you that concerns me." She cast a quick look over her shoulder, and I could see that my suggestion hadn't improved her mood.

"All will be fine, Mutter. You go on." I released her arm and motioned her onward.

I stopped and turned to wait for Mrs. Young. "Mutter is going ahead to the meeting. She will explain that our arrival has been delayed."

Mrs. Young took a little skip to catch up, but the added pressure to her feet caused a limp that slowed her even more.

When I offered my arm, she accepted it and leaned heavily against me. "In the city it is fashionable to arrive a few minutes late—sometimes we don't arrive until a half hour after the appointed time. Making an entrance is considered a good thing."

"That is not our way in the colonies. We believe order is needed in our lives so that we may complete our daily chores with ample time left over to worship the Lord. That is why you hear the bells ring from behind the tailor shop. They help us maintain the schedule for meals, prayer meetings, work—"

"But I didn't hear a bell."

"There is no bell to announce Red Cross meetings or quilting bees—only the routine matters of our life. If we don't arrive and depart from the meetings on time, we cannot prepare and serve meals at the proper hour, and then we would be late for prayer meeting. You see?"

She tightened her hold on my arm until I thought I was surely supporting her full weight.

"I suppose, but I prefer a little more freedom in my schedule."

I smiled and nodded. "Then I would say that living in the city suits you well."

She continued to hobble along, but when I suggested that

perhaps she should return home to soak her feet, she brushed aside the offer. "I will be fine once I sit down."

I agreed that sitting might help for a time, but I wondered what would happen when we headed for home. Experience told me that after she sat for several hours, her feet would hurt even more. When I was ten years old our village cobbler had been ill and couldn't keep up with the orders for new shoes. I wore a pair of too-tight shoes back and forth to school for several days and suffered dearly. Then my mother had me wear a pair of her old shoes. They were too big for me, so she had me don several pairs of woolen socks. Yet even with all the extra layers, I was still in pain. I now understood the importance of wearing properly fitting shoes.

When we finally arrived, I cautioned Mrs. Young that we must enter quietly. "The meeting may be underway." I hoped she would heed my warning. Otherwise, she would likely receive one of Sister Hulda's piercing looks.

The women were chattering when we entered, and I was surprised to see the meeting had not yet begun. All eyes turned in our direction. Mother stood and introduced Mrs. Young, explaining she was a guest at the hotel. First my mother spoke in English, and then in German, for many of the older women didn't speak or understand English.

In fact, the only residents of the colonies who spoke and read the language well were those of us who worked at the hotels, general stores, train depots, and a few other places where speaking English was a necessity in order to conduct business. For the rest, Amana German remained the language of choice—spoken in church, in school, and in most homes. Though there had been some discussion of changing to the English language, there never seemed to be a good time to make the change. The most resistance came from the elderly residents, who said they were too old to learn a new language. And when the younger residents began to age, they gave the same justification. So on it went without change.

Mrs. Young offered a nod of her head and a cheery smile. "Good afternoon, ladies. I'm so pleased to join you. The Red Cross is a noble effort for our country, and it does my heart good to know I'll be able to continue the good work while I'm here in Amana."

The women stared at her, and Sister Hulda poked my mother in the side. "Tell her to speak German, so everyone can understand."

My mother turned to our guest. "Do you speak German, Mrs. Young?"

The woman held her thumb and finger very close together. "Only a tiny bit. I know how to say *good morning* and *good evening*. Oh, and *thank you*. I know how to say that, as well." She beamed at my mother.

"We speak German at our meetings because many of the ladies do not speak English. Ilsa will translate for you, if necessary, though I doubt there is anything that will be of great interest to you."

We sat down and Sister Hulda called for silence. "I have the report to give. You can visit later while you are working on the knitting and sewing."

"What did she say?" Mrs. Young leaned close but whispered loud enough that everyone turned to stare.

"She's going to give a report," I whispered.

The ladies came to attention when Sister Hulda waved the latest bulletin published by the Amana branch of the American Red Cross in front of her. "A quota of forty more sweaters has been assigned to our branch, and we are thankful for the willing hands that completed our earlier quota. Our chapter turned in our sweaters a full month before they were due."

A chorus of satisfied murmurs filled the room before Sister Hulda once again waved the group to silence. "Headquarters announced that sweaters will be accepted in navy blue as well as gray and khaki, but remember that socks must be in gray or white only." She leveled her shoulders in a straight line. "I am proud to announce that all our schoolchildren are members of the Junior Red Cross, and so far they have supplied a quota of ten wool shoulder shawls for Belgian relief." A brief round of applause followed the announcement. "We are instructed to remember that a child, in giving the work of his hands in the Junior Red Cross, is showing love of his country and is being trained in vocational lines."

"Ja. Well, we here in Amana knew the value of children learning a vocation before the Red Cross did," one of the ladies remarked.

Several ladies chuckled, but Sister Hulda motioned for silence. "There is something new to report from the government—something called *Four Minute Men*. These men will deliver four-minute speeches in various moving-picture theaters throughout the country."

"We don't need to know about those, Hulda. Who here goes to see the moving pictures?"

Several ladies glanced at Mrs. Young. Their stares prompted Mrs. Young to once again ask what had transpired.

"The report is about speeches that will be delivered in moving-picture theaters," I whispered. I touched my finger to my lips and hoped she would forgo any further questions until after the meeting.

Sister Hulda pinned Sister Janet with a hard stare. "I know we do not go to the moving pictures, and that's why the bulletin tells us what will be said. If you would just be patient, I'm going to read to you what will be said in the first speech."

Sister Hulda's admonishment quieted the women. "The speech says that we must stop waste and be saving in all things. 'War savers are life savers, and we must adjust to war conditions. The thoughtless expenditure of money for nonessentials uses up the labor of men, the products of the farms, mines, and factories, and overburdens transportation. The great results which we seek can be obtained only by the participation of every member of the nation, young and old, in a national thrift movement.' "

One of the sisters moved to the edge of her chair. "Does that paper name any group that is thriftier than the people of Amana?" She jutted her chin. "I don't think those government men can find a more saving people than Amanans."

Sister Hulda sighed and shook her head. "I agree with you, Sister. We are a thrifty people, but this speech is being made for everyone in the country, not just the people of Amana. I am reading it to you because that is what I am supposed to do."

"Then that is fine. I just don't want anyone to think the people of Amana are not thrifty. There is enough ugly gossip about our people without adding another lie." The sister scooted back on her chair and gave a satisfied nod.

After reading the treasury report, the business meeting was dismissed, and we moved into small groups. Mrs. Young remained by my side. Before I had even wrapped a strand of yarn around my knitting needles, she wanted a full report of everything that had been said. I did my best to translate the events and then turned my attention to Claudia, one of the girls who worked with Sister Barbara in the *Küche*.

The dark-eyed girl edged closer. "Have you had any word from Albert? I've been praying for his safety ever since he departed."

A shade of rosy pink inched up Claudia's neck and colored her cheeks. Although I'd heard several of the girls mention Claudia's affection for my brother, I hadn't given a second thought to the rumors. My brother's good looks and outgoing personality had stirred many a young woman's attention through the years, but none had won his heart. Besides, if Albert had developed an interest in Claudia, he would have told me.

I shook my head. "No letters yet. But I'm sure he has been very busy since his arrival at Camp Pike. I would guess there is much to learn during the first weeks, but I'm hopeful we'll hear from him soon." I dug my needle into the next stitch and wrapped the dark blue yarn around my needle before pulling it through. "We appreciate your prayers for Albert's safety. I do wish he would have chosen to remain at home. I did my best to convince him, but he was determined to serve."

Claudia's needles clicked in a steady rhythm. "I think he is very brave. A true patriot."

I didn't respond. I didn't care if others considered him a patriot or brave, for I didn't consider him either of those things. I considered him a foolish young man who had been swayed by the surge of anti-German sentiment directed at the Amana Colonies. He was certain his service to the country would make a difference, but I was just as certain he'd be proved wrong.

I half listened while the other women chattered and was glad when Sister Hulda adjourned the meeting. "If you've finished your projects, leave them to be packed. If not, please work on them at home and bring them to the next meeting. And if you need additional knitting materials, please remain after the meeting."

Moments later, my mother joined me. With Mrs. Young at

our side, we'd begun to walk home when Mother looped arms with me. "A gut meeting, ja?"

I matched my mother's stride, then tugged her to a slower pace when I noticed Mrs. Young falling behind. "Gut for those who like to dwell on the war. I grow weary of such talk. I wonder how much more we will be expected to sacrifice for the privilege of sending our young men to the battlefield."

My mother pinched my arm and glanced toward Mrs. Young. "You are worried because we haven't heard from Albert. You must be careful when you speak in front of strangers."

I shrugged one shoulder. I'd spoken to my mother in German. "There is no cause for concern, Mutter. Our guest doesn't understand a word I'm saying."

CHAPTER 8

Marengo, Iowa
Jutta Schmitt

I prayed this day would never arrive. But just as morning had dawned throughout the previous twenty-six years of my life, sunlight peeled away the darkness of the previous night and announced the arrival of a new day. However, this day would be different. This day everything would change. This day I would leave my parents and return to Amana.

My feet hit the floor, and an understanding of my future became as real as the cold draft whistling through my bedroom window. I would no longer awaken in this room with my parents nearby, no longer hear my mother's familiar morning greeting, no longer descend the stairs to work in the family bakery. A knot the size of my father's bread dough settled in my stomach. I bent forward and wrapped my arms around my waist, uncertain I could do this. Yet I knew I must not waver.

I was the only one who could save my parents from the threats made against them. A part of me was thankful the elders decided I should live in South Amana, while another part regretted the decision. If I was to conduct this ugly reporting, it should be easier since I didn't know any of the people living in South Amana. On the other hand, it would have been more comfortable to return to familiar surroundings and a few recognizable faces. My father had voiced his disappointment when I'd delivered the news. He'd even asked Brother Herman if the elders wouldn't reconsider. But to no avail. Brother Herman avowed the elders had considered the best use of my talents for the betterment of the community and were convinced my skills could be best used in South Amana. He'd patted my father on the shoulder. "Your Jutta will be under the protection of a fine family. You should thank God for the provision He has made available for her in South Amana."

My father hadn't attempted any further argument. We both knew it would be useless. I shoved my foot into one stocking, then the other, and continued to routinely move through my morning ministrations. Sorrow enveloped me in a tight hold, for I knew my life would never be the same. For years I'd detested the monotony of everyday life, but now that things were changing, I longed to maintain that sameness. A suitcase in each hand, I plodded down the stairs and into the kitchen. I couldn't bear to see my mother's red and swollen eyes or the unmistakable sadness in my father's smile.

Though I failed to maintain a cheerful countenance, it wasn't from lack of trying. I wanted to make my departure as easy as possible—for all of us. My mother stepped to the door and removed her coat from the hook, but I signaled her to stop. "No, Mother. I don't want you to go with me to the train station. Better that we say our good-byes here at home. Father can take me to the depot. Besides, someone needs to look after the bakery."

My mother shook her head. "We can put a sign in the window and lock the door."

"Jutta is right, Eva. It will be easier for her if you say good-bye here. You must remember that she will be back to visit with us."

My mother frowned and wiped away a tear with the corner of her apron. "Only when those evil men want to question her. Isn't there anything we can do, Bert?"

"I have been praying for an answer, but . . ." He shrugged his shoulders and lifted his upturned palms toward the sky. "Nothing. I have received not a word or an idea. It's as if God has turned a deaf ear to my prayers."

If I was going to be at the train station on time, there wasn't time to listen to any more of this hopeless talk. I held my mother tight, told her of my love, and said I would write. "I'll be home to visit soon."

"God be with you," she whispered into my ear. "I will be praying He shows you the perfect way to complete this errand."

Errand? I was being sent to spy on our people, and my mother thought of it as an errand? I shouldn't judge. Perhaps that was how she managed to quiet her fears. Instead of condemning, I should try to do the same.

I hadn't expected anyone to meet me in South Amana. Though the elders had instructed me to arrive on this date, they hadn't designated a particular time for my arrival. I could have written to Brother and Sister Redlich, but I preferred to make my own way. I didn't want to feel obligated to them. It was a silly thought, for my very existence in Amana would make me obligated to them in some fashion. Still, I didn't want to begin our relationship by asking them to break their regular routine for my benefit.

An older man with bushy eyebrows stood behind the ticket window, his thick finger tracing down a ledger of some sort.

"Can you tell me where the hotel is located?" I asked.

His smile was pleasant. "Not so far. You can see it from here." He circled around the counter and walked me to the front windows. "That's it over there—on the corner. If you want to wait, the wagon will be coming from Upper South in twenty minutes. Our driver can take you."

Gripping the handles of my suitcases tightly, I smiled and thanked him. "I think I can walk that short distance."

He chuckled. "Ja. God has smiled on you today. The weather is gut and is not so far to walk."

I wanted to tell him that God hadn't smiled on me at all, that He had turned His face from me. Instead, I mumbled another thank-you and walked out the depot door. Suitcases in hand, I made the short trek, hiked up the front steps leading into the hotel, and pushed down on the heavy latch. A bell jangled overhead when I entered, and a girl about my age appeared from somewhere in the back. Her blond hair had been neatly combed, and the ties of the familiar Amana black cap hung down the front of her bodice. Her smile was courteous but guarded—probably from dealing with demanding hotel guests on a daily basis.

She walked behind the desk and picked up a pencil. "Gut morning. You are in need of a room for the night?"

I shook my head. "I am Jutta Schmitt. The elders have assigned me to work here."

Her blue eyes sparkled, and her lips curved in a broad smile. "Welcome, Jutta! I am Ilsa Redlich." She hurried from behind the desk, but I didn't fail to note the look of surprise. "We are most pleased you have decided to come and work with us."

For a moment I considered correcting her. I hadn't decided to come and work at the hotel—the elders had made the decision for me. But it would serve no purpose to appear displeased or unhappy. "I'm pleased to meet you, Ilsa. I don't know anything about operating a hotel, but I'll do my best to learn. My family owns a bakery in Marengo, so I'm much more accustomed to spending my days baking or waiting on customers."

"I think you will learn quickly. We cook for the guests in the hotel, but we don't bake bread. It is delivered from the bakery each day." She tapped her fingers to her head. "Ach! I forgot that you lived in the colonies before. You know all about the delivery wagons that bring the milk, bread, and meat, ja?"

I nodded. "I remember, but it has been more than ten years since my family moved away, so there is much I've forgotten, too. And I don't think my clothes will be acceptable."

She glanced at my dress. "The rules have eased some—especially since the war. Some of your clothes might be permitted." She pointed to the artificial flowers affixed to my broad-brimmed hat. "But not those."

I laughed and Ilsa joined in. After weeks of worry and anger, it felt good to laugh—even at something as silly as the flowers on my hat. I removed the pins and plucked the hat from my head. "There! That takes care of the hat. Perhaps you can go through my clothing and tell me what will be suitable."

"Ilsa! What's all the chattering out there?"

An angular yet pleasant-faced woman rounded the corner while wiping her hands down the front of her apron. She appeared to be about the same age as my mother. Ilsa waved the woman forward. "Mutter, this is Jutta, our new helper. Jutta, this is my Mutter."

"It is good to have you arrive, Jutta. I hope you will be comfortable and happy living here. You will stay in the small apartment Sister Hulda used before she left us. It is on the other side of the hotel, where we have our apartment—away from the hotel rooms."

I was glad to hear of this arrangement. My mother had expressed concern that I might not be safe if in a hotel room. She would be relieved to know this. "Thank you, Mrs. Red—I mean Sister Redlich."

The older woman tucked a flyaway strand of graying hair behind her ear. "You may call me Sister Marta. We will soon be working elbow to elbow in the kitchen."

I would have preferred to call her Sister Redlich. Sister Marta sounded much too informal for someone the same age as my own mother, but I would do as she requested. I planned to do my best to follow instructions and blend into my new life as quickly as possible so that I could confirm what I'd already told those men from the Iowa Council of National Defense: There was no reason to question the patriotism of the Amana residents.

"We were pleased when the elders told us of your desire to return to the colonies. To have someone return without family is unusual."

She hesitated, obviously hoping I would explain, but I remained silent.

Finally she cleared her throat. "We will do everything possible to make your homecoming easier."

Homecoming. This didn't feel like a homecoming to me, but the older woman's words were enough to make me realize I should be acting pleased to be among them. After all, I had asked to return, and they thought it was because I wanted to be there. If I appeared unhappy, there would be questions, and I didn't want questions.

"I am sure I will be very comfortable among you and your family. I look forward to meeting your husband and . . . and . . . I wasn't told if you have any other family members, but if you do, I look forward to meeting them, as well." My thoughts had been as jumbled as my words, but both Mrs. Redlich and Ilsa appeared pleased by my comment.

"You will meet my husband at the noonday meal. Our son, Albert, has gone to serve in the army, but we are hopeful he will return to celebrate Christmas with us."

Ilsa wrinkled her nose. "Since he hasn't even had time to write us a letter, I'm beginning to doubt they'll let him come home for Christmas."

Sister Marta gave a quick shake of her head. "Now, Ilsa, let's dwell on gut thoughts. I am praying Albert will be home with us."

"And I prayed he wouldn't join the army." Ilsa didn't wait for her mother to respond to the bitter comment. "Come along, Jutta. I'll show you to your rooms, and you can get settled."

After an affectionate pat on my shoulder, Mrs. Redlich agreed. "If you decide to take a rest, the bells will waken you when it is time to eat. We won't expect you to begin your duties until tomorrow."

I thanked her and followed Ilsa to the doorway at the

other side of the large parlor and down a separate hallway. Ilsa glanced over her shoulder. "Your rooms are smaller than most, but I think you'll be comfortable." She grinned. "Less to keep clean."

I agreed, for I hadn't forgotten the cleaning rituals that took place in every Amana home and business during the spring and fall of each year. Truth be told, I was thankful I hadn't arrived in time to help with the fall cleaning and held out hope I would be gone before spring arrived. "I do hope extra help is assigned to assist you."

"Sometimes when others have finished, they will come and help, but mostly it is left to us. To make it more enjoyable, we divide the rooms and try to make a game of it by seeing who can do the best job in the least amount of time."

The game didn't seem like much fun to me, but I didn't say so.

Ilsa stopped in front of a door near the end of the hallway and pushed down on the latch. "These are your rooms." She walked inside and made a sweeping gesture with one arm. "As I said, not very big."

I stepped through the parlor and into the bedroom. The rooms were small, but like all the homes in Amana, they were neat and clean. The multistriped carpet on the floor was much the same as the one we'd had in our parlor at Homestead many years ago. Using the remnants of cloth, a weaver would cut strips and weave the pieces into rugs. "I'm sure I will be very comfortable."

Ilsa glanced at my suitcases. "Once you put some of your personal belongings in here, it will feel more like your own."

Other than clothing, I hadn't packed many personal items. I hadn't planned to bring any, but my mother had insisted. She'd tucked several table scarves and a long linen cloth with tatting along the edges, a small porcelain figurine of an angel holding a child, which had been in my room as long as I could remember, and a framed picture of the three of us taken by a photographer in Marengo several years ago. My mother had placed both my Bible and the *Psalter-Spiel* in my suitcase; I had packed magazines and books I had received as gifts, though I doubted they were allowed.

My mother's decision had been wise, for I saw Ilsa's shoulders relax when I lifted the two religious tomes from my bag. The books seemed to send a signal that I was truly one of them.

"I'll come back and look at your clothes after the noonday meal. We may be able to alter some of them so that they will work just fine." She beamed at me and sat down in one of the chairs. "It won't take long for you to remember all of our ways, and soon you'll know everyone, too. For sure, I want you to meet Garon this afternoon when he brings the passengers to the hotel."

"Garon? Is he another brother?"

"Nein." Ilsa flashed a bright smile. "Garon Drucker is the man I'm going to marry. He is assistant trainmaster and operates the telegraph machine. He also delivers passengers back and forth from the two hotels and to the train depots in Upper and Lower South Amana. The elders consider him a very gut worker." Her eyes reflected her love and pride for the man she planned to marry. "I better go back to the kitchen and help Mutter." She glanced over her shoulder as she reached the door. "I'm glad you're here, Jutta."

Feeling like even more of an imposter than when I'd arrived, I mumbled my thanks and turned back to my belongings. It didn't take long to unpack my two suitcases. After all, I planned to go home as often as possible, and I could always bring any additional items I wanted or needed. Already my heart ached to go home. How would I survive this charade? I paced back and forth while staring at the pale blue walls. Even the wall colors evoked memories of the past. My mother had insisted upon yellow walls in our apartment when we moved to Marengo—at least in the kitchen. The parlor had been painted beige and the bedrooms pale green. She said it made the room look sunny all the time, and she had tired of the Amana blue that was used on most of the walls in the colonies.

As promised, I penned a quick note to my parents and advised them of my safe arrival. A glance at the clock revealed there was time to take my letter to the general store before the noonday meal. Tucking the letter into my skirt pocket, I wrapped myself in my heavy woolen cloak and walked back down the hallway, through the parlor and dining room, and stood at the kitchen doorway. Both Mrs. Redlich and Ilsa were in the midst of meal preparations, and I wondered if I should depart without interrupting them. Before I could make my decision, Ilsa caught sight of me.

"Jutta! Done unpacking so soon?"

I nodded and reached into my skirt pocket. "I have written a letter to my mother and father and thought I would take it to the store for mailing."

Ilsa had already untied her apron strings. "I'll go along with Jutta. I can check to see if we received any mail while I'm there."

I thought Mrs. Redlich was going to object, but she smacked her lips together and appeared to be using her teeth to hold them in check. Ilsa hung her apron on a hook near the kitchen door and pecked a kiss on her mother's cheek. "We won't be long. I'll be back in time to help you finish the potatoes. I promise."

She grabbed her cloak from the hook near the front desk and wrapped it around her shoulders. When we reached the front sidewalk, she looped arms with me as though we were old friends. "I'm so pleased you need to mail your letter. Every day I must wait until Vater gets home before I know if we have received a letter from Albert." She grinned. "But today I won't have to wait so long."

"I hope you won't be disappointed if there isn't any mail." I hadn't missed the sadness in Ilsa's voice when she'd spoken of her brother earlier in the morning.

She shrugged. "If there's no letter, I'll be disappointed no matter what the time of day. It may be better to know earlier in the day—then I won't be so angry when we go to meeting after supper. I probably shouldn't admit this, but sometimes I get very angry with God."

I smiled at her. "It's all right to tell me, because sometimes I get angry with God, too."

"Ja?" Her eyebrows arched high, and she squeezed my arm. It seemed we had formed an unexpected bond. "It's gut to know I am not the only one. Mutter says I must accept God's will. I know she is correct, but that doesn't mean I must like it. Right now I don't think God even hears my prayers."

"Prayers about your brother?"

"Ja. Albert and I have always been very close—always gut friends as well as brother and sister. We shared secrets and were always together—always agreed about everything. Until he decided he should join the army. That I did not agree with at all—and I still don't. I prayed he would change his mind, but that didn't happen. Then I prayed he would fail the physical test they gave him, but that didn't happen. And each day I pray there will be a letter from him, but that hasn't happened, either. I hate this war." She hung her head.

Though I did my best to appear nonchalant, I was surprised by Ilsa's candid remarks. Never had I heard anyone express distaste that a loved one had heeded the call to service. The opposite was generally true. Usually family members couldn't wait to spread the word that their loved one had gone off to serve in the war. Fathers would puff their chests and bluster about the bravery of their sons. Mothers would shed a few tears, but they spoke with as much pride as the men. I thought their behavior odd, but who could blame them? Ever since the United States had entered the war, the country had been bombarded with persuasive speeches, newspaper articles, and posters that extolled the virtues of joining the various war efforts. Perhaps I was as out of step as Ilsa.

Yet I couldn't remain out of step—I must participate in the war effort whether I wanted to or not. And if I couldn't find any true antiwar activities, the Defense Council would be just as happy with lies. The thought made me shiver, and I bent my head against the wind.

"You're cold. You should have worn your mittens." Ilsa pointed down the street. "The store is right up there—on the corner."

I didn't explain that my shiver wasn't from the weather. I smiled instead and tucked my free hand beneath the warmth of my cloak. Minutes later, Ilsa pushed open the front door. The warmth from the potbelly stove mixed with the smells of coffee and spices and the distinct odor of kerosene. As in most of the villages, the kerosene pump was located in the general store in South Amana. I had grown accustomed to electricity in Marengo, but there was no electricity in the colonies. Kerosene lamps provided light, and wood heated the stoves. Large cans of kerosene were brought to the store each week, and assigned portions were pumped for each family.

"Good morning, Sister Ilsa." The storekeeper glanced over the top of his glasses. "You have brought a guest from the hotel to do some shopping?"

"Nein. This is Sister Jutta. She lived in Homestead many years ago and has returned to live among us. She's going to take Sister Hulda's place at the hotel." Ilsa tugged me forward. "This is Brother Peter Tolbert. He takes care of the mail and the store."

"I am pleased to meet you, Brother Tolbert." I reached into my pocket and removed the letter to my parents. "I would like to mail this." I placed the envelope and a coin on the counter.

Brother Tolbert pushed the coin back in my direction. "You must have forgotten that members of the community do not use money, Sister Jutta."

"I would prefer to pay. I don't begin my duties until tomorrow, so it seems only right that I should pay for the postage. My parents gave me the money to pay, and I should honor their wishes."

He nodded. "Is gut to follow the instructions of your parents." Casting a glance toward Ilsa, he nodded toward the rows of wooden cubbyholes along the wall. "Do you see a letter in your family's box, Ilsa?"

She lifted on her toes and leaned across the counter. "I do! I do! Is it from Albert?"

"Ja. I was going to tease you and say it was only an order for your Vater, but then I decided you have worried and waited long enough." He stepped away from the counter and turned to the cubbyhole. "Here you are. It is addressed to all of your family, so I don't know if you should open it or wait until you get home."

Ilsa traced her index finger over the writing on the envelope, then clasped it to her bodice. "I'll wait until I get home. It will be more fun to enjoy it together."

"If you see Garon, tell him I have mail for him, as well."

Her rosy complexion faded to the color of yesterday's ashes. "From the local draft board?"

He shook his head. "You know I cannot tell you who it is from. It goes against the rules."

"Ja, the rules." She turned toward the door. "I will tell him."

I grasped her arm. "What's wrong, Ilsa? Are you sick?"

She inhaled a deep breath of the cold air. "If Garon's mail is from the local draft board, I know he will follow my brother into the army. Over and over I've told him that I don't want him to do this, but he insists it is his patriotic duty. He and Albert are cut from the same cloth: They both think they can change the opinion of the rest of the country if they agree to join the army. But their idea is nothing but foolishness. People will continue to believe the worst about us, no matter how many of our men go. Their willingness to serve will change nothing." Her shoulders drooped in defeat. "Except that they might not return to us."

We were quiet on the way home. I was certain Ilsa was lost in thoughts of her brother and Garon, while I was contemplating the many antiwar comments Ilsa had made to me. The fact that she had done her best to discourage two men from entering the military was a transgression the members of the Iowa Council of National Defense would be pleased to hear. Such information would confirm what they already believed: There were residents of Amana who were not patriotic—at least by their definition. As soon we arrived home, I would go to my room and write down Ilsa's comments. I dare not forget any of them.

CHAPTER 9

Ilsa Redlich

"Mutter, Mutter—a letter from Albert!" My shoes clattered on the wood floor as I hurried through the dining room and into the kitchen, leaving Jutta to follow behind. I did my best to push aside thoughts of Garon's waiting mail as I waved the envelope overhead. "A letter from Albert."

A smile spread across my mother's face. "You have opened it? What does he say?"

"It's addressed to all of us, so I thought I should wait." I shrugged my cloak from my shoulders and draped it over one arm while placing the envelope on one of the worktables. I pointed to my brother's strong handwriting. "See? It says *The Odell Redlich Family.*"

My mother set aside the potato she'd been peeling and examined the envelope. "Ja. You are right. I suppose we must wait until your Vater gets home." She winked and grinned at me. "Maybe since two out of three of us are here, it would be acceptable for us to open the letter. I don't think your Vater would mind."

"Really? You think it would be all right?" I didn't give her an opportunity to change her mind. I ran my finger beneath the seal on the envelope and withdrew the pages.

"Oh look!" There were two letters inside, one with my name and one to my parents. "Albert sent us separate letters—one for you and Vater and one for me." I handed my mother the two pages addressed to them and dropped my cloak across the back of a chair before I unfolded my letter. After quickly scanning it, I sat down to more carefully devour the contents. I glanced at my mother. "He says he has been assigned to work at the hospital."

"Ja, in here, too." My mother pointed at her letter. "That is gut. He should be safe in the hospital."

My mother's idea of safe wasn't the same as mine. I didn't think the hospital was a good choice for Albert. He had no medical training. Besides, Dr. Miller had been assigned to the hospital at Camp Pike for a time. And then they sent him to France. They could do the same to Albert—and probably would. But I wouldn't say that to my mother. Let her believe that Albert was out of harm's way. As for me, I didn't believe it for a minute.

His letter to me contained cheery comments about becoming a soldier and that he'd made the proper choice when he decided to serve. Of course, he hadn't been there for long, and I wondered if he would feel the same way after six months' time. He'd written with as much propaganda as the posters that declared young men who loved their country should sign up to serve. Perhaps someone read the soldiers' mail before it was sent, and Albert had felt compelled to make such comments—to prove his patriotism. Still, I was thankful for the letter and the knowledge that Albert had arrived safe and sound. I smiled at his final remark and waved the sheet of paper at my mother. "Albert says he has eaten all the cookies I sent with him. We will soon need to send him more."

Jutta entered the kitchen and lifted my cloak from the chair. "I'll hang this for you." She smiled at me. "I am glad your brother is doing well."

I thanked her for taking my cloak to the parlor before I turned toward my mother. "Let me read your letter, and you can read mine."

My mother handed me the letter. "We must hurry or the meal won't be ready on time."

"I'd be glad to help while you read the letters," Jutta said as she returned from the parlor. "Tell me what needs to be done." She pointed toward the potatoes. "Would you like them peeled and sliced for frying?"

"That would be very gut. Thank you, Jutta." My mother sat down near me and unfolded my letter.

I was uncertain why Albert had written two letters. They contained much the same information. Perhaps he thought he must write to each of us or he would receive only one letter back. Then again, maybe he thought his promise to write meant he must send individual letters. When I wrote, I would tell him separate letters weren't necessary. Not unless he had something of a private nature to tell me—and I doubted that would occur.

The bell above the front door jangled, and I glanced at my mother. "I'll go. You finish reading." After folding the letter, I placed it on the table and headed into the dining room. From the doorway I could see Garon and Mr. Young deep in conversation. For some reason, their growing friendship troubled me. Garon said most of their conversations were about the telegrams Mr. Young had him wire to business associates. And Garon seemed pleased that Mr. Young would seek him out to send the telegrams rather than the head trainmaster. I thought it odd. When I'd said as much to Garon, he had been hurt. He considered Mr. Young's requests proof of his ability as a telegrapher. I had apologized. Maybe Garon was right. Still, there was something about Mr. Young's behavior that tended to either annoy or frighten me. While I found his wife unpredictable, I thought Mr. Young quite the opposite. He consistently maintained a stern expression as he studied everyone who crossed his path. Mother said it was because he was a lawyer.

I wasn't certain how my mother knew the way lawyers acted, for we had no lawyers in Amana. We weren't a people who settled disputes in a court of law. When a lawyer had been needed to write contracts to purchase our land, the elders had hired one. And when the state of Iowa, through a resident of Iowa County, had sued us, saying the society had exceeded its corporate power in holding real property and conducting secular industries, we'd once again hired lawyers to protect our rights in court. But there was seldom a need for a person trained in the law—not in Amana.

When neither Garon nor Mr. Young looked in my direction, I returned to the kitchen. My mother arched her brows. "We have guests?"

"It is Garon and Mr. Young. Again they are deep in conversation. That Mr. Young, there is something about him."

"Ach! You need to quit with that talk, Ilsa. He is a lawyer. I told you they all watch people and act a little different."

"How do you know this when we have no lawyers living among us?"

"We have had other lawyers stay at the hotel." My mother smiled. "Just as they observe us, I have observed them through the years. And most of them are like Mr. Young—quiet and unfriendly."

"Except with Garon. Whenever Garon is around, Mr. Young has plenty to say to him."

"I think you are making something out of nothing, Ilsa. He rides from the train station with Garon, and they visit on the way. Sometimes they continue to talk when Garon carries his luggage into the hotel. It is nothing unusual. I think you are jealous because Mr. Young takes Garon's time away from you."

"Maybe you are right." I conceded only to stop the possibility of an argument, but I didn't agree with my mother. I was correct about Mr. Young. Of that, I was certain.

Just then Garon strode to the door of the kitchen. He leaned against the doorjamb and nodded toward the parlor. "Mr. Young has returned. He went upstairs to see his wife."

"Ja. I saw the two of you when you came in." I stepped a little closer. "There is mail for you at the general store. Brother Tolbert asked that I tell you."

My mother waved from across the kitchen. "Did Ilsa tell you we had a letter from Albert today?"

Garon reached into his pocket and pulled out an envelope. "So did I." He grinned at me. "Mr. Young needed to purchase some things he'd forgotten and asked me to stop at the store on our way here. When Brother Tolbert showed me the letter, I was thankful we had stopped."

I sighed with relief, happy the letter wasn't from the draft board. "That was the only mail for you? Nothing else?"

His forehead wrinkled, and his eyebrows dipped low on his forehead. "This is the first letter I have received since my *Oma* died in the old country five years ago. What other mail are you thinking I should receive?"

I shook my head. "How am I to know who might write you

a letter?" I didn't want to admit my concern over the draft board. I reached for his letter. "What did Albert have to say?"

He pulled away from me. "I only had a chance to read a little. You can see it after I finish." With a teasing grin, he shoved the letter into his pocket and buttoned his jacket. "Right now I must get back to the station. Mr. Young wants me to send a telegram for him."

"Then you best be on your way." I turned away so he wouldn't see my displeasure. I'd grown weary of constantly hearing what Mr. Young wanted or needed.

"I'll see you at prayer meeting tonight." He pulled his cap from his coat pocket and waved it in the air as he strode from the room.

Once again my mother encouraged Jutta to go to her room and rest or to sit in the parlor, but she smiled warmly and insisted she would rather help in the kitchen. It was at that moment I decided Jutta was going to be a welcome addition to our family as well as capable help with the hotel duties. Not only had we gained much-needed help, but my heart told me that Jutta would become the dear friend I had always wanted. The thought warmed me as we continued to work and visit while preparing the noonday meal. Mother and I explained the hotel routine and the work required each day, and Jutta shared her reasons for returning to Amana. The fact that she had been treated with disdain in Marengo wasn't hard for me to believe. It seemed no one of German heritage could escape rude comments and unkind treatment.

My mother glanced over her shoulder. "It is sad that your parents couldn't return with you."

Jutta nodded her head. "These are difficult times for all of us."

Moments later the bells chimed to announce mealtime. After

stacking the silverware and napkins on top of the dinner plates, I carried them into the dining room and set the tables while Jutta scooped the potatoes into a bowl and Mother sliced the boiled beef.

I heard the clap of the back door, followed by my father's familiar greeting: "It smells gut in here."

I hurried into the kitchen. "Jutta has arrived, Vater."

He unbuttoned his coat and looked at Jutta. "Ja, I see she has. We are pleased to have you with us, Jutta." He chuckled. "I see you are already hard at work." He shrugged out of his coat and hung it beside the kitchen door.

"Thank you for your welcome. I am grateful to have such a fine place to live." She turned toward my mother. "Your wife and daughter have done all of the cooking. I helped only a little with the potatoes. It was the least I could do since Ilsa walked with me to the store."

My mother pointed to the sideboard. "There is a letter from Albert. Sit down and read. There is time before we eat."

My father finished reading the letter and was tucking it into the envelope when Mr. and Mrs. Young appeared in the parlor, along with several other guests. I saw that Mrs. Young spoke with great animation as she accompanied a female guest into the dining room, while her husband sat down in the parlor and became engrossed in some papers. Not until the other guests had been seated and Father called to Mr. Young did he finally put his papers aside and join us. I was surprised that a man of Mr. Young's education and position didn't apologize for his rude behavior, but he made no effort.

We stood at the tables and offered our prayer of thanks. I had noticed previously that both Mr. and Mrs. Young fidgeted when we prayed, and today was no different. I wasn't certain if praying in general created feelings of discomfort for the couple, or if it was only our prayers that caused their restlessness.

As soon as the prayer ended, Mother and I carried the serving bowls and platters to the tables. Although Jutta offered to help serve, Mother insisted she sit with the women. "There will be time enough for serving later. This is your first meal since returning home. You should sit down and enjoy," she said, waving Jutta toward a chair.

I was placing the fried potatoes and onions on the table when Mrs. Young leaned toward Jutta.

"Is this your first visit to Amana?"

Jutta glanced at me, obviously uncertain if talk was permitted during meals. When I merely shrugged, she met Mrs. Young's inquiring gaze. "No. I lived in Homestead for many years. I've recently returned to make my home in Amana, and I'll be working here at the hotel. Beginning tomorrow, I'll be cleaning rooms and serving meals alongside Ilsa and Sister Redlich."

"You're German, aren't you? I can detect the accent in your voice, though it isn't as distinct as the others." She pursed her lips and waited for an answer.

I placed the potatoes on the table with a thud. "Most everyone who lives in the colonies is of German heritage, Mrs. Young, but most of us were born here, just like you. We are Americans." I saw my father's warning look. Silence was preferred during meals, and though we couldn't require the same behavior from hotel guests, we were expected to follow the rules.

"My remark wasn't meant as an insult, Ilsa. I was merely making an observation." Her painted lips curved in a forced smile. "You weren't offended by my curiosity, were you, Jutta?"

Jutta straightened her shoulders, obviously unwilling to give Mrs. Young a direct answer. "My great-grandparents were born in Alsace-Lorraine. And what is your heritage, Mrs. Young? I believe I detect a slight accent in your voice."

I wanted to cheer when Mrs. Young stared at Jutta gape-mouthed. "I am an American, of course, but I have lived and traveled in many countries during my life. What would cause you to ask such a question of me?"

Jutta shrugged. "Like you, I suppose it was my curiosity."

For the remainder of the meal, the woman was clearly disturbed, and she pushed away from the table before dessert had been served. My mother stepped to the sideboard and picked up a knife to slice the cake. "Don't leave just yet, Mrs. Young. I baked spiced plum cake for dessert. I think you will like it."

Mrs. Young pressed her palm to her forehead. "I feel a headache coming on. I must lie down for a while."

Glancing over his shoulder toward the women's table, Mr. Young signaled to his wife. "I'll escort you upstairs once we've finished dessert, my dear."

With a sigh Mrs. Young settled back into her position at the table. My father flinched at the exchange between the couple but remained silent. I was certain he was biting his tongue. During a meal, talk should never take place between the tables of the men and women. For us, it was difficult when such exchanges took place, yet we could not insist our guests remain silent.

Mrs. Young lifted her napkin from the table and returned it to her lap when Mutter delivered the plates of plum cake to our table. Once again Mrs. Young attempted to quiz Jutta about her past, but she met with little success. Jutta's ability to outwit Mrs. Young impressed me. As far as I was concerned, Jutta had sealed a place within our family. She would become more than a friend. She would be as dear to me as a sister.

CHAPTER 10

I didn't see Garon until that evening at meeting. I had hoped he would stop at the hotel when the afternoon trains came through or stop to speak with Mr. Young about sending a telegram, but he'd done neither. After meeting ended, he waved and hurried toward me.

"For a minute I thought you were going to go home without waiting for me." He grinned and tucked my hand inside the crook of his arm. "Where is Jutta? Did you make her work so hard that she must rest? I was sure she would be at meeting tonight."

"She decided to wait until tomorrow. I think she's feeling some sadness and discomfort. She's been away for ten years. To return without her parents or anyone here in the colonies is hard for her."

"She told you this?"

I shook my head. "Nein, but I know that I would feel very

frightened and alone. I know she misses her Mutter and Vater. She has a family picture, and she stared at it for a long time when she unpacked it. If I hadn't been in the room, I'm sure she would have cried."

"Ach! You make such a story out of so little, Ilsa. If she didn't want to leave her family, she could have remained in Marengo."

"Living in Marengo was too hard for her." I explained what Jutta had told us about the threatening men. "Her parents couldn't leave because of the contract on their bakery. They would have been taken to court."

He leaned close to my ear. "Mutter said you are welcome to come for a visit this evening. We had hickory nut cookies for dessert."

"For sure I want to know what Albert had to say in his letter to you, but it would be better if we went back to the hotel. Jutta may need some company."

"So I guess I will have no cookies tonight." Garon grinned as we turned toward the hotel.

I gave him a light jab with my elbow. "I think I can manage to find you a slice of plum cake if it is only your stomach that you are worried about."

His laughter filled the cold nighttime air as we climbed the front steps and entered the hotel. Jutta was nowhere in sight, but Mr. Young was engrossed in a stack of papers he'd spread across a table in the front parlor. He started as we entered the room.

"Back so soon?" He glanced at the clock.

"Our evening prayer meetings last for only twenty or thirty minutes."

"Oh, that's right. I was busy studying some legal papers I'll need for court next week and forgot you wouldn't be gone for long." Mr. Young shuffled the papers into a neat pile and tucked them into a folder he'd placed on the table. "Did you get that telegram sent for me this morning, Garon?"

"Oh yes, sir. After I dropped you off, I returned to the train station. Sent it off first thing. Were you expecting a reply? We didn't get one. I would have brought it to you right away."

I was amazed by Garon's apparent desire to please Mr. Young at every turn. Though Garon was always kind and considerate to all visitors he transported to and from the hotels and train stations, he seemed to have taken a particular interest in Mr. Young. Or perhaps it was the other way around—I couldn't be certain.

I nudged Garon's arm. "I thought you wanted to visit. We can go to our private parlor. Mutter and Vater will join us once they return."

Garon nodded, but his attention remained fixed on Mr. Young. "Wait a moment, Ilsa. I just happened to think that maybe Mr. Young could help Jutta with her problem."

His words perplexed me. "What problem does Jutta have that requires a lawyer's help?"

"With that contract her parents signed. I guess you know about contracts, don't you, Mr. Young?" Garon stepped forward.

Mr. Young gave an unconvincing smile. "I know my fair share." Once again he looked toward the clock. "What's this problem you have? I may be able to give you a little guidance."

"It's nothing," I said, taking hold of Garon's arm and tightening my fingers into a firm grip. "Do not concern yourself, Mr. Young. You have business of your own to take care of."

Garon ignored my remark and continued his rambling. "The girl who arrived this morning to work here at the hotel. Her name is Jutta Schmitt. Her parents are purchasing a bakery in Marengo."

I dug my fingers into Garon's arm with increased fervor. If

he hadn't been wearing his jacket, I'm sure I would have drawn blood. When he flinched and turned, I glared at him. "This is Jutta's private business, Garon," I whispered. "It is not proper for us to discuss her family with a stranger."

Mr. Young leaned forward on his chair, obviously hoping to overhear my comments to Garon. I expected my parents to arrive at any time and interrupt the conversation, but thus far they hadn't appeared.

Garon nudged my arm. "If you are concerned, why don't you go and ask Jutta if she would like legal help from Mr. Young. You said she is sad and wants her parents to move back here with her."

I wanted to throttle Garon. I had never said any such thing. I'd merely told him about Jutta's sad expression before I had left for meeting. Just because I thought she was sad didn't mean that I expected him to interfere.

Mr. Young straightened in his chair. "So Jutta lived elsewhere and has now decided to live in the Amana Colonies? She plans to become a member of your . . . your . . . group?"

Before I could stop him, Garon explained Jutta's circumstances, including the reason why her parents had been unable to return to Amana with her. By the time he stopped talking, my temper had heated to near the boiling point. Where were my parents? Any interruption would have been welcome.

Garon nodded at Mr. Young. "Is a difficult situation because her parents must pay the obligation on their bakery."

"I may be able to help them if their reasons for returning have nothing to do with a lack of patriotism." Mr. Young's eyebrows dropped, and he narrowed his eyes.

My irritation was at a peak, and his arrogant answer annoyed me. "Why is it that you immediately assume there is a lack of patriotism, Mr. Young? Like other outsiders, you forget most of us were born here. Just like you, we're Americans."

Mr. Young yanked on the front of his vest. "Well, if your men are unwilling to serve in the military, it does give rise to the question of patriotism."

"My brother is serving in the army, but I don't believe that makes him any more patriotic than you, Mr. Young."

A deep red blush crept from beneath his white collar until it reached his hairline. "I have a physical ailment that keeps me from joining the armed services, but I serve my country in other ways, Miss Redlich." He'd assumed a formal tone, making his anger all the more evident.

"I'm sorry, Mr. Young. I doubt you meant to offend me any more than I intended to offend you." I tugged on Garon's arm. "We shall leave you to your documents."

Mr. Young jumped to his feet. "Your apology is accepted, and to show there are no hard feelings, I would like to help your new arrival. Why don't you ask her to come and join us? That way she can better explain the particulars to me." He looked at Garon's arm. "And it may save Garon from permanent injury."

I turned toward the door, still hoping my parents' arrival would bring an end to this strange turn of events. I wouldn't want others discussing my personal problems, and Jutta likely wouldn't be pleased, either. We'd begun to form a friendship, and I didn't want Mr. Young and his questions to interfere. If only Garon had kept his mouth shut.

"Go on, Ilsa. Ask Jutta to join us. You said she'd probably enjoy some company this evening." Garon gave me a nudge toward our rooms.

My mind raced with any possible way to avoid the request, but nothing came to mind. Nothing except the possibility of telling a lie. "I'll see if she's awake." I headed down the hall, uncertain what I would do. I could wait a few minutes, return, and tell them she'd retired for the night. I could knock and hope she truly had retired. Or I could let her make the choice herself. When I passed the door leading to our private rooms, I decided I wouldn't venture any further. This could ruin any possible friendship with Jutta. I turned and had taken only a step when I heard the familiar clunk of a metal latch.

My breath caught when Jutta appeared in the doorway. "Jutta. I thought you'd retired for the night."

"It's a little early for bed, don't you think?" She strode toward me and stopped by my side. "I hope your parents weren't displeased that I decided to remain at home this evening."

"No, of course not. They understand this is a difficult change for you." I could feel my forced smile begin to droop. "Garon mentioned your parents to Mr. Young."

Jutta stopped short. "What about my parents?" Her words were laced with anxiety as she clasped her hand atop my wrist. "Mr. Young is not acquainted with my parents. Why would Garon do such a thing?"

"He thought Mr. Young might help them overcome their legal problems."

She stared at me as if she didn't understand a word I'd said. After several moments, I saw a glimmer of understanding in her eyes. "The bakery contract," she whispered.

"Ja. He thought maybe Mr. Young could somehow help them get out of the contract so they could move here with you. Garon knows I am angry that he said anything to Mr. Young. And I am sorry I told Garon. It's just that he inquired about why you'd returned alone, and . . ." My voice faltered as her brows dropped low above angry-appearing eyes.

"And what did you tell him? Did you say I'd received threats? I don't want outsiders to know what has happened to me or my parents, Ilsa. And I cannot believe Garon would speak of my private business to a stranger. I don't want the help of Mr. Young or anyone else." Her hand trembled as she tightened her grip on my arm. "Come on. I will speak to Mr. Young and tell him his help is not needed—or wanted."

Though she attempted to sound brave, her voice quivered, and I was certain her anger had faded to fear. I understood her anger at Garon. The information about her family was not his to share with anyone. Yet I hadn't expected such a strong reaction. Why the fear? Perhaps Jutta was hiding something—something she'd not told me.

Mr. Young was rocking back on his heels with his hands folded behind his back. His dark eyes fastened upon Jutta the minute we entered the parlor, and a ripple of fear raced through me. I hoped that I appeared calm, for my insides were churning like the Iowa River during a summer storm. Jutta squeezed my hand. I wasn't certain if that was a signal that she could deal with Mr. Young, or if she wanted me to come to her aid.

"I understand your parents are having some difficulty with a contract on their bakery, Miss Schmitt. Garon thought I might offer a little help."

Jutta stood straight and met Mr. Young's gaze without flinching. "I thank you for your offer, Mr. Young, but my parents do not want help. They do not wish to avoid their legal obligation and have never expressed a desire to return to the colonies." Her voice remained strong and steady as she spoke to Mr. Young.

As my parents entered the front door, I stepped between Mr. Young and Jutta. "There you are!" I said in a loud voice. "I was becoming worried. I thought we might need to come and search for you." I hoped my interruption would stop any further discussion of Jutta's parents.

"Your Vater stopped to visit with Brother Edwin. Then Sister Barbara said we should walk to their house with them. We went inside and visited for several minutes."

My father rubbed his hands together. "Ja, well, it was too cold to stand outside. And you and Sister Barbara didn't appear to be in any hurry to stop talking." He removed his hat and unbuttoned his jacket. "Since when do you worry about how late your parents stay out at night?" He grinned at me as he removed his wool coat.

"Garon was hoping for a piece of plum cake, but I wanted to be certain Mutter didn't have any plans for the leftovers."

My father rubbed his stomach with his palm. "I have lots of plans for that leftover cake, Garon. We should maybe arm-wrestle to see who gets the biggest piece."

"Come along, then. Let's go to the kitchen and see what we can find for you starving men." Mother waved for us to follow her. "We can get it onto some plates, and I'll let you eat in the parlor if you promise you won't drop crumbs on my rug." Waiting until Garon drew near, my mother grasped his arm. "I understand you received a letter from Albert. You'll have to share it with us."

I was thankful Mother made it clear we would retire to our apartment after she cut the cake. I grabbed Jutta by the hand. "Come along, Jutta. We need to join the others. They may need an unbiased judge to decide if Mutter has cut the cake in equal pieces."

Mr. Young picked up his folder. "If you decide you'd like some help with that contract, Miss Schmitt, just let me know. Garon tells me the bakery is in Marengo. That's not so far, and I'd be happy to speak with your parents about their concerns."

Jutta stopped and glanced over her shoulder. "As I said, there is no need, Mr. Young. My parents are content in Marengo. If Garon led you to believe there was a problem with the contract or purchase of the bakery, he misspoke. My parents have no quarrel with anyone."

"We all have a quarrel with someone, Miss Schmitt. If we didn't, lawyers wouldn't become wealthy men." His eyes remained steely. "If your parents have a change of heart, you come and see me. I'd be willing to look at their contract and see if I can help them."

There was something about the way he looked at Jutta that made my breath catch in my throat. Instead of an offer to help, his suggestion had borne a harsh tone that sounded more threatening than helpful. There was no doubt Mr. Young could be a frightening adversary.

CHAPTER 11

Jutta Schmitt

The moment Garon discovered I was going home to Marengo for a visit, he insisted upon bringing the buggy to the hotel and escorting me to the train station. I'd objected until Ilsa pulled me aside and explained that he wanted to speak to me. I wondered if he hoped to set things aright between us. I knew it was proper to forgive him—Ilsa had reminded me several times, but forgiveness didn't come so easily for me nowadays. Especially when Garon's behavior could place my parents in more danger. Who could say what would come of the conversation he'd had with Mr. Young about our bakery?

The thought of Mr. Young and his beady-eyed stare set my heart pounding. Since that night when I refused his help, I'd done my best to avoid speaking to him. The fact that we were discouraged from talking during mealtime aided my cause, and whenever he packed his bags and headed back to Des Moines, I was most thankful. From all accounts, his brief visits to the hotel were enough to appease his wife, who no longer waited for an invitation to attend quilting bees or Red Cross meetings—much to the dismay of the other ladies, who still had not accepted her presence. Not that I blamed them. Even though Mrs. Young couldn't understand German, her attendance created an air of discomfort at the gatherings. And though she faithfully brought along the needles and thread she'd purchased at the general store, she couldn't sew an acceptable stitch. A fact that set her even further apart from the women.

While the women were willing to freely discuss a new recipe for cottage cheese sausage or wheatless gingerbread that had been served in the *Küchehaas* on Meatless Monday or Wheatless Wednesday, most other matters were whispered in hushed voices in Mrs. Young's presence. Even though she couldn't understand the language, they feared her presence and the tales she might carry. Yet they didn't hesitate to whisper their secrets in front of me. The thought that I could report some of the things they said to one another never seemed to enter their minds, for a sister would never do such a thing to another sister or brother of the community. At least that's what they believed. After each meeting, I hurried to my room and made note of such comments. And though the remarks were few and of little significance, I hoped they might help my family's plight.

After reviewing my notes one last time, I tucked them into a small box beneath my stockings and gathered my bag. Thoughts of the trusting sisters whirled through my mind like a child's spinning top as I hurried down the hallway. Garon was waiting by the front door. I had hoped Ilsa would ride along to the station, but she was nowhere in sight.

"Good afternoon, Garon. I want to tell Ilsa good-bye, and

then I'll be ready to go." I hesitated a moment. "If you are in a hurry, please don't feel obligated to wait for me. I can walk the short distance." Secretly, I hoped he would accept my offer.

"She's in the kitchen." He extended his hand for my bag. "You can leave it with me, and I'll load it into the buggy."

Since I would be gone only three nights, there wasn't much I needed to take along. Besides, I'd left many of my belongings at home. "It's not heavy. I can—"

He extended his hand a bit further. "Don't trust me with it?" There was an edge to his voice that annoyed me.

I kept the bag close to my side. "It has nothing to do with trust, Garon. There is nothing of importance in the bag. However, if there were, you can be sure that I would question whether I should trust you with it." Before he could say anything more, I swept past him and headed into the kitchen. Ilsa's hands were covered with flour and dough. I nodded toward the dough and the large bowl of apples. "Apple dumplings?"

Though I knew Ilsa and her mother were pleased for me, my absence from the hotel would make their days more difficult. All of the hotel rooms were full, which would keep them busier than usual while I was gone.

Ilsa bobbed her head. "The guests like them, and they are easy enough to make. I hope you have a gut visit with your Mutter and Vater, Jutta." There was a wistful look in her eyes. "You are for sure coming back, ja?"

"For sure. I am only sorry that I am going to be away when the hotel is full. It makes so much work for you."

"Mutter and I can handle this. You go and enjoy the time with your parents. Besides, it was not you that decided you would go for your visit the day after Thanksgiving."

She was right on that account. I'd asked the elders for

permission to visit my family when I'd first arrived. And though they'd said they had no argument with a visit to my parents, they wanted me to remain until after Thanksgiving and the annual *Bundesschliessung*—the renewing of the covenant that took place each Thanksgiving Day. When the elders had requested that I wait until after Bundesschliessung, I'd decided they were testing me. They wanted to see if I would attend the solemn service and renew my pledge to live for the Lord and offer the customary handshake. I had not wavered in making my renewal, but my voice had trembled as I lifted my voice and sang the time-honored words that I'd learned years ago:

> "The needy will receive God's help and blessing;
> He satisfies the hungry soul.
> He strengthens those whose flame of faith is lagging;
> To honor Him should be our goal."

Last night as I'd attempted to go to sleep, those words had haunted me and disturbed my sleep. Was I honoring God with my actions? My heart told me no, yet how could I allow my parents to suffer for something they hadn't done? Didn't the Bible say to honor your mother and father? Shouldn't I place the safety of my parents before these people I'd known for only a few weeks?

I leaned forward and placed a fleeting kiss on Ilsa's cheek. "I'll be back before you know I've gone."

Judas had betrayed Christ with a kiss. Was I doing the same to Ilsa? Was I going to show her affection and then betray her friendship? Was I going to report her unpatriotic statements to the men from the Council of National Defense?

Tears threatened, and I turned away, pushing the thoughts of betrayal from my mind. I strode through the dining room and marched past Garon. If I talked, I might lose control. Without waiting for his assistance, I stepped up into the buggy and placed my bag on the floor next to my seat. The brisk wind slapped at my wool cloak, and I pulled it tight around my arms.

Garon hoisted himself up and plopped down with a thud. Reins in hand, he flicked his wrists and slapped the leather straps against the horse's backside. "Looks like the cold air is giving you problems." He pointed to my tearing eyes.

With a swipe of my gloved hand, I wiped away the tears. "You're right. Cold weather makes my eyes water." I leaned back in the seat and hoped he would remain silent for the short ride. I didn't want to visit.

"Until you forgive me, Ilsa will remain angry with me. I was only trying to help you."

"Is that what you call an apology, Garon?" I didn't detect even a hint of remorse in his voice—only anger that Ilsa was angry with him.

"I'm not so sure why I should apologize for trying to help you. Ilsa says I should not have interfered in your business." He hiked a shoulder. "Did you stop to think maybe Ilsa should not have told me about your parents or their contract? If you hadn't told her, none of this would have happened."

I stared at him in disbelief. "So instead of taking responsibility for your bad decision, you now want to place blame on Ilsa because she told you about my parents? Or if that doesn't work, you want to blame me because I confided in Ilsa?" I shook my head. "It is a weak man who cannot admit his own mistakes, Garon Drucker."

He tucked his chin and gave me a sideways glance. "I know I shouldn't have interfered, but I thought Mr. Young could help.

I thought you would be grateful instead of angry. I am sorry for trying to do something to help you. I will never again do such a thing."

Such silliness from a grown man! I sighed as my exasperation mounted. "In the future, I would prefer you ask me before you enter into my business. If you hadn't acted in such a reckless manner, we wouldn't be having this conversation, and Ilsa wouldn't be angry with you."

He stiffened at my words. "You are right. I am sorry. Will you tell Ilsa I have apologized?"

There was no reason to argue any further. Garon's pride would not permit him to offer any more of an apology than he'd just given. And my anger would not permit me to offer any more than what he asked. "I will speak to Ilsa when I return." He hadn't received my forgiveness, but that wasn't what he cared about. It was Ilsa's forgiveness he desired.

"And you will tell her that you have forgiven me?"

"I will tell her that you apologized and promised to never again interfere in my business unless I asked for your help."

"Ja, that is gut. She will be happy when she hears this." He nodded and grinned as he pulled back on the reins.

I stepped down from the buggy knowing we'd both gotten what we wanted. Garon would receive Ilsa's forgiveness while I continued to withhold mine—at least for a while longer.

We entered the train station, and I walked to the window to arrange for my ticket. Garon greeted a young man I'd seen in church on Sundays. After receiving my ticket, I sat down on a bench not far from where Garon and his friend were standing. Moments later Garon pulled a letter from his pocket and pointed to the envelope.

"It's from Albert." I could hear the pride in his voice as he pulled the pages from the envelope.

I turned to look out the window.

"He writes me separately to tell me private things he doesn't want his family to know."

To eavesdrop wasn't proper, but I couldn't resist. His comment aroused my curiosity. Was Garon about to divulge Albert's secrets? Had he learned nothing? A twinge of guilt shot through me as I scooted a little closer to where the men stood. I kept my head bowed so they wouldn't realize I was listening.

Garon unfolded and tapped one of the pages. "He says in the letter that some of the men are not treating him well. They make harsh remarks and treat him with contempt. He's had trouble with only two of the men in his company, but he said that word spreads among the men in the hospital that he is a conscientious objector, and they have made some threats toward him. He says if I receive my draft notice, I should seek God's guidance before I agree to join." Garon chuckled. "He knows I am sometimes a hothead and thinks I could get into trouble."

The other man laughed. "Ja. That is the truth. If one of those soldiers said something you didn't like, you might punch him in the nose, and there would go your enlistment rating as a pacifist. They would be sending you off to fight on the next boat."

"That would not be gut. My Mutter and Vater would be mighty unhappy if that happened. And Ilsa, too."

At the mention of Ilsa's name I pretended to search in the knitting bag I carried with me. I was certain Garon would move further away from me or at least lower his voice, but he simply turned sideways—as if that would block my hearing. Perhaps he was baiting a trap to see if I would tell Ilsa. Then he could accuse me of interfering in his business. He would surely like it if that happened.

"Have you decided what you will do if your notice comes? You should listen to Albert."

"I really want to go. Like Albert, I don't want people to think all the men in Amana are cowards."

"You think I am a coward because I don't want to go to war?"

Garon had clearly insulted his friend. "I didn't say you're a coward, Rinehart, but that is what other people think about us."

"I do not believe everyone thinks we are cowards. There are other people besides us who are pacifists, and they do not fight, either. My Vater says it is important we do not stray from our religious beliefs, even if we are persecuted."

"So you have talked to him about joining the army?" Garon sounded encouraged by Rinehart's comment.

"Ja, when the editor of the Marengo newspaper wrote about the quota of men that must be met for each county. He said that more must go from other towns because the men in Amana are unwilling to serve their country. What he put in the newspaper made me angry, and I wanted to show him we are not cowards."

Garon grunted his agreement. "I understand this. That is why Albert and I both believed we should sign up to serve our country. Now he writes to me and says I should stay at home, but I want to help change how people feel about us."

"My Vater says we should not believe such lies. Maybe he is right. Have people changed how they feel since Albert went into the army? I don't think so. But who can say for sure?" Rinehart shrugged. "Perhaps you will not receive the draft notice and you won't have to make a decision—that would make it easy for you."

"Ja, that would make it easy," Garon said.

"And if the draft notice comes, maybe you should pray and see what God would have you do."

The train whistled as it neared the station, and both men glanced toward the platform. I stood and headed across the station, but Garon hurried to my side before I reached the door. "I hope you have a safe journey." With another shrill whistle and a cloud of dark smoke, the train came to a bellowing stop. "You will remember to speak to Ilsa when you return?"

I nodded. "I will remember."

He held the station door for me and then rushed off to meet any passengers who might need a ride to the other train station or to one of the hotels. I strode down the platform and boarded the train. I sighed as I dropped to my seat, thankful to be alone. Now I must concentrate on what I would tell those men from the Council when they came calling. And I knew they would. My mother had written to tell me they'd again been watching the shop, and another man had stopped in with Lester Becroft to ask when I would return. He even threatened to come to South Amana if I didn't soon return. I'd lost no time sending a letter advising her that I would arrive the day after Thanksgiving.

The train ride to Marengo was far too short—I didn't have nearly enough time to come to any decision. I even tried prayer. But I doubted God wanted to listen to someone like me, a person who would betray good people who loved Him. Not that I didn't love God. I did. But I was sure the people I was willing to deceive were on much better terms with Him than I would ever be.

The train pulled into the station while I continued to weigh what I would tell the men from the Defense Council. Thinking of possibilities was enough to diminish the joy of returning home. I peered out the window and caught sight of my mother standing on the platform, the hem of her coat flapping in the cold wind. She'd tied a woolen scarf around her neck. Still, the sight of her bent figure standing in the cold, damp weather caused me concern. She shouldn't risk a sore throat or cold. Without my presence in the bakery, Father needed her by his side every day. Though I'd been gone only a short time, she already appeared several years older. I couldn't decide if her stooped shoulders were caused by fatigue or an effort to ward off the cold. Either way, the sight of her hunched form saddened me. That brief visit by those angry men had changed all of our lives.

Before I stepped down from the train, I forced a smile and waved at her. She straightened her shoulders and lifted one glove overhead. Bag in hand, I hurried to her side and pulled her into a tight embrace. "It is so good to see you." I leaned back and cupped her cheek in my palm. She looked thinner. "You are feeling well?"

"Ja. Of course. Your Vater said to tell you he is sorry he could not be here to meet you." She gestured toward home.

"I know he must stay at the bakery. I didn't expect both of you to come to the station. In fact, neither of you needed to come and meet me."

"Ach! What kind of welcome is that? To have your daughter come home and no one to kiss her cheek or greet her with a smile? Never!"

"Come on. Let's go inside, where it's a bit warmer." I chided her for standing on the platform, but she dismissed my warnings of catching a cold. "You forget I come from hearty stock—we don't get sick."

"That's what everyone says before they get sick and die." We both laughed. It was an old family joke, and it felt good to share and tease without worrying I would be misunderstood. I directed her to the woodburning stove in the corner. "You need to warm yourself before we walk home." Though it wasn't far to the bakery, I didn't know how long Mother had been standing out in the cold.

She chided me for worrying too much as she extended her hands toward the warmth of the fire. After a few minutes, she glanced around the depot. Most of the passengers had gathered their bags and departed. "I think Lester Becroft and that other man, Mr. Gillman, will be waiting when we get home. They stopped at the bakery to see when you would arrive. They are expecting lots of news from you. I am surprised they didn't escort me here."

I heard the sarcasm in her voice and squeezed her shoulder. "They wouldn't want to be seen in a public place talking to us. They wouldn't want anyone to think they were friends with Germans."

"We aren't Germans," my mother hissed. "We are Americans."

I'd already forgotten the minute-by-minute fear of expressing anything about our German heritage. It was silly. Everyone in Marengo knew which residents were of German descent. In Amana I didn't have to hide my heritage, but I did have to conceal why I was there. No matter where I was, I couldn't be completely honest.

"I think the men will be disappointed with my report."

A flicker of fear shone in my mother's eyes. "I am glad you won't have to say bad things about the people of Amana, but I don't think it will go well when those men return." She shook her head. "I have prayed for God to show us what to do. I told your Vater it would be easier to have them destroy the bakery than to make reports against our own people in the colonies."

I clutched my mother's arm. "Don't even think about suggesting such a thing. They would believe there really is something to hide and that you're trying to protect the people of Amana. Let me take care of this."

She rubbed her hands one last time. "We better go now. Your Vater will begin to worry if we aren't back soon."

Grasping my bag in one hand, I held my mother's elbow with the other. Together we walked toward the bakery.

"I am thankful the elders assigned you to a nice family."

I nodded. "They are good people. I especially like Ilsa. We work well together. She says I don't sound as German as the rest of the people in Amana." I grinned. "I think it's because I have learned to say *mother* and *father* instead of *Mutter* and *Vater*."

My mother chuckled. "And you do not say *ja* or *ach* or *gut* like the rest of us, either. I think it is gut you have learned to speak more like the American people."

I shrugged. "Perhaps. But I sound a little different no matter where I live." I'd written my parents and told them I was comfortable with the Redlich family and enjoyed working at the hotel. Through my letters, I'd awakened their memories about life in the colonies, and I wondered if they were sorry they had left Homestead.

My thoughts were still a jumble when we rounded the corner and opened the door. Lester Becroft and the other man from the Iowa Council of National Defense turned to face me as I stepped inside. Neither appeared happy.

CHAPTER 12

"It's about time you got here!" The man my mother referred to as Mr. Gillman puffed out his chest and strode toward me. "I was about to send Lester to look for you. Thought maybe we were going to have to come to Amana and find you." Lester remained at the end of the counter and prevented any opportunity for me to embrace my father.

Gathering courage, I straightened my shoulders and met the leader's angry glare. "I would think a member of the Iowa Council of National Defense would have more important things to do than worry over someone as insignificant as I am."

He chucked me beneath the chin with enough force to tip my head. "If I didn't know better, I'd think you were trying to insult me. You aren't that stupid, are you, girl?"

"Do not touch my daughter!" My father stormed to the end of the counter, but Lester blocked his path. "You do not need to use force. If you open your ears, you will know that you misunderstood my daughter. We would never insult any of you, would we, Jutta?" He sent me a pleading look.

"My father is right. You misunderstood." I dropped my bag near the wall and unbuttoned my cloak.

The man remained close at my side, the stench of his foul breath filling my nostrils. "I'm sure you got some good information for us, ain't ya?"

Unable to tolerate the offensive odor, I turned my head and inhaled a deep breath. "I have been in the colonies for only a short time, so I think you'll be disappointed with the report I have for you."

His lips curled in an angry snarl. "What's that supposed to mean?"

"The people I've met in Amana have only good to say about this country. I've heard nothing unpatriotic, except a few remarks from visitors who stop at the hotel to eat a meal or spend the night. None of them were residents of Amana or of German heritage."

The man glowered at me. "What about them folks you're living with?"

"We live in rooms attached to the hotel in South Amana. The Redlich family is patriotic, and they love this country. Their son, Albert, is serving in the U.S. Army at Camp Pike, Arkansas."

Mr. Gillman's frown deepened. "If that's all you got to tell us, then you ain't doing what you're supposed to." He inched closer. "I think you know a lot more than what you're telling me. Either you come back here with something more next time, or when you get here, the two of them will be in jail for feeding glass to our soldiers. And don't think we won't rough 'em up before they make it to the jail, neither. You might not recognize either one of them the next time you see 'em if you don't do what you're told."

He sneered at my mother, who had turned as white as fresh fallen snow. "Quit spending all your time with them hotel visitors and get yourself out listening to them Huns—I wanna know what they're thinking and doing."

Somehow I needed to make this man realize that what he wanted was not so easily gained. "You don't understand life in the colonies. I don't make choices about who I see or where I go. I'm assigned a job and a place to live." I was trying to remain calm and explain that to break from the schedule would be impossible. "If I do what you ask, they will become suspicious, and I will learn nothing. You must be patient if you want me to gather the kind of information you want."

"You better figure out a way to do what I'm telling you, or you can believe I'm gonna keep my word. Them two are gonna be in jail the next time you come back to Marengo. Deciding how you're gonna do it is your problem." He pointed a dirty finger at my parents. "And theirs. I don't think they'll enjoy sitting in jail." His eyes darkened. "Now you sure you ain't got nothing you want to tell me?"

Never before had I seen my father appear so angry—the muscles in his jaw were twitching as he attempted to push Lester Becroft from the end of the counter. "You men are cowards. Making threats against women and forcing people to do things you cannot do yourself." Once again he shoved Lester. "And you! What kind of man are you? We give you help when your children are hungry, and this is how you repay us? You may have power in your Defense Council, but you are weak men."

"Watch your mouth, old man, or you won't be able to talk when I get through with you." Mr. Gillman took a long stride toward the counter, his hand balled into a fist. He lifted his arm. "You want this right in the middle of your face?"

"Bert! Stop with this arguing before they hurt you." Tears streaked my mother's face as she pleaded with a frantic urgency.

My heart pounded against my ribs. I'd spoken the truth. There was little to say against anyone in Amana, except Ilsa and visiting strangers, but I had to say something to satisfy this man's anger before he hurt my father. My stomach knotted with regret. "Ilsa Redlich is angry that her brother joined the army." Shame washed over me as I shouted the words.

Mr. Gillman turned, his lips curled in an evil smirk. He motioned Lester to bring him a stool from behind the counter. "And? Go on. What else did this Ilsa say?"

I shook my head. "Nothing. Just that she hoped the war would end very soon so that her brother could come home safe." I met his intense stare. "Lots of people feel the same way. I've heard as much from people who live here in Marengo. They come into the bakery and say they'll be glad when the war is over and their sons or brothers can return home."

"So what you've brought me is worth nothing." The stool clattered to the floor as he jumped to his feet. "Either you come back here in two weeks with some worthwhile information, or you'll see that I keep my promises. Understand?"

I shook my head. "I cannot come back that soon. The elders told me they would permit only occasional visits for the first year. They think I will make a better adjustment to life in Amana if I don't return to the outside so often."

The man remained silent as he weighed my words. I didn't miss the hint of suspicion lurking in his eyes. "I don't think I believe you. If you're not back here in two weeks, they'll be in jail." He watched and waited as though he expected me to change my story.

"I could ask one of the elders to write a letter to my parents stating how often I can come home. Otherwise, I don't know how to convince you. If I don't abide by the rules, they'll consider me unsuitable to remain among them and send me home." That wasn't exactly true, but it wasn't a complete lie.

"I wasn't born yesterday, girl. You could also tell them elders you don't want to come home. That way they'd put anything you want in their letter." Lester bobbed his head in agreement, an obvious lackey within the organization.

"The elders wouldn't lie. They are good men who do their best to follow the Bible's teachings." I folded my arms across my waist. "If a letter won't help, I don't know what else I can do to convince you."

Mr. Gillman looked at Lester. "Guess she must be telling the truth. I don't think she wants the two of them thrown in jail." He kept a steely gaze locked on Lester as if defying him to disagree with his conclusion.

Lester immediately agreed with Mr. Gillman. "Yeah, I figure she's telling the truth. We'll just have to wait, unless you're gonna have her get them fellas to send you a letter."

"Elders," I said, unable to hold my tongue. "They are called *elders*, not *fellas*."

Lester shrugged. "You knew what I meant, didn't ya, Mike?"

The leader grunted. "I want you to play on them elders' sympathy. Tell 'em you ain't never been away from your folks at Christmas. Ask 'em if you can't please come home for a few days after Christmas. If they're such good men, they oughta let you visit your family for Christmas. You write and let your folks know what they say. And don't waste any time. If they say you can't come, I'll be making a visit to that hotel after Christmas to tell them people you're living with that you been spying on 'em."

He grinned, obviously pleased with his plan. "And I'll make up all kinds of things to tell 'em you reported about all of 'em."

I opened my mouth to protest, but he pointed a thick index finger in my face.

"Don't say nothin' more, gal. I'll see you after Christmas— either here or at that hotel. You decide where it's gonna be."

He waved to Lester. They guffawed and slapped each other on the back while they headed for the door. Once they'd departed, I sighed and hurried to embrace my father. "Those men have no honor—especially Lester Becroft. I don't know how he sleeps at night." I forced a smile. "How have you been, Vater?"

"We are getting by. When you were here to help, it was much easier on your Mutter, but we are pleased you are with gut people." He leaned back and looked into my eyes. "That Mr. Young said you were doing very well at the hotel."

My pulse quickened and fear returned. "Mr. Young?"

"Ja. The lawyer from Des Moines. He stopped the other day. I think it was Monday. He said he would try to help us with our contract so we could come and live with you in Amana."

My heartbeat pounded in my ears. I could see my father's lips moving, but the thumping in my chest swallowed his words. "What did you tell him?" When he didn't immediately reply, I clutched his hand. "What, Vater? What did you say to Mr. Young?"

"I told him we didn't have any problems with our contract. There were lots of customers in the bakery, so we couldn't talk. He had to leave to catch his train, but he said he would stop again and talk to us."

"What else? Did you say you'd already paid off the contract on the bakery?"

"Nein. Should I have told him? I am sorry. I didn't know." His eyes clouded with regret.

I shook my head. "No! Do not tell him that. He thinks we still owe money on the contract. If he returns, you should tell him we haven't paid it off yet."

My father dropped to the stool and held his palm to his cheek. "I do not understand. What is this about the contract being paid and not being paid? And why does Mr. Young think we must move to Amana?"

I motioned my mother to draw close and explained what Garon had told Mr. Young. My father shook his head. "You told a lie about the bakery contract?"

Irritation threatened, but I reminded myself that he didn't know the difficulties I'd faced while trying to fit into the life that had been forced upon me. "Father, I am living a lie. I count myself fortunate on days when I can avoid deceit. Do you want me to say that my parents can't leave the bakery because we've been threatened with jail unless they stay there while I spy on the people of Amana?" My words were sharp, and I could see they'd bruised him. "I am sorry, Father. This has been hard for all of us, but it was the only excuse I could think of at the time."

He bobbed his head. "Is all right. We will tell Mr. Young we don't have any problems with the contract and that your Mutter and I have worked hard in the bakery for the past ten years and do not want to leave Marengo. I will tell him we are happy living here, ja?"

"Yes, and we can hope he will not return." I shot a smile at my mother. She hadn't yet removed her coat, and I stepped to her side. Her fingers trembled as she attempted to force the thick buttons through the holes. "Let me help you, Mother." I stepped in front of her and unbuttoned the coat, sad that those men had been able to create such fear among us.

My mother's hands soon ceased their trembling, and a hint of color returned to her cheeks. "I think I should make a fresh pot of coffee." When she looked at my father, he nodded his agreement.

"That would be gut." The minute she'd gone upstairs, my father crooked his finger. "Come close. I don't want your Mutter to hear." He watched the door as I stepped to his side. "I have been thinking about our circumstances. I have some money saved—hidden in our rooms upstairs. I think I should give it to you. When you leave here tomorrow, you should buy a ticket to Chicago. When you get to Chicago, you should buy a ticket to another city—maybe New York. They will never find you in a big city. What can they do to your Mutter and me?"

I stared at him in disbelief. "What can they *do*? Weren't you listening to that man? They will beat you and throw you both in jail. And then they will burn the bakery to the ground or force you to sign it over to one of them so they can sell it—who knows what else they will do. They could even kill you. I heard about a man of German heritage who wouldn't get on his knees to these men, and the next morning he was found hanging in his own house with a note pinned to his shirt that said *Hun lover*."

My father appeared unmoved. "I don't think Lester—"

"Lester? He will not save you. You don't know for sure what they will do. If you don't care about yourself, you must think of Mother. They could do terrible things to her."

He bowed his head and raked his fingers through the shock of thick hair that fell across his forehead. "I feel so helpless. This reporting on our people is a bad thing—I don't like what they ask you to do. Still, I must protect both you and your Mutter.

At night I go to bed and lie awake, thinking and thinking until I have this plan, but you say it isn't gut."

I clasped his arm and rested my head on his strong shoulder. "We must do what they've instructed, Father. If we don't, I believe they will harm all of us. I think our only answer is to pray. Isn't that what you used to tell me? Prayer is always the answer? We must pray that God will keep us safe." I looked into his sad eyes. "And let's pray that God will guard my lips so that I don't bring harm to anyone."

"Ja. You are right, Jutta. We must pray, but I feel I should also be doing something more."

I grinned at him. "You used to tell me that God didn't need help from little girls. Maybe He doesn't need help from grown men, either."

He chuckled and agreed. "I will do my best to let God take over what must be done, but you know how I am."

"I do know—you think the bread will not rise unless you knead it at least one or two times more." I squeezed his arm and then nodded toward the stairs. "I better take my bag upstairs. Mother will wonder what is keeping me."

My mother met me at the top of the stairs. "The coffee will be done soon. We can take it downstairs to enjoy with your Vater, ja?"

I pecked her on the cheek. "That will be fine." I lifted the bag a few inches. "I'll put this in my room, and then I'll be out to help you." The aroma of freshly baked bread drifted from downstairs, a reminder of one of the many things I'd taken for granted during my years at home. But if all went well, perhaps I could come home before long and life would return to normal. Right now, normalcy was a difficult thing to find anywhere in the country. The papers constantly spoke of the changes and sacrifices that must occur to win the war, but I didn't want any more change in my life. I wanted to turn back time and return to the life I'd enjoyed a few years ago, but that was impossible. For now, I needed to enjoy this time with my parents.

The remainder of the day passed in what seemed the blink of an eye. By midmorning on Saturday I felt as though I'd never left the bakery. The three of us had been working together in our usual pattern, with time to visit as we mixed and kneaded the dough. I laughed as my parents joked with each other, and I relished hearing my father retell the stories of his childhood. It didn't matter that I could recite those tales by heart. His deep, soothing voice offered the calm reassurance and familiarity I needed.

I was thankful neither of my parents mentioned Amana or the men from the Iowa Council of National Defense. I didn't want any reminders of the lies and deceit I was expected to execute once I returned to the hotel. For now, I wanted only to pretend that life had returned to normal—that I once again lived upstairs and the war had never begun.

Each time the bell over the bakery door rang, I went to the front of the store to help the customers—just as I had done less than three weeks ago. Few commented that they had missed my presence at the counter, but I hadn't expected much of a welcome. Since the United States had entered the war, only customers of German heritage spoke to us with warmth or kindness. And while many non-German customers continued to purchase their bread from us, they greeted us with a cold and superior attitude. Even their children viewed us with unmistakable disdain. The parents had obviously been teaching them to hate us, as well. That observation added even greater fear and sadness. Conduct such as this had caused our ancestors to flee Germany and come to this country, which avowed freedom. But suddenly there seemed to be little freedom for anyone who had an ounce of German blood running through their veins.

When a young boy walking with his parents spit on the outside of our bakery window, I shuddered with disgust and turned to my father. "What is wrong with parents that permit a child to act in such an offensive manner?"

Sorrow shaded my father's eyes. "Every day it becomes worse. More and more hateful signs are posted, more hate-filled speeches are shown in the moving-picture theaters, and even the newspapers tell children and their parents to hate anyone of German heritage." He shook his head. "Tell me how it helps the war effort if they eat 'liberty cabbage' instead of sauerkraut? Are their children any less sick if they become infected with 'liberty measles' instead of German measles? Last week the schoolteachers marched a classroom of children down the street carrying signs that said they are one hundred percent patriots." He pressed his palm across his chest. "I am a one hundred percent patriot, too. But if I hung a sign on the front window, no one would believe me." He dropped to one of the stools and touched his finger to his head. "My mind cannot understand any of it."

I could see that the frightful changes in the community and the country were taking a toll on my father. "I wish I were here to help you. I know it is difficult for you and Mother."

"Would be gut to have you here. We could use the help even more than before you left."

I arched a brow. My mother had mentioned that there had been less business during the past two weeks, so his comment surprised me. "And why is that?"

"No longer will Mr. Franklin deliver milk to us. He says he was told that he should not sell to my bakery. Now I must go out to the country three times each week to pick up milk from one of the farmers. Then I return to the bakery to make the bread. Sometimes, your Mutter must begin the dough for me." He scratched his head. "I only hope they will not stop the farmer from selling to me."

The reasons for my cooperation with the Defense Counsel continued to mount. My parents couldn't continue under the strain of such mean-spirited actions. Neither their health nor their emotions could withstand this badgering for any extended time.

The bell jangled, and I swiveled toward the door. My breath caught in my throat as I caught sight of Mr. Young entering. My fear soared to new heights, and I instinctively took a backward step toward my father. My heart drummed a staccato beat. "Mr. Young. What brings you to Marengo?"

His lips tipped into a crooked smile. "Why, I've stopped to assist your father with his contract. Didn't he tell you I'd been here and offered my help?" Mr. Young tilted his head and looked at my father.

"Ja, I told her, but we do not need help with our contract, Mr. Young. We do not wish to change anything. Jutta's mother and I want to live here in Marengo and keep our bakery." My father pointed his thumb toward the train depot. "You should head to the depot, or you might miss your train. I thank you for your kind offer, but a lawyer we do not need."

As if he hadn't heard a word my father had said, Mr. Young stepped forward and closed the distance between us. I inhaled a deep breath and met his hard stare. I hoped he wouldn't notice my trembling hands. "I'm sure you recall that I told you the very same thing back in Amana when you offered your help." I latched on to my father's arm and hoped we presented a united force.

"I do recall what you told me, Jutta, but sometimes people

don't say exactly what they mean. I didn't quite believe that you wanted to be separated from your mother and father." He tapped his index finger alongside his right eye. "I could see it in your eyes." He turned his attention to my father. "And what father wants his daughter living with strangers? I'm sure the three of you truly wish to be united, and I want to help."

My father's arm stiffened beneath my hand, and I pressed my fingers into a tighter grip. I wanted my father to remain silent and let me speak to Mr. Young, but I needed a moment to gather my thoughts. How did one convince a man who didn't want to believe what he'd been told? I couldn't tell if he'd detected my fear, but Mr. Young was far too pushy for my liking. My eyes may have betrayed me, but I didn't mistake the false smile on his lips. Our lives were complicated enough without his interference, and I wanted him to move along.

"I am certain you have important matters that await you in your law office, Mr. Young." I hoped I appeared more confident than I felt. "Or if you are returning to Amana, your wife is surely eager for your company. As my father said, we aren't in need of your services."

His smile faded as he dropped his satchel on the counter and opened the heavy metal clasp. Moments later he withdrew an envelope from the bag and placed it on the counter. "I took the liberty of stopping at the courthouse during my previous visit. You were busy with your customers, and I had several hours before my train departed."

My father's eyebrows dipped low, and worry lines formed across his forehead. "For what reason did you go to the courthouse, Mr. Young? You have legal business in Iowa County?"

"On rare occasions I have business in your courthouse, but the reason for my visit was to check the name of the rightful owner of this property. I thought I could write a letter or pay a visit to him and ask if he would consider releasing you from your contract." He removed his hat and placed it on top of the satchel. "After my visit I was somewhat confused, Mr. Schmitt."

The lawyer was baiting us. I hoped my father wouldn't bite. I gestured toward the kitchen. "We have work that requires our attention, Mr. Young."

He leaned forward ever so slightly. "Your work will wait for a moment, Jutta. Surely you're curious about why I was confused."

I shrugged and attempted an air of nonchalance. "Not particularly."

He tapped the envelope. "From my search of the records, it appears that you are the rightful owner of this business, Mr. Schmitt. The property was deeded to you by the previous owner, and the deed has been duly recorded at the courthouse by the registrar. There is no evidence that there is any mortgage on the property." His cunning smile caused a chill to ripple through my body. "Now, why would you and your daughter tell me that you didn't own this property when that simply is not true?"

My father remained silent, obviously expecting me to respond. This was, after all, a lie of my own making. If I didn't have an answer, I knew my father wouldn't have one, either. Fear grabbed hold of me in a viselike grip. I had to come up with a believable reply.

Like a wolf eager to lunge upon its prey, Mr. Young moistened his lips.

My heart quickened when the bell jangled and several customers entered the bakery. "If you'll excuse us, Mr. Young, we must wait on our customers."

His lips curled in a sly smile. "Certainly. In fact, I'll be leaving on the next train. We can discuss this matter when I return to Amana." He picked up the envelope, adjusted his jacket, and tipped his head. "Can't we?" Without waiting for my response he turned and, with a clipped stride, departed the store.

A momentary sense of relief washed over me, but I knew I must come up with some excuse that would hold this man at bay. As I watched him pass by the bakery window, I wondered if he was somehow connected to the men from the Iowa Council of National Defense. Either way, I must be convincing when Mr. Young next approached me. If I was going to persuade him, I must have a flawless answer.

CHAPTER 13

Ilsa Redlich

Until Jutta had gone to visit her parents, I hadn't realized how much I'd grown to depend upon her. She'd been with us only a short time, but already she'd become a respected member of the community and our family. She'd been willing to take on any task without complaint, and she could complete as much work as Sister Hulda ever had, and in half the time. Even my mother was surprised by how easily Jutta fit into the routine of our lives. She said it was because Jutta had lived in the colonies during her early years, but I thought it was because she wanted to prove she still belonged among us. She didn't want the elders to think they'd made a mistake by permitting her return. I was already certain they had made the proper decision.

The only task we both disliked was cleaning room number five, Mr. and Mrs. Young's bedroom. It wasn't a problem if they were gone, but more often than not, Mrs. Young sat in a chair near the window and issued orders. She acted as though we'd never before cleaned a room or made a proper bed. It always took twice as long to clean number five when she was present. And she delivered the same instructions every time. Don't touch this and don't touch that. Or, you may lift this and put it on the bed while you dust, but you shouldn't do so unless I'm in the room. The list went on and on. None of it made sense, but if she even thought we had disobeyed one of her instructions, she burst into one of her tearful bouts. I tried to remember that she suffered from melancholy, but I'd grown weary of her unpredictable behavior.

To make matters worse, she insisted her room be cleaned three times each week. Although we usually cleaned the rooms of long-term guests only once a week, my mother had agreed to Mrs. Young's request. However, Mother hadn't been swayed from the rules when Mrs. Young said she wanted the bedsheets changed two times a week. I had been both pleased and surprised by my mother's determined stance with the woman. Had Mother given in, our time at the washtubs would have significantly increased, a thought I didn't savor. Although Mrs. Young provided a diversion from our usual guests, there were times when her demands grew tiresome.

I placed the cleaning supplies at the bottom of the stairs and headed for the kitchen. Though my mother had set the water to boil, I was pleased to see she hadn't yet washed the breakfast dishes.

I placed my arm around her shoulders. "I was thinking that it might be gut to change our routine. I'll wash the dishes and begin the dinner preparations."

"And I am to clean the rooms?" Her brows lifted high on her forehead.

"Ja. Wouldn't you like to escape the kitchen for a while?"

"So this is a favor you are doing for me?" She chuckled and swiped her damp hands down the front of her apron.

I grinned in return. "Maybe not so much a favor but a reprieve from peeling potatoes and scraping dirty dishes."

My mother nodded. "And this has nothing to do with Mrs. Young and the way her demands sometimes wear on you when you must clean her room?" I started to reply, but she held up her hand. "Before you answer, you should know that Mrs. Young is not in her room. Does that change your mind about exchanging our duties?"

I hadn't fooled my mother in the least. With Mrs. Young out of her room, I'd much prefer cleaning to scrubbing pots and pans or preparing the noonday meal. "It does change my mind, but I won't go back on my offer. If you prefer to switch, I'll remain in the kitchen."

"Nein. And you'd better get upstairs before she returns."

I had walked as far as the stairway before my curiosity got the best of me. I returned and peeked around the kitchen doorway. "Where did Mrs. Young go?" Except to attend the Red Cross meetings or quilting bees with my mother and me, she seldom left the house alone. In fact, I couldn't recall that she'd ever left without one of us or Mr. Young.

My mother tucked a wisp of hair behind one ear as she glanced over her shoulder. "She said she was going to the general store to mail some letters and then take a walk."

"She complains about the cold weather, yet she is going to take a walk?" I shook my head. Hadn't she told me she didn't like to take walks in unfamiliar surroundings? The woman was as changeable as the Iowa weather.

My mother shrugged. "Who am I—or you—to question

what a guest does?" She pointed a finger toward the door. "You're wasting precious time."

I motioned toward the floor. "And you are dripping water." I laughed and hurried to gather my cleaning supplies.

There was no question that the Youngs' room would be first on my list to complete. I knocked on the door to make certain Mrs. Young hadn't returned while Mother and I were visiting in the kitchen. No doubt I would have heard her, but we had a rule about entering rooms: Always knock, and leave the door open while cleaning—especially if there are occupants who insist upon remaining in the room during the cleaning process. Most often our hotel guests busied themselves elsewhere during their visits to the colonies, but Mrs. Young proved to be an exception. She seemed to take delight in being present to make certain everything was done to her satisfaction. She might suffer from melancholy, but it hadn't affected her desire to order me around. Perhaps she'd learned that annoying tendency from her husband, for Mr. Young could be difficult, as well. But unlike his wife, Mr. Young was frequently away, so his demands didn't seem quite so significant.

When there was no answer, I pushed down on the metal door latch, surprised to find it locked. Guests seldom locked their doors when leaving the hotel for brief outings during the day. I dug the keys from my pocket and twirled them until I found the one with a 5 engraved on the end. I shoved it into the lock and turned until I heard the familiar heavy clunk.

After pushing open the door, I stood at the threshold. "It's Ilsa. I've come to clean. Is anyone in here?"

In other rooms it would be obvious if anyone was present, but this was the largest of our accommodations. Besides, Mrs. Young could be hidden behind the dressing screen. Long ago Mother had taught me it was better to be safe than sorry when entering a guest's room. She said she'd once entered a room unannounced and suffered an embarrassing moment. Though she hadn't gone into detail, several years later I heard my father tease her about walking in on a recently wed couple. After that, I was even more careful.

When there was no answer, I removed the cloth from my supplies and dusted the furniture and windowsills—Mrs. Young had a penchant for dusted windowsills and doorframes, and I didn't argue with her. It was easier to simply swipe them down and move along with my duties. After piling the quilts and coverlet onto a chair, I yanked the sheets from the bed, removed the pillowcases, and placed the dirty linens near the door. With a snap of my wrists, I watched the fresh sheet ripple and fall atop the mattress. Once I'd tucked in the edges, I followed the same process with the top sheet. Apparently I'd unfolded the sheet with too much enthusiasm, for several papers on a nearby table fluttered to the floor.

Once I finished making the bed, I stooped down and retrieved the papers, but I stopped short when I noticed the name *Bert Schmitt* printed in bold letters. The words *Iowa County Courthouse* were scribbled below the name. I didn't know anyone named Bert Schmitt. Of course, Schmitt wasn't such an odd name. There were lots of Schmitts who had emigrated from Germany many years ago. There were even some Schmitt families in other Amana villages—but I'd never heard of a Bert Schmitt. I sat down in the chair and stared at the paper. Could he be related to Jutta? Probably a silly thought. After all, how would the Youngs know the name of Jutta's father?

Still, there was a reference to the courthouse in Iowa County, so this Bert Schmitt must live somewhere nearby. I gathered the papers and tapped them on the edge of the table, hoping to get them in some semblance of order. I tried to recall if they'd been scattered across the table or in a neat pile, but I couldn't remember if I'd even looked at the table. Maybe I should stack a few and spread out the rest. I did my best to avoid looking at the other papers. I didn't want to be accused of snooping, but I couldn't help noticing that Mr. and Mrs. Young seemed particularly interested in the war effort. Rough notes were scribbled alongside news-paper clippings that had been pasted to many of the pages, and all of the articles had something to do with the war. Of course, since the United States had entered the war, most everybody was interested, even the residents of Amana.

I shrugged and placed the pages back on the table. Perhaps this was what Mrs. Young did to fill her days. I'd heard some of our guests talk about making scrapbooks in which they kept pictures of important events. Perhaps Mrs. Young was making pages for her own scrapbook.

My back was turned toward the door, and I'd almost finished sweeping when I heard a loud gasp behind me and glanced over my shoulder. With anger flashing in her eyes and fingers clasped across her lips, Mrs. Young stood in the doorway looking as though she'd discovered a dead body. Her hand slipped from her mouth, and she stepped toward me.

"What do you think you're doing in here?" She spat the ques-tion from between clenched teeth.

I stared at Mrs. Young, unable to believe my eyes or ears. The soft-spoken, melancholy lady I'd come to know through the past weeks had disappeared and been replaced by a strident, infuriated woman. Instinctively, I took a backward step. "I'm sweeping the floor." As if to reinforce the truth of my statement, I pointed to the rug.

"You know I don't want you in this room when I'm not here. Why didn't you wait until I returned?"

I shook my head. "I didn't know we weren't allowed to clean unless you were present. You never—"

"My husband gave specific orders when we checked in to the hotel. I know he did." She smacked her lips together, her eyes flashing with a defiant glare.

I knew her husband had never made such arrangements, but I wasn't going to argue the matter. Instead, I decided to turn the tables on her. "If someone must be present when the room is cleaned, perhaps we need to return to our previous cleaning schedule. I'll tell my mother you're dissatisfied. I'm certain she'll be pleased to hear that I'll now have additional time to assist her in the kitchen."

I was bending forward to pick up my cleaning supplies when Mrs. Young grasped my arm. "Wait! I didn't mean to offend you. You surprised me. Don't speak to your mother. I don't want the cleaning schedule changed. I apologize for my abrupt behavior." She opened her purse, withdrew several coins, and shoved them toward me. "Here. Take this for the extra work you perform on my behalf."

I shook my head. "I cannot take your money, Mrs. Young. If you wish to pay extra, you may give it to my father. He will see that it is turned over to the elders. Amana residents don't use money."

"Yes, yes. I forgot." Her fingers trembled as she shoved the coins back inside the bag. "Perhaps there's something else you might like? A new dress or some lace?" She shook her head. "No, of course not. You don't wear lace, and those dull dresses are furnished to you." After a quick glance toward the chest, she clapped her hands together. "I know. What about a toilet and manicure set? You brush and comb your hair, and you file your nails." She glanced at my hands and shook her head. "Perhaps a new pair of shoes."

She had visited the cobbler and knew where the tailor's shop was located. I'd shown them to her when we'd walked through town on one of her first days at the hotel. "All of my needs are provided for, Mrs. Young. I don't want or need anything. If you'll excuse me, I have other rooms to clean."

She clutched at my arm. "Please don't mention this to your mother. I cannot bear to live in a room that isn't clean and tidy."

I sighed. In truth I would have much preferred to clean the room only once a week, but I relented and gave a firm nod. "Whatever you wish."

Thoughts of the papers stacked on the table nagged at me while I continued my morning chores. Once I finished the remainder of the room, I returned downstairs. I was nearing the bottom of the steps when my mother called to me. "Is that you, Ilsa? I need your help in the kitchen."

I placed the cleaning supplies in the small room behind the registration desk, which was now used for storage. "I'm coming, Mutter." I hurried to the kitchen. "What can I do?" I asked as I walked to her side.

She pointed to the grated potatoes that had been formed into fat potato cakes. "The lard should be melted by now. You can place those in the skillet." Once the potato cakes were in the hot grease, she motioned toward the dining room. "You can set out the dishes. I'll keep an eye on the potatoes." She hesitated for a moment. "I thought I heard Mrs. Young return a while ago." Her eyebrows arched and curved into two thin question marks.

"Ja, she is back, all right, and making a fuss because I was cleaning the room while she was out." I hadn't planned to tell my mother, but Mrs. Young's odd behavior had continued to trouble me throughout the morning. "She was very angry, so I told her we would decrease the cleaning to once a week and only when she was present."

My mother picked up the corner of her apron and wiped her hands. "And what did she say to that?"

"She offered to give me money or buy me a gift." I met my mother's surprised look. "And she begged me to keep silent about her angry remarks so no changes would be made in the cleaning schedule." I placed the coffee cups and saucers on the table. "I told her I wouldn't mention anything to you, so I guess you could say I lied to her."

My mother stepped into the dining room. "Ja. For sure, you lied to her, but things like this need to be told. In the future you should not make such promises." She lifted her nose in the air and sniffed. "The potato cakes need to be turned." She scurried back to the stove but soon returned to my side. "Is there anything else you should tell me?"

"While I was changing the sheets, some papers scattered on the floor, but I returned them to the table. I don't think Mrs. Young noticed." I continued around the table placing the silverware at each setting. "Do you know the names of Jutta's parents?"

My mother tapped the side of her head with her index finger. "I am trying to think if I ever heard your Vater use their names." She dropped her hand and shook her head. "I think he only said Brother and Sister Schmitt, but you should ask him. Maybe he knows. Why do you ask?"

"No reason. I was simply curious if you knew more about Jutta's family." I told myself that wasn't really a lie. I did want to know if my parents knew their names.

My mother patted my shoulder. "I know you miss Jutta. You're worried she won't return, ja?"

"A little. I know she misses her parents, but she was frightened and unhappy living in Marengo, so I think she'll come back—especially since her parents want her to be safe."

"Ja, is better for her here, where she doesn't have to worry so much about being mistreated." My mother gestured toward the sideboard. "Hurry and finish setting the table. The bell will soon ring."

I was surprised when Mrs. Young appeared for the noonday meal. She remained silent while we ate, but I noticed her staring at me on several occasions. I tried to tell myself that her actions were normal, that I was simply expecting to see changes in her conduct. After all, Mrs. Young's behavior never could be considered completely normal. She frequently excused herself after eating only a few bites of a meal. At other times she chattered like a magpie and remained until all of the guests departed. To decide what was normal or abnormal behavior would be impossible.

Today she remained throughout the meal and sat in the dining room while I cleared the table. Once we were alone, she clamped her fingers around my arm. "You didn't tell your mother, did you?"

I stared at her hand until she finally released her grasp. "I told you there will be no changes in the cleaning schedule. You need not worry." Before she could ask me anything further, I lifted the stack of dishes and carried them into the kitchen. By the time I returned, she had left the room.

Throughout the afternoon, I stayed close to my mother's side and avoided Mrs. Young. So long as my mother was nearby, I knew the woman wouldn't ask any questions. My task proved difficult, for Mrs. Young spent more time in the downstairs parlor than she had any other afternoon since her arrival. Perhaps she'd discovered the paper work had been moved. Perhaps she planned to accuse me of snooping. Perhaps she would tell her husband, and he would confront the elders. The thought made me shiver.

Not until supper was over and we departed for prayer meeting did I sigh with relief. Normally I enjoyed the warmth and safety of our home, but that afternoon I'd been filled with a disquieting sense of apprehension. We'd walked only a short distance when I saw Garon waiting for us. Seeing him calmed me, and I waved in return.

"That boy does not follow the rules," my father muttered.

"Just like you, when we were in love. You did your share of breaking the rules to see me whenever you could." My mother nudged his arm and smiled. "And if I remember right, my Vater overlooked some of those rules you broke."

"I never broke as many rules as Garon does. He's at the hotel, or Ilsa is at his house every day. Is not gut." He shook his head and clamped his lips together in a frown.

"You're acting like an old man—worse than the elders," my mother teased. "When Garon stops at the hotel, it is because of business. Do you want him to leave the guests standing out in the street? He is supposed to escort them inside and help with their baggage, ja?"

My father's agreement didn't bear much enthusiasm, nor did his sour look deter Garon from loping to my side.

"*Guten Abend*, Ilsa. I am pleased to see you." Garon nodded to my parents as he stopped at my side. "I thought I would walk to meeting with you, if it is all right."

"Ja, it is fine, Garon." My mother bobbed her head and answered before my father could object. "Your parents are well?"

"Ja. They said Ilsa is welcome to visit at our house after

meeting—and the two of you, as well. They said they would enjoy your company, and Mutter said to be sure to tell you she has some crumb cake left from supper that would be gut with a cup of coffee." Garon grinned. "Mutter says that having leftover dessert is one of the rewards of being a *Küchebaas*."

My mother could understand that sentiment, for we often shared leftovers from the hotel kitchen. I wasn't surprised when my father accepted the invitation. He enjoyed crumb cake—or any other dessert, for that matter. And our visit would be viewed as a family visit rather than courting. Either way was fine with me. I knew Garon would find a way to be alone with me for at least a brief time, and I had questions for him.

I followed my mother into meeting, and a short time later I followed her back outside, where we joined my father, Garon, his sister, and his parents. Most nights we would pray and give thanks for a multitude of needs, but tonight the entire time had been devoted to praying for Albert and the other Amanan men serving in the armed forces. Though I was pleased at the outpouring of love and concern for Albert and the other men, I hoped the prayers wouldn't plant more thoughts of becoming a soldier in Garon's mind. He didn't need any additional encouragement to sway him.

Our families joined together, and Garon's parents led the way while Garon and I followed behind. Although we walked at a slower pace, I was certain my parents could hear every word that passed between us.

"I need to talk to you alone," I whispered, hoping neither his sister nor my parents would hear.

He nodded and squeezed my hand. Once we'd gone into the house, the men sat at the table while Sister Barbara prepared the coffee and Mother cut pieces of cake and placed them on blue and white plates. Christina edged to my side and whispered in my ear. "Come and see what I'm making Mutter for Christmas." She clasped my hand and pulled me toward the parlor.

Garon looked up as we passed through the dining room. "Where are you two going?"

Christina touched her finger to her lips and leaned close to her brother. "I want to show Ilsa what I'm making Mutter for Christmas. I'm hoping she can help me with one of the stitches."

Garon pushed away from the table. "I'd like to see, too."

While Garon and I waited in the parlor, Christina scurried to her bedroom. "What is it you need to talk about?"

I hurriedly explained before Christina returned. After blurting out the morning's events, I grasped his hand. "Do you know if this Bert Schmitt is Jutta's father?"

He shook his head. "I don't know, but I can find out and tell you tomorrow morning."

"How can you do that?"

He leaned closer and pecked a kiss on my cheek. "I can't tell you all my secrets. Then you would never need my help."

A sudden sense of panic gripped me as I remembered Garon's friendship with Mr. Young. "You can't say anything about this to Mr. Young. Promise you won't tell him anything I've said to you." I squeezed his hand with all my strength. He yelped and I released my hold. "Shh. Do you want my Vater to come in here?"

"Then you shouldn't squeeze so tight." He glanced toward the dining room, where his mother was pouring coffee. "I am not so foolish that I would ask Mr. Young. What do you think I would say? 'Excuse me, Mr. Young, but Ilsa was cleaning your room at the hotel and was reading some papers and saw the name Bert Schmitt. Can you tell me if that is Jutta's father?' " He raked his hand through his hair. "I am not a fool, Ilsa."

"I'm sorry, Garon, but I'm worried about this, and I know you and Mr. Young have become friendly. I thought you might slip and say something."

He lowered his head and stared at his folded hands. "I know you are still upset that I told him about Jutta's parents and their contract. I won't make the same mistake twice. I promise."

"But you can still find out—about Jutta's father?"

He nodded. "I'll be able to tell you on Monday, for sure."

CHAPTER 14

I was in the small supply room behind the front desk when Garon stopped by the hotel on Monday morning. He quickly surveyed the parlor and foyer as he approached. "Is it safe to talk?"

His secretive behavior caused a shiver to race up the back of my neck. I nodded. "Mutter is in the kitchen preparing the noonday meal, and Mrs. Young is in her room. The salesmen who occupied the other rooms all left after breakfast."

Garon looked toward the top of the stairway. "We should speak softly in case Mrs. Young should decide to come downstairs."

Now I was certain something was amiss, and I grasped his hand. "Bert Schmitt is Jutta's Vater, isn't he?"

"Ja. For sure, that is the name of her Vater. And her Mutter's name is Eva."

I didn't let go of his hand. "Tell me how you found out." I knew Mr. Young hadn't returned to town, so I didn't fear Garon had asked him, but I still wanted to know how he'd gained the information—and how much he'd given in return.

Using his free hand, he pushed his cap to the back of his head and grinned. "I shouldn't tell you my secrets, but it was Brother Peter."

"I should have known!" There was little that escaped the men who managed the general stores in any of the villages. "He took notice when she mailed letters to them. Am I right?"

He chuckled and nodded his head. "Ja, you guessed it. He even wrote it down beside her name in the ledger so he wouldn't forget."

I released his hand, motioned him farther away from the stairs, and lowered my voice a notch. "And what did you tell him in return?"

His head jutted back as if I'd slapped him. "You think I told Brother Peter about the paper you saw with Mr. Schmitt's name?"

Clearly, I'd insulted him. The hurt in his voice was as evident as the sun shining outside the window. "Nein, but that's the problem. I don't know what you told him. And Brother Peter always asks questions. When he gives out information, he expects some interesting news in return. I'm wondering what you had to tell him in order to gain a look at the ledger book."

"You do know him well. And he did ask me questions. He was very interested in Jutta, which isn't surprising. She's new to the village, and nobody knows much about her."

I nodded. "And if he could be the first to know some little piece of information to pass along, it would make him feel important."

"I imagine it would, but I told him I knew less about Jutta

than he did. Otherwise I wouldn't have needed his help to learn her father's name."

I inched closer. "What did he say then? Did he want to know why you wanted Mr. Schmitt's first name?"

"He did."

I gasped and clenched my fingers into his arm. "What did you tell him?"

He shook his head. "I told a lie. I said you were embroidering a Christmas gift for Jutta and wanted to put her parents' names on either side of Jutta's name. I couldn't think of anything else to say."

"That's perfect. And just so it won't be a lie, I'll stitch something for her. I'll have Vater make a small wooden frame, and I'll give it to her on Christmas morning."

Worry melted from his eyes, and his shoulders relaxed. "Gut. That way Jutta won't be confused if Brother Peter ever mentions the Christmas present to her. I was afraid you would be angry and say I'd given a foolish answer." He bent his head and leaned close. I rose up on my toes and permitted a brief kiss, but he wrapped his arms around my waist. "I think I deserve a little more than that tiny peck."

Pulling me tight, he covered my lips with a sweet kiss that caused my heart to quicken. I would have enjoyed having him stay with me the rest of the day, but the sound of footsteps overhead was enough to make us both jump backward.

"Oh, Garon! What a welcome surprise." Mrs. Young stood at the top of the steps looking over the banister at us. "Could you drive me to the general store? I have some errands to complete."

Mrs. Young was leaving by herself again? The woman suddenly had a lot of errands to do. And it seemed strange that she no longer whined about the lack of amusement to fill her day or her dislike of walking about on her own. Perhaps her bouts of melancholy were diminishing. If so, maybe the Youngs would be leaving sooner than expected. The thought pleased me.

"I'd be happy to take you to the store, Mrs. Young, but we'll need to hurry. I must also meet the train."

Mrs. Young skipped down the stairs like a schoolgirl. I glanced at Garon, and he appeared as surprised as I was. She clutched his arm. "Come along, then." She glanced over her shoulder. "You don't need to clean my room today, Ilsa. It can wait until tomorrow."

I didn't acknowledge the remark. Today was the day scheduled for cleaning her room, and clean it I would—whether she liked it or not. We'd already changed our schedule to suit her needs, and I wasn't going to give in any further. I gathered the cleaning supplies and marched upstairs. I'd clean the other rooms first and hope that Mrs. Young would reappear before it was time to clean hers. That way there would be no problem. She could sit in her chair and watch my every move. That thought annoyed me as much as her earlier comment.

I'd finished two of the rooms when I heard the door open downstairs. I scurried to the top of the steps and glanced over the railing. "Jutta! You're back." I rushed down the steps, relieved that she had returned. She smiled in return, but her features were drawn, and I detected a wariness in her eyes that I'd not seen before. "Did you have a pleasant time with your parents?"

"Yes. It was good to see them. They are doing well."

"You look tired. I am guessing you worked in the bakery the whole time you were gone, ja?"

She carried her satchel to the hallway leading to our apartments.

"Let me put this in my room. I'll change clothes, and then I can get to work. The laundry is done?"

I shook my head. "Mutter said we will wash on Wednesday this week because I got behind with the cleaning."

"I'm sorry. If I hadn't been gone—"

"Ach! Don't blame yourself. There were many weeks after Sister Hulda left us that we didn't get the washing finished until late in the week. It is not such a big thing, since we don't have to share our washhouse with any other families." Just as having our own kitchen was an advantage of managing the hotel, so was having a washhouse that didn't need to be shared.

"I'll be upstairs cleaning."

I expected Jutta to come upstairs and help once she'd changed her clothes, but when I had finished cleaning all of the rooms except number five, she still hadn't appeared. I walked down the hallway and stopped when I heard her talking to my mother. From the sounds of things, Mother had put her to work in the kitchen. I had planned to mention the paper with her father's name, but it could wait until later.

I stood outside number five. My earlier irritation had been replaced by a dose of apprehension. There was no answer when I knocked on the door, and I contemplated whether I should enter. Mrs. Young had been clear that she didn't want me in the room. What would Father say if I didn't follow the woman's instructions? I gathered my supplies, turned from the door, and hurried down the steps. Better to check with Mother. If she said to clean the room, there would be nothing to fear.

Jutta was busy preparing crust for dried-apple pies while my mother was writing out a list of supplies she needed from the general store. She glanced over her shoulder when I walked into the kitchen. "All done with the rooms?"

"All but number five. Mrs. Young told me I should wait and clean it tomorrow. She wants to be in the room while we clean, but this is her regular day. Tomorrow Jutta and I will be busy washing clothes and all the sheets and towels. I won't have time to clean her room if I wait until then. What should I do?"

I detected the annoyed look in my mother's eyes. "We cannot always bow to Mrs. Young's wishes. We have other guests to care for besides her. She will complain if we don't clean and complain if we clean when she isn't there. Our agreement was to clean the room today. Go up and knock on the door. If she doesn't answer, go in, change the sheets, clean the room, and come back downstairs."

"Ja. It shouldn't take long." I picked up the cleaning supplies and hiked back upstairs. I was certain Mrs. Young hadn't returned, but I knocked on the door and waited. When there was no answer, I shoved my key into the lock and entered the room. To say it was untidy was an understatement. It appeared she had emptied all of the drawers and tossed the contents onto the bed and table, even onto the floor. Her dresses had been removed from the wardrobe and lay in a heap across the bed. No wonder she'd told me not to clean. What on earth was she doing? Maybe she was preparing to pack her trunks and depart. Then again, maybe people suffering from melancholy tossed their belongings into a state of disarray from time to time. Or perhaps she'd simply misplaced something. I didn't know what any of it meant, but I picked up my supplies, backed out of the room, and locked the door.

My mother's eyebrows arched high on her forehead when I returned to the kitchen. "Done so soon? You weren't gone long enough to take the sheets off the bed."

I quickly explained the mess I'd discovered. "No wonder she told me I didn't need to clean. It would take the rest of the afternoon just to find the top of the bed. I've never seen such a mess."

Jutta continued to crimp the piecrust. "Why would she do such a thing, I wonder."

I shook my head. "I asked myself the same thing. I think they both are strange. Mrs. Young's personality changes like the wind, and her husband isn't much better. He drifts in and out without any set schedule. How does he manage to make a living when he spends much of his time here?"

"Is not our business, Ilsa. Besides, he completes some of his work while he is here. I've seen him with his papers spread out on the table in the parlor more than once. Maybe there is someone at his office who takes care of the business when he is in Amana."

Jutta slit the top of the pies and placed them in the oven. "Maybe he doesn't even have a law office in Des Moines. He could tell us anything."

I grinned at Jutta. "That's true. Maybe he's an out-of-work actor, ashamed to admit failure." I didn't really believe our game of make-believe. If Mr. Young wasn't a lawyer, how would he know how to help with a contract? Yet trying to make sense of such strange people was more fun than scrubbing the floors.

"I think that's everything I need." My mother folded the piece of paper and stood. "Why don't the two of you take my list to Brother Peter while I finish up here."

I shot her a wide smile. She knew how much I had missed Jutta, and she was giving us an opportunity to visit without interruption. We bundled into our heavy capes and pulled on warm woolen gloves. My mother shoved the list into my pocket, and we headed for the door.

Bending my head against the wind, I looked in Jutta's direction as we stepped along the wooden sidewalk. "I have something to tell you, but you must promise you won't tell anyone, because I'm not sure what it means."

Puffs of cold vapor billowed in front of us as we stared at one another. "I promise." When I didn't immediately respond, she grabbed my hand. "What is it?" The words echoed in the frigid December air.

Seeing the mounting fear in Jutta's eyes, I hurriedly told her about finding the paper with her father's name in the Youngs' room. "I wasn't certain of your father's first name, so I asked Garon . . ."

She took a backward step and glared at me. "You told Garon? Why would you confide in him? He's the one who told Mr. Young about the contract. I didn't think you had forgiven him for interfering the first time."

My breath caught. "I know I said I wouldn't forgive him, but he told me the two of you talked before you left for Marengo and that you had forgiven him for his misdeed. That's true, isn't it?"

She nodded but didn't look in my direction. "We talked. I told him that I would speak to you when I returned and ask that you forgive him."

"Gut." A sense of relief washed over me, for I didn't want to think that Garon hadn't told me the truth. "I'm certain he won't say a word to Mr. Young. And he's the only person I know who could find out about your father's name. I didn't want to say anything to you until I knew if Bert Schmitt was your father."

Her breathing slowed a bit, and she gestured for me to continue. When I explained that Garon had asked Brother Peter about her parents' name, Jutta nodded.

"Brother Peter knew because of the letters I sent to my parents?"

"Ja. He wrote their names in the ledger so he would have a record."

"Just like at Homestead. The manager of the general store knows a little about everybody." She turned more serious as we continued to walk. "Was anything else written on the paper in the Youngs' room?"

"Below your Vater's name he had written the words *Iowa County Courthouse*. What do you think it means, Jutta?"

"Maybe something to do with the contract. I can't say for sure."

For the remainder of our walk to the store, Jutta didn't say a word. She'd buttoned up tighter than a high-top shoe. Once inside the store, she stood by the front door while I spoke with Brother Peter and went over the shopping list. Though he made an attempt to draw her into conversation, she didn't respond. I couldn't tell if she didn't hear him or if she chose to avoid the storekeeper. Either way, I was certain my news troubled her.

CHAPTER 15

Jutta Schmitt

Ilsa's news hadn't revealed anything I didn't already know. Mr. Young was determined to stick his nose into my business. I couldn't understand why he was intent on helping us when his assistance wasn't wanted. My thoughts raced as I attempted to sort out the details. When and how had he discovered my father's name? He must have gone to the courthouse before he'd visited the bakery the first time. Had the lawyer been wise enough to know that Brother Tolbert at the general store might keep a log of relatives' names, or had he used some other method to learn my father's identity? And what else did he know?

I'd been more than a little surprised to hear that Ilsa had once again trusted Garon with secret information. I wondered if she would be so trusting if she knew I'd overheard him relating the contents of Albert's letter to one of his friends in the train station. She might think she could trust Garon—I wasn't so certain.

Remaining alert during the remainder of the day and through-out the evening meal and prayer meeting was difficult. My mind continued to hop and skip in every direction while I tried to develop a plan.

As we departed prayer meeting, Ilsa tugged on my sleeve and leaned close. "Come with me to Garon's house. We're going to have cocoa and visit."

I shook my head. "Not tonight. I'm very tired and need to write to my parents. I promised to let them know I arrived safely." I didn't want to tell Ilsa I was trying to figure out why Mr. Young was snooping into my family's business. The less she knew, the better, for I'd decided Ilsa had as much difficulty as Garon when it came to keeping secrets. I was supposed to be spying on the residents of Amana, but now it seemed I was being spied upon. The strange turn of circumstances chilled me even more than the cold night air.

I'd not yet decided what I would tell Mr. Young about the contract. How could I explain a deed being filed with my father's name and still hold to the story that we were paying on the con-tract? I had to come up with a believable story—and then make certain my parents knew exactly what I had told him. There was little doubt Mr. Young would return to Marengo and quiz them. And my story had to be something he couldn't verify through the courts. Otherwise he'd never be satisfied, and these insistent offers to help would continue. A detailed letter to my parents would be required, as well. Could I possibly accomplish all of this without being caught in one of my lies?

While I wrestled to develop a story to tell Mr. Young, I heard the muffled sounds of Ilsa's parents talking in the parlor next door to my rooms. I couldn't make out what they were saying, but I was sure I heard my name mentioned several times. Then again, maybe I was letting my imagination run amok. I sat down at the table and tried to think. When nothing came to me, I resorted to prayer. I was certain God expected to hear from me. The only time I turned to prayer was when I had a problem I couldn't solve on my own. He'd probably begun to turn a deaf ear to my pleas—especially this one. After all, I was asking for help to formulate a lie that would permit me to stay among a righteous people so that I could spy on them.

Except that I hoped to save my mother and father from harm, there was nothing about my request that could be looked upon with favor. "If not for me, I ask that you help me for the sake of my parents. They don't deserve to be injured or thrown into jail." I sat back in my chair and thought about the apostle Paul. He hadn't deserved being thrown into jail, either, but God hadn't saved him. And what about Jesus? He hadn't deserved to die on the cross. So why should God take pity upon my parents? The thought baffled me. I wondered if the elders could answer such questions. Not that I would ask them, of course.

Closing my eyes, I rubbed my temples and willed myself to recall something that would help. No one could have been more surprised than I when, moments later, I jumped up from the chair and shouted, "Switzerland!" Instinctively, I glanced around the room and clapped a hand over my mouth. What if Ilsa's parents had heard me? If so, Sister Marta would soon knock on the door to inquire why I was shouting—or if I was losing my mind.

I couldn't be sure if the thought had been placed there by God, or if it had simply arrived because I'd been thinking about Mr. Lotz, the man who had sold us the bakery. But in case it had come from God, I uttered a prayer of thanks before I removed a sheet of writing paper from the upper drawer of my dresser. I'd need to word my letter carefully. We couldn't afford a blunder—not with a lawyer in pursuit. I assembled my thoughts and then dipped my pen into the bottle of ink.

> Dear Mother and Father,
>   I am sure Mr. Young will come to the bakery and question you, so I am hopeful this story will satisfy his questions about our family. He has not yet returned to the hotel, but I know he will expect an explanation soon after his return. If we are able to tell him the same story, I think he will eventually leave us alone. . . .

After completing the letter, I penned a copy for myself. I'd told my parents to commit the facts to memory, and I must do the same. Long ago I'd discovered the truth was easy to remember, but lies muddled in the brain over time. I couldn't wait until I'd memorized the details of the letter before mailing it to my parents, nor could I chance forgetting any of what I'd written to them. Lawyers were far too clever. We couldn't make any mistakes.

I didn't sleep well last night. An angry Mr. Young had turned my dreams into nightmares filled with jail cells and my parents calling for help. When the morning bells sounded, I'd awakened with a start.

Thankfully, Garon arrived at his usual time and I had remembered to tuck the letter into my apron pocket. He promised he'd leave it with Brother Peter on his return to the train depot in Upper South. I hadn't wanted to ask for his help, but the time to set aside our differences had arrived. To have my parents receive the letter as soon as possible was more important than to remain angry with Garon.

I was thankful there'd been no sign of Mr. Young, for shortly after I'd made my copy of the letter last night, I'd fallen asleep. There had been little time to memorize everything I'd written. Of course, I was the one who'd dreamed up the entire plot. Still, there were details I wanted to commit to memory before speaking to Mr. Young.

A few hours later I was dusting furniture in the main parlor when Garon, along with several salesmen, arrived at the hotel. I breathed a sigh of relief when I didn't see Mr. Young among the group.

"You mailed the letter to my parents?"

Garon smiled, obviously pleased we were once again on speaking terms. "Ja. Brother Peter said it would go out today."

I thanked him and turned when the front door once again opened. I was met by Mr. Young's determined stare. He nodded at me as he removed his black wool overcoat.

I quickly looked away and stepped closer to Garon. "Would you tell Sister Marta I'm not feeling well and must rest for a short time? I'll be out to help with supper preparations as soon as my stomach settles."

His brow wrinkled. I wasn't sure if he was feeling concern or confusion. I certainly hadn't appeared ill when I was speaking to him only a few moments before. "Ja. Of course. I'll go and tell her right now."

Without a backward glance, I scurried to my room. Once inside, I leaned against the door and tried to calm the storm brewing in my stomach. I inhaled a deep breath and pushed away from the door. There wasn't time to waste. I hurried through my small parlor into the bedroom, yanked open the second drawer, and withdrew the letter from beneath my stockings. Dropping to the edge of my bed, I unfolded the piece of paper, traced my finger beneath the words, and scanned the contents.

I'd almost completed reading the letter when a knock sounded on the parlor door. I jammed the letter beneath my pillow and lay down on the bed. "Who is it?"

"It's me. Ilsa. May I come in?"

"Yes. I'm in the bedroom."

The metal latch clunked, and soon Ilsa tiptoed into the room. "Garon said you were not feeling well. Mutter is making you some tea. Does that sound gut?"

"You don't need to worry over me, Ilsa. I'm just having a little problem with my stomach. I will soon be fine. I think a little rest is the best thing, but tell your mother thank you for her trouble."

Ilsa glanced at my feet and frowned. "You should take off your shoes. I'll get a quilt to cover you."

To argue with her would take more time than to do as she said, so I removed my shoes and permitted her to place the cover over me.

She dipped her head in a satisfied nod. "Is gut. You rest now and don't worry about anything. Mutter and I will prepare supper."

I motioned her toward the door. "I will be out to help in a little while."

When she shook her head, I didn't argue further. Once I heard the familiar clunk of the latch, I threw aside the quilted coverlet, sat up, and retrieved the letter from beneath my pillow. Over and over I read the contents of the letter until I had memorized every detail. I shoved it back into my dresser drawer, pulled on my shoes, and folded the quilt. After a quick glance in the small mirror, I tucked a few wisps of hair into place, then straightened my dress and cap, and walked out my parlor door. If Mr. Young attempted to stop me, I'd beg his forgiveness and explain I was needed to help with the evening meal.

There was no doubt he would want to speak with me in private. There was also no doubt that I would do my best to avoid him. I wanted my parents to receive the letter and have time to memorize the contents before Mr. Young appeared on their doorstep.

Throughout the following days, I did my best to avoid both Mr. and Mrs. Young. Each day I hoped he would depart, but each day he remained in South Amana. On several occasions I caught him watching me as I worked in the dining room or parlor, but I'd convinced Ilsa to clean number five ever since Mr. Young's return. I was certain my good fortune couldn't last much longer. But if I could continue avoiding him, my parents would have more time to prepare for his arrival.

I'd finished my work in the dining room when Sister Marta waved her shopping list in the air and gathered her cloak from the hook. "I'm going to the general store, Jutta. I shouldn't be long. You will tell Ilsa if she asks for me?"

"Yes, of course."

I glanced toward the parlor. Mr. Young was watching us. I didn't miss the glint in his eye. He looked like a cat ready to pounce.

"Would you like me to take the list?"

"Thank you for your sweet offer, Jutta, but on my way home, I plan to stop and speak with Sister Hulda about the next Red Cross meeting." She patted my arm and was soon on her way to the store.

I briefly considered asking if I could accompany her, but

she would have thought me foolish. There was work I needed to complete. Hoping to escape upstairs, I made a wide circle around Mr. Young, but he swiveled around in his chair and beckoned to me. "We need to talk, Jutta."

My knees trembled, and I grasped the banister to steady myself. I glanced toward the upper hallway. "I have rooms to clean upstairs. Sister Marta will expect my work to be completed before she returns."

"Then you shouldn't waste time with excuses. It won't take you long to tell me about your parents' bakery and the deed I discovered at the courthouse. I think you were about to explain the circumstances of why the property is already registered in your father's name, yet you said he is still paying on the contract." He rubbed his jaw and looked up at me. "Isn't that where we were at the time we were interrupted?"

When I didn't respond, he pointed to the chair beside him. "Sit down here and let's finish our conversation. I must tell you that I am very intrigued by all of this."

I frowned at him, hoping that I would appear confused. "All of what?"

He grabbed hold of my hand and squeezed until I flinched. "Don't play silly games with me, Jutta. I can be kind, or I can be cruel. It's up to you."

"I don't understand why you care about my parents or their bakery. Why does it concern you?"

"Because I am a patriot, Jutta. And people who tell lies and try to hide things—especially German people who tell lies and hide things—can't be trusted. Tell me, Jutta, are you a patriot?"

"Of course I am." I folded my hands in my lap to keep them from trembling.

He leaned back in his chair and looked down his sharp nose. "Then tell me about the deed to the property."

"My parents purchased the bakery from Mr. Lotz, who had come to Iowa from someplace back east—New York, I think. His family came to this country from Switzerland. When he sold us the bakery, he said he wanted to leave the United States and live the rest of his life in Switzerland—to go and see all the relatives who never left the homeland."

Mr. Young shifted in his chair. "Get on with it—what does that have to do with filing the deed?"

"Mr. Lotz needed money from the bakery to finance his return, but he grew impatient. Once he had enough money to pay for his passage and to purchase a small cottage in Switzerland, he decided to leave. He told my father that he would file the deed, so there would be no problem once he was gone from the country. In turn, my father agreed to continue with the payments until the contract was completed." I inhaled a breath and met his intense gaze. "Mr. Lotz trusted my father, but he said that if my father didn't send the yearly payments, he would return and take back the bakery." I shrugged my shoulders. "And that's how it happened. They are two men who trust each other."

I could see the suspicion in his eyes. "And does this Mr. Lotz still have relatives in Marengo?"

"I don't think so. He had only his wife, and she returned with him. His son died in an accident. I think that's why he wanted to go home to Switzerland. He became very sad after the death of his son."

"And there are lots of people in Marengo who could confirm that Mr. Lotz wanted to go back to Switzerland?"

"I can't say for sure. After he sold the bakery, he and Mrs.

Lotz kept to themselves. I don't know what he told other people. He was a quiet man."

I could tell from his frown that my story hadn't pleased him. A great deal of it had been true—Mr. Lotz and his wife had returned to Switzerland, and their son had died in an accident. But the contract had been paid in full before he left. I hoped there was no way Mr. Young could discover that that particular portion of my tale was a lie. My father had told me no one else had a copy of the contract and the payments had been made directly to Mr. Lotz. The bank had never been involved, and the lawyer who had written the contract died two years ago. I could only hope that the facts were enough to satisfy Mr. Young.

"I'd be interested to know where your father sends his payments, Jutta."

I straightened my shoulders and didn't flinch. "To a post office in New York City."

"That seems strange to me."

I shrugged. "I doubt Mr. Lotz cares what seems strange to you, Mr. Young."

He leaned forward and glared at me. "You're an impudent girl, aren't you!"

I shook my head. "No, but I'm tired of answering your questions when there is no reason for your interference. I've told you what I know. If you don't believe me, then do what you will. I have work to perform."

Pushing to my feet, I forced myself to meet his icy stare. I didn't want him to think I was afraid. I could only hope that my parents would hold up under his examination. No doubt he would be on the morning train for Marengo.

❖

I didn't have to wait long to discover I'd been correct. A letter arrived a few days later. Mr. Young had returned to the bakery and had questioned my father at length. My father's letter stated that he had followed my instructions and had not wavered from the plan. Of course, he had no idea if Mr. Young believed him. As I continued to read, I'd inhaled a deep gasp. The lawyer had asked to see a copy of the contract. Something I hadn't anticipated. My father wrote that he had quickly responded that there had been only one copy and Mr. Lotz had insisted upon taking it with him to Switzerland to protect his ownership until the bakery was paid off. I smiled as I read my father's response. He'd done well.

CHAPTER 16

"Mutter! It's a letter from Albert, and he says he'll be here for Christmas."

I turned from the stove where I'd been checking the chicken stock we would use to boil the noodles. Ilsa pressed the letter into her mother's hand before she whirled around the kitchen and pulled her mother into an embrace.

"Can you believe it? Only one week and Albert will arrive. I can hardly wait to see him." Ilsa moved from her mother's side and wrapped her arm around my waist. "Isn't this wonderful news, Jutta?"

I nodded before I started to roll out the dough. "Yes. To have your family together will bring all of you much joy." I understood Ilsa's excitement. She'd been faithfully writing to Albert and had mailed him cookies on two occasions since my arrival. Each day she prayed for his safety, and each day she hoped for news that he would arrive home for Christmas. I couldn't fault her for being pleased that her prayers had been answered.

Still, I was having difficulty tamping down pangs of jealousy over Ilsa's good news. Only yesterday the elders had again disapproved my request to return home for Christmas. They'd concluded the earliest I should return would be the middle of January. I'd been taken aback when they'd first suggested I wait until February or March. Since receiving their decision, I'd done my best to maintain a good spirit but without much success.

I couldn't explain to anyone what the decision meant to me. My parents could be injured, in jail, or both, by the day after Christmas. And after that, the men from the Iowa Council of National Defense would likely appear on the hotel doorstep. Ilsa had done her best to cheer me, even joking that Pelznickel wouldn't bring me a present on Christmas if my mood didn't improve. She didn't realize that the only gift I wanted couldn't be delivered by Pelznickel.

Though I was happy for Ilsa and her mother, watching them celebrate was like pouring salt into an open wound. Ilsa looked at me and stopped short. "I'm sorry, Jutta. I didn't think about you being away from your family. I was so eager to share the good news that I—"

"You should not apologize. I'm very happy that Albert is coming home. When there is good news to share, an apology is never necessary." I forced a smile. "I look forward to meeting Albert."

"You're going to like him. He's lots of fun and nice-looking, too." Ilsa grinned and winked before she turned to her mother. "Did you finish the letter, Mutter?"

Sister Marta held a finger to her lips. "I'm reading it now, if you will be quiet for a few minutes longer. He says he is looking forward to some Christmas cookies and gut food." She folded the page and slipped it back into the envelope. "For sure, we will see that he has lots of gut food while he is home." She flashed a smile at me. "This is the very best present we could receive."

Ilsa bobbed her head. "Ja. To have Albert home means everything. Pelznickel can take our presents to someone else. Should I take the letter for Vater to read or wait until he comes home for the noonday meal?"

"There is work we need to complete, and it won't be long until he comes home." Ilsa's mother returned the envelope to her. "You can deliver the surprise to him, but now we must finish our work."

I felt like an intruder in a special moment. Witnessing their happiness made me long for home all the more, and I was thankful when Sister Marta said she would cook the noodles. Ilsa hurried back upstairs to finish cleaning the rooms while I set the table. "When you are done with the table, would you make certain the parlor is in order, Jutta? We're expecting more guests on the next train."

A short time later the train whistle echoed in the distance. Garon would pick up the new arrivals in the buggy and escort them to the hotel. I hoped Mr. Young wouldn't be among them. He'd been at the hotel more than usual, and I had been thankful when he departed earlier in the week. Though he'd said nothing more, his presence caused me discomfort. I could feel his gaze on me as I moved about the dining room serving meals or when I passed through the parlor—as if he hoped to catch me doing something improper.

After I'd finished my chores in the dining room, I strode into the parlor and straightened a stack of periodicals that were supplied for the enjoyment of visitors. The noonday bell clanged, and I glanced toward the kitchen. Soon Ilsa's father would be home to register the recent arrivals. I was completing one final check of the room when I glanced out the front window and saw the large buggy used for passenger delivery arrive outside the hotel. Using my thumb and forefinger, I pulled back a corner of the thin, gauzy curtain. My heart plummeted when I saw Mr. Young seated beside Garon. The other passengers, all salesmen, grabbed their satchels and proceeded inside. I released the curtain and hurried back to the kitchen.

I hadn't heard Ilsa's father enter the back door, and he jumped to one side as we met in the kitchen doorway. "I'm sorry," I mumbled, embarrassed by the near collision, and backed toward the parlor.

He chuckled. "No harm done. Are all of the rooms cleaned and ready?" He circled the desk, but his attention remained fastened upon me.

"Ja. Ilsa is still upstairs, but I think she is finishing up cleaning number five. Since it is already rented, she cleaned the others first." Mentioning number five caused me to glance toward the front window. From my vantage point, I could see that Garon and Mr. Young were still engaged in conversation. The sight caused a knot to form in my stomach. Though I was certain Garon would never intentionally do or say anything to harm me, he had what my father referred to as "loose lips." Once Garon engaged in conversation, he forgot to guard what he said. I could only hope my name wouldn't be mentioned during their exchange, for Mr. Young was much cleverer than Garon. My shoulders tensed. What if Garon inadvertently divulged Ilsa had found the paper with my father's name? I wished they would come inside.

At the clatter of footsteps, I glanced toward the stairway and saw Ilsa rushing down the stairs. Her smile faded when she saw the waiting guests circled around the desk. No doubt she was eager to share news of Albert's Christmas visit with her father, but she didn't hesitate at the desk. Instead, she hurried to my side and peered out the window. "Why is Garon still outside?" She didn't wait for an answer. Instead, she gathered her cloak from the peg and rushed to the door.

I watched through the window as Ilsa rushed outside, waving the letter and calling Garon's name. Obviously annoyed, Mr. Young tightened his lips into a thin line as Garon jumped down from the buggy without a backward glance. I breathed a sigh of relief, pleased to see the two men part ways. Wanting to be certain Mr. Young was heading into the hotel, I waited a moment longer. Once he secured his bag from the buggy, I scurried to the kitchen. I had no desire to converse with him.

Sister Marta was dropping noodles into the boiling broth. "Is there anything I can do to help?" Before she could answer, I clicked off a report of the latest arrivals. I'd learned that she always wanted to know how many would be seated for each meal as soon as possible. "Three men and Mr. Young arrived in the buggy. No ladies. Your husband is assigning the men to their rooms, and Mr. Young has probably gone upstairs to greet his wife."

She glanced up from the boiling kettle. "Thank you, Jutta. See that there are enough plates on the sideboard, and then you can slice the bread."

I had hoped to speak with Garon before he departed, but I wasn't certain I'd have an opportunity. He'd probably be gone before I could finish my chores in the kitchen.

After hearing news of Albert's pending visit home, Garon passed through the dining room and into the kitchen. "I am pleased to hear Albert will be home for Christmas, Sister Marta. It will be a gut celebration for all of us. I am most eager to see him."

"Ja. For sure, it will be exciting to see him and hear about his time at Camp Pike." She lifted a bowl from the worktable and dipped a ladle into the kettle of steaming chicken and noodles. "You are welcome to eat with us today. I have plenty."

He shook his head. "Thank you, but my Mutter is expecting me. It smells very gut." He lifted his nose in the air.

Once Sister Marta returned her attention to ladling the noodles, I motioned to Garon. "I want to speak with you about Mr. Young," I whispered once he was beside me.

After a quick glance toward the parlor, he bowed his head. "Not now. He'll be coming downstairs to eat." As if on cue, Mr. and Mrs. Young descended the stairs. "Come to our house with Ilsa after prayer meeting tonight. We can talk then." He strode off without waiting for a reply, but I didn't fail to notice Mr. Young looking in our direction.

I couldn't be certain if he was interested because I was speaking to Garon or simply because Mr. Young watched me whenever he was at the hotel. Either way, his constant scrutiny made me uncomfortable. I retreated to the kitchen and hoped I could remain there until the guests were seated.

Although we sat down to eat a little later than usual, the tolling bell didn't waver from the daily schedule. Even if we'd begun late, we were expected to finish on time. Of course, Sister Marta would never force the guests away from the table, but some things were understood, and most visitors were quick to abide by our rules and keep our schedule. Of course, there were always exceptions—like the Youngs. Since they were here for an extended stay, they felt free to do as they pleased—at least to some extent. And remaining after a meal wasn't unusual for Mrs. Young if she wanted to visit with us. But today it was Mr. Young who lingered.

Even after we'd carried the food from the sideboard and cleared dishes, he remained at the table.

Sister Marta picked up the final dishes as she skirted around him. "Something you are needing, Mr. Young? More coffee?"

I stood at the worktable in the kitchen and observed him shake his head and push away from the table. "No. But when Jutta has a free moment, I'd like to speak to her." He glanced in my direction, and I turned away. "About cleaning our room."

Sister Marta set the stack of dishes back on the table. "Something is wrong with the way the room has been cleaned?" Her back went as stiff as a broom handle.

"No. But I had a question about something that is missing from our room."

Sister Marta glanced over her shoulder. She had visibly paled, but her shoulders remained rigid. "We do not steal, Mr. Young, but if something is missing from your room, you should talk with my husband or me. But this I can tell you—my daughter, Ilsa, is the one who has been cleaning number five. Jutta hasn't cleaned your room since before Thanksgiving."

"I see." He rubbed his jaw and glanced heavenward as though gathering his thoughts. "Well, I have misplaced a book—one that is quite important to me. I thought perhaps Jutta—or Ilsa—had seen it when they were cleaning."

"I see." Sister Marta turned on her heel and walked to the kitchen door. "Ilsa, have you seen a book in number five?" She glanced back at Mr. Young. "What is the title of your book?"

For a split second he appeared bewildered. "Oh, it isn't actually a book, but a journal. It has a brown leather cover and is about this thick." He held out his index finger and thumb and indicated a width of about an inch.

Sister Marta turned back to Ilsa. "A brown leather journal

about an inch thick. It seems Mr. Young has misplaced it and thought you possibly *moved* it."

"Nein, I have never seen the journal, and I do not touch the books and papers in their rooms. Most days Mrs. Young is present when I clean. Perhaps Mr. Young should ask her."

Sister Marta returned to the dining room table. "Have you asked Mrs. Young? Perhaps she put it away for safekeeping."

Mr. Young pushed up from the table. "You are right. I should have inquired of my wife before speaking to you. My apologies. I'm sure we'll locate the journal in due time."

Anger flashed in Sister Marta's eyes as she marched into the kitchen carrying the stack of dirty plates. After placing them near the sink, she turned to Ilsa. "Did you take that man's journal? If you did, you should tell me this minute."

"Nein, Mutter. I would never do such a thing. You know I wouldn't."

"You took that paper from their room. I couldn't be certain."

Ilsa's shoulders sagged under her mother's accusation. "I *read* the piece of paper, but I didn't remove it from their room. Besides, a piece of paper is quite different than a journal or book, Mutter."

"I am sorry, Ilsa, but I had to be certain. Forgive me for doubting you." Sister Marta stepped across the kitchen, embraced Ilsa, and kissed her cheek. She leaned back and looked into Ilsa's eyes. "You forgive your Mutter, don't you?"

Ilsa nodded. "Of course I do." She glanced toward the upper floor. "Mr. Young is a strange man. I'm not so sure I trust him. I would be happier if they returned home for gut."

I nodded and agreed. "If they would leave before supper, it would not be soon enough to please me."

Sister Marta wagged her finger. "You girls must treat all of our guests with respect and kindness." A tiny grin played at the corner of her lips. "For sure they are odd people." She bent her head toward us. "I would be happy to see them depart, as well."

"I think I'll go with you to Garon's house," I said to Ilsa as we walked out of meeting. She was surprised. In the past I'd been quick to refuse, but tonight I hadn't even waited for her invitation.

"Really?" Her eyebrows arched in surprise, and she wove her arm through mine. "I'm so glad. It's time you started to spend more time with all of us."

I was certain she took my offer as further affirmation that I'd forgiven Garon for his past misdeed.

Evenings in the Drucker Küche were a favorite of the young people in the neighborhood. And although Brother Edwin and Sister Barbara were kind people and encouraged the nightly visits, I suspected the young people gathered there because the possibility of a snack was much greater at the Drucker Küche than at their own homes.

While Ilsa busied herself gathering supplies to make popcorn in the fireplace, I pulled Garon to the side and quizzed him. "What was Mr. Young asking you today when you sat in the buggy for so long?"

"You don't need to point your finger at me, Jutta. And you don't need to look so stern, either."

I took a backward step and dropped my hand to my side. "I'm sorry." I tried to smile, but my lips wouldn't cooperate. "I'm worried about your conversation with Mr. Young. I don't trust him." In truth, I wasn't certain I trusted Garon, either. "Mr. Young asks too many questions, and I don't understand why he's so interested in me or my parents." Tears pooled in my eyes, and Garon placed his arm around my shoulder.

"Don't cry, Jutta. There's nothing to worry about." After a reassuring squeeze, he released my arm. "I don't know what to think about Mr. Young. He asks lots of questions. Mostly he wants to know about the people who arrive and depart on the train. He's interested in their names and where they're going, if they've ever visited the colonies before, if they're regular salesmen or new to the Amanas—that sort of thing." He glanced toward the laughter in the other room. "Today he was particularly interested in some people who arrived at Upper and were interested in a quiet meeting place at the hotel. Said they wanted to get in and out of town unnoticed."

My shoulders relaxed a notch. "So he didn't mention my name?"

"Only to ask if you'd gone back to Marengo for another visit."

The stiffness that had fled from my shoulders returned with a vengeance. "What did you tell him?"

"The truth. That you hadn't gone anywhere." He scratched his head. "He also asked if I knew if you had received or sent mail to Switzerland." He frowned. "Do you know someone in Switzerland?"

"I'm not going to answer any questions, Garon. That way, if Mr. Young asks you anything more about me, you can say you don't know."

He chuckled and lowered his head close to my ear. "I will put a lock on my lips." He pursed his lips together and held his fingers to his lips as though turning a key.

With a grin I pushed his fingers away from his lips. "Don't lock your lips too tight because I'd like to know if Mr. Young has given any reason for his interest in me or in any of those other visitors to the colonies. Surely he has mentioned some reason for his inquiries."

He hiked a shoulder. "He said he'd like to write a book one day."

"About what?"

"The different types of people who've come here to live."

I exhaled a whoosh of air. "Why would a lawyer be interested in writing a book about people living in Amana?" I pondered my own question as Ilsa walked toward us, her lips drooping and her eyebrows narrowed into a frown. She latched on to Garon's arm with a possessive hold that surprised me. From the look on Garon's face, her behavior surprised him, as well.

"Are the two of you going to remain by yourselves all evening, or are you going to join the rest of us for popcorn?"

"I was only asking Garon—"

Before I could finish my sentence, she pulled Garon toward the parlor. I followed at a distance and sat by a group of girls on the far side of the parlor. I'd obviously annoyed Ilsa.

On the way home I explained. Although Ilsa professed to accept my apology, it wasn't until several days later that she acted like her old self. Perhaps because Garon had kept his distance from me or because the time of Albert's arrival was quickly approaching.

CHAPTER 17

Ilsa Redlich

"He's here! He's here!" My shouts could probably be heard throughout the hotel, but Mother said I should be sure to let her know when Albert arrived from the train depot. I didn't want to disappoint her. I heard her footsteps behind me. "It's Albert! I can see him in the sleigh." I extended my arm and pointed to the window. "There! On the other side of Garon."

Mother's smile broadened as the sleigh drew near. "Ja. It is Albert. And look! He's in his army uniform."

I peered through the window before I clasped her arm. "Come on! Let's go outside and greet him." I turned and motioned to Jutta. "Come on, Jutta. Come and meet Albert."

She shook her head. "You go on. It's better you have a chance to talk to him first. I'll meet him once he's had a chance to visit with all of you." She waved us forward and turned toward the kitchen. "I'll go and make certain the bread pudding doesn't get too brown."

My mother and I both knew the pudding didn't require a watchful eye. We'd put it in the oven only fifteen minutes earlier, but I sensed Jutta's discomfort, so I didn't press her. Better to let her meet Albert later, when the freshness of our reunion had diminished a little. Right now, it would likely be a reminder of how much she would miss being with her parents for Christmas. Gathering our cloaks around our shoulders, Mother and I hurried out the front door. Tears pooled in my mother's eyes as we waved with excitement.

"Don't cry, Mutter. The tears will freeze, and you'll have icicles hanging from your cheeks. What would Albert think of such a sight?" I giggled and hugged her shoulder as Garon pulled back on the reins.

Before they had come to a complete stop, Albert jumped down and rushed around the back of the sleigh. He kissed Mother's cheek, and after a warm embrace he swooped me into his arms and twirled around. "How is my Ilsy-Dilsy?" After setting me on my feet, he rubbed his stomach and tipped his head toward the front door. "I hope there is some food cooking inside. My stomach is ready."

Mother beamed and grabbed hold of his arm. "For sure, there is. I don't think you will be disappointed. There is ham and potatoes cooked with green beans, just the way you like them." Her gaze traveled the length of his uniform. "Already you look like you have lost weight. I am thinking they need to have some better cooks in the army. Soldiers need muscles."

Noting my mother's worried frown, I tugged on the front of Albert's jacket. "Maybe they measured him wrong and gave him a uniform made for a fat man." I puffed out my cheeks and waddled a few steps for emphasis. Albert laughed, but I could see my antics hadn't relieved my mother's concern. "Don't worry, Mutter. We have bread pudding for dessert. He will surely gain a few pounds by the time he has eaten the noonday meal."

"I hope you remembered to put raisins in the bread pudding."

My mother laughed and nodded. "For sure. You have not been gone so long that I would forget you like raisins in your bread pudding. And there will be raisins in the New Year's pretzel to satisfy you, as well."

Albert's smile dimmed. "I leave before New Year's, Mutter. I must return a week from today." He wagged his finger back and forth. "And before you complain, you must remember we are a country at war. I am thankful I was granted leave to come home for Christmas. We will celebrate New Year's together next year."

My mother's frown didn't leave her face. "If they let you come home by then. I do wish you hadn't—"

"Now, Mutter. Let's not begin talk of what you wish I had or hadn't done. There is nothing to change the fact that I am in the army and must return a week from today. I want to enjoy this time that I have with you." He pointed to the tan burlap bag Garon had lifted from the sleigh. "Otherwise there will be no presents for anyone."

I hopped from one foot to the other, trying to keep warm. Finally I gestured toward the front door. "Come on. Let's go inside before we turn into icicles."

Albert turned to Garon. "Will you join us for the noonday meal?"

"I would like to, but I have to return to the depot. I'll stop by when the afternoon train comes through, and maybe we will have time for a talk. If not, we can visit after meeting tonight."

"Ja. We will have lots of time. I will be here a whole week."

Albert slapped Garon on the shoulder and waited until he stepped up into the sleigh.

"See you later." Garon waved his cap at us as he drove down the street.

We waved in return and continued to chatter while making our way into the house. My smile disappeared when I spotted Mr. and Mrs. Young sitting in the parlor. They'd been nowhere in sight when we'd gone out to greet Albert. No doubt they had heard the commotion and looked out their bedroom windows. Mrs. Young had moved two chairs directly in front of their windows that faced the street. She didn't miss many comings and goings at the hotel. And when her husband was in town, I thought the same could be said for him. The pair seemed to maintain a zealous interest in others, yet revealed little about themselves—behavior I found most odd.

I didn't try to hide my irritation when Mr. Young jumped to his feet and extended his hand to Albert. "Good to have you home for a visit, Private Redlich. I'm Jonathan Young, and this is my wife, Lillian." He gestured for his wife to step forward. "We've been staying here at the hotel since shortly after you joined the army. I know your parents are very proud of the sacrifice you're making to ensure our freedom."

With her lips curved in what seemed a forced smile, Mrs. Young clung to her husband's arm. "We're looking forward to hearing about your experiences since you've left home. We're all eager for news from the men serving our country."

"I'm pleased to meet you, Mr. and Mrs. Young. Thank you for your kind words. I'm sure we'll have time to discuss the war effort during the next week, but the newspapers probably have more information about the war than I do." He looked at the clock and then turned to his mother. "I think I'll take my bags into our rooms, and then I'll be back to visit with you and Ilsa, Mutter."

I was certain Albert's comment was meant to dismiss the Youngs, but they didn't seem to notice. I was setting the table when Albert returned from our rooms. Mr. Young jumped up and waved him toward one of the parlor chairs, but I wasn't going to let Mr. Young have his way.

"Mutter is waiting for you in the kitchen, Albert." I did my best to appear pleasant. "I'm sure you understand, Mr. Young."

He tipped his head and looked at me. "Why, of course." Stepping forward, he patted Albert's shoulder. "We'll make time to talk in a few days—after you've visited with your family."

"You and Mrs. Young aren't going home for Christmas?" We seldom had visitors in the hotel during the holidays. Though I hadn't inquired of the Youngs or my parents, I had assumed the Youngs would depart for home before Christmas. While most guests wouldn't expect to be included in our festivities, the Youngs weren't like most guests. They could very well anticipate spending the holidays in Amana and being a part of our celebration.

"We haven't yet decided. It will depend upon how Lillian feels as the day approaches."

I thought the answer intentionally elusive. Christmas Day was already approaching. Was Mrs. Young going to wait until Christmas Eve to make her decision? Not likely. I was sure Mr. Young simply didn't want to reveal his plans to me. Probably because I'd earlier prevented his visit with Albert. The man could be as irritating as a pair of itchy stockings.

I grasped Albert's hand as he entered the dining room. "There's someone I want you to meet. She's in the kitchen."

"Jutta?"

I grinned and nodded my head. I'd written to Albert and

told him about Jutta's arrival and how her presence had helped me through those first weeks after he'd departed. "She's so nice, Albert. And such gut help. Even better than Sister Hulda, because she can speak lots more English."

"And because she's not so old?" He grinned as he whispered the question.

I chuckled. "Ja, that too. I think you will like her. Did I tell you her parents own a bakery in Marengo?"

"You did." He followed me into the kitchen and placed a kiss on Mother's cheek. "And you must be Jutta. I am very pleased that you have joined our family here at the hotel, Jutta."

"Thank you and welcome home. I am pleased to be here." Jutta leaned down and removed the bread pudding from the oven.

Albert lifted his nose. "I haven't smelled anything that gut since I left home. And I have been thinking about Christmas cookies since before Thanksgiving."

"We have already baked the *Lebkuchen* and *Pfeffernüsse*. And the Marzipan will be ready to bake tomorrow," I said. "We waited to put out the Christmas pyramid until you returned, but we can do that tomorrow, too."

"And don't forget to put ice skating, sledding, cutting pine branches, and a snowball fight on your list." Albert tapped a piece of paper on the counter. "We need to go to the general store for all of the items on Mutter's grocery list and maybe purchase a gift or two." His eyes sparkled as he poked fun at me.

"I know you're laughing at me, but I'm just trying to get everything organized so we can spend lots of time together. Besides, you would be the first to complain if you didn't see Marzipan cookies on the plate."

"Ja. You are right about that." Albert looked toward the other side of the kitchen. "And what about you, Jutta? What cookies do you like for Christmas?"

"I like them all, but *Nuss-Plätzchen* are my favorite."

Albert nodded. "I like nut cookies, too. You like them with hickory nuts or English walnuts?"

"Oh, hickory nuts, for sure," Jutta said.

"Ja, me too. Better flavor." He grinned and settled on one of the stools.

I was pleased to see Jutta relax with Albert. By Christmas I hoped she would feel comfortable enough to enjoy the day with us. It wouldn't be the same as going home to her parents, but I hoped she would consider us a good substitute. Before we could talk further about Christmas preparations, the kitchen door opened and Father blustered into the room, along with a rush of cold air.

"I decided I could leave a little early today. After all, my son does not come home from Camp Pike every day." He strode across the room and wrapped Albert in a bear hug.

Albert returned the hug and laughed when my father pulled a snowball from his pocket and rubbed it on Albert's hair. My mother shook her finger. "Ach! There is no time for such nonsense when I have a meal to put on the table. If you two don't behave, I'll make you leave the kitchen."

Father removed his coat and hat and hung them on the hook by the back door. "You see, Albert? Nothing has changed since you left. Your Mutter still bosses me around the house."

The men didn't wait for further orders from my mother. Instead, they went into the dining room and sat at the table to visit. Before long Mr. Young joined them, and I overheard him asking Albert questions about the war. Although Albert tried to change the subject, Mr. Young consistently returned to that topic.

Mr. Young was in the midst of yet another question when I walked into the dining room and placed several bowls atop the sideboard. "Perhaps if you are so interested in the army, you should consider signing up to join, Mr. Young. I am sure you would be eligible." From my father's sharp look, I knew he disapproved of what I'd said, but that didn't stop me. I was weary of Mr. Young and his interfering ways. "I think you can even request an overseas assignment, can't you, Albert?"

My brother cast a surprised look in my direction. "I'm sure it is possible, but I don't think Mr. Young is interested in joining the army, Ilsa."

Mr. Young straightened his shoulders and tugged on the corner of his vest. "Some of us are required to serve in other ways. I believe I mentioned to you on an earlier occasion that I cannot meet the physical requirements to join the military." He pinned me with a steely gaze. "If I didn't know better, I'd think you were trying to embarrass me in front of your brother."

I shrugged my shoulders. Let him think what he wanted. I longed to ask about his physical ailments, for I'd never seen an indication of such problems or heard of those "other ways" in which he was supposedly serving the country. But before I could say anything more, my mother waved me into the kitchen. It was probably just as well. If I'd said anything more, Father would have chastised me later.

"You need to guard your mouth, Ilsa." My mother handed me the platter of sliced ham. "Mr. Young is a guest, and he was not speaking to you."

I agreed to be more careful, and until the Youngs went upstairs after the noonday meal, I held my tongue. But when they departed for Des Moines the following morning, I wanted to cheer. Now we could enjoy Albert's visit and celebrate without Mr. Young's constant questions. Instead of wishing us a merry Christmas when they departed, Mrs. Young told me I need not clean the room while they were gone. "Consider it my Christmas gift to you," she'd said. Ach! The Youngs—they were such strange people.

After the midday meal Jutta came to our rooms while we placed the nativity figures and candles in the wooden Christmas pyramid, but she remained at a distance. As Albert placed the cardboard crèche on the table, he began to draw her into conversation. "Does your family have a tree for Christmas, Jutta?"

Jutta nodded. "My father cuts fresh branches from a spruce or pine tree, and we push them into a thick wooden pole bored with holes, but we have a crèche like yours. My parents put it under our tree each year."

"We put our pine tree in the hotel parlor," my Mutter said. "But since our relatives came from Saxony, we like to use the pyramid, too."

Jutta leaned forward. "I remember the pyramid from my friend's house when we lived in Homestead. As a little girl, I was always fascinated by how the lit candles in the base would cause the wooden blades on top to turn."

"Ja. Ilsa and Albert were the same way—always watching the pyramid." Mother turned toward me. "If you are going to go and cut branches this afternoon, you better finish cleaning upstairs, Ilsa."

Jutta jumped to her feet. "I can do it. You stay here with your family, Ilsa."

"We'll do it together and be done in no time. There are only a few rooms, and I don't have to do anything in the Youngs' room."

"You should remove the sheets so we can wash them while they are gone," my mother called after me.

We quickly gathered the supplies. Jutta went to one end of the hall and I started at number five. As usual, the Youngs had locked the door. The practice annoyed me. I had hoped that they wouldn't be returning, but Mother told me they planned to come back after New Year's—or sooner if Mrs. Young had a setback with her melancholy. Sometimes I wondered if Mrs. Young truly suffered from the illness or if it was a convenient method of getting her way with her husband.

I glanced around the room as I entered. Ever since the Youngs had rented number five, I never walked into the rooms without feeling discomfort. All appeared in order, although they'd left many of their belongings stacked on the table. Though I didn't look in the wardrobe, I was certain they hadn't packed all of their belongings. It seemed each time Mr. Young returned to Des Moines his wife requested he bring more of her belongings from home. I crossed the room, pulled back the coverlet, and placed it on the chair. Lifting one corner of the mattress, I freed the sheets and walked to the other side of the bed. As I yanked the sheets free, several papers drifted to the carpet. Curious, I leaned down and retrieved the papers.

My heart hammered a new beat as I scanned the papers. Each sheet contained a drawing of some sort of weapon. The drawings were somewhat similar, but I couldn't be certain if it was the same weapon on each page. I couldn't understand the printed information below the drawings and wondered if it could be in some special code.

"Ilsa?" I jumped when I heard Albert call and rushed to the top of the stairs. "How much longer will you be? I think I'll go to the depot and see if Garon can join us." My brother's voice drifted up the staircase. "I'll be back in an hour. You think you will be done by then?"

My hands trembled, and I automatically hid the papers behind my back. My mouth felt like cotton, but I forced myself to answer. "Ja, that would be gut," I croaked.

I could hear Jutta down the hallway as I hurried back to the Youngs' room. I dropped to the side of the bed and continued to stare at the drawings. There were six or seven, all of the pages rumpled and creased. I wondered if Mr. Young had placed them beneath the mattress to press out the wrinkles. I shoved the pages back beneath the mattress—all but one. I would return it once I showed it to Albert. Spreading the clean sheets across the bed, I tucked them beneath the mattress, replaced the coverlet, and rolled up the dirty sheets. After carefully folding the paper, I tucked it into my apron pocket, exited the room, and locked the door. I would return tomorrow.

CHAPTER 18

Jutta Schmitt

As Ilsa had predicted, there were no guests in the hotel on Christmas Eve. She had told me that only a few times had there been visitors at the hotel during the Christmas celebration. And those guests had remained because they'd been stranded due to weather. This year we'd received our share of snow, but it hadn't come all at once. Even tonight as we walked to meeting, flurries were coming down. The moon cast a hazy path through the veil of falling snow, and I wondered what my parents were doing at this moment.

After leaving Amana, we'd attended several different churches in Marengo. And though my parents spoke enough English to communicate with customers, the churches in Marengo were very different—and German was not spoken. So soon we quit going to any church and instead remained at home, where my father read from the *Psalter-Spiel* and the Bible, and sometimes the three of us would sing the familiar hymns of the Amana Inspirationists. Were my mother and father sitting in front of the candlelit tree made of pine boughs singing "Rejoice Ye Heavens"? Or had they done away with any form of celebration because I wasn't with them? I hoped not.

We separated from the men and entered the women's door of the meetinghouse, taking our places on wooden benches worn glossy and smooth from daily use. Even in the meetinghouse, I could smell the scent of pine and spruce, though I was sure it was only my imagination. Tears welled in my eyes as we joined together and sang "All My Heart This Night Rejoices." How good it would be to have my mother and father among this group of colonists, lifting their voices with ours in praise to God.

After meeting we walked toward home with the excited shouts of children surrounding us, each one certain Pelznickel would soon arrive—each one uncertain if the old man in his fur coat and shaggy beard would greet them with a lump of coal, apply a switch to their backside, or give them a juicy orange or some peppermints. Though most children looked forward to Pelznickel's arrival, those who had misbehaved during the year were less enthusiastic. All, however, looked forward to the arrival of Kristkindl. For some, he would arrive late in the evening, for others not until the next day—but for all he would leave a gift. Some would receive a pair of ice skates, others a dollhouse or sled, but for everyone, his arrival brought joy and excitement. The same couldn't be said for Pelznickel's visits.

Garon and Ilsa walked together, while Albert walked by my side and his parents led the way home. I'd been surprised to hear Garon would spend Christmas Eve at the Redlich home, but Ilsa had explained that Garon's family wouldn't celebrate until the next day.

"Pelznickel stopped visiting our house when Christina turned ten years old," Garon said as we turned the corner.

"He still visits our house because Ilsa hasn't yet learned to behave," Albert replied.

Ilsa glanced over her shoulder. "That's not true! If I remember right, you're the one who received coal last Christmas, and I received a bag of candy."

"Ja, but it was a mistake. Pelznickel got confused and gave the wrong person coal. Isn't that right, Vater?" Albert called to his father.

"If there is an argument between you and your sister, you can be sure Pelznickel will bring both of you coal. And maybe a bundle of switches will be included, too."

We laughed and Albert turned up his collar against the increasing snowfall. "Jutta, you are warm enough?"

"Yes, thank you. My cloak is very warm." I briefly wondered what he would have done if I'd said I was cold. "I'm surprised Pelznickel still comes to your house."

Albert grinned. "My Vater loves the tradition. He wouldn't think it was Christmas Eve unless Pelznickel arrived with his sleigh bells and burlap bag."

My foot slipped in the snow, and Albert grabbed my arm.

"Careful. These board sidewalks are slippery when they're wet or covered with snow." He released his grasp but remained watchful as we continued toward the hotel. "What about you, Jutta? Did Pelznickel bring you candy and fruit?"

"When we lived in Homestead he visited, but not since then. I was sixteen when we moved to Marengo, and many of the old traditions were set aside, especially since the war began."

"Ilsa wrote and told me life was difficult for you in Marengo, and that is why you returned to the colonies. I know she is very happy to have you here." He tipped his head. "She thinks of you as the sister she never had. She's written about your kind nature and sweet disposition. I'm sure this change has been difficult for you."

Guilt sliced through me like a sharp knife. If they knew the real reasons for my being in the colonies, they wouldn't think me so sweet and kind. I decided to change the conversation. "Have you adjusted to your life in the army? No doubt you've endured a great deal of change yourself."

"It has been more of an adjustment than I expected, but please don't tell Ilsa or my Mutter. They worry far too much. The hours are long, and the work is hard, but I can handle hard work—I learned about that many years ago." He chuckled, then his laughter quickly faded. "These last weeks it has become difficult to show God's love to the men who choose to label me a coward. At first I was able to push aside the angry words they hurled at me, but as the weeks pass, it is becoming more difficult to ignore them. I do my best, but when everything I say or do meets with ridicule or hatred, it becomes nearly impossible to keep in mind that I should be a reflection of God's love to my fellowman."

"I admire your ability to endure such insults without losing your temper. I think I would want to strike back at them."

"I don't think my sergeant would approve if I punched them in the nose. He would question my status as a conscientious objector."

I giggled. "I didn't mean you should punch them in the nose, but maybe you could remove their shoelaces or cut the buttons off their shirts." I considered the Council members in Marengo. If I possessed the strength of a man, I would do more than cut the buttons off their shirts. I'd let someone else worry about reflecting God's love.

"For sure, my time in the army is teaching me to turn the other cheek and show patience toward my fellow soldiers. I am praying that some of the men will begin to understand that just because we don't believe in war doesn't mean we are cowards." He hesitated for a moment and rubbed his jaw with a gloved hand. "Mostly, my attempts have been unsuccessful, but I am thankful for the few men who have shown me friendship and who understand that I am as much a patriot as any of the other men who wear the uniform."

A gust of wind whipped at my cloak, and I pulled it tight against my body. "That is good to hear. It helps to have a friend you can trust in the midst of difficult circumstances."

"There is gut and bad in most everything, but I do my job and don't complain. The conditions are very poor, but for those of us who have worked hard all our lives and aren't used to fine living, it isn't so bad." He pulled his hat low on his forehead and tucked his chin against the cold air. "The men and their remarks, that is the worst of it right now."

"It sounds frightful to me. Maybe you should talk to Garon a little more and convince him it isn't so good to join. Ilsa worries he still plans to enter if he gets his letter."

Albert nodded. "Garon must make his own decision. I have told him it would be better to wait until feelings against us subside, but only yesterday he said he still wants to serve. Maybe we should all pray that his letter won't come from the draft board."

"Maybe you are right." I didn't mention that my prayers probably wouldn't help a lot.

Once we arrived, Sister Marta served us coffee and Christmas cookies while Ilsa's father told stories and we waited for Pelznickel. Nearly an hour passed before we heard the sound of sleigh bells, followed by loud pounding on the door. Ilsa's father jumped to his feet and opened the door. Pelznickel burst into the room, his eyes flashing from person to person. He stopped in front of Albert and gave him a piece of fruit and some candy. Garon received a sack of candy, and I was surprised when he handed a sack to me, as well. Then he stopped in front of Ilsa and reached into his bag.

When he withdrew a lump of coal, Ilsa shook her head. "I have been a very gut girl, Pelznickel. You must have me confused with some other girl." He frowned and looked back inside the bag. Before rushing from the room, Pelznickel took the coal from Ilsa and replaced it with an orange and peppermints.

"Who was that?" I whispered to Albert, who sat in the chair beside me.

He grinned. "It's Brother Johann. He lives in Upper. He visits most of the houses in Upper and Lower each Christmas Eve. He does a gut job, ja?"

I agreed. Had I been a youngster, he would have frightened me into becoming a better behaved child during the next year. We visited until well after bedtime. Then Garon departed, and I returned to my own rooms. It would seem strange to get up on Christmas morning without my parents. I'd written them a long letter with Christmas greetings, but I'd had no money to purchase gifts. Instead, I'd knitted a pair of gloves for my mother and a woolen scarf for my father. Yesterday I received a letter and small package from my parents. My mother's letter said I should wait until Christmas to open the gift, and I'd followed her wishes. I placed the package on the small table in my parlor, right beside the crèche Sister Marta had given me to make my apartment feel more like Christmas. At least that was what she'd told me when she insisted I take it. And she was right. It did provide a small sense of joy in my otherwise plain parlor.

I hadn't expected to sleep well, but once I slipped between

the sheets, sleep came quickly. However, my slumber was fraught with dreams of men from the Iowa Council of National Defense dragging my parents off to jail. I awakened the next morning with my covers wadded in knots. Ilsa had explained that even though there were no guests in the house and we could have gone to the Küche for our meals, her mother preferred to prepare meals in the hotel kitchen. "She says someone might unexpectedly arrive, and there would be no one at the hotel." However, Ilsa was sure her mother preferred having dinner alone with her family—and I agreed with Ilsa.

After breakfast we attended meeting and returned home to prepare the traditional Christmas meal served in all the colony kitchens: rice soup, creamed chicken over homemade noodles, mashed potatoes, coleslaw, stewed prunes and peaches, and *Stollen*. Albert and his father remained close by while we completed the preparations, and the house was filled with laughter throughout the holiday meal. While we washed the dishes, Sister Marta disappeared, and when we finished our work, she called us to their rooms.

"Come and see what gifts Kristkindl has left in the parlor."

One by one we entered the parlor and took our seats, though I would have preferred to go into my own rooms. The family had done everything possible to welcome me into their celebration, but guilt was stealing my joy.

Sheets were draped over several piles in the parlor. Sister Marta circled the room, pointing at the white lumps. "This one is for you, Albert. This for you, Ilsa. This is for you, Odell." She smiled at her husband before she pointed to another sheet. "And this is for you, Jutta."

I wanted to shout that I didn't want gifts from any of them—

that their kindness made my betrayal all the more difficult. Instead, I smiled. "I did not expect any gifts. You shouldn't—"

"We wanted to include you, Jutta." Brother Odell smiled at me before he strode to one of the chairs and pointed behind it. "It looks like Kristkindl hid your gifts very well, Marta."

Sister Marta laughed and nodded. "So he did. So he did."

All of our gifts were similar. Hand-knit gloves or mittens, sweaters, and scarves, but beneath my sheet I also discovered a pair of ice skates and a framed, embroidered piece that Ilsa had made with my name and the names of my parents. "You can set it beside the picture of your family," she said. I was touched by her thoughtfulness.

And I was glad that I had embroidered pillowcases for her. "For when you and Garon wed," I whispered. She smiled and nodded.

"Now we must go ice skating." Albert stood and rubbed his stomach. "After all the gut food we need some activity, or I will fall asleep."

"You children go and skate. Your Vater and I, we will take a nap."

Albert nudged his sister's arm. "We should stop and ask Garon to come along, ja?"

"Ja, that would be gut, but first we must get our skates from the shed."

Sister Marta leaned forward in her chair. "You could bring me a cup of coffee on your way back through the kitchen, Ilsa."

"I would be pleased to get it for you, Sister Marta." I followed Albert and Ilsa to the kitchen and placed a cup and saucer on the worktable. The coffee would be hot. Sister Marta always kept the pot on the back of the stove for guests who might request a cup. As I gathered a folded towel around the handle, I noticed one of the aprons lying on the floor by the back door. It must have fallen when Albert and Ilsa went outdoors. As I lifted the apron to the hook, a note fluttered to the floor. Probably Sister Marta's shopping list, I thought as I unfolded the paper.

My mouth went dry as I stared at the paper that had fallen from Ilsa's apron pocket. Where had this come from? And what was this strange-looking weapon? Why did Ilsa have it in her apron pocket? I could hear Albert's footsteps at the back door as he shouted to Ilsa to hurry. I shoved the paper into my skirt pocket, picked up the cup of coffee, and hurried back to the parlor, my thoughts in a whirl.

CHAPTER 19

Ilsa Redlich

Holding my skates in one hand, I pulled the shed door closed and hastened after Albert. I leaned down, grabbed a handful of snow, and lobbed it at him. "You could have waited for me. What kind of gentleman are you?"

He laughed and dodged the snowball. "Not a very gut one, but you are too slow. It must be your old age, ja?"

"We'll see who is old once we begin skating. I think you will be sitting down before I am."

Albert opened the back door, and we stomped the snow from our feet. I had expected Jutta to meet us in the kitchen, but she was nowhere in sight. Stepping to the dining room doorway, I peered around the corner into the hotel parlor. "You wait here, Albert. Jutta must be with Mutter and Vater." I turned down the hallway and was surprised when Jutta appeared from her rooms. She hesitated and cast her gaze to the floor.

She looked like a child who'd been caught taking a forbidden piece of candy.

"I needed to put something in my room, but I'm ready."

"Your ice skates?" I tapped the skates I held in one hand.

Jutta touched a finger to her head. "I am not thinking straight. I took them to my room and then left them there."

I waited in the hallway while she returned for her skates. Her earlier excitement had waned, and I wondered what had happened during our absence. I knew she'd received a Christmas gift from her parents and had planned to open it Christmas Day. Maybe she'd opened their gift and was suffering from the remembrance of past Christmases. I couldn't imagine how difficult it must be, but at least she didn't have to endure the daily taunts from those who took pleasure in tormenting anyone of German heritage. If the United States hadn't become involved in the war, none of this would be happening. Albert would be at home where he belonged, Jutta and her family would be together, and Garon wouldn't be talking about joining the army.

Hoping to lift her spirits, I smiled and looped arms with her when she appeared with her skates. "We're going to have great fun. I'm sure there will be lots of others enjoying the ice, and there will be a fire to keep warm."

"It was very nice of your parents to have the skates made for me. They shouldn't have done so much."

"They are fond of you and wanted you to have a gut Christmas with us. Besides, Vater and the blacksmith work together often and help each other when something is needed." I wanted to ask if she'd opened the gift from her parents but decided against it. After all, talk of home wouldn't improve her mood.

Albert was leaning against the worktable, a cookie in his hand, when we walked into the kitchen.

"I was wondering if you were ever going to return. I thought I was going to have to go skating by myself."

I pointed to the hickory nut cookie. "It doesn't look like you have been suffering too much while you waited."

With a chuckle Albert pushed away from the table and strode toward the back door, carrying his skates. He bowed from the waist and made a sweeping gesture with his free hand. "After the two of you."

Fortunately it didn't take long for Garon to decide he would come with us. "Take Christina with you," his mother called as we waited inside the front door. "She should have some fun, too."

I motioned for Christina to hurry and don her cloak while I called to Sister Barbara, "We will be glad to have her come along." Turning back toward Christina, I pointed to my hands. "Get your mittens and scarf. It is very cold."

"And your skates," Albert added.

Pulling her scarf from a hook near the door, Christina flashed a smile. "Garon will bring them. He's always in charge of the skates."

No sooner had Christina uttered the words than Garon appeared with two pairs of skates. "It's gut I am in charge of something. With a mother, a sister, and Ilsa all telling me what is best, I am glad to know I am in charge of ice skates." He grinned and handed the smaller pair of skates to his sister as we departed.

"Maybe because the women in your life know what is best. For sure you need to listen to me when I tell you that going into the army is foolish and not gut for you or anyone else."

"That's not true, Ilsa. The United States needs all of us to do our patriotic duty." Garon straightened his shoulders. "If I go and serve like Albert, it frees other men to go and fight at the front. At least I will be doing something to show the country that even though German blood runs through my veins, I am an American and a patriot."

"If you go into the army, it will not change anything. This war is nonsense. It has done nothing for this country except cause Americans to hate and mistrust one another." Ilsa glanced over her shoulder. "Don't you agree, Jutta?"

She shrugged. "I am no authority on the war, Ilsa. I have learned it is best to not discuss such things."

I nudged Garon. "There, you see? When people are afraid to say what they believe, it is not a gut thing. That's what this war has done—made us afraid of each other. This is what it was like for our forefathers before they fled Germany. Everyone hated them because of their religious beliefs. Now everyone hates us, not because of our faith, but because our distant relatives came from Germany."

"Ach! Stop with this talk, Ilsa. It is Christmas, and I want to enjoy my time at home. Soon I will be back at Camp Pike, where I can listen to much talk of the war. Now I am in Amana. Let me enjoy ice skating and gut food and being with my family."

I bowed my head, ashamed of my behavior. Instead of permitting Albert the pleasure of his time at home, I'd been intent upon convincing Garon he should remain in Amana. "You are right, Albert. I'm sorry. This is a time for happiness, not for talk of war and hatred. Forgive me."

Albert reached back and chucked me beneath the chin. "Only if you let me win my first race down the ice with you."

"I'm not so worried about your forgiveness that I'm going to give you that honor. You'll have to beat me in a fair race or not at all." I grabbed Garon's hand and tugged him forward. "And we're going to beat you to the river, as well."

Christina took my cue and ran behind us, but when I glanced over my shoulder, I could see that Albert remained beside Jutta, the two of them walking at a normal pace. "Come on, you two. Are you so old you can't run in the snow?"

"You go ahead and tire yourself out with running. That way I'll be sure to win on the ice," Albert called.

I cupped my hands around my mouth. "That's the only way you'd be able to win, Albert Redlich." I'd expected my taunt to bring him running, but it didn't. It seemed he and Jutta were becoming friends. Even in the cold snowy weather, the thought warmed me. Maybe one day they could become more than friends. The thought that Jutta could one day become a real member of our family was a wonderful Christmas gift; she would be the perfect sister for me.

As we approached the river, we could see that a number of other people were already on the ice. Garon brushed several flat rocks free of snow and then stooped down in front of me. "Let me help you get your skates on so you'll be ready for that race with Albert." He smiled up at me. "After that, I hope you will spend the rest of your time with me."

I leaned forward as he tightened my skate. "If I didn't know better, I would think you are jealous."

"Ja? Well, that would be true. I never am able to spend much time alone with you, so when we have a chance to be by ourselves, that is what I want." He glanced toward Albert and Jutta as they approached. "But I know you want to be with Albert some of the time. He is your brother, and he has been gone. I promise to be understanding of your feelings."

I placed my gloved hand on his shoulder. "You are very thoughtful, Garon."

He'd finished tightening my second skate and grasped my hand. "Is that why you fell in love with me—or is it my gut looks that won your heart?"

I squeezed his hand and laughed. "I think it was some of both. I just hope you will remember to be considerate of what I want if a letter comes from the local draft board."

He touched his finger to my lips. "We are going to speak only of happy things today. Instead of the draft board, you should speak to me of love. I would be pleased to hear how wonderful I am and how thankful you are that I chose you instead of one of the other girls."

I pushed him backward and laughed when he landed on his backside in a pile of snow. "That's what you get for being so full of yourself. It is you that should be thankful that I gave you a second glance when you first spoke to my Vater."

Laughing, he stood and brushed the snow from his trousers. "Always you must have the last word." He reached for my hand to lead me to the ice. "But I will admit you are right this time. I am very thankful." After a quick glance over his shoulder, he grazed my cheek with a fleeting kiss.

"That was not much of a kiss." I loved teasing with Garon. Other than Albert, he understood me better than anyone. He knew when I was teasing and when I was serious. He knew my likes and dislikes, and he loved me in spite of all my short-comings. Garon was a good match for me—and I didn't want to lose him to the army.

"I could do better if there were fewer people around. Albert might not approve if he saw his sister being kissed." Garon pointed to his face. "I don't want a black eye."

I held out my hand, and the two of us carefully picked our way across the short distance to the ice. "Albert would never do such a thing, but you are right. Word would quickly spread, and my Vater might not be as understanding as Albert. My Vater would never hit you, but he would likely talk your ear off." I giggled. "Instead of a black eye, you would have only one ear."

Garon laughed with me and held his gloved hand to the side of his hat. "Maybe that would not be such a bad thing. When we are married and you are angry with me, I could hear you shouting at me with only one ear instead of two, ja?"

I poked his arm. "I will not be shouting at you." I hesitated a moment. "Unless you really need it." I laughed and motioned toward Albert and Jutta. "They seem to be getting along well, don't you think?"

Garon tipped his head close. "I see that sparkle in your eye. Don't try to make something out of two people who have just met. They are having a gut time. It is nothing more. Besides, Albert must return to Camp Pike, and who knows whether Jutta will stay in the colonies."

I skated forward and then turned a half circle so I could face Garon. He held my hands as I skated backward. "Why would you even think such a thing? Jutta is not going to leave Amana. I can feel it in my heart. She has returned because she loves our ways and believes this is where she belongs."

"That's not true, Ilsa. That is what you want to believe. She didn't come here because she loves our ways. She came here to escape the harsh treatment she received in Marengo. She may return to Marengo after the war is over and the hatred against

Germans has eased. I think she will want to be with her parents and help them with their business. It only makes gut sense."

I didn't want to believe anything he'd said. "Who knows when this war will end. It could be many years. And even if it isn't, I don't think she will want to go live among people who treated her with hatred."

Garon smiled one of his I-won't-argue-anymore-but-I-know-I-am-right smiles. I decided it would ruin our time together if I tried to further defend what I believed. The ice crunched beneath our skates as we crossed the river toward Albert and Jutta. This horrible war had ruined everything—even the possibility of talking to each other without an argument.

Waving my mittened hand high above my head, I called to Albert. "Ready for our race?"

"Ja, but you know I will win, so why should we bother?"

I caught John Miller's attention and he started to make his way down to our traditional finish line. John was our judge every year. I trusted him—probably because back when we were eight years old, I'd threatened to punch him in the nose if he wasn't fair. I'd never had to carry through with the threat, but I still teasingly reminded him each year.

Albert's deep chuckle echoed in the cold air as he took his place beside me and crouched low, his forearm across one knee.

Hoping to keep up with his long-legged stride, I matched Albert's stance. Garon counted to three, and we took off, our skates digging into the ice, both of us eager to win the competition we'd begun many years ago. We always raced a straight line down the river—no twists and turns, nothing that the other could claim as an excuse for failure. Friends lined up on either side, those cheering for Albert on one side—usually all the boys and men—and those cheering for me on the other—usually all the girls and women. I didn't fail to note that Garon was on my side this time with the girls, and the sight of him cheering me on made me try even harder.

Whizzing by the cheering onlookers, I was caught by surprise at the sight of Jutta. She'd clearly taken a spot on the side cheering for Albert. I didn't know whether to feel pleased or hurt. While I liked the idea of Jutta as a possible wife for Albert, I had expected to see her cheering for me. After all, she'd just met Albert. And though we hadn't known each other for long, we were better friends than she and Albert—at least I'd thought so.

Albert's long stride was proving more difficult to match than it had in the past. I tried to gain on him, but he had maintained the lead since the halfway mark. As we neared the finish line, I inhaled a deep breath, bent low, and thrust my body forward.

John waved his arms in an X over his head and then swung them downward as we crossed the line. "It's a tie!" I was certain his shouted decision could be heard by everyone on the river.

"It's not a tie! My head was across the line before Albert's. I know it was."

John shook his head. "The two of you came across together. And if Albert had bent forward a little more, he would have been the winner."

I tightened my hand into a fist and waved it beneath John's nose. "I don't want to punch you, John. It wouldn't be ladylike."

He shrugged and laughed. "Go ahead and punch me if you must, but like it or not, it was a tie, Ilsa."

Garon skated to my side and wrapped his arm around my shoulder. "He's right, Ilsa. It was a tie."

Albert leaned forward and rested his arms on his bent legs. He turned his head and grinned at me. "It was a tie, Ilsy-Dilsy. I could have won, but I didn't want to embarrass you. You better get a lot of practice while I'm gone this winter, or you won't stand a chance next year." He laughed and took off across the ice before I could throttle him.

Jutta didn't follow Albert. Instead, she skated closer while Garon headed toward Albert. "It was a good race, Ilsa. You are a fine skater. I will remember never to challenge you to a race."

"I am a gut skater because Albert taught me." I wanted to ask her why she'd cheered for Albert if she thought I was such a fine skater but decided against it.

"Then he is a good teacher as well as a kind person." She remained by my side as we skated toward Albert and Garon. "I didn't understand how the cheering lines were divided until it was too late to cross over. I should have been on the other side to encourage you. I hope you aren't angry with me."

"I am not angry, but I was surprised when I saw you on Albert's side." I looped arms with her. "I am pleased that you are fond of Albert."

She dropped her hand from my arm. "I didn't say I was fond of him. I said he was kind and a good teacher. I barely know him, Ilsa."

"I am sorry, Jutta. I didn't mean to offend you." I grabbed her hand. "Come on, let's go join Garon and Albert."

Soon we divided into couples, and Garon held me around the waist as we skated side by side. After a short time I pointed toward the fire near the rocks along the riverbank. "My feet are getting cold. Maybe we should sit by the fire for a while."

There were several couples around the fire, but they left soon after Garon and I sat down. Garon placed his arm around my shoulder and pulled me close. "I'm glad to have you alone." He tipped my chin and lowered his head. Our lips melded together in a warm, inviting kiss. The kind of kiss I had expected earlier.

"That was much better," I murmured as his lips once again covered mine. For that short time I forgot my cold feet, the hard rock upon which I was sitting, and even the war in Europe.

CHAPTER 20

January 1918
Jutta Schmitt

Before Albert boarded the train for his return to Camp Pike, he asked me to write to him. I promised that if he wrote to me first, I would answer. Since then, I had worried about my promise. And now there was even more reason to worry, for I'd received a letter from him in last week's mail. In fact, I'd received a letter before Ilsa did, but I didn't tell her, for it would have diminished her obvious pleasure when she received a letter on Monday.

I pored over Albert's account of the train ride that took him through St. Louis and onward to Little Rock, where he'd stayed overnight at the Hotel Marion. My heart skipped a beat when he said the train ride would have been much more enjoyable if I'd been along to keep him company. The day before he departed, Albert said he wanted to become better acquainted when he returned from Camp Pike, and I'd understood his intentions.

We'd communicated well and seemingly become good friends. If I'd met him under other circumstances, I would have been delighted by his words. But given my current plight, his interest in me was cause for concern.

If he knew the real reason I had returned to Amana, I doubted he'd want to receive my letters. And to tell him my actions were necessary to save my parents from jail wasn't possible, either. Even worse, if I carried through with my purpose, I could jeopardize his entire family and other residents of Amana.

Since the day after Christmas, I'd expected a visit from members of the Iowa Council of National Defense. Each time the hotel door opened, my breath caught in my throat. I knew my good fortune could not last much longer. Soon they would appear and expect me to produce meaningful information. And there hadn't been much coming my way. The Red Cross meetings and quilting bees produced little except some new recipes we could cook on Meatless Mondays and Wheatless Wednesdays, or tips for frugal living that had long ago been adopted by our villages. There were varied discussions about the sacrifices being made by the community—the bonds that we purchased, the trees we sacrificed for the war effort, and the business that no longer came to our villages because of our German heritage. And those quiet worries were nothing that the hooligans from the Iowa Council would consider meaningful information.

However, since I found the drawing that had fallen from Ilsa's pocket, I wondered how she'd come to have it in her possession. Had Albert brought it home from Camp Pike and shown it to her? If so, would such an act be treasonous? I didn't want to get Albert into trouble with his superiors. Had Garon discovered it in the train depot? Had one of the Amana residents given it to her? I doubted all of those possibilities, yet if it was a meaningless drawing, why hadn't Ilsa mentioned its disappearance to me? I toyed with the thought that it was simply a paper she'd found on the floor and tucked into her pocket and then forgotten, but like me, Ilsa would have looked at the paper when she retrieved it. And the fact that she hadn't mentioned the drawing was missing gave me greater cause for alarm.

At first I considered telling her I'd found it in the kitchen and asking her why she had it in her possession. But as the days passed, I realized I needed the paper. Other than Ilsa's occasional antiwar comments, that drawing was the only thing of consequence I could report to the Council of Defense members. I didn't want to implicate Ilsa, but what was I to do?

Although God and I weren't on the best of terms, each night I prayed for an answer to my dilemma. I decided that even if He didn't want to help me, He'd surely provide an alternative that would keep me from involving Ilsa. I knew it wouldn't be much longer before someone from the Council of National Defense appeared—or I received word that my parents were in jail. I couldn't remember the exact date that I received my parents' last letter, and the thought that I hadn't received word from them for a while loomed large in my mind. Either way, I must be prepared to supply those men with information that was compelling enough to save my mother and father.

Recent nights were fraught with nightmares of angry men hauling my parents and me to jail or of Ilsa being dragged away from the hotel and calling out to me that I'd betrayed her. In spite of the cold temperatures, each morning I awakened with my nightgown damp with perspiration, and memories of the frightening dreams followed me like unwanted visitors through-out the day.

There had been no definite word from the elders about when

I could plan my next trip home. They'd been vague in their last communication with me, and I wasn't certain if they planned to permit my return home this month or in February. I worried that the men from the Council had returned to the bakery and made further threats to my parents.

When the bell over the front door jangled, I peeked around the corner of the upstairs hallway. My stomach clenched. Though it wasn't the men from the Council, I was disappointed to see Garon escorting Mr. and Mrs. Young into the hotel parlor. We had expected their return prior to the first of the year, but Mr. Young had sent word they would be visiting with relatives and we shouldn't expect them until mid-January. Apparently, their relatives had tired of them, for the middle of the month hadn't yet arrived.

I'd decided Mr. Young must have a prosperous law practice, since he continued to pay for their room here during their absence. He had instructed Ilsa's parents that nothing need be done to the room prior to their return. Sister Marta had expressed displeasure at that, for she wanted the room aired and the furniture dusted. But Ilsa's father told her to do as they'd been instructed. And we had. I'd been more than happy to stay out of their room. I hadn't missed Mr. Young's piercing looks and meddlesome questions.

I hoped Sister Marta would greet them, and when Mrs. Young glanced toward the upper floor, I ducked back and flattened myself against the wall.

"Sister Marta? Is anyone here? Mr. and Mrs. Young have returned." Garon's voice drifted up the stairs. Even though the Youngs didn't need to be checked in to the hotel, and they were still in possession of their key, Garon no doubt wanted to alert Sister Marta of their return. I exhaled when I heard the sound of footsteps below.

"Welcome back, Mr. and Mrs. Young. I hope you both enjoyed a gut Christmas with your families."

Sister Marta's kind words caused shame to grip me like a pinching shoe—but not so tight that it changed my mind. I still had no desire to welcome either of them. I remained at the top of the steps and listened, curious about their early return.

"I'm surprised to see you. My husband said you'd written that you wouldn't return until the middle of January."

"I didn't assume our time of arrival would be of consequence since we paid for our room in advance of our departure."

Mr. Young's haughty attitude hadn't changed.

"There is no problem, Mr. Young. I was merely commenting." Sister Marta's voice remained gentle. "If you'd like to relax in the parlor, I can have one of the girls go dust the furniture and air out the room before you go up."

"That won't be necessary. You can send one of them later in the afternoon, when my wife is there to supervise what she'd like done." Once again, the Youngs were setting their own rules. I wasn't surprised. It seemed they had to control everything.

"Perhaps one of them could come up after the noonday meal and help me unpack my clothing. I do detest unpacking." Mrs. Young sounded on the verge of tears.

Unpacking luggage and trunks wasn't one of the services offered at the hotel. Most guests didn't stay long enough to worry over such things—especially the salesmen. I decided Mrs. Young must have servants to help with such tasks at home. I tiptoed back down the hall and continued with my cleaning.

I was changing the sheets in the room at the far end of the hall when Ilsa called my name. I turned and she motioned toward the stairs. "There's a man downstairs to see you. He said he's a friend of your family."

My fingers turned cold, and the sheet fluttered onto the bed like a cloud floating toward earth. I willed myself to answer, to say something, but my lips wouldn't open and my legs wouldn't move. I stared at her, motionless.

Ilsa stepped into the room and grasped my arm. "Did you hear me, Jutta?"

"Yes." My legs felt wooden as I forced one in front of the other and tried to appear normal.

"Who is he?" Ilsa had taken a backward step and now stood in the doorway.

"How would I know until I see him?" There was little doubt that one of the men from the Council of National Defense was waiting at the foot of the stairs, but I could hardly tell Ilsa.

"Did you have someone back in Marengo that you had planned to marry?"

I stared at her, dumbfounded by the question. "No. Why would you think such a thing?"

"The man doesn't appear much older than Albert, and he's not so bad looking. Not as handsome as Albert, of course, but I thought maybe . . ." The unfinished sentence hung in the air begging for a response.

I shook my head and scooted past her. I hoped she would go back to her duties, but she followed close on my heels. As we reached the top of the stairs, I changed my mind. Maybe it was better if Ilsa remained nearby. Her presence would prohibit any intense questioning from the visitor.

The man stood with his back toward the steps, staring out the parlor window. He didn't turn until we neared the bottom of the stairway. My mouth dropped open, and a gasp escaped my lips. "Kenneth? Kenneth Reeves, is it really you?" I grinned at the sight of his familiar face. He smiled but not his usual smile—not the one I'd grown accustomed to seeing each week when he and his father delivered flour to our bakery. He held his winter cap in his hands, squishing the wool and fur between his fingers. Worry clouded his eyes. He hadn't come for a casual visit. My stomach lurched. Surely he wasn't one of *them*.

"Hello, Jutta. You look fine. It is good to see you." His shoulders were as stiff as his greeting. "I know you are working, but I thought maybe we could talk alone for a few minutes?"

Ilsa glanced back and forth between us. I was certain she expected an introduction, but I didn't know how to explain Kenneth or his sudden appearance at the hotel, so I said nothing. She cleared her throat and gave a slight nod. "I have work to finish. I'll be in the kitchen if you need anything, Jutta."

After mumbling my thanks, I directed Kenneth to the two chairs that sat side by side at one end of the parlor. To sit beside him on the couch would be improper. On the other hand, I needed to be close enough to hear and to avoid the possibility of anyone eavesdropping on our conversation. The chairs were the best choice. My position there provided a good view of the front porch, parlor, hallway, stairs, and dining room.

I waited a moment, but when Kenneth didn't speak up, I took the lead. "How are my parents? Have you seen them this week?"

He nodded. "A few days ago. The bakery is still open, although business is not as good as in the past."

I had hoped for more information, but I didn't press him. "What brings you to South Amana, Kenneth?" I doubted he was just passing through and had merely stopped for a visit.

In spite of the coolness of the room, perspiration dotted his upper lip, and he unbuttoned his coat. "I'm feeling a little warm." He attempted a smile but failed. "I have a message, but it's not from your mother or father. It's from members of the Iowa Council of National Defense."

My breath caught in my throat, and I clutched the corner of my apron. "You're one of them?" I shook my head. "I never thought you would join such a group. How can you take their side against us? We were always good customers, always paid our bills on time, and treated you and your father with kindness and respect. The claim they have made against us is a lie—we would never put glass in our bread." I sucked in a breath of air. "You have known us all the years we've been in the bakery. Do you believe we could do this horrible thing?"

He bowed his head. "You don't understand, Jutta. One of the leaders approached my father and said we were needed as members of the Council. They wanted information on the stores where we make deliveries."

"They want you to report on everyone?"

He locked his fingers together. "Not everyone. They're mostly interested in the businesses operated by anyone of German heritage. Since all of the store owners and managers know and trust us, the Council thought we would be a good choice to find out if there were any traitors. They gave us a list of different questions to ask, and then we are to report the answers to them."

My anger swelled until I thought I might explode. Clenching my jaw, I forced myself to remain calm. "And you agreed to become one of their members and to do this?"

"I had no choice."

"There is always a choice, Kenneth." I spewed the words at him, unable to contain my fury.

He leaned close, his gaze now steady. "Who are you to judge me? You made the same choice, didn't you?"

His angry words pierced me. I might not be a member of the

Council, but I was spying on my own people. "Tell me what you know about the choices I have made." I had no idea how much he'd been told about my return to Amana. Now that the Council of National Defense ruled my life, I didn't trust anyone.

He sighed. "I know that you are here to gather information on these people, and that makes you even worse than me." I expected him to appear smug. Instead, sadness shadowed his features. "I am sorry, Jutta. I know you don't want to be involved in this prying and reporting any more than I do." He hiked one shoulder. "Right or wrong, we are doing what we must in order to protect our families." The sadness I'd detected only moments ago had disappeared. "I was sent to tell you that the Council has become impatient with you. They expected you to return home the day after Christmas."

"I told them it was impossible to return so soon. I can't make them understand that there are rules here. I cannot come and go whenever it suits them. You can tell them I will come home as soon as the elders give me permission. Try to make them understand, Kenneth."

At the sound of a closing door, we both glanced at the stairs, and I held a finger to my lips. "Don't say any more about this until we are alone."

He gave me an I'm-not-a-fool look that made me realize he'd probably begun his work as an informant long before I had. I wondered if he'd already told those hateful men things about my parents and our bakery. Perhaps he was the one who'd suggested that we put glass in our bread. The very thought caused me to look at Kenneth in a different way. I must remember that he was one of them. He may not have joined voluntarily, but he was a member of their group. His first allegiance would be to his family and the Council, not to me. I couldn't expect him to plead my case with any vigor.

Mrs. Young was clutching her husband's arm as they descended the stairs. Hoping to avoid any communication with them, I turned toward Kenneth. I doubted my behavior would be successful, but I was pleasantly surprised when the Youngs walked by us without a word. Kenneth focused intently upon the couple as they exited the hotel. He twisted around and continued to watch them as they strolled past the front window.

Mouth gaping, he turned back toward me. "Is that Jonathan Young?"

My heart slammed against my chest like an anvil striking iron. "How do you know Mr. Young?"

"There was a big meeting of the American Protective League in Des Moines that members of the local and state chapters of the Council of Defense attended. The American Protective League has much more power than the local defense councils. Mr. Young was at the meeting. I wouldn't have noticed him, but he was arguing with several very important men, and I asked who he was. One of the men told me he's a lawyer in Des Moines and that—" Kenneth stopped short and clasped his palm over his mouth. "I shouldn't have told you that. Promise you won't tell."

Though my heart continued to pound an erratic beat, I didn't answer his plea. "So Mr. Young is a member of this American Protective League?"

"I can't say for sure if he is or he isn't. He was at the meeting. That's as much as I know. Promise you won't tell." Panic shone in Kenneth's dark eyes, or maybe it was fear. Probably some of each.

"But if he was at the meeting and talking to the men in charge, he must be a member, don't you think? Did you hear any of their argument?" I didn't want to end the conversation without more information.

"No! I didn't hear anything they said. Promise you'll keep this to yourself." His earlier boldness disappeared, and he wilted into the chair. "If they found out I told you, there's no telling what would happen to me."

"I am guessing they would treat you the same way they have threatened and bullied me and my parents. If they don't throw you in jail, they will force you to tell lies and betray your friends in order to benefit their so-called patriotic agenda." I shrugged one shoulder. "They are men who seem to take pleasure in intimidating others."

"Will you promise not to tell anyone what I've said about Mr. Young?"

I met his frightened eyes. "Will you promise to do everything you can to protect my parents from harm?"

He bobbed his head. "You tell me what I should say, and I promise I'll repeat each word to the Council members." For the next several minutes, I gave Kenneth instructions. When I had finished, he clasped his hands together, leaned back in the chair, and shook his head. "So you have nothing to report on *anyone*? They aren't going to be happy. Isn't there something of importance you can tell me?"

For a moment I considered the drawing, but I quickly decided I wouldn't entrust something that could prove valuable to Kenneth. "No. I want you to do exactly as I've said. Tell them I will continue to listen and watch for any signs of unpatriotic behavior and that I will be home as soon as I gain permission from the elders. You must convince them to keep my parents from going to jail, Kenneth. If they appear unmoved, tell them you're certain I'll have news that will please them when I come home."

He stood and rubbed the back of his neck. "I don't know how you expect me to convince them when you've told me nothing that will help."

"Tell them Mr. and Mrs. Young are staying at the hotel and that I think Mr. Young is a German spy." Kenneth didn't laugh. "I'm sorry, Kenneth. I shouldn't joke. I am as worried as you are about their reaction. But the people of Amana love this country, and they are doing everything possible to help the war effort. Your Council is misguided to think there is anything unpatriotic going on among these people."

"You promise you'll say nothing to anyone here or in Marengo about the meeting in Des Moines or Mr. Young?"

"I promise, Kenneth."

He buttoned his coat, and I walked alongside him to the door. "Even if I can't convince them to keep your parents out of jail?"

"You will convince them. I'm sure of it." I turned and walked back upstairs.

Late that night, after I had prepared for bed and repeated my prayers, I lay in bed and thought about my conversation with Kenneth. His accusation that we both had made the same choice pained me. I wanted to believe our decisions were different, that he was worse than I was because he'd joined the Council, but were we so different? If those men had insisted I become a member, what would I have done to save my family—and myself? Just like Kenneth, I'd been without the courage to do what I knew was right. Even now, guilt weighed heavy on my conscience. I doubted I would ever possess the faith to believe God would protect my family and I could simply refuse the demands of the Council.

Suddenly I sat up in bed. If Mr. Young was a member of the

American Protective League, had he been sent here to spy on the people of Amana? If so, why did the Council need information from me? I dropped back on my pillow. Perhaps the two organizations didn't share information. I wished I had asked Kenneth. Still, the fact that Mr. and Mrs. Young planned to remain in Amana the entire winter was reason enough to believe they were hoping to uncover some type of unpatriotic behavior within the colonies.

I shivered at the idea and tucked the Dutch blue quilt tight beneath my chin.

CHAPTER 21

Ilsa Redlich

Remaining in the kitchen the day before while Jutta had conversed with her visitor had been difficult. My mother had gone to the general store, while I busied myself in the kitchen. I hoped someone would come into the hotel. A guest in need of a room would have permitted me an opportunity to observe what was going on in the parlor, but no one had arrived.

While I mixed the ingredients for the spice cakes we would serve for dessert at the evening meal, I wondered about the man who had come to see Jutta. From the greeting they'd exchanged, I was certain she knew him—and that she considered him a friend. Although she said there had been no man who'd captured her interest back in Marengo, I wondered if she'd been completely honest with me.

From the tone of Albert's recent letter to me, I thought he'd developed an interest in her—one that could possibly lead to something beyond friendship. My mother said it was my imagination, but I knew the special looks and gestures people exhibited when there was more than a passing interest. Garon and I had used some of the same behaviors when we began to move beyond friendship. Besides, I knew Albert better than anyone, and I was positive I hadn't misinterpreted the meaning behind his words. For sure, I didn't want Albert to be hurt by Jutta.

I poured the cake batter into two large sheet pans specially made by the tinsmith for the hotel. They were larger than a regular cake pan but not as deep, so we could serve more pieces of cake from the same amount of batter. I turned at the sound of footsteps in the dining room.

Jutta greeted me as she stepped to the worktable and stared at the filled cake pan. "It is Wednesday, Ilsa. Did you make the cakes with regular flour?"

I clapped my hand across my lips. It was clear I hadn't used the rye flour. My anger flared at the error. "I forgot it was Wednesday. These silly wartime rules accomplish nothing. Do they really think the war can be won if we go without meat on Mondays and don't use wheat flour on Wednesdays? It is nothing but foolish regulations made by the same men who send our fathers and brothers to be killed in a war that has nothing to do with this country."

"Whether we think the rules are foolish or not, we cannot serve the cakes for supper, Ilsa. The minute the hotel guests take a bite, they will know we aren't following the rules of Mr. Hoover and his Food Administration. Your family could get into trouble. And it could cause problems for all of the villages." Jutta tapped the edge of the cake pan. "We must throw this out and make cakes with rye flour."

"Nein! Ever since President Wilson appointed this Mr. Hoover and his Food Administration, we are expected to live by more and more silly rules. I will not waste. How is that helping to win the war?" I grabbed the pan and shoved it into the oven. "To waste food helps no more than saying a blood sausage is a 'victory sausage' or having children sing about 'patriotic potatoes.' How can a potato be patriotic?"

Although I could see the concern in Jutta's eyes, she giggled at my remark.

"We may think it is silly, but there are many people who are convinced by such methods. My mother told me that everyone in Marengo goes to hear those Minutemen speeches at the moving-picture theater."

I stared at her in disbelief. "Your Mutter and Vater attend?" We'd heard talk of the speeches and some of the hateful remarks being made against anyone of German heritage. I didn't know what surprised me more—that they would go to see a moving picture or they would listen to the half-truths of those speeches.

"Sometimes you must do things in order to maintain peace, Ilsa. My parents have a business that will be ruined if they don't comply with what is expected of them. They would be viewed as German sympathizers if they did not attend." Jutta leaned across the worktable. "And you must think the same way, Ilsa. We don't know anything about the people who take their meals in the hotel dining room. To disobey the rules is asking for trouble, and your family could be reported as German sympathizers. You can't risk that possibility."

I wanted to stand my ground and say such a thing would not happen, but I knew she was correct. "Then we will make something else for dessert tonight, but we will save this for tomorrow night." I couldn't let my stubborn nature cause trouble for everyone. "We can mix oats with butter, molasses, and sugar and spread it over spiced apple slices." While I gathered the oats and other ingredients, Jutta lifted a large crock from the shelf.

"So tell me about your visitor from yesterday," I said. "Who is he?" This was our first opportunity to speak privately since the day before.

Jutta didn't look at me. Instead, she fixed her gaze on the oats she was pouring into a large tin measuring cup. "His name is Kenneth Reeves. His family delivers flour to our bakery in Marengo, and he was passing through Amana. From my parents he learned I was here, so he decided to stop and say hello." She poured the oats into the large mixing bowl and measured the sugar.

After Jutta's free-flowing advice only a short time ago, her current response seemed much more guarded. It didn't make sense that a deliveryman would make a special effort to stop and visit with her. I couldn't imagine Albert or Garon doing such a thing. Then again, men on the outside were much different—at least that's what I'd observed among the salesmen who stayed at the hotel. "Where was this Mr. Reeves going?"

"Going?" She appeared startled by my simple question. "I'm not sure. I didn't think to ask."

Her reply surprised me. That was the first thing I would have asked any unexpected visitor. "He had news from Marengo?"

"Not much. He said that business at the bakery isn't as good right now, but it had declined before I left, too. Some people don't want to buy from a bakery owned by people of German heritage." She shrugged. "To try and change their minds is about impossible. Especially with all the anti-German banners and posters in every store window. Even the children who used to stop by the bakery for a free piece of warm bread on their way to school now call us Huns. When that first started, it brought tears to my father's eyes." She straightened her shoulders and headed toward the door. "I'll go to the cellar and get some apples."

"Better take a bowl with you."

She shook her head and flapped the skirt of her apron. "I can carry them in here."

I didn't argue, but I thought a bowl would be easier. Jutta had been gone only moments when I heard Garon talking outside the back door. I peeked out the kitchen window and saw him deep in conversation with Jutta. He was leaning close, and they appeared to be whispering. He patted her arm in a familiar manner before she finally opened the cellar doors and disappeared from sight. My stomach flip-flopped, and I thought I might be ill. Did Jutta have feelings for Garon? Even more important, did Garon have feelings for Jutta? At the sound of his knock on the back door, I returned to the worktable and called for him to come in.

"You let all those who knock enter without first looking to see who is there? What if I was a hobo in search of a free meal?" His eyes twinkled with mischief, and a smile split his face.

"I don't have any need to worry about hobos in the middle of winter. They won't arrive until warmer weather." I continued to mix the crumbly mixture that would top the apples.

"Smells gut in here." He lifted his nose and sniffed. "Spice cake?"

"Ja, but we won't serve it until tomorrow." I explained my mistake. "Jutta thought I should throw them away, but I refused. Our people have never been wasteful, and I would rather break the rules than throw gut food in the garbage." I arched my brows, waiting to hear if he would support my behavior.

"If you decide you must heed Jutta's advice, you must first tell me." His tone had changed from playful to serious.

His stern words of caution surprised me. "Why?"

"Because I will eat the cakes to hide the evidence." His rumbling laughter filled the kitchen, and I slapped his arm.

"That was not funny, Garon. You frightened me with your harsh warning."

He leaned forward and pressed a kiss on my cheek. "I am sorry if I frightened you. I was only playing."

I tightened my lips into what I hoped looked like an angry scowl. "Well, it wasn't funny." I nodded toward the window. "I see you and Jutta now share secrets."

His brows lowered, and he appeared confused. "You are referring to me talking to her by the cellar doors?"

"Ja, I am referring to you talking to her by the cellar doors." I mimicked his words and tone.

He grinned. "You are jealous." Leaning forward until he was looking into my face, he lightly pinched my cheek. "You are, aren't you?"

His delight at my jealousy annoyed me. I wished I hadn't said a word, yet I wanted to know why he was whispering with her. "What if I am? Is it wrong for me to be worried when I see the man I am to marry secretly sharing words with another woman and patting her arm? What if you saw me behaving in such a manner with Theo or Werner? What would you think of that?"

"I would know you were being kind to two fellows who don't have a chance of winning your heart."

He stepped behind me and wrapped his arms around my waist while I tried to continue working. When he leaned down and kissed my neck, I dropped the mixing spoon onto the counter and pushed him with my elbow. "Stop, Garon. What if someone would see you?"

"No one will see. There is no one here." His breath tickled my neck.

Once again I told him to move, but I didn't want him to stop. Instead, I wanted him to remain close and continue reassuring me that he loved only me. My heart fluttered and my pulse quickened as he grasped my shoulders and turned me toward him. After lifting my chin with his index finger, he lowered his head, and I leaned into the warmth of his embrace. My jealous thoughts evaporated like a mist as he captured my lips in a warm and tender kiss.

At the heavy thud of the cellar doors, I pushed Garon backward. "That will be Jutta."

"I don't think she will be surprised to know that we steal a kiss from time to time." He winked and moved closer, but I placed my palm against his chest to hold him at bay. Garon continued to move toward me, and I placed my other hand on his chest and pushed back.

Jutta stopped short when she entered the kitchen with her apron full of apples. I was certain we made quite a sight. Me, with both hands against Garon's chest while he leaned forward, pushing against my efforts. I withdrew my hands and took a backward step. Garon lurched forward and was forced to catch himself against the worktable to avoid dropping to his knees. I stifled a giggle and glanced at Jutta. "We were having a discussion, but I think Garon lost his balance."

Moving farther into the kitchen, Jutta placed the apples on the worktable and grinned. "It looks like it could have been a dangerous conversation."

Since Garon hadn't yet answered me, I decided it best to address the question to both of them. "I asked Garon what you and he were discussing before he came into the kitchen."

Jutta glanced at Garon. "I asked him about the telegrams he sends for Mr. Young. I was curious why a man who owns a business in Des Moines would need to send telegrams from Amana. I was also curious about what they said and who he was sending them to."

Her answer surprised me. Of all the things I could have imagined, asking about Mr. Young and his telegrams hadn't been one of them. "Why do you care about the telegrams?"

She shrugged her shoulders. "I think both Mr. and Mrs. Young are rather odd, and I was being . . . nosy."

I giggled. "You are becoming more and more like me, Jutta. Garon accuses me of being the nosy type."

Garon shook his head. "Only a few times have I said you are nosy."

"Ja, a few too many, I think." After flashing him a grin, I turned back to Jutta. "And what did you find out about the telegrams?"

Garon pushed away from the table. "I am standing right here. I can tell you what I said."

"You didn't tell me when I asked you earlier, so I thought it would be easier to get an answer from Jutta."

Jutta picked up a knife and began to peel one of the apples. "He said he didn't know what they said. None of them made any sense, and they were sent to different places, mostly on the East Coast. Right, Garon?"

He gave one firm nod. "You see? It was nothing of interest or importance."

I nudged Garon with my elbow. "How could you send telegrams if you didn't know what messages they contained? That makes no sense."

He shook his head. "I could *read* them, but they were just a bunch of words that didn't create real sentences."

"Like what? I don't understand."

Garon yanked his wool cap from his pocket. "I didn't under-stand, either. That's what I'm trying to tell you, Ilsa. It would be words like 'forty think muscle metal,' or something like that—just gibberish that doesn't mean a thing."

"Maybe it has to do with his legal cases, and he doesn't want anyone to know. That's possible, isn't it, Jutta?"

Jutta picked up the bowl of apple peelings. "I've never had anything to do with lawyers or the things they need to keep pri-vate. But I do think the Youngs are a strange couple who exhibit peculiar behaviors. And I do wish they would leave Amana."

Garon tapped his forehead. "Sometimes I think women have more imagination than men." He grinned. "Either that or you just have too much time to sit around and think, while men must always be working." With a loud chuckle, he took several long strides toward the back door while ducking his head.

"You had better run, Garon Drucker." I picked up one of the apples and waved it overhead. "Best to remember that I can hit a target when I want to."

His snorting laughter rang in the crisp winter air as he loped across the backyard.

The bell over the front door jangled, and Jutta swiped her hands down the front of her apron. "You finish the dessert. I'll go see who it is."

Moments later she returned with a grim look on her face. "It was Mr. Young. He was looking for Garon. He has another telegram to send."

A chill that was colder than an Iowa snowstorm raced down my spine. Any other day, Jutta's comment wouldn't have caused me concern, but today's conversation made me wonder if there was more to Mr. Young and his telegrams than either Garon or I imagined.

CHAPTER 22

Jutta Schmitt

For more than a week, my mind had been turned upside down in a jumble of confusion. I didn't know whom to trust or what to believe. I'd considered everything Garon had told me about the telegrams and Mr. Young, and I'd done my best to piece together Ilsa's comments and behavior. I wanted to believe they were both unaware of the many possibilities those telegrams presented. And then there was the drawing I'd found from Ilsa's pocket. Was she as innocent as she pretended, or were she and Garon somehow working with Mr. Young? The idea seemed impossible, yet this war had done strange things to people. I was living proof of that.

Several letters from Albert had already arrived, and I was pleased to read that one of the new arrivals assigned to the infirmary had been especially kind to him. Though not a pacifist, the new arrival exhibited God's love to Albert. And just as Albert had done with me, he'd been quick to assume the best of this Private James Higgins. I hoped he hadn't misplaced his trust in the young man.

Albert's letters told of long hours working in the pneumonia ward, and I wondered if he'd considered he might contract the illness from one of the patients. If so, he didn't mention such fear, only how much the men had suffered. I hadn't failed to note the shakiness of his script when he'd written that four young men had died several days earlier, and it had taken great effort on his part to return to the infirmary the following morning.

In his most recent letter, he'd written that he was learning a great deal while aiding the doctors. He didn't complain about changing bed linens or mopping floors, but he did reveal that he disliked moving the bodies of dead soldiers from the ward. *Even before they could set foot outside the country, their parents receive word of their deaths. There is nothing pleasant about watching young men die,* he'd written. Then he had apologized for the somber tone of the letter and said he was thankful he could confide in me. Those words caused a stab of remorse in my heart, for I wasn't worthy of Albert's trust.

As I washed my face and recited my morning prayers, I added a prayer that I wouldn't be compelled to betray Albert. My gaze settled on the letter I'd been writing to him. There wouldn't be time to finish it this morning. I buttoned the bodice of my dress and tucked the stationery into the top drawer of my chest before I hurried from the room.

Both Ilsa and Sister Marta were already at work in the kitchen. "I'm sorry I am so late. I couldn't get to sleep last night, and then I didn't hear the morning bell." I lifted my apron from the hook and dropped it over my head.

The fat sizzled and popped as Sister Marta emptied a bowl of sliced potatoes into two large iron skillets. "No need for apologies. Sometimes we all need an extra few minutes of sleep." She glanced in my direction and smiled. "I am sure you were excited about your trip home today."

"Yes. I am eager to see my parents." My impatience to return home had increased with each passing day.

Ilsa sliced the bread that had been delivered by the bakery wagon only a short time ago. "Your Vater will meet you at the train station?"

"Or perhaps my mother."

As soon as the elders had sent word I could return to Marengo for a weekend visit, I had written to my parents, but I hadn't received a letter in return. However, my mother had met me at the station the last time I'd gone home, and I knew from her earlier letters that they were both eager for another visit from me. I had hoped the elders would permit me to remain longer than the weekend, but I didn't ask for additional time. I didn't want to give them cause to think I was unhappy living here, for other than missing my parents and having to spy on the Amana residents, I was content in this peaceful village.

I was somewhat apprehensive to return home, because I was certain the bullies would expect me to bring information they could use against the people of Amana. Yet, even if I could endure handing over the notes I had maintained, I doubted they'd be incriminating enough to suit the men.

Last night I'd decided that before I departed, I was going to ask Ilsa about the drawing I'd found in her apron pocket. I didn't plan to report her to the Iowa Council of National Defense, but I hoped she would give me a bit of information that would appease them. Still, I would need to be careful, for there was no telling what reaction my questions would elicit.

Once we'd completed breakfast, Ilsa and I gathered our cleaning supplies. At the top of the stairs, she walked to the right and I turned to the left. I had nearly completed my duties in the second room before I finally gathered enough courage to speak to her. Propping my broom in the doorway, I walked down the hallway and was surprised to see the Youngs' door ajar. Prior to their departure the day before, they'd repeated their instructions to refrain from entering the room during their absence. Careful to keep my breathing shallow, I tiptoed the remaining distance to their doorway and peeked through the opening.

Ilsa stood facing the table near the windows. I could hear the rustle of paper, and my mind raced with a multitude of thoughts. Was she working in concert with the Youngs on some sort of government project? Was she a spy for the American Protective League or Council of National Defense? Both ideas were preposterous, yet there was the picture I'd found. Why else would she be interested in the Youngs' belongings? After one look at the scene before me, I decided this was not the time to speak with Ilsa about the drawing.

Holding my breath, I backed from the doorway and made a slow turn. The floorboard creaked beneath my right foot, and my stomach instantly clenched in a tight knot. Eyes wide, Ilsa swung around, and we locked eyes. "What are you doing?" My voice quivered as I asked the question.

She barreled across the room, grabbed the door, and swung it wide. "You're supposed to be cleaning down the hall. Why are you standing here spying on me?"

My jaw dropped, and I took a backward step, surprised by

her accusation. "I wasn't spying on you, Ilsa. There was something I wanted to ask you before I left for Marengo, and when I came down the hall, I noticed the Youngs' door was open. I was going to pull it closed, but I saw you inside going through their papers."

"I wasn't going through their papers." She jutted her head forward and planted her hands on her hips.

I was astonished that she would tell me an outright lie. Surely she knew that I'd seen what she was doing. I considered letting her lie stand but quickly decided against it. What was the worst that could happen? She couldn't tell her parents I'd been spying on her when she'd been in the Youngs' room. They knew she wasn't supposed to be in there. It would be best to simply confront her with the truth.

"You *were* going through their papers, Ilsa. I saw you. I don't know why, but you must have some reason." I reached into my pocket and removed the drawing. "And I'm sure there is also a good reason why you had this in your apron."

She reached for the drawing, but I withdrew my hand before she could retrieve it. "Did you take this from Mr. Young's papers?"

She bowed her head. "Ja. I was changing the bed, and I saw it under the mattress. I had planned to ask Albert if he'd ever seen such a weapon at Camp Pike or if he knew why Mr. Young would have such a drawing."

"What did Albert tell you?"

She shook her head. "I lost the drawing before I could ask him. I've been looking all over since I discovered it was missing. I was afraid it had dropped from my apron and Mr. or Mrs. Young found it. How long have you had it?" Concern shadowed her eyes and added a hint of gray to the usual pale, powdery blue shade.

"While Albert was still here for his Christmas visit."

A frown creased her forehead. "And you waited all this time to ask me about it?"

"There never seemed to be a good time to discuss it with you." I didn't add that I still remained uncertain I'd made the right decision. Anger flashed in Ilsa's eyes, and I realized it would be unwise to say I feared trusting her. I inhaled a ragged breath. "Last night I decided I should talk to you about the drawing before I went home for my visit."

Ilsa pointed to the paper. "I am thinking I should return it."

"Do you believe that is wise? If they know it has been taken and it reappears during their absence, they will know one of us has been going through their belongings." I nodded toward the table. "What else did you find?"

She studied me with a worried look. Either she wasn't sure she could trust me or she was embarrassed to admit she'd been snooping. Finally she sighed. "You have said you think Mr. and Mrs. Young are an odd couple, ja?"

I nodded. "They act very strange."

Ilsa motioned me into the bedroom. "Look at these papers. All of them about the war and different kinds of weapons. And look at this." She pulled a map of Europe from beneath one stack of papers and slapped it on top of the pile. A variety of marks had been placed on towns and cities throughout Germany and the surrounding European countries. Another map of the United States had marks placed on towns, as well—most of them along the East and West coasts. "What do you think all of this means?"

"I'm not sure. With the maps and newspapers, it could mean

they want to learn about the progress the Allies are making with the war, but I don't know about the weapons and those papers with all the figures written on them. It is very strange." A lump the size of a watermelon settled in my stomach. I was now certain that Mr. Young was gathering information for the American Protective League and was likely one of their most important members. Only a man with influence and power could have so many vital documents.

That thought alone was enough to make me take a backward step. I clasped a hand to my midsection. "You must be careful to put everything back exactly as you found it, Ilsa. If they discover anything disturbed, there could be trouble."

"You worry too much, Jutta. I don't think they will recall exactly how they left the papers on the table. And what trouble can they cause?" Ilsa shoved the papers back onto the table in a disorderly fashion. "If they move out of the hotel, it will be better for all of us. They make even Mutter uncomfortable. And for sure there would be delight at the quilting frame if Mutter announced Mrs. Young had departed for gut."

"Still, you should try to get everything back in proper order. I've heard stories about members of the Iowa Council of National Defense and American Protective League causing trouble for people they think aren't patriotic. I've wondered if Mr. Young is a part of that group and if he is here to spy on our people."

Ilsa gasped and her eyes opened as wide as white china saucers. "But these papers have nothing to do with us." She rifled through one of the stacks. "I don't see one thing about any of our people. Besides, they have no power over any of us who live in the colonies."

From what I'd seen of those insolent bullies, I was certain they wouldn't give a second thought to wreaking havoc in Amana or anywhere else. None that I'd met could be considered merciful. "Just because there isn't anything in this room that mentions the colonies or gives a list of names doesn't mean they aren't seeking information against us."

"For sure, I think they are strange people who are overly interested in the war, but I don't think you are right about them. What is there to tell about our people except that we are patriotic and do our best to help with the war effort?"

Without divulging my own particular problems with the Iowa Council of National Defense, I'd done all I could to warn Ilsa. I wanted to tell her about these people who made up lies against good citizens in order to make themselves appear more patriotic or to increase their stature within their frightening group, but I wasn't ready to answer the questions she might ask about how I'd gained such knowledge.

"What about that drawing? Do you plan to keep it or give it back to me?" Ilsa pointed to the paper I still held in my hand.

"Why don't I burn it? Then there will be no evidence to prove that you took it." I held my breath and hoped she would agree. If the men in Marengo couldn't be appeased any other way, the drawing might prove beneficial. I wasn't certain how I could use it without implicating the Youngs or Ilsa, but if that drawing was the only way I could keep my parents out of jail, I'd be forced to use it.

"Ja. I think that is best, too." Ilsa made one final attempt to straighten the papers. We backed out of the room while giving it one final assessment. "I will miss you while you're in Marengo, but I hope you find your parents well."

"Thank you, Ilsa." I brushed a quick kiss on her cheek. "I will miss you, as well." I gestured toward the far end of the hall. "I'd better hurry and finish my cleaning, or I won't be done before time to leave."

"Don't worry, I'll finish for you. You should go and get ready." She smiled and I wondered how I could have ever thought Ilsa wasn't a true friend.

Guilt nagged me once I departed for Marengo. Especially when I remembered Ilsa's reminder to burn the drawing that was now tucked into my pocket. While I stared at the fallow fields awaiting the warmth of spring and the cut of a plow, I prayed I wouldn't need to use that drawing. To sacrifice Ilsa for the safety of my parents wasn't a choice I wanted to make.

Maybe I could make up a story about the drawing, but if Mr. Young was an important member of the League, he would surely be informed of any suspected traitors. That thought was enough for me to imagine his dark, beady eyes boring into me as he reviewed the drawing. My hands trembled, and I patted the pocket of my skirt to make certain the paper was still there.

During the rest of my short journey, I prayed the bullies would not appear, that my parents would say there had been a misunderstanding among the members of the Iowa Council of National Defense and I could return home, that the war had ended and I could once again live without fear. I knew the war would not end before I arrived home, but I believed there was a strong possibility God would keep those intimidating thugs away from our door—if not for me, then to protect the people of Amana from my possible betrayal.

As I stepped down from the train in Marengo, excitement mounted at the thought of seeing my mother and father. I glanced about the small train depot, surprised that I didn't see either of them. With my shoes tapping on the tile floor, I hurried through the compact train station and out the front door. A bright winter sun shone on the layer of snow that blanketed the countryside. I cupped one hand above my eyes and continued to search for my parents. Perhaps they'd been delayed with extra bread orders, but I couldn't deny the sense of disappointment that washed over me. What had my mother said the last time I'd come home? To return home without someone to greet you with a hug and a kiss would be very sad? Today I knew she had spoken the truth, but I did my best to push aside any feelings of unhappiness. The bakery wasn't far. The walk wouldn't take long. Besides, I needed more time to think.

I waved and spoke to several customers I saw along the way, but each one turned away as if I were invisible. Their behavior caused me to pick up my pace. Mother had written that she and Father seldom left home. I now understood why. I'd been there only a few minutes, and already I wanted to hide inside the bakery.

Exhaling a cleansing breath as I rounded the final corner, I again shaded my eyes against the blinding snow in order to gain a better view of the bakery. In truth, I had hoped to capture a glimpse of my mother or father, but the sight that greeted me wasn't of my parents. I clapped a hand across my mouth and blinked hard at the sight. The bakery was streaked with red and black paint. Heart pounding, I broke into a run. A silent scream lodged in my throat as I drew closer and saw the shattered front window and the ugly words spelled out with the red and black paint. Shards of broken glass clung to the wooden window frame like the jagged teeth of a wild animal still seeking its prey. From the street I could see destruction inside.

Hands trembling, I pushed open the door. My feet crunched

on a mixture of broken glass and snow that had drifted through the unprotected window. I raced up the back stairs, shouting for my mother and father. Though I wanted to believe I would find them sitting in the parlor drinking a cup of coffee, my heart told me they wouldn't be there.

With a shove of my hip, I pushed open the door at the top of the steps and was greeted by silence. Like the bakery, the rooms had been ransacked. Drawers had been pulled from the chest and dumped on the floor, belongings from the wooden chest had been tossed about, dishes lay broken on the floor, and even the sofa and chairs were slit open.

The door to my parents' bedroom was closed. I tapped on the door out of habit—I had never entered their room without permission. Though I didn't expect an answer, I waited a brief moment before I turned the knob and opened the door. The same destruction confronted me there. Tears rolled down my cheeks when I saw the chest my grandparents had brought from Germany now reduced to a pile of wood, good for nothing but kindling.

The familiar sound of bells from Mr. Reeves' flour wagon sent me rushing to the upstairs window. Kenneth and his father weren't far from the bakery. In my haste to speak to them, I tripped on a piece of wood in the parlor. Had I not grabbed hold of the banister, I would have tumbled headfirst down the steps, but I didn't permit the near accident to slow me down.

Running down the steps and jumping over the wreckage in the bakery, I ran out the front door and chased after the wagon. "Kenneth! Mr. Reeves!" They both turned on the wagon seat. My skirt whipped around my legs as I raced after the wagon. "Wait! I need to speak with you."

The horses slowed, though they didn't come to a halt. I panted for breath as I trotted alongside the moving wagon. "My parents. Are they in jail? Do you know what happened?"

Mr. Reeves wagged his head. "Nope. Not sure 'bout nothing, Jutta. Don't know what happened to your folks, but the store was all tore up when we come by here maybe 'bout a week or so ago." He rubbed his jaw. "You recall exactly when it was, Kenneth?"

Kenneth shook his head. "No, not for certain. Sure sorry about all that damage, Jutta. Looks like the bakery is pretty well ruined."

"Our rooms upstairs are no better. They destroyed all our furniture, but I can't find any sign of my parents. Have you heard anything about where they might be? Did those men come and lock them up in jail? You must know something."

Kenneth nudged his father. Still holding the reins in his hand, Mr. Reeves leaned forward and rested his arms across his knees. The horses slowed to a near stop. "I heard your folks run off somewhere after a visit from some members of the Council a few weeks ago. All that damage happened after they disappeared. Guess it was their way of getting back at your folks for taking off like that."

"But you're sure they're not in jail?"

Mr. Reeves tucked his head against the cold wind that whipped down the street. "They ain't in jail around here. If you're smart, you'll head back to the Amana Colonies before they find out you're in town. Word has it that your folks are probably hiding out in the colonies, and I think you'll be the one in jail if the Council leaders get hold of ya."

Little wonder no one had acknowledged me a short time ago. What if one of those people had sent word to the Council leaders? Someone would soon arrive at the bakery. "Thank you for speaking to me, Mr. Reeves. You can tell your defense group that I have seen nothing of my parents, and I know they are not in the Amanas."

Mr. Reeves frowned. "It isn't *my* defense group, Jutta. Like Kenneth told you, we all have to take care of ourselves however we can. Your folks are good people, and I sure don't like what happened at the bakery, but I had to join. I couldn't take a chance on losing my business. I have a family to support."

How could I fault Mr. Reeves? I'd been trying to protect my parents and our bakery by moving to Amana. But my move hadn't saved my family. I lifted my arm in a halfhearted wave. "Thank you for talking to me. Please tell those men that my parents aren't in the colonies."

He pulled his wool hat down on his head. "You best get on out of town as soon as you can."

I heeded his words and ran back to the bakery, picked up my small bag, and hurried to the train station. "When is the next train to South Amana?"

The clerk pointed to the train schedule. "Be about an hour. You want a ticket?"

I removed the coins the elders had given me for my ticket and shoved them across the counter.

"Got any baggage?"

"Just this, but I will carry it with me." I lifted my small bag high enough for him to see before taking a seat on one of the benches that faced the tracks.

It would be too dangerous to go back to the bakery. In truth, it was probably dangerous sitting in the train station. If one of those thugs spotted me, they probably wouldn't care if I was at the bakery or sitting in the train station. They'd haul me off to ply me with questions and toss me in jail when they'd finished.

Perhaps the people milling about the train station would provide cover.

I kept my head bowed and refrained from looking around but knew my clothes would alert anyone who entered the station that I was from the colonies. Everyone in Marengo knew the plain clothing and calico prints worn by the Amana women, although the dark prints wouldn't identify us for much longer. The last shipment of necessary dyes had been delivered to Baltimore in the summer of 1916 on the *Deutschland*, a German submarine that had run the British blockade to make the scheduled delivery. However, there would be no more products arriving from Germany. Unless something unexpected should happen, the calico mill would be another casualty of the war.

When I heard the hoot of the whistle and the rumble of the approaching train, I breathed more easily. Still, I wouldn't feel completely safe until I was away from Marengo. I pushed to my feet, eager to board the train. In spite of the cold, I decided to go outside, where I could more easily hide from view.

I'd taken only a step when I felt strong fingers clasp my shoulder. My stomach lurched as I twisted around and came face-to-face with Kenneth Reeves. Tears of relief pooled in my eyes, and I lifted my hand to my lips. "I thought you were one of those bullies who came to our store," I whispered through my trembling fingers.

Kenneth glanced over his shoulder. "One of the leaders of the Defense Council sent me. They saw you outside the bakery. He said to tell you that if your parents are in the Amanas, it will mean trouble for all of them, and it would be better if they came back to Marengo." He sighed. "You will be closely watched, Jutta, so don't attempt to go and see them."

I motioned for Kenneth to follow me outside. The noise of

the hissing train mixed with the voices of disembarking passengers to create a clamor that masked our conversation. With a careful step, I turned and headed for the door, relieved when I heard him follow after me. He came alongside as we cleared the doorway and pointed to an inset along the side of the brick building.

"How can I go and see them when I have no idea where they are?"

He stood facing me, using his back to block the gusting wind. "You must not take this matter lightly, Jutta. The leaders of the Council are very angry. They expected you to provide information that could be used to prove the people of Amana support Germany in the war. They know that without jail as a threat to your parents, you aren't going to help them."

"Even if my parents were still in Marengo, I couldn't tell those men from your Council anything they want to hear. They want to label the people of Amana as unpatriotic and punish them because they are conscientious objectors, but the colonists have done a great deal to support the war effort."

"I'm not defending the actions of the Council or the American Protective League, but—"

I held up my hand to stop him. He might not be defending them, but he was their mouthpiece. "You can remind the Council of the many black walnut and larch trees that the Amana people willingly cut from their land to make rifles and flagpoles—trees they planted when they first arrived in Iowa. You can remind them of their purchases of war bonds. You can remind them how Amanans constantly exceed the Red Cross quotas. Would they do such things if they hoped for Germany to win the war?"

I looked up into Kenneth's eyes. "Can't you see that you

have taken up with weak men who use ugly schemes to make themselves appear brave patriots? If they are so brave, why don't they go and fight in the war and leave us alone? Tell them I asked you these questions, Kenneth."

He shook his head. "It would only cause more trouble for you."

"Ha!" I whipped my hand through the air. "How can I have any more trouble? Our home and our bakery have been destroyed, and I have no idea if my parents are even alive. What more can these men do to me?" I forced back the tears that threatened to spill down my cheeks.

He hiked one shoulder. "Maybe nothing to you, but what if they started a fire in one of the villages? Do you want your angry words to push them toward more destruction?"

The thought caused me to shudder. "Nein," I whispered, slipping back to the German language that had once again become so familiar to me.

"And you shouldn't speak German, Jutta—only English."

The conductor took his place alongside one of the passenger cars, and I grasped Kenneth's arm. I decided I would make one final attempt to get information from him. "Isn't Mr. Young providing plenty of details about our people to the Council? I think it should be enough to have one of their members living in our hotel."

Kenneth paled at the mention of Mr. Young. "You promised you wouldn't mention I told you about him."

"I have kept my word."

The conductor shouted the familiar "All aboard," and Kenneth stepped to one side. "You should get on the train."

"You will ask them about Mr. Young?"

"I can't. It would cause them to ask too many questions. I

don't want to become more involved than I already am. I don't like being the one they send to talk to you, but I have no choice." He shoved his hands into his coat pockets. "Be careful, Jutta. You never know who is watching or listening."

His warning was as cold as the icy wind that swept across the wooden platform.

CHAPTER 23

Only when I was on the train did I allow myself to think about all that had happened in the short time since I'd left South Amana. I closed my eyes and pictured the destruction I'd witnessed in our bakery and apartment. I prayed in earnest that my parents were safe and the Council hadn't taken them to a jail in some distant town. I wanted to believe Kenneth and his father had spoken the truth—that my parents had fled before the destruction occurred. But how could I completely trust them? Like everyone else, they were trying to protect their own family and business—and they weren't German.

As I settled against the leather seat, I understood why I hadn't received a letter from my parents recently. Either they were in jail or they'd found a hiding place. But where would they go, and who would welcome them? I tried to think of anyone who would give them shelter. I was certain there was no one in Marengo.

Besides, the risk would be too great to remain there. The likely place would be the Amanas, but I was sure they wouldn't seek refuge among the colonists.

Before I had returned to Amana, my father mentioned money he had saved, and he'd encouraged me to purchase a train ticket to Chicago or New York. Could my parents have boarded a train to some distant city without sending word to me? To think of them doing such a thing seemed impossible, yet I could think of no one who would risk offering them shelter. Fear and sadness now pervaded my thoughts like an unwelcome storm. I folded my arms tight across my waist. Never had I felt so alone in all my life.

What had this war done to everyone? Spying on one another and reporting falsehoods to gain favor and be lauded a "patriot" had spread through the country like an epidemic. And I was a part of it. Like so many others, I had become embroiled in the heinous activity. But when I forgot my own involvement, I was repulsed by the very idea that friends and neighbors would turn against each other. I should go before the elders and admit my lies and ask forgiveness. I should beg them to let me remain in the village, but the thought of admitting I had been less than truthful when I asked to return to Amana was far too daunting.

What would I do if they asked me to leave? I couldn't return to Marengo. And there was no place else to call home. For now, my decision was clear. I must remain silent.

I started when a woman leaned across the aisle and touched my arm. "Excuse me, do you live in the Amana Colonies?"

Kenneth's warning rang in my ears. I nodded my head, afraid I might slip and say *ja*. No doubt *ja* wouldn't be considered English.

The woman smiled. "You live in Homestead?"

I shook my head. "No. South Amana."

"I'm going to Homestead." She folded her hands in her lap. "I do enjoy shopping at the general store. They have the best selection of lace I've ever seen. My husband says I shouldn't be worried about lace when the country is at war, but I don't see how it helps the war effort if I look dowdy. Don't you agree?"

I wanted to tell her she was asking the wrong person, for our people never adorned their dresses with lace and frills. Instead, I decided a neutral yet tactful answer would be best. "I am sorry, but I don't know much about adding lace to dresses or how to best help the war effort. But I do agree that the Homestead store has a lovely selection."

A slight blush colored the woman's cheeks. "I forgot that you folks never wear any of the lace you sell in the store." She turned in her seat, her feet in the aisle as she leaned even closer. "Isn't that difficult? To see all those beautiful fabrics and laces and yet wear such plain clothing yourself?" As soon as she'd uttered the words, she covered her lips with her fingers. "Oh, I do hope I didn't insult you. You look perfectly lovely in your plain dress, I just . . ."

"You did not offend me." I smiled to assure her. "Our people are quite content to wear unadorned clothing, but we are very thankful for those who purchase such goods from our stores." I hoped my answer would be enough to halt any further questions.

"Some of my friends won't shop in the Amanas anymore. They're angry because your men won't go and fight in the war. They say it's unpatriotic."

She obviously thought her comment might come as a surprise. As if we didn't know that there were both people and businesses that had discontinued purchasing from the colonies. When I didn't respond, the woman continued to stare at me. Was she one of those people Kenneth had mentioned? I didn't doubt the Council had enlisted women to spy on their neighbors. They had manipulated me easily enough. I brushed my hand down my dress and felt the bulge of paper in my pocket. I must keep my promise to Ilsa and burn the drawing.

The woman cleared her throat. "What do you think about your men refusing to fight?"

"If you have questions about our faith, you should speak to one of our leaders in Homestead. If you ask at the general store, someone can direct you to one of the elders."

"That won't be necessary. I'm more interested in purchasing some beautiful lace than talking about religion with one of your elders." She turned and leaned back in her seat. For the rest of the journey, she remained completely silent.

I was thankful for the quiet, but her questions had set me on edge. Was she one of those spies working for the Council or the American Protective League? Could I trust anything she'd said? I disliked the overwhelming feeling of distrust. Would I feel this way for the remainder of my life? Always uncertain if I could trust what others said or did? I prayed not.

"South Amana!" The conductor shouted the name of the village several times as he strode down the narrow aisle.

The train lurched and hissed before it finally came to a halt in front of the familiar train station. The woman smiled and bid me good-bye, but I worried she might sneak off the train after I'd passed through the station. Until the war began, I'd never considered myself a suspicious person, but now I'd become wary of everyone who spoke to me. I didn't like the feeling.

Holding my woolen cape tight against the brisk cold wind,

I clasped the travel case with my free hand and stepped off the train. As I approached the station, I glanced over my shoulder at the hissing train and caught sight of the woman still seated on the train. My worries had been unfounded, and for that I was grateful.

"Jutta! I am surprised to see you back so soon." Garon stood behind the counter near the telegraph equipment. I wondered if he was sending another telegram for Mr. Young, for he usually wasn't at the train station after supper. My stomach growled at the thought of food. Perhaps there would be some leftovers at the hotel. He stepped from behind the counter and drew near. "Something is wrong?"

"Yes. Very wrong. My parents are missing."

His jaw dropped and disbelief shone in his eyes. "How is that possible? Could no one tell you where they are?" He reached to take my bag. "Perhaps they've gone to visit relatives. Did you write for them to expect you?"

"They haven't gone to visit relatives. We have no relatives in this country, and I don't think they sailed for Germany." I gave him a halfhearted smile as weariness settled across my shoulders like a heavy weight. I didn't have the strength to relate the details twice. As if he understood, he grasped my elbow. "Come. I will take you back to the hotel so you can talk to Ilsa's parents."

I glanced over my shoulder as he helped me up into the buggy. "You were sending another telegram for Mr. Young?"

"Ja. I told him I didn't have much time before prayer service, but he insisted it needed to be sent right away."

"Maybe he should learn to tap out the telegrams himself."

"Brother Milton says that with what Mr. Young pays to send

all these telegrams, the village can afford to purchase new equipment in no time."

"It would seem that is quite true."

Garon chuckled. "Brother Milton exaggerates. It's just that Mr. Young sends more telegrams than any other person who has visited the colonies." He grasped the reins and gave them a flip. "Of course most people don't stay at the hotel for so long, either."

"But I thought Ilsa said there were families who stayed for most of the summer."

"You're right—there are a few—but they write letters instead of sending telegrams, so I don't see them much. I'd forgotten."

We were silent for the remainder of the short distance to the hotel. I wanted to ask Garon what the telegram said, but if it was like the others, it didn't matter. Even if he told me, it would make no sense.

He offered his hand and assisted me down from the buggy before grabbing my case. When I reached to take it from him, he shook his head. "I want to go in and hear what happened." He hesitated a moment. "If you have no objection."

"No. You are welcome to hear everything I know, though there is much that I can't answer."

"Jutta! What are you doing back so soon?" Ilsa scurried from the dining room, where she'd been clearing the dishes, and wrapped me in a warm embrace. "This is a gut surprise."

I slipped my cloak from my shoulders. "No, not so good."

Sister Marta stood framed in the doorway between the kitchen and dining room with a look of worry in her eyes. "You are pale, Jutta." She stepped forward and placed her hand to my forehead.

"No fever." She took my cloak and handed it to Ilsa. "Hang this on the peg." Taking my hand, she led me to one of the dining room chairs. "Come and sit down over here. I will fix a cup of tea. Have you eaten supper?"

"I would be grateful for a cup of tea. I will eat later."

"Is that Jutta I hear talking in there?" Brother Odell's question was followed by the familiar sound of his heavy footsteps crossing the parlor floor. "You missed us too much to remain gone for even one night?" His eyes twinkled with merriment but soon faded when he looked at our dour faces. "What has happened?"

Once everyone was seated, I described what I'd discovered upon my arrival in Marengo. They listened without interruption. When I finished, Ilsa touched my hand. "So that is why you didn't receive a letter from your Mutter this week, ja?"

"I am thinking that is the reason, but whether they left Marengo on their own or if they are in jail, I am not certain."

A frown settled across Ilsa's forehead. "You do not trust what Kenneth Reeves told you?"

"I don't know who to believe anymore." I looked at Ilsa's father. "Kenneth said I should be careful—that I might be followed if they truly believe my parents are being hidden somewhere in the colonies." I folded my hands in my lap. "But if they have my parents in jail, there would be no reason for them to watch me, ja?" It had been a long and frightening day, and my thoughts jumbled together like twisted yarn. I wanted Brother Odell to agree with me so I wouldn't have to worry about strangers constantly watching us or coming into the villages and causing trouble. Yet I didn't want to think of my parents confined in a jail, either.

Brother Odell leaned forward and placed his forearms across

his knees. "It serves no gut purpose for us to worry, Jutta. I understand you have deep concern for your Mutter and Vater. We will all be praying for their safe return. Before prayer service, I will go and speak with the elders to explain what has happened and to warn there is a possibility of trouble from these outsiders."

Ilsa's mother reached for my hand. "You were wise to return as soon as possible. We are most thankful for your safety."

Obviously they hadn't understood the amount of destruction these people could accomplish in a short time; they hadn't seen the condition of our bakery and home. If they had, they wouldn't be so calm. "If they come to the colonies, they could set fires or destroy the woolen mill. What if they cause an explosion at the flour mill? They are dangerous men."

"We cannot adopt a spirit of fear. It is not the way of the Lord. You must remember what the Bible says in Second Timothy: 'For God hath not given us the spirit of fear; but of power, and of love, and of a sound mind.' "

"I understand, but I am not so sure those men in Marengo are making their decisions with a sound mind."

Ilsa's father grinned. "That may be true, but we will trust the Lord to watch over us and protect us." He pushed up from his chair. "I will go now and speak to the elders. It is gut to have you home, Jutta."

Home. The word sounded strange to my ears. I wasn't sure where my home was anymore. It surely wasn't in Marengo, yet it didn't feel as if it were here, either. Not without my parents. I silently repeated the Bible verse Ilsa's father had spoken to me. I didn't want to be fearful. I wanted to believe God had given me a spirit of power and love, but right now I didn't feel strong. Right now, I felt weak and angry and fearful.

Ilsa's father lifted his coat from the peg. "I will go directly to meeting after I speak to the elders. I will tell the elders of your great concern for your Mutter and Vater as well as for the villages. You must pray for strength and trust God, Jutta." He waved at Garon. "And you should return the buggy to the train depot."

Garon glanced at the clock and jumped to his feet. "Ja. I must hurry or I will be late for prayer meeting." He buttoned his coat while following Brother Odell toward the back door. I was surprised he didn't trip over his feet when he turned to wave at Ilsa.

"Ilsa will sit here with you while you finish your tea, Jutta. I need to go to our rooms and prepare for meeting."

I heard Ilsa's mother greet Mr. and Mrs. Young, who had come downstairs and were now seated in the hotel parlor looking at magazines.

Ilsa scooted her chair close to my side. "Do you think your parents will be able to repair the bakery?"

Keeping my voice low and careful to speak in German, I described the full extent of the damage. "I doubt they would ever want to return to Marengo. Their safety is the most important thing right now."

"You should try to think of any persons who might have taken them in. Do they have friends elsewhere that they might have gone to stay with?"

Before I could reply, Mr. Young closed his magazine and placed it on the table. "You ladies have forgotten the governor has issued an order that only English should be spoken." He pinned me with a dark stare. "You need not worry. My wife and I won't report you, but you really should be more discreet. You never know who might be listening."

Forcing every ounce of civility I could muster, I said, "Thank you for the reminder, Mr. Young."

I wanted to add that our conversation had been private and not intended for his ears, but I was certain that wouldn't be well received, especially when I noticed his lips tighten into a smug smile. What was he thinking? I knew it couldn't be anything good. His dark eyes remained fixed upon me. I rested my hand against the pocket of my skirt. The thickness of the folded paper gave me a strange sense of comfort. I had promised Ilsa I would burn it, but perhaps that had been a mistake.

There would be surprise and anger among the members of the American Protective Society if they discovered a man in Mr. Young's position would be so careless with wartime documents. If he wanted to report us for speaking German, I could contact those hooligans in Marengo and tell them I'd discovered the drawing lying on the floor of Mr. Young's room. With the paper to prove my truth, he'd be hard-pressed to deny the allegation! If the drawing helped to save us from those professing patriots in the Iowa Council of National Defense, it would be worth it.

I tamped down the fear and guilt that started in my toes and climbed to the pit of my stomach when I recalled Mr. Young's smug look. My thoughts were not pure or kind or filled with love for my fellowman. They were not what the Bible instructed, but neither were Mr. Young's. Of that I was certain. Though I understood my behavior should be based upon the Bible rather than on Mr. Young's actions, I wasn't so sure the Bible teaching would win this time. Men like Mr. Young had caused me to lose my parents, and I was unwilling to let him or anyone else take anything more from me.

At the chiming of the village bell, I exhaled a deep sigh. Time to gather for evening prayers. Was that God's way of telling me my thinking was wrong? A sign to turn loose of my anger and the desire to strike back? If so, I would ignore it, for I wasn't going to let these men win so easily. How could I simply do nothing when my parents could be sitting in a jail somewhere? Maybe those who had lived here for all their lives could trust God to take care of everything, but I was determined to do my own part—if I could find a way.

CHAPTER 24

The last month had passed in our regular Amana routine. Except for the arrival of several guests who had never before roomed at the hotel, little had changed since my return from Marengo. For the first several days I worried the thugs from the Defense Council would arrive, and I had startled each time the bell over the front door jangled. I feared they would suddenly appear and tell the elders I was a fraud—that I had agreed to move to the colonies in order to spy on my own people. But after several days passed and no one except hotel guests appeared, I convinced myself the members of the Defense Council had found someone else to harass.

Even though my parents' whereabouts remained unknown to me, I continued to hope I would find some way to locate them. So far, it had proved an impossible feat. Each week the elders assured me there was no reason to worry over their safety or whereabouts.

They reminded me that God would make provision for them. Nevertheless, I continued to scour the Bible and read of the many martyrs who had died for their beliefs. God hadn't interceded for them—why should I trust He would protect my parents?

As if to confirm my fears, several articles attacking the Amanas and our beliefs appeared in the *Marengo Sentinel* and the *Cedar Rapids Republican*. There was little doubt the editorials would stir up further anger and resentment toward all people of German heritage—especially when the "Comments of the Week" column reported that the District Exemption Board had taken all of the draft registrants from Amana out of Class 1 and put them into deferred classes. From the tone of the article, it seemed there might be a group that would seek to secure a reversal of the board's decision. The newspaper hadn't been content to simply report the decision and the possibility of an appeal. Instead, it branded the men of Amana as *slackers*, yet another ugly label to add to the ever-increasing list of insults.

With the escalating anger and hatred directed at all people of German heritage, fear for my parents' welfare intensified. Unless they were in jail, they would have written to me by now. They would want to ease my worries, assure me of their safety, and offer words of encouragement. Even Mr. Reeves' statement about my parents fleeing town before the incident at the bakery had failed to convince me, for I knew my parents would never permit me to suffer such anxiety.

I had received letters during the past two months, but all had been from Albert. Each time I entered the general store and Brother Tolbert waved an envelope in my direction, my heart quickened, but by now I knew the letters would be from Albert and not my parents.

As our letters crossed back and forth in the mail, I was

thankful for Albert's friendship and also pleased to read that Private Higgins continued to show him friendship and kindness as they worked together at the Camp Pike infirmary. In his latest letter, Albert told me the two of them had begun praying together each evening, and both of them were praying for the safety of my parents. His letters urged me to remain confident and to trust God. I was amazed that he continued to be concerned for my well-being while he suffered daily insults and discord at the camp.

Though his prayers and concern warmed my heart, they created another layer of guilt. With each passing day, I knew I should reveal the truth about myself, but each time I made an attempt, the words stuck in my mouth like a lump of cold mashed potatoes. Before going to prayer meeting this evening, I had promised myself I would speak up, but once again my tongue refused to move. Several hours ago, I dropped into bed feeling the weight of failure resting heavily on my chest.

No matter how hard I tried, I couldn't push aside the guilt. I had sat mute while two elders and other members of the group had once again prayed for the safety of my parents and had thanked God for my increasing faith. At that point, I should have spoken up, told the truth, cleared my conscience—but I hadn't. I'd remained as silent as a doorpost.

I had flinched when one of the elders stopped me outside the meeting. "We are all thankful God brought you back home to us, Sister Jutta."

If only they knew the truth. That single thought continued to plague me, and I knew it wouldn't stop until I confessed. But how and where did I begin to ask forgiveness for agreeing to sacrifice the people of Amana for my own family?

I slid from beneath the thick quilts and dropped to my knees. First, I must ask God to forgive me and ask for courage to speak.

When the time was right for me to speak, surely God would give me a nudge.

I'm not certain when I finally fell asleep, but when the morning bell rang, I longed to cover my head and remain in bed. I forced my feet to the floor, washed my face, recited my morning prayers, and slipped into my dress. I continued in a daze while we prepared breakfast, thankful I had grown accustomed to the schedule. As in the previous week, there were several men at the far table.

"More salesmen," Sister Marta remarked when I commented on the new arrivals. "Most of them just passing through to buy from others. Our hotel is gut enough for a bed and food, but few of them will purchase our flour and woolens. Most of their companies would rather buy inferior products and boycott us. That is, unless they want our lumber to make rifles—then they forget boycotts and our German heritage." She slapped her palm across her lips, and fear shone in her eyes. "I should not have said such a thing."

With a pat on her shoulder, I picked up a platter of sliced bread. "You need not worry, Sister Marta. I have thought the same thing." There had been a time not so long ago when I would have considered her words a possible antiwar comment. One that I could write in my notebook and present to the Defense Council in the hope of keeping my parents safe. Now I no longer needed to keep notes on such comments. Though it didn't relieve worry for my parents, there was freedom in knowing I wouldn't be forced to report on anyone living in Amana, especially the Redlich family.

Ilsa had gone upstairs when Garon arrived to take passengers to the train station. He grinned and tapped his index finger alongside one eye. "Looks like you did not sleep so well."

I nodded and continued dusting the parlor furniture. While the men went upstairs to gather their belongings, I motioned to Garon. "Why so many new salesmen during the last month?"

"Probably replacements for men who have gone into military service. A few still place small orders at the woolen mills." He shrugged. "I had one who was in the train depot all afternoon one day last week. The only time he left was when I brought him to the hotel for the noonday meal. He said he was waiting for another salesman who never arrived."

Could some of these men be a part of the Iowa Council of National Defense? Perhaps they'd been sent to spy on us—to see if my parents were hidden somewhere nearby. "Strange that he would remain at the depot. You should have told him you would bring his friend to the hotel when he arrived."

Garon bobbed his head. "Ja, I did tell him that, but he said he was fine to stay there. I think he liked watching people come and go, and when it was quiet, he would talk to me. He liked watching me send and receive telegraph messages. He said he enjoyed the sound. It reminded him of clicking dance shoes."

After Garon and the salesmen departed, I completed my chores in the parlor, then trudged upstairs to clean the rooms the men had vacated. I had neared the top step when Ilsa signaled for me to remain quiet and join her by door number five. I did my best to avoid any squeaky floorboards as I drew to her side.

I tipped my head close to her ear. "What are we doing here?"

She flashed me a warning look and tapped her index finger against pursed lips. Exaggerating my lips, I mouthed the word *what* and arched my brows to emphasize my question. Ilsa cupped one hand behind her ear while using her free hand to point toward the Youngs' door. "Listen," she mouthed.

I held my breath but didn't hear a thing. I shrugged my shoulders and shook my head, but she motioned for me to wait. Then I heard it—Mrs. Young. She was singing a German folksong. And she was singing in *German*! I shot a wide-eyed stare at Ilsa and pointed down the far hallway. Careful to keep to the strip of carpet and walk on tiptoe, I made my way to one of the empty rooms. Ilsa followed me inside.

We stood in the doorway watching for any movement from the Youngs' room. "She said she didn't understand German. Have you ever heard her speak anything other than English before today?"

Ilsa shook her head. "Nein. I couldn't believe my ears. Especially after Mr. Young told us we should speak only English. When she first arrived, I took her to see the village. She mentioned she had traveled to many countries, but she told me she did not understand or speak German."

Mr. Young had been at breakfast that morning, but Mrs. Young hadn't come downstairs. She continued to seek a special favor from time to time, and occasionally one of us would relent and carry coffee along with a slice of bread and jam to her room. "Where is Mr. Young?" I hadn't seen him leave with the salesmen.

"He came through the kitchen after breakfast and spoke with my Vater. The two of them walked out the back door while you were in the parlor. He hasn't returned." Ilsa had barely finished speaking when the downstairs bell jangled. As motionless as two statues, we stared at each other while Ilsa's mother greeted Mr. Young.

"My wife and I will be departing for a few days, Mrs. Redlich."
Mr. Young's deep voice drifted up the stairs.

"I am surprised. Yesterday your wife said she wished to attend
our special Red Cross meeting later this afternoon."

When Mr. Young cleared his throat, I wondered if Sister
Marta's comment had annoyed him. "An unexpected matter has
come up. We should return within a few days."

His shoes hit each step with a determined thud, a definite
indication the conversation had ended. We ducked into the bedroom, but at the clunk of the door latch, Ilsa peeked around the
corner. "I wonder if Mrs. Young was still singing her German
tune when he entered the room."

"If so, I'm certain she stopped the moment she saw him." I
gestured toward the door. "You had better get back to cleaning
your rooms or you're not going to finish before time to help with
the noonday meal." Without waiting for her response, I turned
and yanked the dirty sheets from the bed and tossed them to
the floor.

"I'd rather wait until they're gone," she whispered.

I grinned. "You don't need to whisper. I don't think they
can hear you."

"I'm not so sure. Who would have ever thought Mr. Young
could have heard us talking in the dining room when you returned
from Marengo?" She tapped the back of her cap. "I think that
man has eyes in the back of his head and ears like a hawk."

I stifled a giggle. "Ja. I think he takes pleasure in surprising
people."

"Or scaring us." Ilsa edged toward the door. "I hope they
don't come out of their room while I'm in the hallway."

"Then hurry up and move." I shooed her with my hand.
"Go on."

Ilsa scurried out the door, and all remained quiet until I heard Mrs. Young complaining to her husband a short time later. "I don't know why you can't go by yourself, Jonathan. You know how I dislike rushing around. My hair isn't even properly combed. Why can't we wait until the afternoon train?"

"I'll explain later. Talk will only slow our departure. Come along now, or we'll miss the train."

Mrs. Young continued to express her discontent over the unexpected travel, but Mr. Young didn't relent. He called a farewell to Sister Marta as the bell jangled over the front door. I rushed down the hall and peeked out the window overlooking the street. Mr. Young had a firm hold on his wife's elbow and was rushing her toward the depot. He truly wasn't taking any chances on missing the train.

I backed away from the window and called to Ilsa. "They're gone."

She poked her head around the doorway leading to number seven. "Ja, and glad I am to see them both leave. Maybe they won't come back."

I shook my head. "They didn't take their belongings, but we will both enjoy the time they are away. And it is one less room for you to clean."

Ilsa nodded. "Ja, but I am thinking maybe I should go in there and see if Mrs. Young has a German songbook."

"I am thinking you should stay out of their room." I didn't want Ilsa stirring up any trouble with Mr. Young. He hadn't bothered me for some time now. Once confirmed that my father's statements regarding the bakery contract matched my own, his attempts to "help" my parents move to Amana had ceased. From time to time I wondered about his involvement with the American Protective League and if he might know of my parents' whereabouts, but I'd likely never know the answer to that. I didn't doubt his dislike for me. He'd attempted to accuse me of stealing a journal from his room, and if he was aware the drawing was missing, he'd likely accuse me of taking that, as well.

"Ja. I am sure he gave Mutter orders that the room should not be entered. I'll be happy to let the dust settle on the furniture." She giggled as we both returned to our work.

Once we finished, we carried our supplies downstairs and stored them in the small room behind the front desk before donning our aprons.

"There are potatoes to be peeled." Sister Marta pointed to the basket of potatoes she'd carried from the cellar earlier in the morning. "No need to peel all of them. We will be two less for the midday meal." She glanced up from the worktable and visibly paled. "I was busy baking the pies and forgot to come upstairs and tell you that you should not go into the Youngs' room. They left earlier in the day."

"No need for worry, Mutter. I saw them depart and was sure they wouldn't want me in the room. I won't go in to clean until they return."

Sister Marta sighed and placed her open palm across her bodice. "Gut. I don't want any complaints from either of them. I'm sure Sister Hulda will be most pleased to hear that Mrs. Young won't be present for the Red Cross meeting."

"I think Mrs. Young makes Sister Hulda nervous. Ever since the meeting last month when Mrs. Young corrected her about the number of socks we had knitted." Ilsa giggled. "I never saw Sister Hulda so flustered."

Sister Marta bobbed her head. "Ja. After the meeting Sister Hulda told me I should explain to Mrs. Young that she shouldn't speak out during the meetings since she isn't a member of our chapter."

Ilsa's eyes widened at the revelation. "Did you tell Mrs. Young? What did she say?"

"I didn't say she couldn't speak at the meetings, but I suggested she should consider making any suggestions or corrections to Sister Hulda in private." Sister Marta continued slicing the ham while she talked. I stopped to watch, always impressed by her ability to make such even cuts. Whether she sliced bread, meat, or vegetables, the cuts were always even and precise.

"Did your words anger Mrs. Young?" I picked up a knife and sliced the potatoes Ilsa had pared. My slices were no match for Sister Marta's.

"I don't think so, but it's hard to say. She didn't comment one way or the other." The spoonful of lard Sister Marta scooped into the hot skillet skittered and danced across the pan until it melted. "I thought we would discover if she had taken the comment to heart when we attended the meeting this afternoon."

I slid the pile of potatoes into the hot grease while Ilsa seasoned the green beans with a heaping spoonful of bacon grease. "I'll be pleased to celebrate Mrs. Young's absence with Sister Hulda. For the first time since she arrived, we will be able to converse without worry about what we say."

Sister Marta nodded. "And we won't have to speak in English. The old women will be able to understand. Ach! They will be so happy today."

Holding a large metal spoon overhead, Ilsa spun around. "Oh, Mutter, you will never guess what we heard when we were upstairs cleaning the rooms." She poked my arm. "She won't believe it, will she, Jutta?"

"For sure, she will be surprised."

Sister Marta settled a fist on each hip. "Why don't you tell me, and then we can see if I will be surprised?"

Ilsa glanced about the room as if she expected to see some strange person suddenly appear in the kitchen. "Mrs. Young was singing."

Sister Marta frowned. "Ja? That is not so hard for me to believe."

"In German. She was singing in German." Ilsa punctuated each word with a swing of her spoon.

"Nein. I cannot believe this. She does not understand German. She told us so when she first arrived. She said she understood only simple greetings. And when we were speaking in German at the first meetings she attended, she was completely confused—she didn't understand a word. Don't you remember, Ilsa?"

"I remember what she *said*. That doesn't mean she was speaking the truth. We both heard her singing. Didn't we, Jutta?" Ilsa sprinkled the beans with salt and pepper and gave them a stir.

I nodded. "She didn't sound like someone who had trouble with the language, Sister Marta."

"I am guessing she has asked someone to teach her a German song so she can impress the women at one of the meetings. She is a woman who needs to be noticed, don't you think?"

Ilsa nodded. "She is a woman who wants to be noticed, but she is also a woman who told a lie. I think she speaks German as well as all of us."

I wasn't positive who was correct, but a trickle of fear raced up my spine as I considered what Ilsa said. How many private matters had been discussed in front of her while thinking she didn't understand? "What about Mr. Young?" I whirled around to face Ilsa. "Do you think he understands German?"

My head pounded as I considered what that might mean.

As a member of the American Protective League, Mr. Young's services would be quite valuable if he could understand German. And if he didn't, having a wife to interpret for him would be the next best advantage.

Both Ilsa and Sister Marta shook their heads. "Nein," they said in unison.

"But we didn't think Mrs. Young could speak, and she does," I argued.

"You and Ilsa think she does. I think she learned a simple folksong. We will see who is correct when she returns." With a big smile Sister Marta said, "I have a plan."

CHAPTER 25

Ilsa Redlich

For the first time since they'd arrived at the hotel, I was eager to see Mr. and Mrs. Young. Now that I'd heard my mother's plan, I was impatient to put Mrs. Young to the test. Each time Garon brought passengers from the train station, I rushed to the window and scanned the arrivals, hoping to see them. Thus far I'd been disappointed, and today didn't prove any different. From my vantage point upstairs, I captured a glimpse of the oversized buggy, but today there were no passengers, not even any new salesmen.

Garon jumped down from the wagon, and I scurried to the first floor to greet him. "No passengers today?"

He looked over his shoulder. "Not unless they are invisible." With a chuckle, he strode toward me. After a quick glance at the kitchen, he wrapped me in an embrace and lowered his head, his lips meeting mine in a warm and inviting kiss that left me breathless.

I placed my hands on his chest. Even through his heavy wool coat, I could feel the thump of his heart pounding a rapid rhythm that matched my own. "Mutter is in the kitchen. She could walk in here at any moment." My warning had little effect. He dipped his head, and once again our mouths melded together in a lingering kiss that I hoped would last forever.

It wasn't the clicking of my mother's footsteps that tore us apart, but the pounding of horses' hooves and shouts of approaching riders. Garon grasped my hand, and we rushed to the front window.

"What is all the noise out there?" My mother hurried toward us, her eyes wide with curiosity. She leaned over my shoulder, and we watched the riders dismount and tie their horses outside the hotel. "They don't look like our usual customers." With a quick step, she crossed the room and took her position behind the front desk. "You should stay here in case there is trouble, Garon." Her eyes shone with a hint of fear.

Garon and I continued to watch from behind the gauzy curtains that covered the windows. The men huddled in a circle, and several turned up their collars against the wind that blustered through the village carrying light snow and a freezing chill. "They look like a rough group." I was careful to keep my voice low. I didn't want to further alarm my mother.

Garon's head dipped in a quick nod. "I don't recognize any of them. We can hope that they are only passing through and are stopping for a meal." Using his index finger, Garon opened the curtain a mere slit.

They didn't look like the type of men who would stop in Amana for a meal—or anything else, for that matter. Yet if they had a lame horse or needed a blacksmith, that would give them cause to stop before going further. "Maybe you should go out and see if they need help of some sort."

"We will wait to see if they come into the hotel. There is no need to invite trouble into our midst." My mother's strident objection surprised me. She was the one who frequently fed hobos and other transients passing through our village. Something about these men had clearly fired an inner alarm.

"They are looking our way, and one of them has taken the lead." I glanced at my mother and back to the group of men. "They're coming inside." Garon and I pulled away from the window and hurried to the front desk, Garon taking his place on my mother's right and I on the left.

The door opened and five men entered, stopping only long enough to stomp most of the snow from their boots. They showed no concern for the mess they'd created. I frowned at them, stepped to the storage room, and gathered a mop and bucket. I thought when they saw the cleaning equipment we might receive an apology, but none was forthcoming.

Before I could move toward the end of the counter, my mother grasped my arm. "Wait here, Ilsa. We can clean after they have departed." She was careful to speak in English but kept her voice to a whisper.

"How may I help you gentlemen?" she asked, still holding my arm. "We have several rooms available, and our midday meal will be served in half an hour."

"We ain't got any interest in eating with Huns or sleeping in your filthy beds, neither. We was told we'd find Garon Drucker at the train depot, but he wasn't there. Fella over there said I'd find him here." He pointed a thick finger at Garon. "You Drucker?"

"Ja, I am Garon Drucker. Do you need a telegram sent or something taken to the depot for shipment?"

One of the men who had been standing at the rear of the group stepped forward and yanked open his coat. A shiny badge was attached to the front of his inner jacket. "You're under arrest."

The bucket that I had been holding clattered to the floor, and the mop landed with a dull thud. My head swirled and I thought I might faint. The two largest men rushed forward and grasped Garon by his upper arms. Garon flinched, and the men wrenched his arms backward until he let out a yelp.

"Don't mind a bit if you wanna keep fighting us. I enjoy showing you Huns we can lick all of ya." A trickle of tobacco juice rolled down the side of his mouth as he tossed his head back and laughed.

Garon relaxed his arm but maintained a steely look at the larger of the two men. "What is this about? I have done nothing wrong."

"Shut up! You know good and well why we're here."

"No, I don't." Garon twisted around, and the man wrenched his arm until Garon shouted in pain.

My strength returned, and I slapped my hand on the front counter. "You must explain what this is about. You can't just walk in here and drag one of our people off to jail."

My mother nudged me and hissed for me to keep quiet. "Please, may I ask by what authority you are arresting this young man, and for what reason? We are gut citizens. I think my request is proper and should be simple for you to answer."

The man who'd revealed his badge met my mother's gaze. "We don't have to tell you nothin', but since you asked so nice, I'll tell ya. This here warrant is to arrest Garon Drucker for treason against the United States of America."

I leaned against the front desk. Otherwise, I knew I would drop to the floor. "Treason? That isn't possible." I pointed toward Garon. "He wants to join the army. Does that sound like a man who would do anything to harm his country?"

Garon bobbed his head. "You can check at the local draft board. They have my papers—all signed and official."

One of the men holding Garon spit on the floor. "The army don't want the likes of you, Drucker. And as far as I'm concerned, they oughta lock up all of you Huns. You make my skin crawl."

My mother leaned forward. "Please! Tell us what you believe he has done."

"We ain't required to tell you nothin'!" one of them hollered.

The obvious leader waved him to silence. "Don't have any particulars, just the warrant. I'm taking him to the jail in Marengo for now. Don't know if they'll send him someplace else or not."

The two men holding Garon pulled him toward the door.

Garon turned to look over his shoulder. His complexion was as white as the snow that layered the ground. I pushed away from the desk, but my mother placed her hand over mine.

"You can do nothing except make matters worse, Ilsa. We will get help once they are gone."

I knew she made sense. I couldn't possibly force those men to release Garon, but it seemed wrong to stand there and watch them haul him away without doing something. Yet, I knew this was a matter the elders would need to handle.

Garon's smile was a brave yet feeble attempt. I could see the worry in his eyes and knew it matched my own.

The minute they cleared the door, I watched them force Garon atop one of the horses, and then with a triumphant yell they thundered out of town.

In only minutes my father raced into the house. "I heard a commotion and went to the door of the shop. Did I see Garon with those men on horseback?" He panted to catch his breath.

"Ja." Tears rolled down my cheeks. I reached for my father's hand. "You must go after them, Vater. They are going to put Garon in jail. They say he has committed treason."

"Treason? How did Garon commit treason? That is impossible."

"That's what we tried to tell them. I told them that he wanted to join the army, but they didn't listen." I clutched his arm. "They are going to put him in jail in Marengo."

My father squeezed my hand. "I will go and speak with the elders. They will know what we should do." My father motioned to my mother. "I will see if they want us to ring the emergency bell so our people can gather at the meetinghouse to pray for Garon."

My father had been gone for only a short time when Jutta returned from the general store. Snow clung to her cape and shoes, but unlike the men, she took care to brush off as much as possible before she entered the hotel. Her gaze fell on the puddles of melted snow that had been tracked through the parlor. She wiped her shoes on the mat and transferred the basket from her arm to the front desk.

"Who made this mess?" She shook her head. "Someone without good upbringing, for sure." She reached into her basket and withdrew two letters. "From Albert—for you, Ilsa, and one for you, Sister Marta." She beamed at me, but when I didn't reach for Albert's letter, her smile faded. "Something is wrong?"

"Ja, something terrible." I pointed to the floor. "The mess was made by a group of men who came and arrested Garon—for treason."

Jutta gasped, her eyes wide with disbelief. "I saw riders as I was leaving the store, but I didn't see Garon among them. I wondered what they were doing in town."

During the next several minutes, Mother and I explained what little we could about the incident and expressed our hope that the elders would go directly to Marengo and arrange for Garon's release. Jutta hung her cloak, and we continued to talk while we shelved her purchases.

We had completed the task and had also cleaned the floor in the front parlor by the time my father returned. "The elders from South are going to Main Amana to meet with the elders there and see what they recommend." The village bell tolled in the distance and my father gave a firm nod. "We will go to the meetinghouse and pray." He stepped behind the counter and withdrew a key from the drawer. "I will lock the door. Marta, put a sign in the window that says we will return in one hour."

Though I had thought it impossible to experience deeper despair, my father's report caused anguish to grow until it sat like a heavy stone in my chest. I had hoped the men would immediately ride to Marengo, but instead, the elders would ride to Main, and we would pray. As we walked down the steps, I came alongside my father. "Do you think they will hire a lawyer to help Garon?" I swiped away the tear that trickled down my cheek.

"I think they will do everything possible to protect him. They don't believe he has done anything that could ever be considered an act of treason, but until all of the facts are known, it is impossible to know. Right now, it is best that we pray—for Garon's safety and for the elders to make wise decisions." My father yanked his hat low on his forehead.

My insides trembled. "Has anyone spoken to Garon's parents? They need to know what has happened."

"Ja, I stopped and told them before I came back to the hotel. After prayer meeting Brother Edwin is going to take a horse from the barn and ride to Marengo." My father rubbed his palm along his jaw. "I don't know what to think of the cruelty taking place around us. First Jutta's family and now Garon—who will be next? How much must be sacrificed before the country accepts that the people of Amana support America in the war."

I longed to accompany Brother Edwin to Marengo and make certain Garon hadn't been injured. Instead, I walked with my family to the meetinghouse, where we entered our respective doors and settled on our benches before lifting our voices and hearts in unified prayer for Garon's safety. I hoped he could somehow feel our presence with him through our prayers. As we departed the church, the older members gathered around Garon's parents to offer consolation while the younger ones drew near to me and promised continued prayer for Garon. I was thankful for their support, but it did little to erase my fear.

When we returned to the hotel a short time later, Jutta grasped my hand. "Why don't you go and rest. I can clean the rooms by myself today." She walked down the hallway with me, and I clung to her hand, needing to feel all the warmth and support she could lend me.

"I do not think I can survive if something terrible happens to Garon," I whispered as we entered the apartment.

"You will survive. Do you not remember the passage the elders read to us in meeting?"

"Ja, I remember. I learned those verses when I was a little girl. 'My grace is sufficient for thee: for my strength is made perfect in weakness. Most gladly therefore will I rather glory in my infirmities, that the power of Christ may rest upon me. Therefore I take pleasure in infirmities, in reproaches, in necessities, in persecutions, in distresses for Christ's sake: for when I am weak, then am I strong.' " I rambled off the verses, then attempted a smile. "I think the apostle Paul was much stronger than I am. I find no pleasure in persecution or distress."

"I think you are much stronger than you know." Jutta looked into my eyes and squeezed my hand. "Remain steadfast and know that God will take care of both you and Garon. When I am consumed with worry for my parents, I push aside my concern and remember all the things I love about them. Don't dwell on the unknown. Instead think about what you know to be true."

"I'm not sure I can do that."

"Yes you can. Tell me what first drew you to Garon and why you love him. Can you do that?" She led me to the sofa in our parlor, and we sat down side by side.

"Ja, of course. I have known him since he was a little boy." I gazed into the distance, a smile pushing at my lips. "Even when we first began *Kinderschule*, he told me that when he was old like his Mutter and Vater, he was going to marry me." I laughed at the remembrance. "Garon can make me laugh when I want to cry. He understands my heart better than anyone, and he has always forgiven me when I've wronged him. He has a gut heart, and he loves me." I bowed my head. "And he loves God."

"And God loves him."

Sympathy shone in Jutta's eyes. More than anyone else, she understood my anguish. She'd been told to pray and trust God for the safe return of her parents, and now I had been told to do the same for Garon. But sometimes prayer didn't seem like enough. Sometimes trust seemed too difficult. Sometimes it seemed God needed my help.

CHAPTER 26

Jutta Schmitt

Panic gripped me like a vise. What if Garon's arrest had something to do with me? Were the actions of the men from Marengo a further retaliation for my lack of cooperation with the Defense Council? Throughout the afternoon I wrestled with every possible scenario. One minute I convinced myself that his arrest had surely taken place because of me. The next minute I decided that if this had anything to do with me or my parents, the Defense Council wouldn't have arrested Garon—they would have arrested me. I remained upstairs cleaning the rooms so Ilsa could rest and pray. I hoped her prayers would meet with more success than my own, for I'd still heard nothing from my parents.

As I changed the beds and swept the floors, I harbored secret thoughts that Garon might capture a glimpse of my parents or perhaps overhear some discussion of them. But as soon as those thoughts came to mind, guilt attacked me. Such selfishness! Even during the distress of others, I was thinking of myself.

I still hadn't admitted my lies and deceit to anyone. Oh, I'd knelt beside my bed and asked God to forgive me, but I hadn't spoken to the elders or Ilsa and her parents. I hadn't revealed my secrets to them—or asked for their forgiveness.

It had been easier to go to God—after all, He wasn't surprised to hear my confession. He already knew what I'd done, but to tell the people who had opened their home to me or to tell the elders who had welcomed me back to the colonies had been impossible as yet. The need to tell them nagged at me, but thus far I'd been unable to conquer my latest fear—yet another fear that had grown out of my selfish nature. I worried the elders would ask me to pack my bags and leave. If that happened, where would I go—especially with my parents still missing? The very thought knocked the wind from my chest. Such a decision would be fair and just. My coming to South Amana had placed all of the colonies in danger. When the time came for me to reveal the truth, I prayed the elders would allow me to remain in South Amana—at least until my parents were found. If not, I would leave without argument—it was the least I could do. By the time I gathered enough courage to tell the truth, perhaps I would have a plan for my future.

I continued through the rooms, and when I had dusted and changed the bed in the final room, I walked past number five, thankful the Youngs had not returned. Holding my cleaning supplies, I grabbed the railing with my free hand and hurried downstairs. I swiveled around when the front doorbell jingled.

Mrs. Young strolled across the threshold, her husband following close on her heels. I silently chastised myself for thinking about them. Though I knew it was silly, it was as if my thoughts had caused their return.

Mr. Young stepped alongside his wife. "Why the frown, Jutta? If I didn't know better, I'd think you were unhappy to see us."

I shook my head and forced a smile. "Welcome back." I was thankful they continued upstairs without further conversation.

They had climbed only a few steps when Mr. Young stopped and peered over the railing. "You may come up and clean and help my wife unpack. And our room will need to be dusted and aired."

"There won't be time before supper. I must help in the kitchen." I met Mr. Young's hard stare. "I'll try to come up this evening." Without awaiting his reply, I turned and strode to the kitchen.

I expected him to call after me, but he didn't. Likely he'd wait and mention my abrupt response during the evening meal so he could embarrass me in front of the other guests. He seemed to take pleasure in such ill-mannered behavior.

Sister Marta was combining the ingredients for tonight's liver dumplings when I entered the kitchen, but she glanced up at me. "All done with the rooms?"

"Yes, for now. What can I do to help?"

Her brows furrowed. "What do you mean 'for now'? There is a problem?"

I shrugged. "The Youngs have returned and want special treatment. As usual." There was little doubt Sister Marta heard the disdain in my voice.

"She needs someone to unpack her clothes. Am I right?"

I grinned and checked the large pot of water on the stove. "You are right. And they want the room dusted and aired. I told them they'd have to wait until after supper. I am sure Mr. Young will mention it when they come downstairs to eat."

"Ach! They will not be happy with supper, either. Neither of them likes liver dumplings. They complained the last time I prepared them."

I remembered, and the thought of their displeasure delighted me. I was attacked by a fleeting sense of guilt, but even that did not erase my pleasure. I couldn't wait to see their faces when we delivered the serving bowls to the sideboard.

Sister Marta looked up from her mixing. "Did Mr. Young ask about Garon?"

"No. That is strange, don't you think?" I'd been so unhappy to see the couple return, I hadn't thought about Garon's absence at the train station. Following Sister Marta's direction, I added salt to the kettle of water. "Brother Milton must have given him some reason for Garon's absence at the train station. If he told Mr. Young of Garon's arrest, it seems Mr. Young would have mentioned it when they arrived."

Perhaps Mr. Young had known of Garon's arrest before he ever returned to the hotel. If he was a high-ranking member of the American Protective League, it made sense that he would know. In fact, he probably knew more about Garon's welfare than any of us. Maybe I *should* go upstairs and help Mrs. Young unpack her clothes.

Once supper preparations were well underway, I suggested exactly that. "Maybe the Youngs won't be so unhappy over the liver dumplings if I air their room and help them unpack."

Sister Marta appeared to take a survey of what needed to be accomplished before the supper bell would ring. "Ja. Maybe that would be gut. I don't think Ilsa will want to spend time with them this evening—especially if they begin asking questions about Garon."

"As soon as I finish, I'll return to set the tables." I scurried out of the kitchen, collected my cleaning supplies, and dashed upstairs. I tapped on the door. "Mrs. Young? I've come to clean the room."

At the sound of footsteps crossing the room, I took a backward step and waited until the door swung open. Mr. Young stood in the doorway with his lips curled in an expression that more closely resembled a sneer than a smile. The afternoon light streamed through the west window and rested on his shoulder.

"What a pleasant surprise, Jutta. My wife is weary, and your help will be greatly appreciated." He stepped to Mrs. Young's side and placed a fleeting kiss on her cheek. "I'll return in a short while. I'm going to the train station and have Garon telegraph a message for me."

Though I attempted to withhold my surprise at his remark, my mouth dropped open. It seemed he didn't know about Garon—or was he merely acting innocent to see if I would tell him? Either way, I knew I must say something. "Garon isn't at the train station. Didn't Brother Milton tell you?"

"No. He was busy at the ticket counter and waved us toward another fellow who was driving the buggy. I asked him about Garon's whereabouts, but he said he didn't know. Not a very friendly young man. In fact, I was going to mention his attitude to Brother Milton." Mr. Young's eyebrows knit in a frown. "So where is Garon? Has he been assigned to some other work? I need him to send a message."

"We think he has been jailed in Marengo."

Mr. Young arched his brows, and I thought I detected a flicker of surprise in his dark eyes. "Jailed? When? For what reason?"

"A group of riders burst through the doors of the hotel earlier today and said they'd come to arrest him for treason. They flashed their badges and forced him to ride out of town with them."

"And no one has done anything to help him?" The urgency in his voice matched the concern that now shone in his eyes.

His alarm surprised me. "The elders will decide what is best." I lifted one of his wife's dresses and shook it out. Before I hung it in the wardrobe, I glanced over my shoulder at Mrs. Young. "This may need to be pressed before you can wear it, but perhaps the wrinkles will fall out."

Mr. Young stepped in front of his wife. "You are worried about wrinkles in my wife's dress when one of your friends has been hauled off to jail? You think God is going to protect him? Is that it?" His thin mustache twitched, and he pointed his index finger beneath my nose. "If that's what you believe, you're going to be sorely disappointed. Garon needs the help of a lawyer. I will ride to Marengo and see to this situation."

I shook my head. "You should first speak to the elders and see what plans they've made before you take matters into your own hands." His plan to assume responsibility for Garon's welfare both offended and startled me. Who was he to assume such a role? Why did he feel such urgency? Had those men arrested me or Ilsa, would Mr. Young have been concerned? Would he have felt compelled to ride to Marengo and use his legal skills to free one of us? I doubted it. His resolve was based upon something deeper than Garon's welfare, of that I was certain. I wondered if he feared Garon would reveal information that had been contained in the many telegrams he'd sent. Still, if he was a ranking member of the Protective League, he shouldn't be concerned.

His wife stepped to one side and grasped her husband's arm. "She's right, Jonathan. These people like to take care of problems in their own way. You shouldn't force yourself upon them." Suddenly the voice of reason, Mrs. Young continued to talk to her husband. Her calm demeanor and thoughtful insight belied the traits she'd exhibited over the past months. Her sad and mel-ancholy behavior had been replaced by clarity and assurance. Though I wanted to believe Mr. Young truly cared about Garon, I wondered if his concern had more to do with those telegrams than Garon's safety.

Mr. Young placed his palm atop the pile of papers arranged on the table. "I will speak to the elders, my dear, but it is imperative I do all I can to help Garon." He settled stern eyes on his wife. "You do understand that I know what is best in this situation, don't you." It was an unwavering statement, rather than a ques-tion, to which his wife gave a slight nod.

I didn't understand why he would know what was best in this situation, for he didn't know the particulars any more than we did. He gathered his hat and coat. "Please continue with your cleaning duties, Jutta. My wife will instruct you on what needs to be done."

"You might wish to speak with Brother Redlich. He may have more information from the elders."

He gave a slight nod—the only acknowledgment that he'd heard my suggestion. I wasn't certain how he intended to travel to Marengo. There wouldn't be another train for hours, and I doubted Brother Samuel would be easily convinced to furnish a buggy or horse to a visitor at this hour of the day.

I continued to unpack Mrs. Young's dresses while she sat near one of the windows overlooking the street. "Your husband's concern for Garon surprises me."

"He is a lawyer. It's his job to overcome injustice."

Mrs. Young's comment carried the same tiny accent that I'd noticed when she first arrived at the hotel. The accent she attributed to her years of travel and occasionally forgot to hide.

Though she watched my every move, she remained unusually quiet while I dusted the room.

"Jutta! I need you to help in the kitchen," Sister Marta called from downstairs. "You can finish cleaning after supper."

I pointed toward the other side of the room. "Would you like me to open the windows so the room can air? You can wait in the hotel parlor if you think you'll take a chill."

Mrs. Young waved me toward the door. "No, you can go on and help Mrs. Redlich. I believe I'll rest until time for the evening meal."

There wouldn't be much time for resting. The supper bell would ring in half an hour.

Sister Marta peeked in the oven to check the potatoes as I entered the kitchen. "Mr. and Mrs. Young are happy?"

I shrugged as I drew close and told her of my conversation with Mr. Young and his reaction to the news. "I think Mr. Young has gone to Marengo."

"So Mrs. Young is alone up there?"

I nodded. "She said she wanted to rest until supper and refused my offer to air the room."

Sister Marta smiled. "Then it is a gut time for our test to see if she understands German. And I know exactly what I will do—she won't be able to resist."

I wasn't sure the timing was perfect, but I trusted Sister Marta knew what she was doing. "Follow me to the front desk—you'll be able to hear from there." After a final check of the food, she motioned me forward.

With an ear cocked toward the upstairs, I held my breath and waited until Sister Marta reached the upper floor. After knocking loudly, she waited until the door opened. Then, speaking in German, she said, "Your husband has been thrown from a horse, and his leg is broken. Do you wish our doctor to care for him?"

Even from below the steps, I heard Mrs. Young's gasp. "Of course, you should have the doctor care for him!" she shouted. "Where is he?" I heard the clatter of her footsteps on the stairway. Sister Marta was following close behind Mrs. Young, who appeared panic-stricken. She still didn't realize she'd responded to a message spoken in German. She'd been too worried over her husband's condition. Exasperation shone in her face as she neared the bottom step. "Didn't you hear me? Where is Jonathan?"

"I don't know where he is, but I think he is probably just fine." Once again, Sister Marta spoke in German, but this time Mrs. Young remembered to look confused.

"You know I don't understand German."

"Well, you understood just now when I stood outside your door and told you your husband had a broken leg. It was obvious you understood every word." Sister Marta continued to speak in German.

"This is not humorous, Mrs. Redlich. What is this game you are playing with me?"

"It is not a game but a way for me to discover the truth. Why is it that you want to hide the fact that you understand our language? Is it because you are embarrassed you are a German-American?"

"How dare you say such a thing. I am not a German, and you should be ashamed of yourself. Holding yourself out to be a woman who believes in the Bible and one who supposedly follows God's ways, yet you tell lies."

Sister Marta remained calm. "If you had told the truth, you wouldn't have understood one word I said about your husband. It was a test, Mrs. Young, and you failed."

"I did not fail. When we first arrived, I told you I understood a little German." Mrs. Young narrowed her eyes and pinched her lips into a tight seam.

Sister Marta now stood at the bottom of the stairs, her hand resting on the sturdy rail. "You said you understood simple greetings, nothing more. What I spoke was far more than a greeting. During our times together, you have asked me to interpret many less difficult comments than what I said upstairs. You are a fraud, Mrs. Young."

The woman paled and grasped Sister Marta's arm. "Please do not tell my husband of this mistake. He will never forgive me." Her eyes shone with fear.

"Why did you lie to us? Surely you knew it wouldn't matter to us if you spoke German."

"My husband insisted." Her gaze flitted back and forth between Sister Marta and me. "He didn't want to deal with all the hatred that is directed toward German people."

The halting words didn't ring true. I was sure she was hiding something more.

"Please promise you won't say anything to my husband. He will be extremely unhappy with me."

Sister Marta shrugged. "I see no reason to mention it to your husband." She hesitated a moment. "Unless it should prove necessary for some reason in the future."

Apparently Sister Marta's answer satisfied Mrs. Young, for she turned and ascended the stairs.

"There is something very odd about all of this. The Youngs are a strange couple," I said as we returned to our duties in the kitchen. I was certain we were both thinking the same thing— trying to recall all the comments we'd made in front of Mrs. Young, what the ladies at the sewing circle had discussed in her presence, and whether any of our comments might have been repeated to anyone else.

Soon after I finished setting the table, the village bell tolled, and I began filling the serving bowls. "I wonder if Mrs. Young will decide to tell her husband what happened."

Sister Marta shook her head. "I don't think so, but for sure I will tell mine. I do not like any of this."

CHAPTER 27

Ilsa Redlich

When Jutta knocked on the door and called me for supper, I jumped to my feet and rushed to the other side of the room. I didn't take time to put on my shoes or offer a proper greeting as I yanked open the door. "Has there been any word about Garon?"

Jutta stepped inside the parlor. "No, but Mr. and Mrs. Young returned. When Mr. Young learned Garon had been arrested, he said he was going to ride to Marengo."

"Mr. Young?" I rubbed my forehead. Why would Mr. Young hurry to Marengo? Granted, he did have a tendency to poke his nose into matters that didn't concern him. He'd been quick to visit the bakery and question Jutta's parents, even though she'd refused his offer of help. For sure, I didn't think the elders would want him overriding their decisions. Even though my mother said lawyers acted in strange ways, I thought Mr. Young's behavior went beyond strange. And the same could be said for his wife.

Jutta pointed to my shoes beside the bed. "You better put those on. I don't think your mother would like you serving the guests in your stockings."

I glanced down. "You're right. I don't think she would be pleased."

While I shoved my feet into my black leather shoes, Jutta plopped down beside me. "Let me tell you what happened while you were resting."

She settled a little closer and told me how my mother had tricked Mrs. Young into admitting she could understand German. I gasped, surprised that my mother would do such a thing. "I never thought my Mutter would lay such a trap."

"Neither did Mrs. Young. She even said your mother lied to her." Jutta chuckled. "When Mrs. Young realized she'd been caught in her own web, she decided to point a finger at your mother."

"I am sorry I missed out. It would have been exciting to see Mrs. Young trying to take back all of her lies." I reached up and pretended to gather words from the air and stuff them into my mouth. "And I can only imagine what Sister Hulda is going to say when she discovers the truth about Mrs. Young." From the start, Sister Hulda had been opposed to the idea of Mrs. Young's attending our Red Cross meetings. This would prove her resistance to outsiders had been justified. No doubt other members of the Red Cross would be doing their best to remember every word they'd uttered in the woman's presence.

Evening shadows danced on the blue plaster walls as I followed Jutta down the hallway. I was still digesting the news when Mrs. Young emerged at the top of the stairway. Her normally pale complexion appeared ghostly in the fading evening light.

She gestured to us. "I won't be joining you for the evening

meal. I'm not feeling well, and I plan to rest. Perhaps a plate in my room later?" I could hear the question in her voice and glanced at Jutta.

"Yes. When I come up to finish cleaning, I will bring you a plate." Jutta continued toward the kitchen.

I stared at Jutta, surprised by her generous offer. She hadn't even attempted to convince the woman to come downstairs. I arched my eyebrows. "You are most kind to a woman who has been living a lie with us."

Jutta grinned. "Not so kind. We are having liver dumplings for supper. She will not be pleased when she sees what is on her plate."

My mother looked up as we entered the kitchen. "You are feeling a little better, Ilsa?"

I shrugged. "Maybe a little, but I would feel better if someone would bring us news of Garon."

"All we know so far is that our elders from South rode to Main Amana to seek advice." My mother motioned for me to fill the milk pitcher. "All of this changes nothing for us. We need to be sure supper is served on time. Besides, the mind doesn't wander when we keep our hands busy."

My mother glanced toward the back door. "Your father must have been delayed at work. We will begin without him. I can keep a plate warm for him."

Three salesmen clomped down the stairs and took their seats; my mother signaled that we would begin. All of them were what my mother referred to as *regulars*. She considered salesmen who had been coming to the hotel on a regular schedule for at least a year our *regulars*. Those who'd been renting rooms from us for less than a year, she referred to as *possibles*. And those who switched back and forth between our hotel in Lower South and the hotel in Upper South, she referred to as *impossibles*, for she would never know whether she should expect them or not.

And though Mother might deny it, she made certain the regulars received a larger portion of dessert and an extra cup of coffee at every meal. The regulars understood the routine: They arrived on time, sat at the men's table, remained silent while we said our prayers, and didn't talk during mealtime. The regulars made our work less stressful, and Mother thought they should be rewarded in some small way.

This evening was no different from other evenings when only the regulars were present. They dished up hearty servings, emptied their plates, and then disappeared to the parlor or to their private rooms.

We were clearing the dishes when my father entered the back door and placed a quick peck on my mother's cheek. "I am sorry to be late, but—" The bell over the door jangled, and my father crossed the kitchen. "Continue with what you are doing. I will go see who is out front." He returned almost as quickly as he'd departed. "It was Mr. Young. He rode to Marengo, but they would not give him permission to speak with Garon."

My mother wiped her hands and walked to the oven, where she'd kept a pan of food warm for my father. He pulled a stool to the worktable and settled. She arched her brows. "Does Mr. Young expect supper?"

"Nein. He said he was going to bed and didn't wish to be disturbed." My father shook his head. "He will wake up hungry in the middle of the night, but who am I to tell a grown man what to do?"

"I suppose that means if Mrs. Young wants something to eat, she must come downstairs." I glanced at Jutta.

"For sure. If I go up there with her supper, I will disturb Mr.

Young, and I have no desire to anger him. If Mrs. Young is hungry, she can come down." Jutta removed her apron and hung it on the hook near the door. "That means I finish cleaning their room tomorrow rather than this evening. For that I am pleased."

My chest felt heavy, and my breath came in shallow gasps as I dropped to one of the stools and listened to the talk swirl around me. Garon was sitting in jail, and my parents and Jutta were worried about supper and cleaning rooms. How could they continue their routine as if nothing had happened?

My father motioned for my mother and Jutta to sit down while he ate. "I was late for supper because Brother Edwin stopped to tell me that he rode to Marengo and was able to talk to Garon." He took a bite of his dumplings. "I think that is part of the reason they refused Mr. Young's visit."

I sighed with relief and drew closer, leaning my elbows on the worktable. I didn't want to miss anything my father had to report.

He swallowed and pointed the fork tines toward the plate. "Gut dumplings. I hope you made extra."

Jutta grinned. "You can have Mr. Young's share, since he isn't going to eat."

While the others continued to chatter, my thoughts were of Garon and the men who had hauled him off to Marengo. One of them had said he was guilty of treason, yet how could they accuse someone like Garon—a man who wanted to join the army and serve his country—of treason? It was beyond reason. It had been obvious those men hadn't wanted to hear Garon's explanation— they had taken pleasure in their assigned duty. Their treatment had been rough and unrelenting while they'd been in our hotel. I could only imagine how they must have treated him when they had him alone in Marengo. In spite of the warmth in our kitchen, I shuddered.

My father leaned toward me. "For now, they are going to keep Garon in the Marengo jail, but he has not been harmed. Brother Edwin was told nothing more about why Garon had been charged with treason."

"I am thankful to hear he hasn't been injured any further." My fear bubbled like a boiling kettle. I swiped a tear trickling down my cheek. "I had hoped for more news."

My father reached across the table and patted my arm. "There is more, though I am not sure it is what you want to hear. Brother Drucker tells me there will be a meeting on Monday with the elders, some men from the American Protective League, and the men from that Iowa Defense Council."

I gasped. "The men who came here and arrested Garon?"

"I am not certain it will be the same men, but they are all part of the same group." He squeezed my arm. "They will also bring Garon with them."

Knowing they would bring Garon gave me hope. Surely they wouldn't harm him if they'd agreed to return with him on Monday. "Do you think that means they will release him?"

My father shook his head. "I think that is doubtful. If they did not think he was a traitor, they would not have arrested him. But Brother Drucker said he had been assured they will bring Garon here, and we are going to have a meeting so that everyone can be heard. The elders have called for special prayer meetings each day. We will ask God for protection over all of the colonies and ask that the truth be revealed to these men."

Mother turned from the sink. "The special prayer meetings will be gut. To join in prayer is the best thing we can do." She sent me a look that meant I should hearken to her words.

I knew she was correct, but at times prayer didn't seem enough. I longed to do something more substantial—something that would relieve the ache in my heart.

Jutta drew closer to the worktable. "I am surprised Mr. Young was unable to gain information from those men. That's what lawyers are supposed to do, is it not?"

My father shrugged. "These men from the Defense Council take the law into their own hands, and it seems they do not have to answer to anyone—even lawyers. I am amazed at the power they possess."

My mother dried the remaining kettle and placed it on the shelf. "Does Mr. Young plan to be present and help Garon on Monday?"

"We did not tell him about the meeting. Who can say if he will be here or not? For sure, I do not know. He may be upstairs packing as we speak."

My mother cast a worried look at my father. "I thought you said he was going to bed."

My father nodded. "He did say that, dear wife. I meant only to point out that I have no idea what Mr. Young has planned for Monday or even for the next few hours."

"So the elders have arranged for another lawyer to help Garon?" My mother hung the towel on a peg.

"Nein. Brother Edwin said they came and talked to Sister Barbara while he was gone. They have decided to wait and see what takes place at the meeting on Monday." My father raked his fingers through his thick hair.

"Who will attend the meeting, Vater?"

"I do not know. The men at the jail sent a paper with Brother Edwin. They have listed the people they plan to have in attendance from their Defense Council and the Protective League. The elders will choose who will be present to speak for Garon."

Though I wasn't surprised the elders would decide, it provided little solace, for only God knew if the elders would choose the proper people to speak—the ones who could help to free Garon.

After prayer meeting, Sister Barbara invited us for coffee and cake. "Please come," she urged. "We have more news."

Once we were gathered around the table, Brother Edwin took a piece of paper from his pocket. "The elders have decided who will attend the meeting on Monday." He unfolded the paper with a deliberate assurance. "The elders will be present, of course. Brother Ernst will take charge. Garon's Mutter and I, the three of you." He pointed to my mother, father, and me. "And you, too, Jutta. Also they have selected Brother Milton."

My mind whirred with questions. The list seemed an odd group. I understood why Garon's parents would be included, and I assumed the elders included me and my parents because of my betrothal to Garon. But I wasn't certain about Jutta, and Brother Milton was a complete mystery. Brother Milton was the supervisor at the train station, but Garon hadn't required instruction for several years. Nowadays, the two of them conducted their work with little need for communication.

Creases etched my father's forehead. "I don't understand why the elders have asked for Jutta to be present."

Brother Edwin removed his pipe from his pocket. "The elders didn't request Jutta or Brother Milton. It was the Defense Council that requested their presence."

Jutta stared at Brother Edwin, her lower lip tucked between

her teeth and her complexion as white as the sheets we gathered from the clotheslines on washday. Concern shone in her eyes, yet she didn't utter a word.

I could no longer bear the deafening silence that hung in the air. "But why would they request Jutta or Brother Milton? It makes no sense."

Brother Edwin tamped the tobacco into his pipe with practiced precision. "I wish I knew, but I have no answers for your questions, Ilsa. I've told you everything we know."

Though Garon's parents did their best to appear calm and cheerful, I didn't miss the looks that passed between them. I was certain their fear ran as deep as my own. If all went well, this meeting could mean Garon's release, but if it didn't go well, who could say what lay in store for any of us.

While we drank our coffee, my thoughts continued to whir, and I longed to return home. By the time we finally departed, I worried there was more to this than any of us imagined. Perhaps all of the villages were in jeopardy. There was no way to know what plans these men might be devising against any of us.

I turned toward Jutta when we entered the hotel. "Do you think this has something to do with your parents' bakery? I can think of no other reason why those men are interested in having you present. And how would that link to Garon?" A recollection of Garon and Jutta whispering by the cellar doors came to mind, and I wondered if they had shared other secrets. Did those talks have something to do with Garon's arrest? Perhaps Jutta wasn't the friend I had thought.

Pain flashed in Jutta's eyes when I refused her outstretched hand. "I do not believe Garon's arrest has anything to do with my parents' bakery, Ilsa. Surely you know that I would tell you if I had any information about his arrest."

When I didn't respond, Jutta turned and walked toward her rooms as though pushing her feet through a heavy winter snow. I wanted to believe she was my friend, but I couldn't forget seeing her whispering to Garon at the cellar steps or erase the nagging thought that she and Garon might have lied to me.

CHAPTER 28

Jutta Schmitt

For the last three nights, I chased sleep like a starving dog pursuing an elusive bone. There had been brief occasions when exhaustion won out, but my fatigue increased with each passing day. Fear mixed with guilt and together they concocted an overpowering potion that didn't permit rest. Perhaps once I spoke to the elders this afternoon, I'd finally be able to sleep. I had made my request in secret after prayer meeting on Thursday night. I'd had no choice.

I hadn't missed the questions in Ilsa's eyes. She didn't trust me—of that I was sure. And though speaking to the elders today would likely mean the end of my life in South Amana, there was no other way to right any wrongs I'd caused. The truth must be told, although I doubted anything I had to say would help Garon. I was sure Ilsa thought Garon and I shared secrets that were connected to his arrest, but my lies and deceit had nothing to do with his confinement. At least I prayed they did not, but I'd been haunted by the fact that the Defense Council had placed my name on their list.

I could only hope they hadn't devised a story that went beyond the lies I'd already told. If so, I didn't know how I could refute them. Once everyone knew my return was merely a ploy to uncover any anti-American activity within the colonies, it would be difficult to convince anyone to believe me.

During the past several days, the kitchen had been unusually quiet during meal preparations, and this morning was the same. I had become accustomed to the silence observed during our meals, but the quiet that now permeated the kitchen disturbed me. Except for Sister Marta's occasional requests, silence reigned. Ilsa spoke to me only when forced to answer a direct question. Otherwise, she deferred to her mother. I had tried to draw her into conversation on two separate occasions, but she ignored my attempts. She clearly wanted to avoid me, so I granted her wish. Once I spoke to the elders, I might try again. Everything would come out at tomorrow's meeting, but I wished I could explain it to Ilsa beforehand.

I wanted to believe that if our positions were reversed, I would give Ilsa an opportunity to speak with me. Unfortunately, I wasn't certain that was true, for I'd come to the realization that until faced with a situation, I didn't know how I would react. Six months ago I would have laughed at the thought of returning to Amana and reporting on the colonists. However, the threat of harm to my parents had quickly changed my mind. I wanted to believe I was courageous, yet during these past months I had learned I lacked sufficient courage to trust God. Even now when I considered what might happen when I spoke to the elders, all thoughts of bravery escaped me. Instead, I trembled with fear.

I took my place on one of the long unpainted benches along the women's side of the meetinghouse. I found comfort in the silence and simplicity that surrounded me: the whitewashed walls, the well-scrubbed pine floors, the plain table and chairs positioned to face the congregation. The meetinghouse contained nothing to distract me this morning from the worship of God, nothing but my own fearful thoughts.

Flanked by elders on either side of him, the presiding elder took his place at the plain wooden table. Together with all of those present, I knelt and rested my forearms on the bench while we prayed in silence. I prayed for my parents' safety; I prayed for Garon's well-being; but mostly I prayed for myself. When I lifted my head, I silently chided myself. Even my prayers had become selfish.

For the remainder of the service, I did my best to keep my thoughts on God. I sang the hymns, listened to the readings, knelt for prayer, and listened to the elder's reminder that true harmony of spirit can be obtained only through genuine humility of the heart and subjection of one to the others. "You must remember that you should rid yourself of willfulness and selfishness. . . ." His words cut like a cold winter wind, and though I joined in the final hymn, heard the benediction, and filed out of the meetinghouse with the other women, the only thing racing through my mind was the need to rid myself of selfishness.

After we finished the noonday meal, I waited until Ilsa and her parents retreated to their private rooms, and then I departed for the meetinghouse to speak to the elders. My heart pounded as I entered the women's door and saw the men sitting at the front of the church. The presiding elder motioned me forward. "Please sit, Sister Jutta."

The men folded their hands and peered at me, a frightening picture of intimidation. I followed their example and folded my hands, uncertain if I was expected to be the first to speak. One of the elders cleared his throat and leaned slightly forward. "You may explain your reason for requesting this meeting with us, Sister Jutta."

"Thank you." My mouth turned dry. Now that I was sitting before them, I wondered if I could actually reveal the truth. I lowered my head and inhaled a deep breath. *Do not be afraid. They will forgive you.* The words echoed deep inside and gave me the confidence to speak. "First, I want to thank you for granting me permission to return to the colonies. I have found peace and kindness among our people."

They smiled and nodded. "This is gut," the presiding elder said before pausing. "This is what you wanted to meet with us about?"

"Not exactly." I withdrew my handkerchief from my pocket and clutched it between my fingers. "I have come here to tell you that I have done something terrible." All of them leaned in my direction. "I have deceived you." I inhaled another deep breath. "When I asked to return, I wasn't truthful about the reason."

The presiding elder shifted in his chair. "You were not fearful of being assaulted by men in Marengo?"

I bobbed my head. "There were some threats and insults against me, but that is not the true reason I returned. I came back to spy and report on the people of Amana—to tell the Defense Council of any anti-American activity I observed within the colonies." The silence was deafening, and I longed to run from the room.

"Why would you agree to do such a thing, Sister Jutta?" The question from an elder at the far end of the row broke the silence.

My words came in a rush as I explained the threat to my parents, the possibility of their going to jail, and the loss of our bakery. "I wanted to protect my parents," I whispered.

"Is gut to want to take care of your Mutter and Vater, but not at the expense of others, ja?"

I bobbed my head. "I was wrong, and I wanted you to know the truth before the meeting with the Defense Council tomorrow."

"You were afraid they would tell us?"

"I don't know if they will tell you, but I didn't want anything they said to surprise you. I thought it best for you to know beforehand." I wrung the handkerchief into a knot. "I don't know if it will help for you to know this, but I have never made any unfavorable statements about the colonies or anyone who lives here. I told those men that the Amana people are patriots who support the United States in the war against Germany. They have not been pleased by what I have reported, and I believe that is why they destroyed my parents' bakery."

"It is gut to know that you did not tell lies about our people in order to serve your own purposes, Sister Jutta, though it saddens my heart to know that you did not truly wish to return to live among us. Sister Marta and Brother Odell speak highly of your work at the hotel. They have come to think of you as a daughter." He rubbed his forehead. "They have even suggested that you move into their apartment with them."

I swallowed the lump in my throat. "I came here for the

wrong reason, but after living here for these past months, it is my very deep desire to remain in the colonies—at least until my parents can be located." I hesitated for a moment. "If you decide that I must leave, I will understand." My final statement was no more than a whisper, but several of the elders acknowledged the comment with a slight bow of the head.

After I answered their numerous questions, the presiding elder nodded toward the door. "We will need to discuss what you have told us before we come to a decision, Sister Jutta. You may wait in the adjacent room."

As I waited, the minutes seemed to crawl by like hours. I had told myself I would accept the elders' decision with grace and thanks, but when they finally called me to rejoin them, all thoughts of grace fled from me. Fear had escalated to new heights, and I wasn't certain I'd be able to thank them if they told me to pack and leave. *Where will I go? Where will I go? Where will I go?* The thought pounded in my head like a drummer thumping an insistent beat.

I returned to my seat and stared at a spot just above the presiding elder's head. I flinched when he placed his Bible on the small wooden table. "We have arrived at a decision, Sister Jutta. A unanimous decision." He glanced first to his right and then to his left. The elders each gave a nod of agreement. "If it is your genuine desire to make your home in the colonies, we have agreed that you may stay. If and when your parents return, you may reassess your decision on where you choose to live."

"Thank—"

He held up his hand. "Let me finish. You may stay, but you must go to the members of the Redlich family and tell them the truth. They deserve to know. Then we will speak to them and see if they desire to have you remain at the hotel or if we should seek other work for you." He inhaled a deep breath and placed his hand on his Bible. "If you have not asked God to forgive you for what you have done, it is most important that you seek His forgiveness above all others." He turned a steady gaze upon me. "You understand this?"

I nodded. "I have asked for God's forgiveness, and I am willing to ask the same of Brother and Sister Redlich and Ilsa."

A white-haired elder who sat to the right of the presiding elder tapped the table. "You are certain you have said nothing against any person or group of people who are members of this community, and you have not given anyone cause to question our patriotism?"

"I am certain. If anyone should claim such a thing, it is a lie." Now damp with perspiration, the knotted handkerchief rested in the palm of my hand.

"You may return to the hotel, Sister Jutta. Please do as we have instructed regarding the Redlich family. We will expect you to be present for the meeting tomorrow and to speak the truth if you are questioned."

"You may be sure that I will do as you ask." I pushed to my feet. "Thank you for your kindness. I did not expect or deserve to be treated with such goodness and grace."

"We have listened and followed the guidance of the Father. Though you came here under a cloak of deceit, He has shown you the truth. He has forgiven you and expects no less from us."

His words wrapped around me like a warm cloak. I wanted to remain and thank each of the elders, but I doubted such behavior would be looked upon with favor. Besides, I knew I would shed tears if I attempted to speak any further.

When I neared the door, the elder called out to me, "Do

not forget your promise to speak to Sister Marta and Brother Odell."

I waved and nodded. How could I forget such a thing? In some ways it would be even more difficult to tell them the truth—especially Ilsa. I doubted she would be so quick to forgive. I entered through the back door, thinking Sister Marta might be alone in the kitchen, but when I opened the door, three sets of eyes turned toward me.

"We are enjoying some dessert, Jutta." Brother Odell pointed to the leftover bread pudding. "Ilsa knocked on your door, but there was no answer. We didn't know you had gone out." He glanced toward the backyard. "Is very cold to be out for a walk, ja?"

I wiped the snow from my shoes and removed my cloak. "I went to the meetinghouse for a talk with the elders." All three of them arched their eyebrows. Had the circumstances not been so serious, I would have laughed at the sight. "I needed to tell the elders I had lied when I asked to return to the colonies." I inhaled a deep breath. "And I needed to ask for their forgiveness."

Ilsa dropped her fork. "And did they forgive you?"

I nodded my head. "Ja, they did. I have also asked God for His forgiveness, but now I must confess to you, and I hope you will find it in your hearts to forgive me, as well. If you do not, I will understand."

Sister Marta reached for my hand. "You are pale, Jutta. Perhaps you should wait and tell us later."

"No. If I wait, it will be too hard to gather my courage again." I glanced at the three of them. They had been so kind and had opened their home and their hearts. Now I must tell them how I had taken advantage of them. "I came here to spy on the people of Amana—for the Defense Council." After I had blurted out the ugly truth, I held my breath.

Ilsa covered her mouth and laughed. "This is a joke."

Her laughter ceased when I shook my head. "It is no joke, Ilsa." I went on to explain the circumstances that had taken place: the visits from the bullies, the threats they made regarding my parents, and my eventual agreement to return and meet their demands.

Ilsa's lips curled in disgust. "How could you do such a thing to us? We opened our home to you. I thought of you as a sister—I even prayed that you and Albert would fall in love and one day marry." She scooted from the stool and stepped behind her father as if to place as much distance between us as possible. "You are a liar. You betrayed all of us!"

Sister Marta gestured for silence. "Let Jutta finish what she has to tell us. You are too quick with your words of condemnation, Ilsa. You need to harness your tongue."

Ilsa folded her arms across her chest in a defiant gesture. "You scold *me*? What about Jutta? Do you have no anger for what she has done?"

Brother Odell turned to Ilsa. "First, we must let her finish. We don't know if any harm has occurred."

I shook my head and repeated what I'd told the elders: that I had said only good things about the people of Amana and their support for the war effort. "I am ashamed of what I did, but I feared for my parents. Even though I had hoped to protect them, I couldn't find it in my heart to speak against anyone."

"Because there is nothing you could have said to hurt any of us. Otherwise, you would have done what was asked." Ilsa's eyes flashed with anger.

"That is not true, Ilsa. I could have told them about the comments you have made against the war; I could have told that you didn't follow the prohibition against baking with wheat flour on Wednesdays; I could have told how you've attempted to sway Garon against joining the army. All of those things would have pleased the members of the Defense Council, but I could not, because you have become like a sister to me, as well." I met her gaze. "I cannot change what has happened, but I am asking for your forgiveness."

Brother Odell nodded his head. "God has forgiven you, the elders have forgiven you, and we forgive you. I am thankful you did not speak against us and that no harm came to the villages because of your actions."

"What about Garon? He is in jail. What part do you have in that?" Ilsa's question was laced with anger. "The Defense Council placed you on their list. For sure, I think you had something to do with his arrest."

"No. I have never said anything about Garon, and I promise you that his arrest has nothing to do with me. Once my parents disappeared, they no longer had any power over me. I think my name is on the list because I work here, and they hope to frighten me into telling them something, even if it's a lie."

"If you've done nothing wrong, why would they believe they could frighten you?" She clenched her jaw and tightened her lips into a thin seam.

"They could threaten to tell the elders that they sent me here to report on the colonists. They are men who will say anything they believe will serve their purpose."

Ilsa shook her head. "And it seems you do the same. Tomorrow we will see who is telling the truth." She turned and stalked from the room.

For now, the knowledge that I had received the forgiveness of the elders, Ilsa's parents, and God would have to be enough.

A flood of relief washed over me, for I could now live free of the lies and deceit that had haunted me since my arrival. And though I longed for Ilsa's forgiveness, I couldn't fault her. I had betrayed her trust.

CHAPTER 29

Ilsa Redlich

The night before, after I returned to my room, I shed tears of anguish and loss along with tears of bitterness and anger. How could Jutta have done this to me—to Garon—to all of us? We had offered her kindness, and I had considered her as dear as a sister. I had shared my deepest dreams and fears with her. And for what? To receive her betrayal?

Sleep eluded me as my anger continued to swell and subside throughout the night. I asked God's forgiveness, but otherwise I avoided prayer. Most of all I avoided opening my Bible, for I didn't want to read words that might encourage me or change my mind.

Until I knew the truth, I would not apologize to Jutta.

That morning my mother drew near when Jutta went into the dining room to set the tables. "You need to apologize and ask Jutta's forgiveness."

"I asked God's forgiveness last night. If what Jutta has told us is true, I will speak with her after the meeting. First, I want to be certain she deserves my forgiveness."

My mother gasped. "*Deserves* your forgiveness? I cannot believe you would say such a thing, Ilsa Redlich. Do you deserve God's forgiveness? Did you deserve to have Christ die for your sins? I am ashamed!"

Using the long-handled fork, I turned the sizzling bacon. "For causing you shame, I am sorry, but it does not change my mind. I will wait to offer my forgiveness. Garon's life may be in great danger because of Jutta's coming to live with us. If so, I don't know if I can forgive her."

"To have an unforgiving heart is not what the Bible teaches. If you do not forgive, bitterness will take root in your heart, and in the end, you will suffer greater consequences than Jutta will."

Rather than achieving the desired effect, my mother's admonition only annoyed me. She could quote the Bible and warn me of terrible consequences, but it wouldn't change my decision. I was not prepared to forgive Jutta—not now, possibly never.

I was thankful when Jutta returned to the kitchen, for it would stop the talk of forgiveness. In fact, it stopped all conversation. The three of us worked in silence as we completed preparations and ate our breakfast.

There were few guests, and for that I was thankful. All of the salesmen departed as soon as they'd eaten their breakfast. Mr. and Mrs. Young retreated to their room, but a short time later Mrs. Young appeared in the kitchen and announced that she and her husband were going on an outing and wouldn't return until late in the afternoon. I was pleased to know they'd be absent, though I thought a daylong outing in February rather curious.

Even more, I thought Mr. Young would want to be present for the meeting.

"I thought your husband would remain at the hotel to provide help to Garon if a lawyer is needed."

Mrs. Young hesitated for a moment. "I believe the elders advised my husband his help was not needed. Jonathan is not one to insert himself where he isn't wanted." Keeping her gaze fastened on her hands, she pulled on her gloves. "I do hope all goes well."

"Since when doesn't Mr. Young stick his nose into the business of others?" I whispered to my mother. "And it is quite cold to go on such an outing, don't you think?"

My mother shrugged. "I am thinking Mr. Young may feel insulted that the elders did not ask for his help, so they prefer to be gone for the day. Perhaps they are going to take the train to Iowa City or Cedar Rapids for some shopping or to visit the library. I recall Mrs. Young mentioning she wanted some good books to read."

"If they want to shop or visit a library, it seems they would return to their home in Des Moines. I truly do not understand why they continue to stay here. I don't believe one word they say."

My mother frowned. "That is unkind, Ilsa."

"Perhaps, but she lied about speaking German, didn't she?" I rested my elbows on the worktable. "And the other day when I said something about children, she wrinkled her nose and said children are a nuisance! Does that sound like a woman who suffers from melancholy because she has been unable to bear a child of her own?"

"Is true that she hasn't ever mentioned her desire for children."

I nodded. "And she didn't even want to look at Sister Rose's newborn daughter at the Red Cross meeting last week."

My mother lifted another stack of dishes into the sudsy water. "I thought perhaps it grieved her to see the baby."

"Maybe, but I don't think so."

My father strode into the kitchen and joined us. "What am I hearing? Talk of babies?"

"No need to worry." My mother grinned at him. "We were discussing Mrs. Young." She gestured toward the coffeepot. "You need more coffee?"

"Nein. I wanted to tell you the meeting with the men from Marengo will take place in the dining room."

"Here? In the hotel?" My mother gasped. "Why would they want to meet here? That is not a gut idea. We have guests upstairs."

My father rested his hands on the worktable. "The elders would have preferred another location, but there are trains due to arrive, and we cannot leave the hotel unattended. Since we must all be present, they decided this would be the best place."

She shook her head. "I am surprised the Defense Council agreed. I don't have the wisdom of an elder, but I think having such a meeting in the hotel is a foolish decision."

"We can take turns at the front desk. The parlor is available for anyone they don't want in the dining room, and one of the men from Marengo is bringing some sort of divider we can place between the rooms."

My mother pressed her fingers down the front of her dress. "What time will they arrive?"

"They should be here by eight o'clock. They want to begin early so the matter can be settled by suppertime."

"Suppertime? Am I to serve them the noonday meal?"

Frustration shone in her eyes. "You should have told me before now, Odell. How am I to prepare for so many extra people when you give me no notice?"

"The elders gave me strict instructions. And you need not worry about the noonday meal. They are making arrangements to have soup and bread delivered from one of the kitchen houses."

"Tongues will be wagging once all that food is delivered to the hotel." My mother frowned. "I can only imagine what stories will be traveling from house to house."

"Gossip is frowned upon," my father said with a grin.

Mother placed the dried dishes on the shelf before she turned toward my father. "The elders can frown all they want, but that doesn't stop gossip."

Jutta folded the dish towel and hung it over the drying rack. "What about cleaning the rooms?"

My father motioned to me. "Both of you should go upstairs and begin your cleaning. I will come for you if you are needed at the meeting."

I stopped short at my father's instruction. "I would prefer to clean the parlor and wait down here so that I can see Garon when he arrives. Who can say when I will have an opportunity to see him again?"

"The parlor will need to be cleaned," he agreed, "so you may remain down here until Garon arrives. Is true we do not know what will happen, but we must remember to trust God, Ilsa."

I nodded and murmured my thanks. While Jutta gathered her cleaning supplies and retreated upstairs, I dusted the parlor furniture—very slowly. I didn't want to complete my task before Garon arrived. Not since the fall housecleaning had the parlor been dusted so well. It was when I pulled aside the curtains and swiped the windowsills for the second time that I saw the men from Marengo arriving. There were two men on horseback, while Garon and several others rode in a buggy.

Keeping my eyes fixed upon Garon, I said, "They're here, Vater. And the elders are arriving, as well. Mutter is right. For sure, the tongues will be wagging when all these people are seen."

My heart thumped and my palms turned damp as the men mounted the steps. I rushed toward Garon when he entered the front door, but one of the men held out his arm and stopped my advance.

"Get away from the prisoner." His lips twisted in an ugly snarl.

Garon attempted a smile, but I could see fear clouding his eyes. His hands were tied behind his back, and I doubted he'd seen soap or water since they'd taken him into custody. One of the men yanked Garon's hat from his head. His hair was matted and dirty, and I wondered if he'd been forced to sleep on the floor.

My father stepped from behind the desk and approached the men on either side of Garon. "My daughter is betrothed to Garon, and since his hands are tied, I do not think there is any harm if she wishes to greet him. Even if he should try to escape, I'm sure the two of you would have no trouble detaining him, ja?"

The two men glanced at each other, obviously embarrassed to admit their loutish behavior was unnecessary. "She can tell him hello, but this ain't no tea party we're bringin' him here for. When a man's accused of treason, he loses his rights to be treated fair."

My father frowned at the men. "I thought to lose his rights, the accusations had to be proved. No one has found Garon guilty of anything—you are the only ones who think he has committed a wrongdoing."

The man scratched his growth of beard. "Yeah, well, we're

the ones that count, so I'm saying she can tell him hello, but that's as far as it goes." With a glare in his eyes, he motioned me forward. "And don't be talking in that ugly Hun language of yours, neither. Speak English."

"We know we are to speak English." It would have been satisfying to tell him that he didn't speak very good English, but I refrained. Instead, I greeted Garon while the two of them stared at us. I longed to touch him, but when I reached out my hand, the man pushed me back.

"No touching, neither." He looked at my father. "Where we s'posed to have the meetin'?"

My father directed the two men and Garon into the dining room. Soon the other men from Marengo entered with the elders and Garon's parents. A rough wooden screen was placed in the doorway between the dining room and the parlor, though it didn't hide much. With little effort, anyone in the parlor could see and hear everything going on behind the makeshift partition.

The men insisted that everyone on their list must be present in either the parlor or dining room. Jutta was summoned from her cleaning duties and took a seat beside me in the parlor. Brother Milton settled on the couch. My parents took up their station behind the front desk. In addition to the elders, Garon's parents were granted permission to remain at one of the tables in the dining room for the entire proceeding.

I had no idea who was speaking, but one of the men from either the Defense Council or the American Protective League said it was time to begin. "The charges against Garon Drucker are as follows: That he has on at least twenty occasions sent coded telegrams that could assist the enemy in the war effort. That we have an agent of the American Protective League who will testify that Garon Drucker personally sent these telegrams, using the telegraph equipment at the South Amana train station. Unless such information can be disputed with ample proof, Garon Drucker will be held in jail until the court assembles to judge his crimes."

"I have already told you these accusations are false. I know nothing of military—"

Chair legs scraped on the wooden floor. "You need to shut your mouth unless you're told to speak." I couldn't see who had given the order, but for sure it was one of bullies.

While we waited in the parlor, a member of the American Protective League explained that Garon had tapped out those coded messages. His voice was loud and clear. "I arrived in South Amana and passed myself off as a salesman traveling to several towns along the line. While I waited for the train, I positioned myself near the window so I could hear the tapping of the equipment. Although the messages made no sense, I wrote down every word that was sent."

"And you are considered an expert with Morse code?"

"I am. But since the messages made no sense, they were turned over to military specialists, who were eventually able to break the code."

I wasn't certain who was speaking, but from the tone of the questions and answers, it was the men from Marengo who were talking.

"And why were you sent to South Amana? In other words, why did anyone think the messages were coming from the telegrapher in this particular place?"

The man cleared his throat. He was probably smirking, pleased to point a finger at Garon. I leaned forward to listen. "We received word from the East Coast that there were messages coming from someone in this area. I can't reveal the particulars, or future operations could be placed in jeopardy."

I grimaced. This man sounded much more educated than the thugs who had hauled Garon into the hotel. He also sounded as though he knew what he was talking about.

"And what did those messages say?"

"The expert who decoded the telegrams informed us that those messages contained formulas for poison gas, development of sophisticated flame throwers, and other weapons that would be very helpful to the German military." There was a brief pause, and I heard the shuffle of papers. "I was astonished at the information he was sending—and we've now discovered that some of those telegrams were being sent to German spies working in large eastern cities. Two of them have been apprehended. We've also learned that information about the German army was being transmitted by that same telegraph to the National Headquarters of the American Protective League."

"What? I am confused. What does this mean?" I recognized Brother Edwin's voice and was thankful he'd interrupted, because I was confused, as well. "Are you saying there are two people reporting information—one to the Germans and one to your Protective League?"

"Not two men—only one. Your son was obviously working as an informant for both sides. I'm sure he was receiving a great deal of money for his efforts."

"This is nothing but lies," Garon shouted.

"You will remain quiet or I will have you removed from the room," the man from the League replied in a threatening tone.

"My son didn't mean to offend you, but you must understand that these charges are completely false. Garon would never do any of these things. And he has no need for money. We live in a society that provides for all of our needs."

"He may not have needed it to support himself, but maybe he was looking to get out of here and begin a new life—one where that money would help him to start over elsewhere. It makes perfect sense."

"It makes no sense at all. I do not under—"

"I am trying to explain. If you and your son would cease with your interruptions, I will continue."

Brother Edwin mumbled an indistinguishable reply, but I assumed he promised to be quiet, because the man cleared his throat.

"As I was saying, there were messages going both directions. There wasn't concern when the Protective League was receiving information, for we assumed it was coming from one of our informants in this area. But when we discovered the same telegram was being used to send secrets to the Germans, we knew we had a traitor of the worst sort on our hands."

Brother Milton rested his elbows on his knees and covered his face with his hands. "Why would Garon do such a thing?"

His hands had muffled the question, but it had been clear enough. My anger soared like a bird taking flight. I scooted to the edge of my chair. "He did not do anything," I whispered. "How can you so easily believe he is guilty of these charges?"

Brother Milton uncovered his eyes and cupped his jaw in one hand. Was it shame or disappointment I saw in his eyes? "You can hear what that man said, Sister Ilsa. They have proof."

I glanced over my shoulder at Jutta. "This must be connected to the telegrams Garon was sending for Mr. Young."

"I think you're right, but I have heard that Mr. Young is an important member of the American Protective League. If so, he wouldn't help the Germans—he would be helping the United States." Jutta twisted the tie of her bonnet and stared at the upper hallway. "Yet if Mr. Young is an important member of the League, why wasn't he included in this meeting—especially since he is staying here at the hotel? And if these men believe it is a double informant at work, it surely must be Mr. Young, not Garon."

"You must say something to one of the elders." Intent upon convincing Jutta, I pushed aside all memory of the unkind behavior I'd directed at her the previous night.

"Me?" Her eyebrows arched high on her forehead. "Perhaps it would be better if you told your Vater. Then he could speak to the elders."

I could understand Jutta's reluctance. Only yesterday she had faced the elders and confessed her offenses. No doubt she would prefer to remain invisible during this proceeding, but Garon's future was at stake. I must convince her to tell what she knew. In the end, it might not help Garon, but we needed to try.

"Please, Jutta. I know I was wrong last night. I should have forgiven you. Perhaps this is God's way of showing me that my behavior was displeasing to Him, but you must speak up. If not for my sake, do this for Garon. He does not deserve what is happening to him."

"I gave my word to the person who told me about Mr. Young that I would not reveal his name. They will ask me how I came by this information." She squeezed my hand. "You know they will insist I tell them." Jutta's eyes welled with tears, but she finally gave a slight nod. "When there is an opportunity, I will speak to the presiding elder, but if this information doesn't help Garon, you must not hold it against me."

"You have my word." I brushed a fleeting kiss on her cheek. "Thank you. And please forgive me for my actions."

Her lips curved in a faint smile. "We shall put the past behind us and move forward."

A short time later, one of the elders appeared from behind the screen. "We are going to take a short recess." He strode toward my mother and father. "A cup of coffee would be appreciated if you have the time, Sister Marta."

She waved toward Jutta and me, and we hurried from our places on the couch. "We will serve coffee to the elders. You will help me in the kitchen, ja?"

I poked Jutta in the side and nodded toward the elder. Her jaw clenched, but she took a hesitant step in his direction. "May I have a word with you regarding what has been said in the dining room, Brother Ernst?"

The elder nodded at Jutta, and though I wanted to remain and make certain she told him everything about Mr. Young and the American Protective League, I followed my mother toward the kitchen. My heart thumped in overtime when Garon looked up at me. I wanted to rush to his side and console him, tell him everything would be fine, but I knew any attempt would be thwarted by the men sitting on either side of him. I flashed an encouraging smile before I disappeared into the kitchen.

I had placed cups and saucers on the sideboard and was pouring cream into a pitcher when Jutta entered the kitchen. "Brother Ernst asked that we prepare coffee for everyone, not just the elders."

Sister Marta nodded. "I expected he would want us to offer hospitality to them. I have already placed another pot on the stove."

While my mother carried the coffeepot to the dining room, I pulled Jutta aside. "Well? What did Brother Ernst say?"

She glanced toward the dining room. "I didn't recognize any of those men. They aren't the ones who came to our bakery."

"I don't think it matters—they all belong to the same groups. What did Brother Ernst say?"

She turned away from the men in the other room. "When the elders are given their turn to speak, he is going to ask if Mr. Young is one of their members."

"That's all? I doubt they'll tell him the truth—especially if they are trying to protect him for some reason."

"I believe he understands it is important. Besides, I am sure Garon will explain he sent those telegrams for Mr. Young. We must have faith that God will protect Garon."

I couldn't argue against Jutta's declaration, but having faith or trust didn't seem enough. Even prayer seemed negligible. I wanted to do something significant. "Sometimes I think God needs a nudge—a little help. I would never want my Vater or the elders to hear me say such a thing. They would think all of their Bible teaching has fallen on deaf ears." I glanced into the dining room and then back at Jutta. "Do I make any sense to you?"

"Ja, but sometimes when we try to help God, I think we can make matters worse. Sometimes we need to give Him a little elbow room to complete His work. If they don't give Brother Ernst or Garon an opportunity to speak about Mr. Young and his role in sending the telegrams, then we will march into the dining room and make them listen to me."

I bobbed my head, pleased with Jutta's plan. One way or the other, we would see that Garon didn't return to jail.

CHAPTER 30

Jutta Schmitt

After everyone had finished their coffee, we took our places in the parlor and once again strained to hear every word. The man from the American Protective League said he had completed his comments, and now Brother Ernst could make a statement or begin questioning any witnesses he wished to call on Garon's behalf.

Before beginning, Brother Ernst thanked the men for agreeing to meet in South Amana. His voice was clear and kind. "We have been patient while you set forth all of these accusations, and I know you will permit us the same opportunity so that we may discover the truth."

One of the men from Marengo grunted something about Huns, but another told him to be quiet.

Ilsa clutched my arm, and I could see the fear in her eyes. Proving anything to these men would be difficult. They wanted to believe the worst of Garon—of all of us. Still, when presented with the truth, attitudes could change. Ilsa's attitude about me had certainly changed since last evening. I could only hope that the elders would have the same success with these men.

Brother Ernst's clear voice drifted across the partition. "Garon, tell us about the telegrams that you are supposed to have sent to these informants in the eastern cities."

Ilsa's fingers tightened around my arm as Garon acknowledged he had sent the telegrams but that they had been sent on behalf of Mr. Young, a guest in the hotel. "I did not understand what any of those messages meant. None of them made any sense to me. I am a telegrapher, and it is my job to send the messages I am given. If I had known they had anything to do with the war, I wouldn't have sent them."

"Tell me," Brother Ernst started, "is Mr. Jonathan Young a member of your American Protective League or the Iowa Defense Council?" His voice didn't waver as he asked the question.

Chairs scraped on wood and murmuring voices drifted toward us. "The lawyer from Des Moines?" the man in charge asked.

"Ja, that is the one," Brother Ernst replied.

"Yes, he is a member, one who is highly acclaimed in our organization."

"Then he is a man with access to much information, I would guess?"

I wanted to applaud Brother Ernst for his quick thinking. If the League was going to accuse Garon, then they needed to have answers for Mr. Young's actions.

"Y-y-yes, I would say he has had more access than most. He is a lawyer, and his services are used at all levels. His early requests for top security clearance were denied for a time but later were approved. He has done much to aid the League."

Perhaps that denial had been the incident Kenneth Reeves

had observed when he'd attended the meeting in Des Moines—the one he'd described to me. I didn't doubt for a minute that Mr. Young would be angered by such a refusal. He wasn't a man accustomed to rejection.

"I believe that Mr. Young and his wife are guests here at the hotel. Perhaps this matter could be easily resolved if we asked him to join us." Brother Ernst appeared from behind the partition. "Would one of you go to the Youngs' room and ask him to come down?"

Ilsa jumped to her feet. "They departed this morning on an outing. We don't expect their return until later this afternoon."

My heart plummeted when I heard the chairs scrape across the floor and murmurs from the men in the dining room. I feared they would leave and take Garon with them. One of the men moved the partition. "If it's going to take Mr. Young's presence to get to the bottom of all this, then maybe we should wait and finish up on another day."

Brother Ernst held up his hand. "If we are not to complete the matter today, I request you release Garon to our safekeeping."

One of the hooligans shook his head. "Naw, that ain't a good idea. He'd be gone before morning. You can't trust these Huns."

Ilsa rushed toward Garon, but her father stepped forward and grasped her arms before she could reach him. She twisted away and turned toward me, desperation shining in her eyes. "What about those drawings and the other papers we saw in the Youngs' room, Jutta?" She waved toward the men. "Tell them." Before I could speak, she waved toward the upstairs hallway. "Go and see for yourselves. They have stacks of pictures. I found drawings of weapons under their mattress when I was changing the bed. Isn't that right, Jutta?"

355

Sister Marta gasped and covered her mouth. "You were going through their belongings, Ilsa?" Her muffled question went unheeded.

One of the rough-looking men from Marengo appeared eager to rush upstairs, but the well-dressed man who had been asking the questions waved him toward the dining room. "Go sit down with the prisoner." He glanced at Ilsa and, in an unexpected gesture of kindness, told her she could visit with Garon while he checked the room. Turning in my direction, he motioned me forward. "Please take me upstairs to see those papers and drawings you were talking about."

I hadn't been talking about the papers and drawings, but I didn't correct him. He gazed down at me. "I'm Fred Gillett. What's your name?"

Brother Ernst stepped forward. "This is Sister Jutta Schmitt."

Mr. Gillett frowned. "Schmitt? I believe I've stopped at a bakery in Marengo owned by people named Schmitt. Would those be relatives of yours?"

There was no reason to fear speaking the truth to this man. "My parents own the bakery, but there is little left of it. Your members destroyed the bakery, and my parents have disappeared."

"I am sorry for what happened to your bakery, though I had nothing to do with that incident. The members of the local Defense Council in Marengo have been warned they are to take no further actions of this sort unless so directed by the American Protective League."

He obviously thought his statement should make me feel better, but it didn't. "No one should have the authority to destroy the property of others. My parents are loyal to this country, yet I have no idea of their whereabouts. I was threatened that if I did not come to the colonies and make reports against the citizens of Amana, our bakery would be destroyed. All because we are of German heritage. What kind of country is this that persecutes us simply because our ancestors came from Germany?"

I wasn't certain if he would answer me or send me off to jail with Garon. He hesitated for a moment before he spoke. "We are at war with Germany, and we are trying to protect this country."

"With such behavior, Germany does not need to worry about destroying the United States. People like your men from the Defense Council and your Protective League will do it for them. You cannot judge us as enemies because our ancestors came here from Germany." I could see that my boldness startled him, and Brother Ernst, as well, for he shook his head and held his index finger against his pursed lips.

"I will not argue our methods of defending this country with you, Miss Schmitt, but I am sorry for the destruction of your parents' business. What has happened to you is shameful, and I will see what I can do to help once we have resolved the problem now facing us."

I thanked him. Though I disapproved of his group, if he could reunite me with my parents, I would be grateful. Brother Odell withdrew the key from the hook near the front desk, but Brother Ernst took it from his hand. "Sister Marta and I will accompany you upstairs with Sister Jutta. It would be improper for her to be alone with a man."

I marched up the steps, the rest of group following close behind. Expecting the door would be locked, I stepped aside for Brother Ernst, but when he pushed down on the latch, the door swung open. The Youngs had always made a practice of locking their door if they were to be gone for any length of time. What were they up to?

Brother Ernst motioned us inside, and I scanned the room.

The stacks of papers that usually covered the table and overflowed onto the floor had completely disappeared. It took only a glance around the room to reveal the Youngs had realized something was amiss and had removed the incriminating papers from the room. They'd likely stuffed the piles of papers and drawings into their suitcases. Mr. Young could have taken them out of the hotel while Mrs. Young came to speak with us in the kitchen early this morning. She had stood in the doorway, blocking our view of any activity near the stairway or front door.

A wave of nausea swept over me. Without those papers, we couldn't prove what we'd said. I hurried to the bed, hoping I might find one of the drawings or maps hidden beneath the mattress. Perhaps they'd forgotten some. I glanced over my shoulder at Brother Ernst and shook my head. "Nothing."

Sister Marta rested her palm along her jaw and appeared uncertain whether she should be relieved that we weren't going to rummage through a guest's room or worried that we'd found nothing of consequence. I strode across the room and opened the wardrobe. The Youngs' clothing was inside, and the large trunks they'd arrived with were still here. Surely they would return.

"Ach! I told them not to burn paper in the fireplace." Sister Marta frowned and marched to the fireplace. "That is why we have the wood. Look at all this mess they have made."

I stooped down near the fireplace. From the appearance of the charred remnants, it appeared they'd been burning newspapers, but I couldn't be certain. Had they burned those stacks of papers rather than packing them?

Mr. Gillett stared into the fireplace. "It doesn't appear there's going to be much we can do until Mr. Young returns."

After seeing the room, I doubted Mr. Young's return would assist us in any way, but I wasn't going to say so. If there was no proof remaining in their room, Mr. Young wasn't going to furnish it to Mr. Gillett or any of those other men. Obviously, Garon's arrest and the trip to Marengo had served to alert Mr. Young to clear his room of any connection to the war or his spying activity. And if these rooms were any indication of Mr. Young's plan to protect himself, Garon would be the sacrifice.

Ilsa visibly paled when we returned to the parlor and Mr. Gillett announced there was nothing but the couple's personal belongings in the rooms. She hurried to my side and leaned close to my ear. "He's lying, isn't he?"

"No. Everything we saw there is gone. From the looks of the fireplace, they burned many of the papers and no doubt took the rest with them. I even looked under the mattress."

"Then we have no way to prove Garon's innocence. I gave them hope, and now . . ." Her voice trailed off as she traced her fingers along the folds of her dress.

"There is still hope, Ilsa. When Mr. Young returns, they will question him and perhaps he will say something that will permit the truth to come out." I knew the chances of such good fortune weren't likely. After all, Mr. Young was a lawyer. He'd been crafty enough to realize he needed to remove the papers from his room and crafty enough to leave town for the day, and he'd surely be crafty enough to avoid a misstep when being interrogated. Especially since the men asking the questions didn't make their living working in courtrooms.

"Garon's Mutter can't stop weeping, and his Vater just stares across the room. I want to console them, but what can I say? They had some hope when Mr. Gillett went upstairs to find the papers, but now they fear Garon will be returned to jail—or worse."

"What do you mean, 'or worse'?"

Tears trickled down Ilsa's cheeks. "One of those men from

Marengo laughed and said they could save the county some time and money on the return to Marengo. He patted his jacket." Her eyes glistened. "I think he has a gun in his pocket."

I clutched her hands and squeezed tight. "Mr. Gillett will not permit such a thing. I don't think Mr. Gillett is a bad man—just misguided in his thinking." Though I wasn't certain I was completely correct about Mr. Gillett, I wanted to give Ilsa hope. And I wanted to believe I was right about the man—both for Garon and for myself. I wanted to believe Mr. Gillett would keep his word.

As time for the noonday meal approached, Brother Ernst drew near. "One of the elders has taken the buggy and will go to each of the Küches and collect the food the Küchebaases were instructed to prepare." A slight smile played at his lips. "There will be less talk this way."

The announcement eased Sister Marta's concerns. We had received extra bread from the bakery wagon before the men arrived from Marengo. It seemed Brother Ernst had thought of everything, and though I admired his efforts, I doubted his attempt to still any wagging tongues would be successful.

Sharing our meal with these uncouth men proved uncomfortable, but after a stern warning from Mr. Gillett, they ceased their rowdy talk and ate in silence. For some, it appeared more difficult than others, for they were obviously accustomed to taking their meals in more boisterous surroundings. When the meal ended, we cleared the tables, and while the men adjourned to the parlor or outside for a breath of fresh air, we hurried to wash the dishes.

Ilsa remained somber, unwilling to believe there was any hope for Garon. She lifted a stack of clean bowls to the shelves along the wall and shoved them into place. "How I wish I had that drawing," she muttered. "If you hadn't burned it, we could show it to Mr. Gillett."

I fell against the worktable as I spun around. "The drawing! That's it, Ilsa. I still have it."

"You do?" She crossed the room in four giant steps. "Where is it? We need to show them." She grabbed my hand and began to pull me toward the dining room.

With an abrupt yank, she stopped in her tracks. "Wait! Why do you still have the drawing?"

I didn't fail to notice the suspicion that shaded her question. I knew what she was thinking. All the anger and doubt she'd experienced last night when I'd revealed my reason for coming to Amana had returned to haunt her—and me. She hadn't had enough time to fully regain her trust in me. This revelation could sever any hope of future friendship. Yet what would be worse? The end of a friendship or the end of Garon's freedom? Besides, I had already admitted I still had the drawing.

"I won't lie to you. I kept it in case I might be able to use it as a way of protecting my parents. Had it been the only means to save them, I think I would have shown it to those men. But it wasn't necessary. My parents were gone when I returned to Marengo, and the bakery had already been destroyed." I was certain she wanted to ask me if I had planned to implicate her, but she sealed her lips into a thin line—likely afraid of what I might answer. "None of this matters right now, Ilsa. Come with me, and we'll get the drawing."

She shook her head. "No. I think it is better that you go and tell Mr. Gillett and the elders. Ask them if it will help to see the drawing. Otherwise, there is no need to give it to them." She shrugged. "Who can say? If they don't think it is enough evidence, we may be able to use it in the future."

I didn't argue with her. The idea made little sense to me, but to argue would only make matters worse between us. I approached Brother Ernst with the news. He nodded and waved me forward. "We are ready to begin, so you can come into the dining room and tell us about this drawing."

Standing in front of the group wasn't what I had hoped for, but I took my place and answered Brother Ernst's questions. Hope gleamed in Sister Barbara's eyes as she straightened her shoulders and looked at me. Garon's father didn't appear quite so confident.

Mr. Gillett pushed away from the table. "So we are off to another room to look for papers." He glanced toward the men on either side of Garon. "Remain with the prisoner."

"Off on another wild goose chase," one of them muttered, but he was forced to retract his comment when we returned a short time later.

Holding the drawing, Mr. Gillett examined it and shook his head. "This is a weapon I've never before seen, but military experts will know. This isn't something that should be in the hands of anyone other than the military." He leaned back in his chair. "Still, I don't know how you can connect this drawing to Mr. Young. If we'd found it in his room, it would be difficult for him to explain, but I believe he will say that he's never before seen it, and there is no way to repudiate such a statement."

"But there is," Ilsa said, rushing from the parlor and past the divider.

Rather than admonishing her for the interruption, Mr. Gillett motioned her forward. "And what is that?"

"There's writing on the back." She motioned for him to turn over the drawing.

For a moment he studied the bold script. "And how do we

know this is Mr. Young's handwriting? Knowing the circumstances, I'm certain he wouldn't freely give us a sample of his handwriting. If he did, he could disguise it enough that it wouldn't match what is written here."

The sound of a creaking drawer and the shuffle of papers could be heard in the parlor. Moments later, Brother Odell appeared. "Excuse me, but I have a letter written by Mr. Young. He wrote to me asking to rent the upstairs room. Perhaps you could compare his letter to the writing on that picture."

"I think that would prove to be most helpful." Mr. Gillett examined the envelope and withdrew the letter. After turning the drawing facedown, he placed one of the written pages alongside it on the table.

Together with several of the other men, Brother Ernst leaned over his shoulder and tapped a finger on the table beside the letter. "I think these look like the same person's writing, Mr. Gillett."

"I agree. It is obvious to me that Mr. Young is connected to this drawing, and that he is the one who should be charged with treason." Mr. Gillett pushed away from the table. "Although I doubt Mr. Young will show up at his law office in Des Moines, we will be on the lookout for him." He raked his fingers through his hair. "I don't think you'll see either of them back in the Amana Colonies. Mr. Young is too smart—he wouldn't take such a risk."

Sister Marta stepped forward. "But what about their belongings? Surely they'll return for those."

Mr. Gillett shook his head. "No. They left them so all would appear normal. They are quite shrewd." He nodded toward Brother Ernst. "I believe we can consider this meeting concluded and the charges dismissed against Garon."

"Aw, now I ain't thinkin' he's been completely cleared of the charges," one of the men from Marengo lamented.

Mr. Gillett shot an angry look across the table. "And I don't believe I asked for your opinion. Untie his hands."

The man, though obviously not in agreement, did as Mr. Gillett ordered.

Once Garon was released, Ilsa rushed to his side. Had the elders not been standing nearby, I was certain she would have kissed him. There was no doubt their life together would prove a strong union.

CHAPTER 31

The days passed and life returned to normal. Soon after the meeting when Garon had been freed, the elders instructed Sister Marta to pack up the Youngs' belongings. We carefully folded Mrs. Young's gowns and Mr. Young's suits, as well as the rest of their clothing. Ilsa noted that we didn't come across any of Mrs. Young's jewelry, a fact that confirmed our belief the couple would never return.

A story appeared in the newspaper crediting the Iowa Defense Council and the American Protective League with the discovery of a double espionage plan that involved a lawyer from Des Moines. A description of both Mr. and Mrs. Young followed, with a request that anyone with knowledge of their whereabouts should contact authorities immediately. There had been no mention of Garon's arrest and subsequent release or the part we had played in uncovering Mr. Young's anti-American activity. The

American Protective League and the Defense Council took full credit. And that was fine with those of us who knew what had truly occurred. Mr. Gillett hadn't promised our efforts would be acknowledged to the public.

I was disappointed that there'd been no mention of my missing parents in the newspaper, for Mr. Gillett had promised he would issue orders to the defense groups that my parents should be permitted to return home safely. After a week passed, one of the regulars arrived at the hotel with a newspaper tucked under his arm.

He'd handed me the paper and pointed to an article. "This have anything to do with you?"

I devoured every word of the item and thanked him.

"Thought you might want to see this, too. They've got these posted all over Marengo and at a couple of the other stops along the way. Saw a few in Cedar Rapids earlier in the week."

The posters stated that by order of the American Protective League, Bert and Eva Schmitt were hereby permitted to return freely to their home in Marengo, and under order of said League they should be permitted to conduct business without harassment or interference of any person or organization. Any such harassment against them would be punishable by imprisonment. The poster bore the name of Fred Gillett, president of the Iowa American Protective League, and was stamped with an official emblem. I was thankful Mr. Gillett had kept his word.

His efforts to help had far exceeded my expectations, but I doubted the posters and newspaper articles would reunite me with my parents. If they were in hiding, how would they ever see the notices? And I doubted the posters would be displayed beyond Iowa City and Cedar Rapids. If my parents had gone to

Chicago or some other distant city, they would never know it was safe to return.

The immediate pleasure I'd experienced upon seeing the posters soon gave way to sorrow. To live in this state of expectancy, never knowing if I'd ever again hear from my parents, seemed the cruelest of punishments. Was I to go on with my day-to-day life as though nothing had happened? My stomach knotted at the possibility. How long could I do such a thing?

"Pray." That single word remained the constant response I received from the colonists when I lamented there'd been no word. I often considered telling them that I had been praying ever since I arrived in South Amana, but I held my tongue. I knew their intentions were good—they wanted me to place my burden at God's feet and trust He would answer. I did believe God would answer my prayer, but unless it meant the return of my parents, I wasn't certain I would be willing to accept the outcome. Of course, I didn't share that thought with anyone. I didn't want the colonists to think I possessed a superficial faith.

I was upstairs cleaning when I heard the jingle of the front door. "Ilsa, Jutta! There are letters from Albert." Garon's voice drifted up the steps, and both Ilsa and I rushed down the hallway from opposite directions. He laughed as we came together at the top of the steps. "If ever I want to make sure you two come when I call, I'll be sure to mention Albert's name." He waved the letters overhead. "One for each of you."

"I received one, too." He patted his pocket. "It was not an easy task convincing Brother Peter to let me deliver your letters." His eyes sparkled as he grinned at Ilsa. "But for you, I persisted."

"And what did your letter say?" Ilsa asked as she bounded down the steps.

"Albert wrote that he thought I made a wise decision." He beamed at her. "He said he thinks marriage to you is a much better choice than going into the army."

Ilsa grinned. She glanced around before pushing to her toes and accepting his kiss. I looked away, embarrassed by their show of affection, though they seemed comfortable to share a kiss in front of me. Perhaps because they were seldom alone and they knew I wouldn't tell. Ilsa's hands remained flat against Garon's chest. "Did he say he would come home for the wedding?"

"He said he would request a leave. He wants to be here, but he can't say if he will be given permission to come home." Garon covered Ilsa's hands with his own and looked into her eyes. "For sure, he is happy that we are going ahead with the wedding."

Ilsa nodded. "Ja, but it will not be the same without Albert."

"Who can say? Perhaps the army will give him the leave he requests. We will pray for a good result." I hoped my light-hearted tone would help ease Ilsa's disappointment. "Let's get a cup of coffee and read our letters." I didn't know if Sister Marta would approve. We had already enjoyed our midmorning coffee along with a slice of bread smeared with rhubarb jam, but she'd gone to visit with Sister Hulda about the next day's Red Cross meeting.

I quickly scanned the contents of my letter while Ilsa checked to see how much coffee remained in the pot. As usual, Albert had sent separate pages: one I could share with his family and one that was for me alone. I didn't think Ilsa realized Albert had taken up this practice, but it seemed he needed to write to me of happenings that he feared would worry his parents and Ilsa. I quickly removed the letter he had marked *For your eyes only*, and tucked it into my apron pocket.

"There isn't much coffee left," Ilsa called from the kitchen.

"You and Garon share it. I had enough earlier this morning."
I sat down at the dining room table and began to read my letter. I
didn't expect anything of consequence—Albert saved those items
for my personal letter. In this one he spoke of the weather, training
exercises, and the medical guidance he continued to receive at the
infirmary. The spirit of the letter was cheerful, especially when
he wrote of Ilsa's wedding. No doubt Ilsa's letter contained much
of the same. Most of the time the letters were nearly identical,
but he knew they would be shared, and there was only so much
information one person could write—especially when you didn't
want to worry others.

Once Ilsa had read her letter, we exchanged. As expected, they
were almost word for word. I returned her letter and pushed up
from the table with a grin. "I'm going to go up and finish cleaning. I'm sure the two of you can find something to talk about in
my absence."

I waved as I scurried up the steps and returned to the room.
Removing the rest of Albert's letter from my pocket, I dropped
to one of the chairs. My heart plummeted. His letter detailed the
long hours he'd been required to work at the infirmary. He never
wanted to appear tired or complain—such behavior was sure to
draw criticism from the other men.

Through his letter, I could feel the weariness of his body
and his heart.

Each day I wonder how we will meet the demands. More
and more men are being shipped overseas, and that leaves fewer
of us to work in the infirmary. There have been several cases of
influenza, and there is worry of an epidemic. All precautions
must be taken. I do ask for your prayers that I may keep a good
spirit and be of comfort to those who are ill. I had one young

soldier who was very ill ask me how he could be assured of going to heaven if he died. I counted it a great honor to read to him from the book of Romans. Before he died, he accepted Jesus as his Savior. I am thankful I was here to talk with him.

I am truly pleased and give thanks to God that Garon was released from jail and that he and Ilsa have set a date for their marriage. They are a good match, and I am hopeful I will be home for their wedding.

I continue to be thankful for the friendship of Private Higgins. Although some of the men taunt him, he has proven to be a true friend. He has even convinced some of the other men to change their attitude toward me. For that, I am also grateful.

Though letters do not suffice for gaining knowledge in person, I eagerly look forward to the day when I will return home and we can learn even more about each other. I believe one day we might be a good match, as well. I do hope this does not offend you or frighten you, for if you have interest in another, I will not interfere. However, it is my hope that I can always count you as a friend.

Please write and tell me what you have heard regarding your parents and their welfare. As usual, I ask you to keep this information to yourself, for my parents would needlessly worry. I hold you in my thoughts and prayers.

Faithfully yours,
Albert

Before I folded the letter and returned it to my pocket, I reread it to the final paragraph. Would Albert and I make a good match? I had enjoyed his company during the Christmas visit and thought him a fine man with a quick smile and a gentle heart. To think of him as a part of my life gave me pleasure and brought an unexpected smile to my lips. Of course it was impossible to say what the future might hold for us. Without doubt, I would be pleased to explore the possibilities when Albert returned home.

In the meantime I was thankful for his friendship and the privilege of praying for him.

Later that night after I slipped into bed, I drifted off to sleep remembering Albert's words about the future.

I don't know what awakened me—the pounding at the front of the hotel or Brother Odell's shouts to be patient, that he'd answer the door in a minute. I wrapped my robe tight around me and peeked out my bedroom door.

"Probably a traveler who lost his way," Brother Odell called to his wife.

"Or one of those hobos looking for a free night in a warm bed. Be careful and see first who is out there before you open the door, Odell."

"Ja, ja. I will be careful." His suspenders snapped as he lifted and then dropped them onto his shoulders. "Stay in your rooms," he called over his shoulder.

By now, both Sister Marta and Ilsa had arrived at the doorway leading into the hall. I walked down the hallway and joined them. The three of us peered into the darkness, the only light being the flicker of the lamp Brother Odell carried with him.

"Mark my words, it is going to be one of those hobos begging for food or a blanket." Sister Marta shook her head. "And you know your Vater won't refuse help."

"Neither would you, Mutter." Ilsa giggled and grasped her mother's arm. "You are full of resolve when you aren't face-to-face with those men who beg for a handout."

"Ja, ja. Come in, come in." Brother Odell's welcome drifted to our ears.

"You see? I told you, Ilsa. Your Vater cannot say no to them. You can be sure they will leave a mess for us to clean in the morning."

"Jutta! Come! Your Mutter and Vater, they are here!" Brother Odell hesitated only a second. "Jutta! Did you hear me?"

For a moment his shouts didn't register, and I remained frozen in place. My parents? Downstairs? Impossible. The thoughts skipped through my mind like autumn leaves in a gust of wind.

Ilsa pushed me forward. "Go—see if it is truly them."

Without further urging, I clutched my robe to my body and hurried into the parlor. My heartbeat pounded in my ears until I thought I might faint. *Please, dear God, let it be them.* Brother Odell lifted the lamp, and I stopped in my tracks, unable to believe my eyes.

"Mother! Father!" I rushed forward and embraced them, tears streaming down my cheeks. "I cannot believe it is you."

"What's all the commotion down there?" One of the hotel guests stood at the top of the stairs. "I can't get any sleep with all the noise. What time is it?"

"Three-thirty. All will soon be quiet. We had some unexpected guests arrive."

"Yeah, well, I need my sleep."

My father apologized for the intrusion and begged the man's forgiveness before he motioned that we should keep our voices down. "We need to talk quietly," he whispered.

Brother Odell waved us to the desk. "Here is the key to number five. There is enough room for all of you to sleep up there, Jutta. Go and visit with your parents." He patted my father's shoulder. "We will talk more in the morning."

"Ja. And my thanks for taking gut care of our Jutta while we were gone. She told us of your kindness before we left Marengo."

"She has been a fine addition to our home." He pointed to the upstairs. "Sleep well."

I led my parents upstairs. We wrapped ourselves in quilts to keep warm until my father started a fire. "I want to know everything that happened. Where have you been?" I was careful to keep my voice low. I didn't want to disturb any other guests.

"We will tell you, Jutta, but you must promise you will tell no one—not even these people at the hotel. It must remain our secret, for if you tell, it could cause great harm."

"I promise, Father."

"We had been receiving more and more threats because those men were unhappy that you could find nothing to report on the people here in Amana. They promised to destroy the bakery and either take us to jail or harm us if they didn't soon hear something they considered worthwhile."

I nodded, my heart breaking. They'd been living in fear since the day I'd left Marengo, and I could see how it had aged my mother. Deep lines creased her forehead and gray now streaked her dark brown hair. Strange what fear could do to our bodies.

"So you decided to leave before they could hurt you?"

"Ja. And we have been hiding at a farmhouse outside of Cedar Rapids ever since."

I frowned. "I don't understand. How did you get to a farmhouse, and why—"

My father held up his hand. "I will explain. You remember Henry Reeves, who delivered our flour?"

"Oh sure, I remember. Kenneth came to the hotel, and—"

"I know, I know. But do not judge too harshly just yet. Mr. Reeves was very sad for what was happening to us. He told me he had joined that Defense Council because of the threats made to him if he didn't join, and he told me he was being forced to report on any of his customers who were of German heritage."

I bobbed my head. "And I told Kenneth what I thought about his family doing such a thing to us. We were good customers—"

"Jutta! You must stop interrupting. I am trying to tell you that they helped us. Mr. Reeves brought his wagon in the middle of the night and hid us in the back, all covered with his flour bags." My father grinned. "We looked as white as snow when we arrived at his brother's farm near Cedar Rapids. They agreed we could stay with them. They were gut to us."

"It wasn't bad for us, Jutta. A few times we had to hide in the barn, but mostly we stayed in the house with them. Later, Mr. Reeves' brother told us about the posters, but they decided it would be best if we waited to be sure it wasn't a trick to try to find us and put us in jail. Once they were sure it was safe, Mr. Reeves came to Cedar Rapids to get us."

"I don't understand why it is such a secret. The Protective League has agreed you were treated unfairly, and—"

My father shook his head. "If those men in the Defense Council discover Mr. Reeves helped hide us and that he brought us back to Amana, he could suffer the same damage to his business. He and his family would be considered anti-American for helping us at a time when we were considered traitors. Don't you see, Jutta? The danger has been lifted from our heads, but not from his, so we must never whisper their names to anyone."

I leaned back in the chair, ashamed of the things I'd said to Kenneth Reeves and thankful for the help he and his father had given my parents. I recalled the day I'd been in Marengo and run alongside their wagon. Though they'd spoken to me, they'd been careful to avoid drawing any attention that might connect them to my parents or to me. And to think that while I was harboring ill feelings toward Kenneth and his father, they had my parents safely hidden in Cedar Rapids. "That was so good of them. Perhaps one day there will be a way we can repay their kindness."

"I would like that." My mother glanced around the room as she settled back in the overstuffed chair. "This is a very nice room we have for tonight."

"And what of tomorrow? You have made plans?" I glanced back and forth between them, uncertain what they might say. After reestablishing my bond within the colonies, I didn't want to leave the Amanas. Yet our months apart now seemed like years, and I knew I couldn't bear to live away from my mother and father, either.

They looked at each other and smiled before my father spoke. "What would you think if we told you we would like to return to live in the colonies?"

Even though my father's question didn't surprise me, his news sent a thrill through me. Though they had worked hard to own their bakery and live in the outside world, they'd never truly adjusted to life in Marengo—none of us had experienced the same peace we'd enjoyed while living in Homestead. "I would be very pleased to hear that. And I think the elders will welcome you back, though you may not be able to return to Homestead. What would you think of living in one of the other villages?"

My father shrugged. "As long as our family can be together, we will be pleased to live in whatever village the elders decide is best. But for now, I think we should go to bed. Tomorrow is a new day." He bowed his head. "But first let us thank God for His protection and for bringing us back together."

As tears glistened in my father's eyes, I realized I had never before seen him cry.

My heart felt as though it might burst as I silently joined my father in prayer. God's faithfulness had prevailed, and He'd blessed me beyond all I'd imagined. I was now reunited with my parents, and together we would begin our life anew in the Amana Colonies. And who could say? Perhaps when Albert returned from the army, we would establish a special bond of our own. For now, I would look forward to that day with great anticipation.

SPECIAL THANKS TO . . .

. . . My editor, Sharon Asmus, for her generous spirit, excellent eye for detail, and amazing ability to keep her eyes upon Jesus through all of life's adversities.

. . . My acquisitions editor, Charlene Patterson, for her enthusiastic encouragement to move forward with this series.

. . . The entire staff of Bethany House Publishers, for their devotion to making each book they publish the best product possible. It is a privilege to work with all of you.

. . . Brandi Jones, Amana Heritage Society, for tirelessly answering my many questions, for private tours, and for reading my manuscripts for technical accuracy.

. . . Lanny Haldy, Amana Heritage Society, for meeting with me and taking precious hours away from other tasks to provide information, answer questions, and make recommendations.

. . . Mary Greb-Hall for her ongoing encouragement, expertise, and sharp eye.

. . . Lori Seilstad, fellow author and friend, for her honest critiques and friendship.

. . . Mary Kay Woodford, my sister, my prayer warrior, my friend.

. . . Tracie Peterson, friend extraordinaire.

. . . My husband, Jim, my constant encourager, supporter, advocate, and the love of my life.

. . . To my readers, for your e-mails of encouragement, your expressions of love, and your eagerness to read each book.

. . . Above all, thanks and praise to our Lord Jesus Christ for this miraculous opportunity to live my dream and share the wonder of His love through story.

NOTE TO MY READERS . . .

If you have not yet had an opportunity to visit the Amana Colonies, I encourage you to do so. You won't be disappointed! However, if you are unable to visit Iowa and would like to learn more about the Amana Colonies and the people who settled there, please visit their Web site at: *www.amanacolonies.com/* or the Web site of the Amana Heritage Society at: *www.amanaheritage.org/* or the Web site of the National Park Service at *www.nps.gov/history/Nr/travel/amana/learnmore.htm.*

More from Judith Miller!

In the face of an uncertain future, can their restless hearts find peace in the quiet life of the Amana Colonies?

Somewhere to Belong by Judith Miller
DAUGHTERS OF AMANA

When an outsider betrays her trust, must her whole community suffer the consequences?

More Than Words by Judith Miller
DAUGHTERS OF AMANA

When three cousins are suddenly thrust into a world where money equals power, the family's legacy—and wealth—depend on their decisions. Soon each must decide what she's willing to sacrifice for wealth, family, and love.

THE BROADMOOR LEGACY by Judith Miller and Tracie Peterson
A Daughter's Inheritance, An Unexpected Love, A Surrendered Heart

If you enjoyed *A Bond Never Broken*, you may also like:

Laughs and sparks fly in 1890s Texas as one couple tries to make their dreams become reality before they lose each other—and their sanity.

Serendipity by Cathy Marie Hake